THE CHRESTOMATHY OF DESIRE

Works by D. J. Butler

LEGACY OF THE CORRIDOR

THE CHRESTOMATHY OF DESIRE

A collection of speculative fiction by

D. J. Butler

HEMELEIN PUBLICATIONS

This book is for Rob Howell,
who kept asking me for short stories.

TABLE OF CONTENTS

LEGACY
OF THE CORRIDOR

Welcome to the tenth volume in the Legacy of the Corridor series! We're coming up on the fifth anniversary of the first volume in just over a year. Way back in 1994, M. Shayne Bell put together *Washed by a Wave of Wind,* an anthology of short works by authors from "The Corridor", an area that covers Utah, most of Idaho, parts of Wyoming and Nevada, stretches south into Arizona, parts of southern California, and parts of northern Mexico, and stretches north of Idaho and Montana into the area around Cardston, Alberta, Canada. For those unfamiliar with this Corridor, it was settled primarily by Mormon pioneers, members of the Church of Jesus Christ of Latter-day Saints.

Shayne's anthology highlighted science fiction and fantasy works by authors from this area, as the Corridor contained an unusually high number of successful genre authors—for the population in the area—both members and non-members of the predominant religion. Was it something in the air? Something in the scenery and elevation? Something in the water? No one has figured that out yet, though several essays have pontificated on the topic.

That legacy continues today with an impressive list of award-winning and successful genre authors such as:

Jennifer Adams · Lee Allred · Jay Boyce
D. J. Butler · Orson Scott Card · Michael R. Collings

Michaelbrent Collings · Ally Condie · Larry Correia
Kristyn Crow · James Dashner · Steve Diamond
Brian Lee Durfee · Sarah M. Eden · Richard Paul Evans
David Farland · Nancy Fulda · Diana Gabaldon
Jessica Day George · James Goldberg · Shannon Hale
Mettie Ivie Harrison · Tracy Hickman · Laura Hickman
Charlie N. Holmberg · Christopher Husberg · M. K. Hutchins
Raymond F. Jones · Matthew J. Kirby · Martine Leavitt
Tricia Levenseller · Gerald N. Lund · Lisa Mangum
Gama Ray Martinez · Brian McClellan · Stephenie Meyer
L. E. Modesitt, Jr. · Brandon Mull · Jennifer A. Nielsen
Wendy Nikel · James A. Owen · Lehua Parker
Janci Patterson · Steven L. Peck · Aprilynne Pike
Ken Rand · Brandon Sanderson · Caitlin Sangster
J. Scott Savage · D. William Shunn · Jess Smart Smiley
Eric James Stone · May Swenson · Howard Tayler
Brad R. Torgersen · Nym Wales · Rick Walton
Dan Wells · Robison Wells · David J. West
Jack Weyland · Carol Lynch Williams
Dan Willis · Julie Wright

That's a big list of names, and it only barely scratches the surface.

Hemelein Publications created this publication series to highlight authors from The Corridor, both well-known and lesser-known, in order to highlight the amazing creativity found among this large and expanding group of authors. We think Shayne did a wonderful job drawing attention to these amazing writers back then, and we want to continue what he started.

You can learn more about the Legacy of the Corridor publication series, as well as about many other awesome books, on the Hemelein Publications website:

http://hemelein.com/go/legacy-of-the-corridor/

Joe Monson
Managing Editor
Hemelein Publications

MERE PULP FROM A GIANT AMONG AUTHORS

JOE MONSON

We are back with the second collection-of-interesting-name from the inimitable Dave Butler. He writes a wide variety of stories, from sword and sorcery to flintlock fantasy to space opera to time travel to steampunk to nonfiction about all of those and more. He's also very musically inclined, wrote a soundtrack to go with his *Witchy Eye* novel, as well as various other filk songs (six of which are found here in this volume). Throughout all of it, you'll find threads of optimism, hope, and adventure, stories where the good guys always win (if, perhaps, not in the expected way). I think these qualities are what has his works on my "must read" list.

I first met Dave over a decade ago at Life, the Universe, & Everything, an annual science fiction and fantasy symposium held in Provo, Utah. I don't remember if he had his guitar with him then, but he can often be found at conventions quietly strumming out a tune while chatting and joking with other authors, readers, artists, and anyone else who stops to listen. He has a (usually) quiet presence, despite his gianthood, and he smiles freely as he moves from topic to topic. And he knows a lot about a lot. *A lot.*

He's incredibly well read, and he consumes books on a wide variety of topics (he mentions the books he's reading in his newsletter; go sign up for it on his website), including both ancient and modern history, religions, culture, and more (too many to list here). He uses that knowledge to build up the foundations and flesh-out of all of his fiction, whether in a short story or a novel. He's at least passingly familiar with several different languages—a few of which he speaks—and I've lost track of how many different languages he's learned to create more believable worlds, or just for fun. He's a scholar and a gentle(giant)man.

As a fellow Kovel Award winner, it's been great fun to work with him while putting together this volume. Within, you'll find tales of science fiction and fantasy adventure, intrigue, love, mystery, and more, which sounds like a strange mix unless you know Dave. There are stories from *Witchy War, Abbott in Darkness, Time Trials,* and (my favorite) the *Hiram Woolley* series. There are several standalone works, too. There are filk songs. There are several essays about his works and the writing business in general. In short, there's something for everyone here.

Take some time today and immerse yourself in this chrestomathy. You know you have greatly desired it, almost as much as Galadriel desired the One Ring. The major bonus with this collection over the One Ring is that this collection is not evil. Read it today. You won't regret it.

Joe Monson
May 2025

The Greatest of
These Is Hope

Sometimes, you think you're being invited to have a story published in an anthology of upbeat science fiction organized by a big-name fantasy writer, when in fact, you're just being invited to submit. And sometimes, you help a couple of friends who were also invited to submit to contact the editor to be able to send in their stories on time. And sometimes, those two friends get their stories into the anthology, while you are told that your story was the one that barely didn't make the cutoff. But then sometimes Ed Willett comes along and puts the story you wrote into a Shapers of Worlds *anthology, because Ed is a mensch.*

S hepherd: *And now abideth faith, hope, charity, these three.*

    The Ecumene Shepherd stood at the front of the long Ecumene Community Hall, atop the short minbar tower. His avatar had a thick grey bar across the top of its block-like head, which Izzy thought must be a skullcap, and wore black. The avatar's mouth was a flat, serious line.

All the avatars had block-like heads, including Izzy's. That was just how avatars looked. The blocky head of Izzy's avatar was a sunset gold, with curlicues meant to approximate the look of her real, wildly curly, hair.

Shepherd: And sometimes . . . the greatest of these is hope.

Behind the Shepherd rose a dark-blue panel spangled with silver and gold dots. The dots slowly revolved around a central point, slightly to the side of one of the fainter stars. This was an image of the night sky, but not any night sky Izzy had ever seen—it was the night sky of Earth. Mom and Dad hadn't ever seen it, either—Izzy's family was four generations off-Earth.

But that revolving night sky of Earth was one of the symbols of the Ecumene.

Rowland-Beta, sometimes called Elizabeth's World, had its own night sky, with a dense skein of stars that came and went and thick smeared bands of various colors and large patches of void. Izzy liked to sit on the broad, flat space on top of the kelp-processing tanks with Mom, Dad, and Bear, turn off their station's lights, and watch that sky. There wasn't another station in sight of them in any direction, so with the lights turned off, the night became glorious.

Everyone on Elizabeth's World lived this remotely. That was why the Ecumene Community Hall was virtual, located in a walled-off section of the Sphere where many of the controls were disabled, to prevent vandalism. During sermons, like this one, communication abilities were limited, to avoid disruptions.

The Ecumene and the government had controlled spaces in the Sphere. Outside those controlled spaces, the Sphere was where children met and played.

"Burp!" Bear yelled, but no one in the Sphere could hear him.

The Shepherd interrupted a description of Eli and his favorite activities —which conspicuously left out his love of griefing in the Sphere and all the dirty jokes he'd learned from his older brother, Tim—to quote scripture again.

Shepherd: Call on Him in fear and hope. Lo! The mercy of the Infinite is nigh unto the good.

Viv (group PM): I miss Eli.

The other participants in the funeral couldn't see the group chat, which made it much more discreet than a whispered conversation. Izzy snaked a hand to her keypad and quietly typed a response.

Izzy (group PM): I do, too.

Izzy had never met either Viv or Eli, or the fourth member of their group, Ahmad, in physical space. Their families all operated stations thousands of kilometers apart, but the children met in the Sphere to heap up mountains, go into the cubes to mine Unobtainium and Handwavium, which allowed them to build fantastical devices in the Sphere, and fight Stalkers. Rowland-Beta itself had no mountains, and indeed virtually no dry land, no rare elements, and, of course, no Stalkers. Most of the planet's devices were tools used in cultivating and processing kelp.

Now Viv sat on a virtual pew two rows ahead of Izzy and to the right. Ahmad sat somewhere behind the girls. Izzy knew that because Ahmad had told her; her avatar was frozen in place during this part of the service and couldn't turn its head.

Eli lay in the coffin in front of the Shepherd.

"Juice!" Bear yelled. The only juice he knew was a sweet distillate from kelp.

The station shook. Not the Community Hall, which was virtual, but Izzy's family's station. Over the Shepherd's muscular voice, she heard large waves slapping against the side of the station's tanks. She heard Dad curse and slip out of his Sphere-helm, then run to the station's control room.

His avatar remained poised and solemn, sitting on the other side of Mom. For the funeral, the family's avatars all wore black.

Ahmad (group PM): Did you guys feel that?

Izzy (group PM): Whoa.

The tremors had been getting more frequent, and bigger. Since virtually everyone on Elizabeth's World lived on floating stations, the tremors manifested as waves. It was a tremor that had killed Eli, apparently; a tsunami had swept him from his family's station, and he had drowned in the kelp.

At least, that's what Viv had heard from her parents. Izzy's parents had said nothing, but had forbidden Izzy and Bear to go outside alone. Bear, who could barely talk, really shouldn't be outside alone anyway, but Izzy was eleven years old, and the sudden restriction on her liberty chafed, however sensible it was.

But how big must a tremor be to throw waves against Izzy's station and also Ahmad's? Or could there be two tremors at the same time?

Either possibility seemed ominous.

Shepherd: Let us say the prayer for the dead together. Be exalted and sanctified His great name in the world He created . . .

The communication controls relaxed, and members of the congregation recited along. Izzy's text scroll filled with multiple versions of the prayer, some misspelled, some using variant words, and a few in different languages. She copied and pasted the prayer herself, mechanically, one line at a time, from an open file.

Viv (group PM): This really makes me want to go griefing. Just find a building somewhere and trash it. A whole village. A castle.

Izzy (group PM): You can't grief in here.

Viv (group PM): Duh. Meet me at ZL 1200?

ZL 1200 was a time, midday at the zero-longitude line of Elizabeth's World. The place of the meeting would be the same place they always met.

Izzy (group PM): I'm in. Ahmad?

Ahmad said nothing. Izzy couldn't look for his avatar or the avatars of his two mothers. Instead, she checked the scroll and realized that none of Ahmad's family were saying the prayer for the dead.

Viv (group PM): He's just glitching. I bet he meets us.

WHEN IZZY ARRIVED at Mount Mountain, Viv was waiting. Her avatar had orange hair and literal cherries on its creamy cheeks. Ahmad was nowhere in sight.

None of the children had ever seen a mountain in real life, because Elizabeth's World had no mountains. Ahmad claimed he had once stood on an island, but Izzy was skeptical. So, when they had decided to build a meeting place in the Sphere, it had seemed natural to make it the most earthy, the most mountainous, the most kelp-free place they could possibly contrive. Mount Mountain was a forest of steep, needle-like spires, thick with vegetation. The others told Izzy it also echoed with the cries of the seventeen species of birds they had created and given homes on Mount Mountain, but Izzy had an old Sphere-helm, with limited audio capability. The resolution was so bad it made voices, birdsong, and avalanches all sound the same, so she just left the audio off.

Bear liked to listen to the audio when he was in the Sphere and would yell "burp!" every time he heard any sort of Sphere-sound. Apparently, that was what it all sounded like to him.

Izzy: No news from Ahmad?

Viv: Nothing. I've been looking at the map, and there's a river valley about two hundred klicks from here, full of defenseless villages and herds of cattle. Easy pickings.

Izzy: Maybe we should wait for Ahmad?

Viv: Not too long.

While they waited, Izzy walked in circles, looking for her friend. Viv stepped to the edge of Mount Mountain and began work on another peak.

Viv: I'm going to name this one Eli Hill.

Izzy: Good idea.

Izzy helped. They were experienced builders, and the mountain didn't take long. When they had finished, and filled its cliffs with nests full of an eighteenth species of bird that Izzy named Eleazarids, also after Eli, Ahmad still hadn't shown up.

They gave up on him and went griefing.

Running to the location Viv had chosen took about fifteen minutes. The avatars in the river valley were all in sleep mode, or just walking in circles. A few NPCs resisted, but they were weak. With their wide silver swords, Viv and Izzy smashed fences, cut holes in the walls of houses, and massacred herds of cattle and sheep. Every time she came across a chicken, Izzy picked it up and hurled it onto the nearest rooftop. The two girls carried out their mayhem with eggs and chickens raining from the sky.

When they had carved a path across the cluster of villages and were turning to cut through again, they met another avatar. It stood in their path, flickering as if the user's connection was weak.

Viv: Ahmad?

But it was Eli's avatar. Sandy brown hair, dots for freckles, a permanent grin.

Had Eli looked like that in real life?

Izzy: Viv . . .

Viv attacked. Her blocky avatar blocked Izzy's view, but around the bobbing rectangular head, Izzy caught glimpses of Eli's digital body, marked by star after star as it took blow after blow, until virtual Eli fell to the virtual ground and his flickering eyes were replaced by flickering Xs.

Izzy: Viv!

Viv abruptly vanished.

Izzy stood looking at the avatar until she felt her station rocked by three big waves in quick succession. "Izzy!" she heard Dad yell. "The coupling with the processor is broken! I need the welding gear and the rappelling harness!"

She disconnected.

Izzy told Mom about seeing Eli, and Mom gave her a hug.

She didn't get on the Sphere for a few days, and no one suggested she should. There was plenty for her to do, helping Dad fix the processing-tank coupling, and then fix it again when another wave broke the weld.

Dad looked a lot at the horizon as they worked. There were dark circles under both his eyes and a patchy beard starting to sprout on his jaw.

An ethernote from Ahmad reassured both her and Viv that he was alive, his family's station had just lost power briefly, but she and Viv both answered so briefly they were almost curt.

A guest came to dinner, and Izzy was surprised to see that she recognized him: it was the Ecumene Shepherd. She'd never seen him in the physical world, but she recognized him by his similarity to his avatar. He was dressed in a black cloak and tunic, and where the avatar had a thick grey band across the top of its head, the Shepherd had eyebrows thicker than his thumbs, running in a single bar from ear to ear at the base of a deeply wrinkled forehead.

Not a skullcap, after all.

The Shepherd smiled a lot and had kind eyes.

Izzy's parents seemed to expect him, but no one had given Izzy any warning, and no one explained why there was an Ecumene Shepherd on the station for the first time ever.

The small talk the adults made over dinner was elliptical. Their voices were subdued.

"Any sign of the wormhole re-opening?" . . . "PlanSec doesn't have any evacuation capacity, that's not what they were made to do!" . . . "Not enough metal to build that colony ship Patel was talking about, I heard." . . . "We could put something in orbit, but it wouldn't hold everyone." . . . "The tremors are getting worse. Forget about plate shifts; if the planet goes, being in orbit won't be safe enough."

Did they think she was too young to understand? Or were they trusting her enough to show her their own fears? Izzy's stomach hurt.

Mom smiled at her and held her hand.

Over steamed kelp-noodles and chunks of fried eel, the Shepherd turned to Izzy. "I hear you saw your friend, Eli."

"The Sphere was glitching, that's all. I'm not stupid. Eli's dead."

Dad chuckled grimly and looked out the window.

Bear yelled, "Burp!" He wasn't wearing his Sphere-helm, so maybe he just recognized the word *sphere* and gave his usual war-cry.

The Shepherd nodded. "Only, your mother ethered the Sphere techs, and they can't find a record of the glitch."

Izzy felt very small. "Did you come out here to call me a liar?"

The Shepherd shook his head, eyebrows furrowing. "Your friend Viv saw it, too. I believe you both."

Izzy shrugged, chewing a mouthful of kelp. It had a mild, salty taste, under a chutney of hydroponically grown tomatoes. "Then the techs missed the evidence of the glitch."

The Shepherd nodded. "Or maybe what you saw was something else."

"A ghost?"

"The line between a ghost and an angel can be very fine."

Izzy put down her fork and knife. "If Eli came back as an angel, worse luck for him. And for Viv, who chopped the angel to bits."

"If Eli came back as an angel, maybe he was sent to help us. For instance, maybe he came to bring you feelings of peace and comfort."

"And we killed him." Izzy picked up her knife and fork and took another bite of food. "But it was just a glitch."

The station shook once during dinner, throwing a bowl of legumes across the floor, and twice after. When Mom flew Roo out to deliver the Shepherd to his flyer, Izzy stood in an observation bay with Dad and watched.

Roo was the utility vehicle that Mom and Dad used to reach remote combines or, occasionally, shuttle to other stations. It was a small flyer, shaped like an eggplant, with a pocket containing four seats. Roo was also the name of the AI that flew the utility vehicle. Mom landed Roo alongside the Shepherd's flyer, riding at anchor, and tethered the vehicles together. Then the pocket opened and the Shepherd stepped across into his own craft.

Dad snorted and walked away.

Izzy watched until Mom and Roo had returned to the station's dock and the Shepherd had disappeared over the southern horizon.

Where was her friend Eli?

"DAD," Izzy asked, "is the planet going to blow up?"

She asked it when Bear wasn't around. He was too young to worry about this sort of thing.

Dad looked up from the processing unit he was tinkering with and wiped sweat from his eyes, smearing grease on both his cheeks in doing so. "Look, all this god stuff . . . you don't have to believe it."

"That's not what I was saying." Izzy handed her father a spanner.

"I figure the real meaning of it is, live your life from moment to moment as if the whole world could end. Because you could die, from moment to moment, and then your world would be over. So, live as if you were about to be judged at all times."

"By a god?"

"Or by people. Because you might have a heart attack, or a stroke." Dad sighed. "Or you might get knocked off your station by a bad wave and drown in the kelp."

Like Eli had. "Dad, is Rowland-Beta going to blow up?"

"Someday. Maybe tomorrow. Maybe in a million years, maybe in a billion."

"So, there's no hope for any of us."

Dad gripped a bolt with the spanner and grunted while he forced it to turn. The dented protective plate popped off, and he set it aside. "In the long run, as individuals?" He considered. "We all die. But the species gets better. There's always hope for our children."

"And for us? On Elizabeth's World?"

"Smart people are working on it." Dad grinned, but his eyes were flat. "There's always hope."

Izzy took a deep breath. "There sure are a lot of tremors."

"There sure are." Dad picked up the replacement plate and snuggled it into place.

"BE CAREFUL OF A BIG WAVE, MIRIAM."

"I know you'll protect us."

Dad watched, sitting on a catwalk above the rest of the family. Mom sang over three short candles, one red, one white, and one black. Even unlit, the candles smelled of citrus and spice.

"One light is the Bridegroom," Mom sang, as she lit the first candle. "Sing it with me, one light is the Bridegroom."

"One light is the Bridegroom," Izzy and Bear sang together.

"One light is the Bride." Mom lit the second.

"One light is the Bride."

"And the third light is Secret Wisdom, watching over them both."

"The third light is Secret Wisdom."

"Secret Wisdom watches over us now," Mom said. "She gives us what we need. What do you need, Bear?"

"Juice!"

At least he hadn't said "burp."

"And what do you need, Izzy?"

Izzy hesitated. "I want the tremors to stop. Or I want us all to get away from them."

Mom looked thoughtful and was silent for a time. "And what does Eli need?"

"Juice!" Bear offered again.

What *did* Eli need? What would Izzy need, if she and Eli traded places? "Maybe he misses his friends."

"Let's pray for those things." Mom smiled. "For the tremors to stop, and for Eli not to miss his friends anymore."

"Juice!"

"And for juice."

Mom and Izzy and Bear joined hands and prayed without words for a long time.

Waves rocked the station violently that night, and tore up kilometers of kelp, but not until the entire family was inside and safe.

In the middle of the night, Izzy awoke to the sound of footsteps. The station rocked, and she saw Dad's shadow, pacing past the opening to her sleeping pod.

IZZY RETURNED TO THE SPHERE. She met Ahmad and Viv to add more to Mount Mountain, and to repair some damage that had been done by griefers in their unusually long absence. Eli Hill, standing at the edge of Mount Mountain, had been gnawed by hostile pickaxes down to a nub.

While they rebuilt, they had to fight off Stalkers. The Stalkers were pink, simple-faced marauders. They were operated by central processing, rather than by a live user, and all they did was march toward an active user's avatar and attack it when they arrived. Their attacks were clumsy, and they were usually unarmed, so experienced players killed Stalkers by the thousand.

Izzy and her friends killed several hundred while repairing Eli Hill, and then dug a moat around Mount Mountain to protect it. They dug the moat down to the substratum, then obliterated the stairs by which they'd descended into the moat, and then used all their combined Unobtainium to make an invisible bridge at an agreed spot.

In the century and more since humans had left Earth, they had never yet encountered an *intelligent* species from another planet. Plants and animals, yes, but nothing that could communicate, or, apparently, think.

Everything that had evolved off planet Earth was either a cow or a Stalker, was how Izzy had restated this fact to her Sphere-tutor, Ms. Wilson. Eventually, she had been able to make Ms. Wilson understand what she meant.

After the others had to go (the sun set earlier in their longitudes), Izzy stayed, replacing nests, layering on additional tiers of shrubbery, and widening the protective ditch even further. While she was hacking away at the edge of the moat, she found a trail she had never seen before.

Out of curiosity, or hoping it might lead to a new source of Unobtainium to replace what they'd used, she followed it.

At the end of the path, though, and not very far from Mount Mountain, was a structure. It was long, black, and rectangular. Izzy couldn't tell at first glance what it might be made of, but it hung suspended in mid-air.

Izzy knew of no way to hang a structure above the ground in the Sphere. Surely this oddity must conceal a source of a rare material.

On the structure's underside were red markings in a square around an opening. The structure was low enough to the ground that Izzy could walk underneath it, and then jump up into it.

Inside the structure was a room, and a small console, like a table. Standing on the other side of the console was her friend Eli.

Eli: You have sufficient breathable atmosphere?

The avatar wasn't flickering anymore, but it shifted left and right, as if the user were new to the game's controls.

Eli: You have enough food?

Izzy put her fingers to her keypad.

Izzy: Here? In the Sphere? I don't need food. I was looking for somewhere to mine Unobtainium.

Eli took a few moments to respond.

Eli: Not in this simulation. On the planet.

Izzy: There is air, and plenty of food and water.

Eli: Why are you all frightened?

Eli didn't sound lonely. Izzy didn't like the questions he was asking, but they weren't the questions of a lonely person.

Was the Shepherd right? Could this be the ghost of Eli, or his . . . angel?

Izzy: Are you frightened?

Avatars couldn't change expression, so Eli stared without responding for a few moments.

Eli: I am safe.

Was Eli safe because he was dead, and not exposed to the tremors and the waves they caused?

Izzy: Do you have air, and food, and water?

Eli: My vessel has more than enough.

What kind of vessel sailed through the lands of the dead?

Izzy: Is it cold where you are?

Eli: It is very cold.

Eli moved forward, edging around the table. Out of reflex, Izzy pulled her avatar back, and promptly fell down through the hole in the floor. As she tumbled to the ground in the Sphere, Izzy felt her chair in the station topple sideways and heard Mom shout.

Izzy cut her connection before she hit the ground.

THE SHEPHERD RETURNED to the family station two days later, and this time Izzy's parents looked surprised. Mom took Bear and hid, somewhere down in the engine rooms where Izzy couldn't see them.

Dad took Izzy out in Roo to meet the Shepherd and the man who had come with him.

"Roo," Dad said. "Land alongside the open hatch of that flyer."

"Acknowledged." Roo followed Dad's instruction, and Dad tethered the two vehicles together with Roo's magnetic arms.

In the Shepherd's open hatch stood both the Shepherd and a man in a plain blue suit, with his name on a black tag on his chest. They wore safety harnesses, anchored to the flyer; Izzy and her father were belted into Roo's seats. The man in the blue suit wore a large pistol, strapped to the outside of his right leg in a glossy black holster. Izzy tried not to stare.

The starry symbol of the Ecumene, painted and static, surrounded the opening.

"Sure, my daughter is happy to talk to PlanSec," Dad said. "Just as soon as you tell me why."

The newcomer didn't smile. "We haven't been able to communicate with the Galactic Main since the wormhole collapsed, Mr. Reiter."

Dad laughed. "You think Izzy can help you with that?"

"Hear him out," the Shepherd said.

"What is PlanSec?" Izzy asked. It had something to do with the government of Elizabeth's World, but she wasn't sure what.

"Planetary Security." The Shepherd smiled at her. "You don't hear from them often because Elizabeth's World is such a safe place."

As he spoke, a wave threw both vehicles into the air and spun them 180 degrees. The Shepherd cried out, but no one fell into the water. Dad looked up at the station, hulking above them with its various pods, platforms, and connecting catwalks.

"Go on," Dad said.

The motion of the vehicles had thrown Dad's jacket open, and Izzy now saw that he, too, was carrying a pistol. She's seen it for years in the locked emergency compartment, and he'd taught her to use it, shooting at birds and at floating objects, but she'd never seen her father carry it to a meeting with another person.

She fixed her eyes on the Shepherd and his companion.

"We've detected a tight-beam transmission from off-world," the PlanSec man said. "It was aimed at this station."

"Nothing else out here for thousands of kilometers," Dad said. "But I didn't receive any transmission. I didn't even detect one."

"It wasn't in one of our standard frequencies," the PlanSec man said. "We only caught a small part of the transmission, but the data looked like Sphere-code."

"Izzy plays in the Sphere." Dad's voice sounded tense. "So does Bear. That's Barak, my son. I believe he knows two words. Are you saying my kids are communicating with the Galactic Main? My wife and I attend an Ecumene service, from time to time . . . does that mean we might be receiving messages?"

Dad's hand shifted perceptibly closer to his pistol.

"I'm saying we want to ask," the PlanSec man said.

He, too, moved his hand to his belt, not far from his weapon.

"I'll talk to them." Izzy nodded at the PlanSec man. "I'll talk to you."

The Shepherd knelt, bobbing up and down slightly in her view as the two vehicles moved on waves not quite in sync. His safety harness pulled his tunic as he did so, exposing soft brown belly. "I know you saw someone surprising in the Sphere."

"Your dead friend," the PlanSec man added.

Izzy felt the skin at the back of her neck prickle. "Is that what this is about?"

"Maybe," the PlanSec man said. "Did you talk to your dead friend?"

Izzy nodded slowly. "He talked about breathable air. And he said it was cold where he was, and he wanted to know if I had food."

"Food?" PlanSec asked.

Izzy nodded again. "I think maybe he was hungry."

"Anything else?" PlanSec asked. "Any talk of rescue? Discussion of planetary stabilization? Coordinates for other habitable planets? Any mention of the Governor, or Planetary Security, or the Ecumene?"

Izzy shook her head to all the questions.

"I don't think Eli knows anything about those things," she said. "Eli liked griefing and dirty jokes."

Dad snorted.

The PlanSec man took a deep breath, exhaled, and shook his head. Izzy kept her eyes on his pistol until he had disappeared into the vehicle, and then stared at the vehicle until it had crossed the horizon.

She didn't stop trembling for three hours.

VIV SENT HER ETHERNOTES: *Come join us at the Sphere. Mount Mountain feels empty without you. Ahmad is a terrible griefer, he wants to fill up his inventory instead of just smashing stuff. Come baaaaaack!*

Ahmad ethered her, too: *Hey, where are you? I like Eli Hill, good job with the new bird species! Why does Viv like breaking everything to bits, when we can take it and use it ourselves?*

Izzy didn't answer.

She didn't get any ethernotes from Eli.

The waves got bigger and more frequent. Dad stopped sleeping. Mom lit more candles.

"JUICE!" Bear said.

It was the middle of the night and he woke Izzy up. She rubbed her eyes and stared through the transparent ceiling of her sleeping pod. A brilliant crimson band crept overhead, punctuated by distant stars here and there.

"Juice!" Bear said again. Then he added, "Eli!"

"Go to bed," she told him. "It's late."

Bear reached under her light coverlet and grabbed Izzy by one foot. "Eli!" he said again.

The name brought Izzy fully awake. She'd never heard Bear say Eli's name before.

Where would he have heard it? At Eli's funeral? But that had been in the Community Hall, and Bear imitated all the low-res noise he heard in the Sphere as "burp." From Izzy's own lips, in some casual discussion of what she did in the Sphere? From Mom or Dad?

It didn't matter. "Go to sleep."

She rolled over and tried to find sleepiness again.

"Burp!" Bear said, and then she heard his feet padding away across the station.

Izzy was just beginning to drift off when it occurred to her that Bear had left her dormitory and walked *away from* his own sleeping pod.

"Bear?" she leaped from her bed.

She ran down the hall. Dad lay crumpled against a control console, snoring erratically. Beside him, on the console, stood an open bottle of kelp-liquor, half empty, and his pistol. She wanted to stop, to hide the gun and the bottle, but she was afraid Bear might be headed for the outside.

The door to her parents' sleeping pod was shut. All over the station, lights were off, and the celestial glow shone down through the transparent ceiling, lighting her path.

The one light that was on shone in the ladderway leading down to Roo's port. Izzy stuck to the balls of her feet but ran faster.

"Coordinates acknowledged," she heard Roo say.

What coordinates could Bear give Roo? Burp-juice-burp-Eli? Izzy threw herself down the shaft of the ladderway, sliding down the ladder's rails rather than climbing down its rungs. She landed heavily and off-balance, just in time to see Roo's pocket begin to close.

Izzy lurched to her feet and threw herself down the dock, falling down the short stairs and into the pocket just as the transparent shell of the pocket shut.

Bear sat in the pilot's seat, his hands on the steering controls.

"Bear, what are you doing?" Izzy smiled at her little brother, trying to make light of the moment. "Roo, open the pocket."

"Please fasten all safety restraints," Roo said. "Launching in ten seconds."

"Roo, override!" Izzy said. "Roo, stop!"

"Nine," Roo answer, "eight . . ."

Izzy quickly shoved Bear into the pocket's second seat and buckled him in, and had just enough time to dive into the pilot's chair and fasten her own harness before Roo left the dock.

Roo's acceleration to maximum speed was so gradual that Izzy scarcely noticed it. But by the time she gave up trying to find a manual override or activate the comms, which absolutely refused to cooperate, the utility craft was skimming above the water at 300 kilometers per hour.

The waves were enormous. Looking over her shoulder, she saw the station heaving up and down so violently it seemed about to flip upside-down.

"Roo, go back!" she said to the vehicle.

"Where are we going?" she asked it.

"I'm going to tell my dad!"

Roo ignored her.

Bear promptly fell asleep.

In less than an hour—travelling always due west, Izzy could tell by watching the moving crimson band overhead—lights appeared ahead, just above the water. She had studied the charts, and she knew that there was no station here. What, then? Some craft in transit, or some bioluminescent sea dweller, come up to the surface for air?

But the lights were stationary, and the color was a deep red, not the blue or white she usually saw in eels and crustaceans. And as Roo drew closer, she saw that the red lights were embedded in the underside of a long black cylinder. It was enormous, ten times longer than the station was across, and smooth and black, and it hovered above the water without any visible means.

Izzy felt as if her heart had stopped beating.

Encircled by red lights, on the underside of the cylinder, was an opening. Roo decelerated, positioned itself beneath the opening, and then rose vertically into the cylinder. Within the cylinder was darkness.

"Initiate docking procedure," Roo said.

"Where is this?" Izzy asked.

"This is Eli's house."

THE POCKET'S transparent shell opened, and there was a black staircase, leading up.

Should she leave Bear, or bring him with her? Neither seemed safe, but she picked Bear up and slung him over her shoulder. It seemed like a way to honor his part in bringing her here.

At the top of the stairs, she found herself in a room.

The only thing in the room other than herself and Bear was a console.

Bear woke up, and she set him down. "Juice," he observed.

"Juice," Izzy agreed.

An opening appeared in the wall, and a being came out. It slid forward slowly, moving by rolling a hedge of muscular tentacles beneath itself, and came to stand on the other side of the console.

Izzy had been here before.

"Eli," she said. "This is Eli's house."

The being was slightly shorter than Dad, and broader, and covered with wrinkled yellow skin. It had a skirt of tentacles ringing its upper body as well as the mass of tentacles beneath it, and something that looked like a face in between. Its eyes were large and unblinking, and its mouth was a birdlike beak.

The being stood still for a few moments, then reached forward and touched the console. A synthesized voice poured out, low-resolution and deep, but understandable.

"Izzy. I have peaceful intentions toward you. I have peaceful intentions toward your family. I have peaceful intentions toward your whole people. I am like you. I live in isolation. You farm kelp. I mine cosmic dust. I watched you. Your planet is dying. You are cut off from your other planets. I tried to reach your people's communications. I failed. Then I connected with your simulation. I have capacity in my vessel to hold the entire human population of this planet. I am here to help."

"Burp!" Bear hollered.

Izzy's heart beat so fast she could barely breathe. "What's your name?"

The being touched its console repeatedly, with both upper and lower tentacles. The motions reminded Izzy of typing.

"My name is hard to say," the voice said. "Please call me Eli."

"Eli." Bear nodded, and hugged Izzy's leg.

Somehow, Izzy managed not to cry.

Eli-the-Dust-Miner touched the console again. "And this is my family."

Another opening appeared in the wall. From it emerged three beings that resembled Eli-the-Dust-Miner. One was his size, and faintly green. The other two were smaller, closer to Bear's height, and bright-pink.

Bear rushed three steps forward, stopped, then shook a fist in the air. "Juice!" he said. "Burp! Eli!"

One of the pink creatures clung to its green parent, but the other came to meet Bear halfway, upper tentacles trembling with excitement. It made a noise that sounded like squealing.

"May I use the comms in Roo?" Izzy asked. "In my vessel? I want to contact my parents."

"Yes," Eli-the-Dust-Miner's synthesized voice said. "Tell them we are coming."

Izzy nodded. "I'll tell them there is hope."

STUPID GOAT

This is a prequel to Time Trials, *which I co-wrote with M.A. (Mike) Rothman. "Stupid Goat" was packaged into a novella-like introduction to* Time Trials *that contained the first chapters of the book, this story, and another story, "Rise of the Administrator," written by Mike. It's not about the our-time characters who get snatched up into the alien gauntlet to defend the value of the human race, but some of the then-time characters they encounter in the book. And, of course, we get to see the monsters.*

S tupid goat," Badis muttered. "You're not worth it."

"Badis!" Antal called in a loud whisper. "Badis, aren't these the canyonlands?"

Badis shook his head to chase away the distraction of his friend's question. He crept forward on the balls of his feet and the knuckles of one hand. In his other hand, he held a coiled lariat. He and Antal had come following a stray goat; with no hunting to be done, this was a task that fell to them, as young men of Ahuskay village.

The goat was a cross-eyed and ill-tempered nanny named Tammint. She had a propensity to bite and kick the people of Ahuskay, and to wake them in the middle of the night with unprovoked bleating. The news of her disappearance had been greeted with relief by several of the village's children.

Unfortunately, Tammint also gave abundant, fat-rich milk, so the Tribespeaker had pulled Badis and Antal from their fishing and sent them to bring her back.

A dry wind blew, scouring the skin of Badis's face.

Tammint chewed placidly and stared at Badis with one eye. Her head was oversized and the eye within it oversized again, so that Badis had the impression that the face of some much larger beast, streaked with brown and white and studded with rolling bloodshot eyes, had been stitched on the neck of a simple goat. She stood on a slab of yellowish rock and behind her, the ground yawned open.

They had indeed reached the beginning of the canyonlands.

"Shh," Badis said. He shook out the coil of rawhide and prepared to throw it over Tammint's neck.

"Lemta says the Ametsu will eat your liver from your body while you're still alive."

"Shh." Badis rotated his arm in a gentle stirring motion, preparing to throw the lariat. "We're not here to fight the Ametsu. Besides, one of the Ametsu has been to Ahuskay village this season. The tribe has paid the blood price." Badis flinched, remembering the surprised expression of Ayrad and Kella's look of terror as the Ametsu had broken their necks in turn. Badis had fled to avoid witnessing any further than that. "The Ametsu will not take us."

"Lemta says the Ikeyu are even worse."

Badis shook his head, wishing Antal would shut up. In the orange light of the setting sun, both boys' complexions were a dark, burnt red. They wore linen kilts and each had a knife on a strip of rawhide around his waist, but they were otherwise unarmed. Should Badis have brought a spear? All the talk of Ametsu was making him uncomfortable.

"How could they be worse?" His voice cracked slightly. "The Ametsu kill us and eat our livers."

"Or eat them while we're still alive," Antal pointed out.

"Just so," Badis agreed. "What would be worse than that?"

Tammint took two small steps forward, and the chasm leading into the canyonlands gaped at her hoofs.

"The Ikeyu eat human brains."

Badis threw the lariat at precisely the wrong moment. The word 'brains' soured his aim, and the lariat skidded into a patch of tall grass shy of the runaway goat. Tammint blurted out a groan of objection and leaped out of sight, down into the ravine.

"Curse you, Antal!" Badis snapped.

Antal's eyes turned to water and his knees knocked together. "Don't curse me, Badis. We're friends."

"Don't be a child," Badis grumbled. "You're not cursed. I just want you to shut up when I'm trying to catch the goat."

"But you said it," Antal whimpered. "You said I was cursed!"

"You're not cursed. I didn't mean it, I take it back." Badis spat over his right shoulder. Spitting drove out the demons, but also it would show that he really meant what he said. He embraced Antal, who trembled. "Come on, we have to follow the goat."

"Perhaps we won't be able to find Tammint in the darkness of the canyons," Antal suggested.

"It's not that dark yet." Badis collected the leather and stepped down into the ravine. The crack in the earth sank steeply and he could barely make out Tammint's hindquarters in the gloom, scrambling deeper into the canyon.

"How much is one goat really worth?" Antal asked.

Badis ignored his friend and followed the nanny. The crack poured quickly into the top of a stone chimney. The goat, sure-footed as all her kind were, sprang down the rock by leaping from one barely-visible crack to the next. She climbed almost as fast as falling, and where the chimney ended on a scrub-covered hillside, tucked almost out of sight, around the chimney's corner, Tammint stopped to crop at yellow grass. Her tail waggled at Badis and Antal, taunting them.

"I'm not as good a climber as you are," Antal said.

"We have the rope." Badis quickly secured the leather around his friend's chest and lowered him down the chimney until he reached the point where he could find handholds and footholds unaided. Then Badis slid down the stone himself, slowing his descent by means of his feet on opposite walls.

Tammint had moved on, but there was enough light that Badis could follow her tracks down the hill and into the next ravine. Antal jogged at his shoulder. Ahead of them, the evening's first bright star shone in the eastern sky. It had to be the Hunter's Dog, which Badis found appropriate.

But then the canyon turned just a bit to one side, and the Dog disappeared.

A trickle of water splashed across their feet as the canyon walls rose.

"Why does one goat matter so much?" Antal asked. "We might die."

"We won't die."

"We might," Antal said. "There are Ametsu who eat livers and Ikeyu who eat brains living down here in the canyonlands. They might kill us."

"It's our task to live," Badis said, "and also to get the goat."

"Easier to be certain I'll live if I don't have to chase a cranky nanny through the darkness," Antal grumbled.

Ahead, Badis saw the shadowed outline of Tammint standing on a boulder in the middle of the canyon. He slowed his pace and scanned the shadows, looking for a way to take the goat from the side. He saw none, and prepared his lariat again.

"Do you like milk?" he asked his friend. "Then it's your task to care for the goat."

"At what price?" Antal asked.

"We take a risk," Badis agreed.

Badis threw the loop at Tammint. He dropped the leather line neatly around the goat's neck and pulled. Only when he had tugged and failed either to budge the beast or shake any sound from it did he walk in for a closer look.

The silhouette he'd seen belonged, not to a goat, but to a gnarled chunk of dried tree trunk.

"Curse me," he growled.

"No," Antal begged. "Don't curse either one of us, please."

Badis sighed and spat over his shoulder. As if to mock him, Tammint bleated from the darkness of the ravine ahead.

"I don't think I like milk that much," Antal said.

Badis freed his lariat from the tree trunk, looped the rope again to be able to throw it, and continued on into the darkness.

The two young men of Ahuskay village descended deeper into the canyonlands. The air became rich with moisture and Badis's nostrils filled with the scents of watercress and citrus. They made their way slowly, as much by feel as by sight; the stars that now shone clearly overhead showed a spinning slice of the sky, now the Hunter, now the Bull, now other constellations.

Tammint's pace also slowed, but Badis missed two more casts with his rope and began to despair of catching her. Antal murmured beneath his breath, no longer articulating his fears loudly enough for Badis to hear them. Still, Badis felt the complaints, like the constant slap of a brisk rain, or the snoring of a hunter lying on his back.

Then Badis saw a light. He stopped Antal with a hand to his friend's chest.

"Is that fire?" Antal asked. "It must be the Ametsu."

"It could be a fire laid by men," Badis said.

"Men could be robbers," Antal pointed out. "Who else would be in the canyonlands?"

"Perhaps young hunters," Badis suggested, "looking for a lost goat."

"Where is Tammint?"

Badis looked and bit back another curse. The stray beast stood out against the light as she approached it. Squinting, he could make out a rough wooden shelter against the rock wall of the canyon. Did he see a leg as well, the leg of a man sitting in the shelter? The goat wandered toward the leg.

Then a shadow lurched forward. A man seized the goat by its foreleg and dragged it into the shelter. But the size of the man, relative to the goat . . . he had to be a head taller than Badis, and Badis was accounted tall by the hunters of Ahuskay village. And the man's head . . . Badis had a hard time putting into words what he had just seen.

"The man had the head of a bull," Antal said. He shook violently. "He was a giant. He is a giant. He has horns as long as my arms."

As long as Antal's legs, Badis wanted to say. But he held his tongue and forced himself to control his breathing. "I will go closer for a better look."

"What?" Antal snapped. "Why?"

"I like milk."

"But the Ikeyu eat brains!"

Badis shrugged, throwing the gesture invisibly into the darkness. "Perhaps the Ikeyu will have sated itself on the goat's brains, and at least I can bring the flesh back to the village to eat."

"*Human* brains, Badis!"

Badis clapped Antal on the shoulder. "If the Ikeyu eat my brains, make sure to ask them to at least give you back the goat."

He did not feel the bravado he effected, and he wished again that he had a spear. Badis had never seen one of the Ikeyu before this night, and he didn't know whether Antal was right that they ate the flesh of men. Or their brains.

And he didn't especially like milk, either.

But he was a hunter of Ahuskay village, and his people's lives depended on milk and meat as they depended on tubers and gourds and grains. He would not let them down.

He slung the coiled rope over his shoulder, took a deep breath, and walked toward the light. The sand crunching under his feet was loud in his ears, drowning out even the noisy rush of his own breathing. The light came from a small fire of gnarled sticks on a sand bank above the bottom of the ravine. Badis walked in the bottom of the canyon, circling out to place himself in front of the shelter beside the fire, so he could approach as conspicuously as possible. Around him, he heard the lowing of cows, then saw their bulky, shadowed masses, then smelled them.

Had he been mistaken? Had he seen, very briefly, the shadow of a cow, and taken it for the shadow of a man with a cow's head? He almost laughed.

As he climbed the sandbank, though, he saw the Ikeyu. There were two of them, sitting beneath a rough wooden canopy lashed between two trees and a low ledge in the cliff, to make a sturdy lean-to against the rain. The Ikeyu sat with their backs against the stone. They had the heads of bulls, with massive horns stretching out parallel to their shoulders, so that they rattled against each other when they moved. Their bodies were the bodies of men—very tall and strong men—wearing kilts and sandals.

On the sand between them lay Tammint, legs trussed together and body in shadow, bleating irascibly.

The two Ikeyu ate from bowls with their fingers. Something smelled pungent.

Badis stopped at what he judged was the edge of the firelight and raised a hand. "Greetings!"

One of the Ikeyu dropped his bowl and snatched a club from the ground. His comrade placed a hand on his chest to restrain him.

"Who are you?" the second Ikeyu called. His voice was a low rumble, like that of a moaning cow.

Badis took slow steps forward. "I'm peaceful."

"Robbers may say they come in peace," the Ikeyu said.

"My name is Badis. I'm looking for my lost goat, and I think you may have found it." Badis gestured at Tammint. Should he mention Antal? But if the Ikeyu wanted his friend to come forward, Badis didn't think Antal would. In fact, Antal might already be running home to Ahuskay village. "I'm alone."

Both Ikeyu grunted, and made no move to stand. "I'm Rooget," said the Ikeyu.

The other Ikeyu laid down his club. "I'm Shorim."

"I'm glad you caught my goat," Badis said. "Her name is Tammint. She's ill-tempered and disobedient, and I have been following her for several hours."

"How do we know she's your goat?" Rooget asked. "Does she have a marking? I didn't see a marking. How are we to know she's not a wild goat?"

Badis hesitated. The people of Ahuskay village didn't mark their beasts because the next nearest village was several days' journey distant, so there was thought to be no need.

"She looks like a wild goat," Shorim said.

"One way you can know that she is my goat," Badis said, "is that you can check for yourself that she's female. If that goat is a billy, it's not mine."

"The goat's a nanny," Rooget confirmed. "But perhaps you are keen-eyed, and noticed from far away that her horns were relatively thin, suggesting a female."

"I'm not especially keen-eyed," Badis said.

"Perhaps you just guessed," Shorim added. "You would be right half the time, guessing."

Badis considered. "You're large and dangerous and you outnumber me."

Rooget frowned, his muzzle turning down slightly. "Are you trying to impress us with your courage?"

Badis's throat felt dry. "No. I feel frightened. But I'm willing to talk to you even though I'm frightened, because my people need their goat back."

Shorim snorted. "If your people needed a wild animal, would you not be willing to risk a conversation with us?"

Badis sighed and shook his head. "Yes, but . . . that's my goat. How can I prove it to you?"

"Do you know any secrets about the nanny?" Rooget asked. "A subtle marking on her belly, or a scar on her leg?"

"No," Badis admitted.

"Is the goat trained?" Shorim pressed. "Perhaps it will jump or sit at your command."

"Do you train your cattle to jump and sit?" Badis shot back.

"That's a fine point," Rooget conceded. "But my cattle know me. Does this goat know you?"

Badis ran his hands through his hair. "I don't know. Maybe."

"Let's find out," Rooget said. "We'll untie the goat and you call her. If she comes to you, then she's your goat and you can take her home. But if she doesn't, then she's our goat and we'll eat her."

"Also," Shorim added, "we'll eat you."

There was a sickening pause. Tammint bleated.

Then both Ikeyu laughed.

"No," Rooget said. "We don't eat humans."

"The Ametsu do," Badis said.

"We aren't Ametsu," Shorim pointed out.

"Is there no other way I can have my village's goat back?"

"No," the Ikeyu said together.

Badis nodded. "Release the animal, then. I'll call her."

He had been chasing the goat all evening and into the night across the desert. Of her own volition, the beast would clearly never come to him. On the other hand, perhaps now she would rush to his side for protection from the Ikeyu.

And there seemed to be no other way.

The Ikeyu leaned forward, rattling horns and bumping shoulders as they unwrapped the ropes binding the nanny's legs together. Then Shorim lifted Tammint; she looked like a kid in his hands. He stood her on all fours, still restraining her.

"Are you ready?" Rooget asked.

"Come here, Tammint," Badis said. "Come!"

Shorim released the goat.

Tammint bleated, and stood still.

"Come, Tammint!" Badis called. "Come to me!"

The goat turned to Rooget and scratched her head against his leg as if he were a tree.

"Shall we make our goat into a stew?" Shorim asked his companion. "Or just roast her over the fire?"

"Curse you, Tammint!" Badis snapped. "Come to me, you stupid cursed goat!"

"What are you doing?" a new voice thundered.

A third giant strode out of the darkness onto the sandbar. Like the two Ikeyu, he was broad-shouldered and muscular, and he wore a kilt and sandals. His head looked nothing like a bull's, though; he had a snout that might have resembled a jackal's or an anteater's, with long teeth, and tall, upright ears that were square at their tips.

An Ametsu.

In his right hand, the Ametsu held Antal by the ankle. Antal hung upside down and swung from side to side as the Ametsu moved and turned. Whimpering sounds came from Badis's friend.

The Ikeyu scrambled to their feet, the sudden motion sending the goat trotting away in alarm. Tammint stopped at the edge of the light, barely visible.

"We found this goat," Rooget said. "The human says it's his, but we were making him work for the animal."

"The human came in a pack." The Ametsu turned and glared down at Badis. "Where are the others? What are you doing here? Are you spies? A war party?"

Badis's knees shook. He tried to explain, but couldn't control the sounds coming from his mouth.

"I know your face," the Ametsu said. "What village are you from?"

Badis stammered nonsense syllables.

"He told us he was alone," Shorim said.

The Ametsu raised Antal higher off the ground, turning to face the Ikeyu. "Does it look as if he came alone?"

"The curse!" Antal shrieked at Badis. "You cursed me!"

"Don't hurt my friend!" Badis yelped.

The Ametsu roared. With a single step, he leaped to the stone wall of the canyon. At the same time, he spun Antal about his head like a bull-roarer. Antal screamed for a brief second, and then the Ametsu hurled Antal head-first into the cliff face and the scream ended.

Badis stared.

The Ametsu seized Antal's body again. Raising it overhead, he sank his teeth into Antal's side, tearing out flesh and the liver beneath. Blood poured down the Ametsu's face. This was the thing Badis had not witnessed about the deaths of his friends Ayrad and Kella. This was what he had only known from the descriptions of others.

Badis vomited.

Then he ran.

He didn't pick a direction or think about direction, he simply turned and fled. He heard roaring behind him and felt his feet thrash the sand and stone. He passed through a wall of cattle and ducked and dodged around them. Leafy branches struck him in the face and he scrambled through brambles that tore at his skin. He splashed twice through brooks of running water. After a minute of running, or maybe two, he became aware that he heard the bleating of a goat ahead of him.

A pale splinter of silver starlight fell down into the bottom of the canyon. He could barely see, but he could hear Tammint ahead of him, also running, and he followed the sound. But what about the Ametsu and the Ikeyu?

He stopped to listen. Over his own beating heart, he could hear heavy feet crashing. He couldn't be certain how many of the giants were following him, or how far back they were.

The leather rope still rode on his shoulder. Badis quickly stretched it across the center of the canyon. Mostly by feel and keeping the line hidden in shadow, he anchored each end around a heavy boulder, just a few paces short of a jagged nest of rocks, and pulled the line taut.

Then he followed Tammint again.

The goat was climbing now. It had found a ribbon of sandy path that climbed back and forth up the canyon wall. This was not the route by which Badis had come into the canyonlands, but it was far too late to worry about that now. Badis kept his body low and scurried up the path as quickly as he could. The nanny was bleating less and so was harder to follow, but she had also tired out, so Badis began to gain ground.

He watched the canyon below. Once he rose above the level of the ravine floor, he saw the canyon as two silvery walls bordered by ghostlike white tree branches and separated by an impenetrable river of murk.

His heartbeat slowed and he remembered Antal. His complaints on the way into the canyonlands; he'd only proceeded because Badis had bullied him into it. The look of fear on his face as he bewailed having been cursed. The final scream.

Badis shuddered.

He *had* cursed his friend, and his friend had died.

He heard the soft scrape of hoof on stone above him, and looked at Tammint. On the other hand, Badis had also cursed the goat. Was the goat about to die? Would he and the goat die together?

His hands trembled and he forced himself to take deep breaths.

The Ametsu came sprinting up the canyon below. He ran faster than a man, with longer strides. Seeing the monster, Badis realized how high he'd come on the wall. Another minute of creeping and he'd be out of sight, over the rim of the canyon. Now he held perfectly still, trying to avoid attention, and praying to his dead ancestors and every god he knew that his simple trap would work.

The Ametsu was racing at full speed when he suddenly plunged forward, diving headlong into a tangle of shadow that Badis knew to be a heap of sharp rocks. An immense cracking sound and the rumble of sliding rock rose from the ravine, and then the scene was still. The trap had worked, the monster had been brought down.

Badis counted all his fingers slowly.

There was no sound from below. Was the Ametsu dead? Was he unconscious? Was he injured?

He wasn't immediately following Badis, which was perhaps all Badis could hope for. Careful to keep his steps on sand and to avoid sending any rocks or other rubbish skidding down into the canyon, he resumed his climb.

At the top, the trail evaporated into scrub brush. Tammint waited there, but now Badis had no rope to tie around her neck, and he was too tired to carry her. He stood, swaying on his feet, and considered his options.

He examined the night sky to find the way westward.

He spat over his right shoulder.

"Stupid goat," he finally said. "Cursed beast. You aren't worth it."

But he grabbed Tammint by the horns and began the long, slow struggle to drag the nanny home.

THE CUNNING MAN AND THE JUPITER KNIFE: FIVE THEMES

The Association for Mormon Letters invited me to write a blog post upon the occasion of the publication of the second Hiram Woolley novel, The Jupiter Knife. *Here it is.*

The *Cunning Man* and *The Jupiter Knife* are two novels set in 1935, co-written by me (D. J. Butler) and Aaron Michael Ritchey. Their protagonist is a Lehi sugar beet farmer named Hiram Woolley, who is also a practitioner of his Grandma Hettie's traditional magical lore, and who uses that lore to fight the demons of the Great Depression.

Aaron and I had a great time writing these books and are grateful for the reception they've had. I believe that one of the strong points of the novels is their themes, and, with that in mind, I want to identify what I think some of the books' recurring themes are:

The connections across generations matter. Hiram is a wounded man in part because he was unloved son of an unfavored wife in a polygamist marriage. Another character, learning this of him in *The Cunning Man*, speculates that his own abandonment is what causes Hiram to refuse to abandon others. Lacking a biological son, Hiram is raising as his adopted son Michael, whose father, Yaz Yazzie, died fighting in the Great War with

Hiram. All Hiram's skills and power were transmitted to him by his grandmother.

The past is always with us. Hiram remembers a world that was pre-industrial, a world more strongly rooted in community and family, a world in which ordinary people turned to arts that his contemporaries would describe as magic, for assistance and comfort. In that world, the lines between faith and magic were different from what they appear to be in 1935, and perhaps didn't exist at all. Hiram knows that his origin and his people's origin lies in that older world, which is the source of some of their weaknesses, and also many of their strengths.

There are secret worlds within the world. Hiram lives at the dawning of mass media, which tries to present a unified culture and vision of the world. As a keeper of secrets himself, both sacred and magical, Hiram knows that the mass media vision is at best an approximation and at worst a lie. His allies and his enemies both are similarly inhabitants of the secret worlds within the world, and Hiram strives to defend people who are innocent, and ignorant of these microcosms, from the evils that can pour forth.

We all stand across thresholds. Hiram was born in polygamy but lives in a world in which it is illegal. He was raised entirely by women but is an adult who is surrounded by men. He was taught magical lore as a child but encourages his son to master the techniques of science. The freely-practiced charismatic gifts of his youth have been supplanted by an increasingly layered structure of church governance. Hiram lives constantly with the tension that he has one foot at all times in the future, and one in the past.

Righteousness matters, and so does the definition of righteousness. Hiram is a paladin, a holy warrior whose magical powers depend not on his own will, but on his being right with God. Hiram's God is the God of the Epistle of James, and the Sermon on the Mount, and Hiram's understanding of righteousness is quite specific: pure religion and undefiled, visiting the fatherless and the widows in their affliction. This gives him a mission, it answers moral dilemmas, and it endows Hiram with power to act in a fallen world.

OTHERS EAT THE SHEEP

This one is new. My friend, Father Gabriel, suggested the subject matter to me, after delivering a lecture on the Penitentes of New Mexico at my house.

I don't actually know when Wales, Utah got electricity.

Hiram Woolley shifted from one foot to the other. He stood beside Bishop Pritchard near the foot of the coffin, within arm's reach of the line of mourners approaching to see Sister Bevan's body. Behind him, a waist-high wooden rail separated most of the room from a low dais containing a lectern, a table for the weekly sacrament of bread and water, and a handful of folding wooden chairs. Hiram's son, Michael, hulked as inconspicuously as he could at the end of a pew alongside which the mourners, having paid their respects, shuffled out.

Hiram had been introduced to the congregation as an assistant to the Presiding Bishopric. This was strictly true, though of the three men in the Presiding Bishopric, only John Wells, with his old-world English sensibility, knew that Hiram was here. Michael had been referred to as Hiram's "driver", which was also literally true. The fact that Michael was Navajo and

Hiram was a sugar-pale white man helped reinforce the not-quite-lie that covered the real reason for their participation.

Standing didn't make Hiram feel uncomfortable. The fact that he wore a dark suit and a thin black tie, on the other hand, left him off-balance and out of his element. He couldn't even wear his Fedora, out of respect for the dead, and held it pressed against his chest. The lump in his jacket pocket burned in his consciousness like a beacon, though he told himself that his generally rumpled appearance probably hid it fairly well.

Beyond the tall, narrow windows of the room lay the heavy darkness of winter night. The waxy smoke from the four kerosene lamps lighting the chapel tickled Hiram's lungs and painted a thin layer of residue on the wooden ribs vaulting toward the peaked ceiling. Two lamps burned on hooks behind Hiram, to his left and right, and one hung beside each door at the back of the hall. Wales, Utah, was a village on a byroad's byroad, and electricity had not yet touched it. Neither had the broader currents of American culture, much, a fact which Hiram found generally comforting.

Except that John Wells had heard that here, among the third-generation Welsh immigrants, many of whom still said "bore da" to each other each morning, there worked a monster.

A Sin Eater but also, perhaps, something darker.

Hiram took a deep breath to steady himself. The Bevan family had told him nothing when he'd offered his condolences. Now Ifor Bevan, Sister Bevan's burly oldest son, lurked near one of the lamps at the back of the hall, gripping the lapels of his black wool jacket with white-knuckled hands and staring at Hiram through slitted eyes.

Hiram tore his gaze from Ifor and fixed it on the coffin. The casket was open and Sister Bevan lay peacefully, her hair as white as her dress. Even in death, her wide mouth was fixed in a kind smile and her eyes seemed to twinkle. Hiram focused his attention on her feet, lidding his gaze to disguise the fact. The Sin Eater would be interested in Sister Bevan's right ankle.

Hiram and Michael had stood vigil all night, concealed and watching the doors, but the Sin Eater had not appeared. This was the Sin Eater's last chance, and then Sister Bevan would be driven to the cemetery and lowered into the earth.

Was the Sin Eater a local man? Was he itinerant, traveling to Ephraim and Nephi and Panguitch to offer his services?

Hiram was not terribly disturbed at the idea that a Sin Eater was at work among the congregations of rural Utah. He was unconvinced by the

Sin Eater's central claim—that he could bear away from the deceased, in a vessel of bread, all the dead person's sins. The Sin Eater claimed to absorb the sins of the departed loved one. In reality, Jesus bore mankind's sins, and no other man could do the work. But Hiram didn't think it did harm for a Sin Eater to offer a little consolation to the grieving family, even if the consolation was not strictly doctrinal.

What worried him, and worried Wells, were the reports that more was at work here. Reports of unsettled dead, of livestock massacred and drained of blood, of children missing. All in the Sin Eater's wake.

The lamps at the back of the hall were both snuffed in the same instant, plunging the room into shadow. Heads turned to look at the cause, but Hiram had expected something of the sort. If Ifor Bevan hadn't doused the flames himself, he'd ordered someone else to do it.

He remained focused on the casket instead.

A hand deftly ducked beneath Sister Bevan's ankle, beneath her pure white skirt, and snatched up a spherical loaf of crusty bread hidden there.

Before he could properly see anything about the Sin Eater's person, Hiram took two long steps forward. Hiram raised his hat and placed it over the Sin Eater's face, and then he punched the Sin Eater in the stomach.

"Pap!" Michael yelled.

The Sin Eater sprawled to the floor, dropping the loaf and clutching her belly.

The Sin Eater was a woman.

"Brother Woolley!" Bishop Pritchard snapped.

She wore a severe gray skirt, low-heeled black shoes, and a red shawl. Her black hair was pulled into a bun at the nape of her neck, and gray eyes blazed furiously at Hiram to either side of a long, thin nose.

"Everyone stand back!" Hiram cried.

Michael swept to the door nearest him. Ifor Bevan tried to stand in his way, but Michael was a head taller and fifty pounds heavier and swept the smaller man aside without effort. When Bevan snarled in protest, Michael pulled a pistol from his jacket and pointed it at the ceiling.

The pistol that had belonged to Michael's birth father, and then to Hiram.

"Get everyone out of here!" Hiram shouted.

"You struck a woman!" the Sin Eater whimpered.

"I rather doubt I did." Hiram pulled his hat onto his head.

The congregation was folding itself in a tight pocket around Hiram.

"Michael!" Hiram called.

"Everyone out!" Michael fired a shot at the ceiling, and the crowd condensing around Hiram hesitated, breaking into particles.

"Why do you hate Sister Bevan?" The Sin Eater climbed to her feet, laboring with each motion as if in great pain. Hiram wished he had the pistol himself. "Why do you wish her to suffer for her sins?"

"Jesus suffered for her sins," Hiram said, his voice softer than he intended. "If Sister Bevan hasn't already repented, she will."

"Not everyone is saved." The Sin Eater cracked the knuckles of each hand, slowly.

"But there is only one Savior," Hiram told her. "And you know it."

"Everyone out!" Michael shouted again, but no one paid him any mind.

"Are you calling me a fraud?" the Sin Eater asked.

"I think you're something worse than a fraud," Hiram said. "Why don't you show yourself?"

Hiram felt cool air. Over the heads of the crowd again clustering about him, he saw the top of the chapel door open.

"Get away from the Sin Eater!" Michael called. "Get out of here and go home!"

"Surrender," Hiram suggested. "Come with me, and leave these people in peace."

"You urge the shepherd to leave his flock." The Sin Eater smiled, showing teeth.

"Some men protect the flock," Hiram countered. "Others eat the sheep. Only the former are shepherds."

"Pap!" Michael slammed the door shut. "There's something out there!"

A shriek pierced the smoky air from near one of the windows. A woman wearing a dark green hoop skirt seventy years out of fashion collapsed.

"You didn't warn me anything like this might happen!" Bishop Pritchard hissed.

Hiram pushed the Bishop back and then stepped toward the Sin Eater, drawing a lamen, a written paper amulet, from his pocket. He wasn't certain it would contain the Sin Eater, but he hoped it might at least reveal her true face.

The Sin Eater leaped forward, jaws gaping. Two rows of long, yellow, pointed fangs opened as wide as a bear trap and a fetid wind of reeking wet air washed over Hiram.

Hiram punched her in the face, knocking her to the ground.

The crowd surged toward the windows and doors. Dull thuds and a racket of scratching filled the air. "Bar the doors!" Michael bellowed. "Stay away from the windows!"

Ifor Bevan took a swing at Michael and Michael laid him out with a single left-handed punch.

The Sin Eater lay on the floor, face down. "You would hit a woman?" she asked slowly.

"I'm pretty certain I haven't," Hiram said. Stooping, he tucked the lamen into the neck of her dress, beneath her bun of hair.

Even before he stood, he saw her disguise fall away. His fingertips grazed the back of a neck that was gray and scaly, and the Sin Eater that had seemed to be five feet tall lay across eight feet of floor.

Hiram took a deep breath and stepped back. Bishop Pritchard mumbled incoherently and fled across the dais toward a window. Following him with his eyes, Hiram saw pale faces, slack and peeling with rot, bob outside in the darkness. Hands like flippers, whose fingers seemed to have lost all independent power of motion, slapped at the glass.

The congregation mostly surged in a choppy pool of humanity in the center of the room, though a knot of men clustered at each door, barring entrance to the horrors scraping outside. Michael yelled direction at the men guarding the doors. Bishop Pritchard, gibbering with fear, nevertheless dragged a woman away from a window toward the huddled mass in the center.

Hiram stood alone at the front.

Alone with the Sin Eater.

"Do you have a name?" he asked. "Do you have kin?"

The Sin Eater climbed slowly to its feet and swung to face him. It had a snout like a snub-nosed alligator, but with six eyes: two facing forward, like a lizard's, two on its cheeks facing to the sides, and two where two nostrils should be, blinking slowly above long yellow teeth.

"Do you care?" the Sin Eater asked.

"No," Hiram said. "I care only that you leave."

But it was half a lie. He prized knowledge, from whatever source he could get it.

"You hit hard," the Sin Eater said.

"God will hit you harder," Hiram told it. "Repent now or flee the light."

The Sin Eater's attack came so fast that Hiram didn't see it. The monster struck him in the chest and hurled him through the railing, smashing a length of it to splinters. Hiram banged against the sacrament table and rolled across the dais, losing his Fedora in the process.

He scrambled to his feet despite a wave of pain that engulfed his left side. He expected to be seized by the monster, but instead, the Sin Eater bounded into the pews, snuffling after something on the floor.

The loaf.

The men at the doors yelled. Michael bellowed at them, encouraging them with words Hiram wished his son didn't know, as the forces outside pushed. The doors bowed inward, buckled, and even slipped open momentarily before collapsing shut again.

The crowd in the center of the hall reared back from the Sin Eater, gasping and weeping. Bishop Pritchard stood at their head, arms raised ineffectuality.

Hiram took the lantern nearest him from its hook and stepped wearily to the sacrament table. "Sin Eater!" he yelled.

The grey beast rose from the pews and turned to face Hiram, brandishing in long-nailed hands the round loaf of crusty bread.

Hiram slammed the kerosene lantern onto the sacrament table. The tame dancing flame became a sudden pyre, a tower of light jetting three feet into the air. He reached into his pocket and pulled out the loaf of bread hidden there.

It was the same loaf he had plucked from Sister Bevan's coffin scant minutes before the funeral had begun, substituting it with another.

He raised the loaf high. "This is what you came for, child of Satan."

The Sin Eater snuffled at its own loaf, the eyes at the tip of its snout dilating and blinking as it did so. With a sudden roar, it tossed the loaf aside.

"Thief!" it bellowed.

Hiram picked up a wooden splinter, heavy and sharp as a dagger.

"You can't have Sister Bevan," he said. "There's only pain for you here. Leave now."

He laid his loaf, the bread the monster had used for whatever sorcery it performed, onto the flame.

The Sin Eater bounded forward and Hiram leaped to meet it. The monster was focused on the flame rather than on him, and in its distraction, Hiram jammed his splinter into the beast's throat.

Then he wrapped his arms around the monster's chest.

The reptilian death-stink of the beast and the crisp stench of burning bread mingled in his nostrils. The Sin Eater tried to lunge forward and Hiram let himself hang like a dead weight, dragging the monster down. Falling together, they fell short of the table and struck the edge of the dais on the way down.

Hiram's vision swam, blurring into a river of stars. The beast roared, clawing at him with the long nails on hands and feet. Hiram squeezed harder, but the Sin Eater finally ripped him away by brute force and tossed him onto the front pew.

Hiram struggled to sit or stand but failed. He fought to inhale and his ribs felt as if they might burst through his skin.

The Sin Eater pounced on the flame, smacking its claws into the fire until the light was doused, leaving only a single lantern dimly lighting the chapel. The monster scooped the bread from the sacrament table into its mouth, throwing back its head and roaring. Black powder fell from its jaws, sprinkling its massive shoulders.

"Ash!" it cried. "Ash, all ash!"

"Soon . . . you too," Hiram grunted.

The Sin Eater spun on Hiram and stalked toward him, growling and snapping its jaws. "I will not go alone!"

"No," a voice said.

And with the voice came light.

Hiram blinked. His eyes filled with tears, and for a moment, he couldn't see. Covering his face with one hand, he slowly forced his eyes open to peer between cracked fingers.

Between him and the Sin Eater stood Sister Bevan. She turned to look at Hiram, her wide mouth smiling kindly and her eyes twinkling.

"No," Sister Bevan said again. "You cannot have Hiram."

The Sin Eater screamed and fell to one knee, tucking all its eyes into the crook of one arm. "But the others!"

"What others?" Sister Bevan's voice was mild but echoed with great volume.

A second figure in white stepped down from the sacrament table, as if the table were the bottom rung of a ladder or the lowest step of a staircase. Hiram didn't recognize the figure's face, but it was a man, and like Sister Bevan, he glowed from head to foot.

Then a third figure stepped down.

Then a fourth, and then came a stream.

The Sin Eater staggered to its feet and lurched away. Before it could run, the white figures seized it. They raised it above their heads, more figures joining as the procession moved forward. Were twenty angelic beings crowded beneath the Sin Eater's squirming, roaring body? Thirty?

They carried the monster toward the door where Michael stood.

Hiram tried to stand but couldn't. He lay across the back of the pew and reached a hand toward his son. "Michael!"

Michael put his pistol away and shoved his way into the knot of men around they door. They stared, terror writ openly on their faces, as the Sin Eater and its captors advanced. Michael shoved and dragged them aside, and finally stood back himself, dropping to his knees and averting his face as the figures in white arrived.

Untouched, the door opened.

Hiram dragged himself across the pew, staggered over the aisle, and finally pressed himself into the window.

Across the snow-covered churchyard, he watched shambling, white-clad bodies turn and walk toward the procession of light. They moved stiffly and slowly, but somehow the procession itself slowed to permit their approach. The lumbering, shambling bodies reached the glowing white beings and melted into them, one at a time, and with each addition the marchers glowed more brightly.

Then the last of the shuffling attackers disappeared, absorbed by the angelic host.

For a moment, poised at the edge of the churchyard, Hiram thought he saw Sister Bevan turn and look back at him.

The Sin Eater shrieked, a strangled, tortured sound.

And then the procession was gone, and the Sin Eater with it. The only light illuminating the chapel came from the single remaining lantern hanging from its wall hook.

Hiram flopped onto his back and concentrated on his breathing. Carefully, he examined himself for injuries. His ribcage ached, and he expected to have a spectacular bruise on his side in the morning, but he didn't think he had any broken bones, and he wasn't bleeding.

A hand offered itself.

"Brother Woolley." The speaker was Ifor Bevan.

Hiram took the proffered assistance and climbed to his feet. In the corner of his eye, he saw Michael, keeping a close watch on Ifor.

"Please call me Hiram."

"I didn't know," Ifor said.

"To be honest, I didn't either."

"Was that woman always a monster?" Ifor shook his head. "Disguised as a woman? Or did she become a monster?"

"I don't know." Hiram shrugged, then winced as the gesture shot pain down his ribs on both sides. "I find I just do the best I can, without ever knowing for sure. Judgment belongs to God."

Ifor looked at his feet. "So does salvation."

"So does salvation," Hiram agreed. He offered Ifor his best grin, shook the man's hand, and limped to the dais, looking for his hat.

AUTHOR'S PREFACE TO
WITCHY EYE

Witchy Eye got a second edition. I should acknowledge the enduring interest of readers, and the strong and persistent support of my editor and publisher, Toni Weisskopf. The second edition had to differ from the first, for contractual reasons (we wanted to start giving away the ebook first edition for free online, so the second edition had to differ from the first). One of the two things I added to the book for the second edition was this author's preface.

I get asked, *Where did the Witchy War come from?* I've answered the question many times, on panels, in interviews, and in podcasts, but for the sake of all those who just read the books without hunting down all the author's media appearances, I'll set forth some answers here, too.

I say "some" answers because I think there are multiple explanations or sources, some of which may even elude me.

One way to answer the question is in terms of what I was reading at the time I began the project. I had finished my second novel (as of now, unpublished, but it garnered me my first agent), and was casting about for a new project, and several different streams of my reading collided.

One stream was the Brothers Grimm stories, which I was reading to my children. We had already read the Uncle Remus tales and were trying to find something equally deep and gritty, and the German stories fit the bill nicely. As it happened, I was reading at the same time a history of the Thirty Years War (I forget which one, I own several), and I had an embarrassingly late epiphany. I had always loved the setting of the Grimm tales, but never really understood it. It wasn't just the early modern technology, which I think of as the Froggy Went a-Courtin' tech level, at which a cavalier might ride with both a sword and a pistol by his side. It was also the delightfully patchwork political framework, in which a bishop and a lord mayor and an emperor might all interact. And it was also this setting that seemed to have a frontier element, in which towns were hacked out of deep, gnarled forests, and castles clung to perilously steep mountainsides.

Somehow, in my youth, I had never realized that this fairytale land was early modern Germany, as part of the Holy Roman Empire. Suddenly, at the age of nearly forty, my eyes were opened.

I thought, aha, what a great setting, I should set my next book in this land. I began imagining fallen cavaliers who would be armed with sword and pistol both, and dangerous princesses concealed from overbearing emperors, and oathbound, mystery-bearing monks.

As I was sketching out ideas for the story, I finished the history of the Thirty Years War and picked up the next book from my bedside stack, which happened to be David Hackett Fischer's *Albion's Seed*. This is an anthropological history of the four great English migrations to North America (the Roundheads, the Cavaliers, the Quakers, and the Scotch-Irish). Each migration gets a detailed two-hundred-page discussion of the many features distinguishing it from the others: marriage ways, food, ideas about law, hierarchy, and freedom, clothing and architecture, religion, naming patterns, and much more. Then the historian shows the continuity between the English source of the migration and the practices of the emigrants after their arrival in the New World.

I read *Albion's Seed* and I thought, wow, I wish that roleplaying game settings were this detailed. Wow, I wish fantasy novels had this much world-building background in them. Wow, someone should really take this stuff and use it as the backdrop for a series of books. A series of fantasy books. American epic fantasy, using the many American cultures (not just the four English migration streams) rather than halflings and ogres and elves. And that series should incorporate American legend and folklore—mound-builders, giants, standing stones, lost civilizations, Americans living within the framework of the Biblical epic, and all that.

I would love reading those books, I knew.

But who would write them, if not me?

Another stream that flowed into these waters came from my own life. We have three children. Our son was born with one ear stuck to the side of his head, from having been pressed against the wall of the womb; it gradually opened, remaining, perhaps, slightly asymmetrical to this day. One of our daughters inherited a recessive trait in my wife's family, resulting in a glorious shock of curly, ungovernable hair.

And our other daughter has eyes that dilate at different sizes. My brother noticed this when he was visiting us and she was only weeks old, resulting in a rushed trip to the doctor to make sure she didn't have, for instance, a concussion. She was fine; her eyes simply dilate to different sizes. From that time, I began calling her my "witchy-eyed child," or even just "Witchy Eye." So when I began putting together an American epic fantasy with fairytale and quest elements, partly inspired by the Brothers Grimm tales that I was reading to my children, I decided that I would build the story, in a sense, around my children.

Around three children, each with strange gifts and a curious facial quirk, and their connection with their strange, magical father and their powerful, regal mother. Around three children whose quest would require them to gain self-knowledge and learn the lost secrets of their ancestors to be able to vanquish evil and take their place in the world.

There are many other streams flowing into this story. How I see the Bible and the spiritual inheritance of mankind is no doubt one. I read the Venerable Bede and Gerald of Wales and Geoffrey of Monmouth and grew interested in the conciliar model of Christendom described by those writers. My love of languages and cultures is absolutely another key thread. Ancient Egypt has always been a fascinating subject of study to me, and you should definitely hear an echo of the father-son divine dyad Osiris and Horus in Peter Plowshare and Simon Sword. I recall also a map in an article in *National Geographic*, showing the water systems of North America. I stared at the map, realizing that everything between the Rocky Mountains and the Appalachians was one giant basin, and that the Ohio and the Mississippi were a single river system draining that basin into the Gulf of Mexico. *And if that river system had a god?* I asked myself. *What would that god look like?* What lies behind the intersection of the Teays River, Doggerland, and the Apocalypse of John's vision of "a new heaven and a new earth"? Was the character of Thalanes inspired by the various priest characters of Katherine Kurtz's Deryni books, great favorites of my youth?

Does the character of Captain Sir William Johnston Lee partly reflect Charles Portis's Rooster Cogburn, a delightful discovery of my adulthood?

I started writing *Witchy Eye* as a young adult novel. I had written, as I recall, three chapters when my friend Michael Dalzen, who was in my writing critique group, the Story Monkeys, said, "Dave, I think this the book where you should just really let loose and write the story you want to write. It shouldn't be YA, write for grownups. Don't worry about losing your readers, pull no punches, put in there exactly what you would want to see."

Which was great advice.

So I took it.

THIS EDITION of *Witchy Eye* contains not only this preface, but also a short story written for the purpose, called "Calvin Calhoun Sees the Lights of Atlanta." It's a story about young Calvin, that sets up a comment he makes in the book, and also answers an important question. What had young Calvin ever done to make his grandpa Iron Andy see that he was going to be a hell of a feller? What feats had Cal accomplished, in his modest way, that would make the Elector willing to entrust his own sacred charge to the young man of eighteen?

Calvin Calhoun Sees the Lights of Atlanta

Calvin Calhoun is one of the romantic heroes of the Witchy War. He remains stubbornly faithful to an unrequited love, and he risks and stretches himself to grow, first into the "hell of a feller" his grandfather sees he can become, and then into Iron Andy's proxyholder in the parliamentary knife-fighting in Philadelphia, and then finally (spoilers) into the Calhoun Elector fighting the great battles as the Empire comes crashing down.

Such a character deserves backstory. Cal has a line in Witchy Eye *about having seen the lights of Atlanta, and having been mistreated by strangers only on account of his Appalachee origins. That gave me enough hook. Plus, I wanted to explore where his characteristic tomahawk and moccasins came from.*

T he boy at the end of the bar was nearly man-height, though he could only have been twelve years old. He had long red hair, pulled back behind his head in a loose queue. His face was bony, eyes protruding and nose less like an eagle's beak and more like a hatchet's blunt curve. He wore a gray match coat over a loose hunter's shirt, and an old fowling piece leaned against the plank beside him. Thin lips pressed together in pride, he guided a ha'penny across the scarred wood with one finger.

It was midafternoon, and the tavern was slow. Gospel Boots Johnson set a tankard in front of the boy and filled it as full as he judged he could, without spilling. Small beer, scarcely any alcohol at all in it. Then he spooned in a great dollop of molasses, leaving the spoon behind.

The boy nodded. He stirred his beer, making a show of having no urgency.

Boots took a bucket and rag from beneath the counter and set to work casually on a sticky spot. "Heading into the city?"

The boy shrugged. "Followin' friends." His voice was a high-pitched Appalachee whine. "Where'er they go, I reckon."

"Come far?" Boots asked. "I don't expect you're from around here."

The boy took a sip of the beer. His hand shook as he drank, and Boots saw skinned knuckles and dirty nails. It was by an act of will that the boy kept his sip small. "Up Nashville way."

"All two hundred fifty miles on foot?" Boots didn't ask, *and alone?*

The boy nodded.

"Listen," Boots said. "I have this bread." He left the rag where it was and collected a breadboard behind the bar. It held a quarter loaf, a bit of hard cheese, and a knife. He set it in front of the boy.

The boy's eyes widened, but he shook his head. "I'll drink what I've paid for."

"You're not following me," Boots said. "This is left over. It's only good for attracting mice. I was about to throw it to the pig, only the pig's already eaten, so this food would only get trampled into the mud. Why don't you do me this service, friend? Just eat this bread and cheese so I don't have to see it go to waste."

"Hey, Gospel!" one of the muleskinners in the corner bellowed. "You going to fill up my beer, or do I have to wait for your wife to squeeze out another little Johnson, and then sit patient while that squirt learns to walk so it can come serve me?"

"The latter!" Boots barked back.

"Be about ten minutes, then!" a second muleskinner roared.

The caravan men, regulars who worked the triangular trade between Chattanooga, Birmingham, and Atlanta, all burst into laughter.

"Lord hates a man as can't do an act of service when it's called for," the boy said. "And the prodigal son wasn't above eatin' a little pig food."

"Thank you." Boots nodded and waddled over to deal with the merchants.

He filled the muleskinners' mugs and came back to the counter to find that the boy had neatly sliced himself a wafer of bread and a morsel of cheese and was slowly nibbling both. "If you ain't hungry enough now," Boots said, "please take whatever's left with you for the road. I've been to Nashville, folks there were always kind to me. Maybe I know your people."

"Elector Calhoun's my grandpa," the boy said. "Name's Calvin. Calvin Calhoun."

"Sweet Beulah," Boots said. "That's some people you've got. Good to meet you, Calvin. My name's Gospel Boots Johnson. Folks call me Gospel or Boots, to taste."

"Sounds like a Roundhead name," Calvin suggested.

"It does," Boots agreed. "I'm Pennslander by birth, but my mother was born in the Covenant Tract. Who are these friends you're following?"

Calvin sipped his beer and looked Boots in the eye. "They ain't really my friends. I'm followin' a passel of Ferdinandians leadin' a herd of cattle down from Chattanooga."

"Looking to buy a few head?" Boots asked.

"I ain't really followin' the hidalgos as such," Calvin said. "Those cows are Calhoun beasts. They got stole from under my nose by some Polk boys. And you know how those Polks can be."

"Tell me."

"Ordinarily, fair's fair," Calvin said. "You swing me round the one side, and I'll swing you round the other. But the Polks as stole my family's cattle headed right off to Chattanooga, like they weren't even fixin' to hold on to the animals. Like they weren't fixin' to give us a chance to steal 'em back. So I didn't even tell my grandpa, I jest followed the Polks."

"Your people don't know you're here?" Boots gulped. The Elector Calhoun had a reputation for ferocity in defense of his own, and Boots had sudden mental images of war breaking out in Appalachee over the missing boy.

"I reckon not," Calvin said.

"And the Polks must have sold the cattle to the Ferdinandians," Boots said.

"In Chattanooga. Afore I could do anythin' about it." Calvin grimaced.

"This is a lot of work to go to for some cows," Boots said. "And danger. How many Ferdinandians are there?"

"I make 'em seven, by their tracks," Calvin said. "They're my family's cattle, Mr. Gospel. And the one . . . well, the one is my own heifer, Red Sally. I've been trackin' her in particular. She's got a trick to the one hoof you can't miss. She's my first cow, gift of my grandpa hisself, and I don't plan on losin' her."

"Listen," Boots said. "I don't know how you aim to drive a bunch of cattle by yourself all the way back to Nashville."

"With difficulty," Calvin said. "But I've driven cattle afore."

"Maybe there's an easier way." Boots jerked his thumb over his shoulder. "The building next to this one is the sheriff's office. Why don't I take you over there, you can swear out a warrant, and then the sheriff and his man can go seize the herd? They have your brand on them?"

"They surely do," Calvin said. "It's sometimes called a flyin' C on account of it looks like a letter C with wings. Only what it really is is a C with an E stuck on its back backward."

"E-C for the Elector Calhoun?"

"That's it," Calvin agreed. "Highland heraldry, my grandpa'd call it."

Booted nodded. "Going to the sheriff will be less dangerous for you. And once you've got the cattle back legally, we can write to the Elector to get him to send help. Or I can help you hire someone."

"I confess these sound like city ways." Calvin's expression was openly dubious. "You reckon it could work?"

"It's how it's supposed to work," Boots said. "Shall we go talk to the sheriff?"

Calvin hesitated, weighing something internally. Finally, he produced a dull silver shilling and set it on the counter. "I'll come with you, Mr. Gospel, iffen first you can sell me the biggest bottle of the hardest alcohol you've got. Whatever I can git for this shillin'. Homemade, for preference. The rough stuff. The stuff as gits you drunk by the second sip and blind by the third."

"Promise me it isn't for you," Boots said.

"Not me, Mr. Gospel. I been studyin' to take up the New Light, so I've mostly entirely given up drink."

SCATTERED autumn rains and the usual traffic had churned up the dirt street beyond the tavern's door. Boots looked down at Calvin's feet, half-fearing he'd find the boy unshod, but Calvin wore heavy black leather shoes that plowed efficiently through the mud, though the street sucked at his heels as he slogged forward.

The sheriff's door hung open and Boots knocked as he entered. "Sheriff Perkins!"

Calvin followed him with slight hesitation.

The cells in back held a single prisoner, a scruffy leatherstocking Boots didn't recognize. A deputy named White leaned against the wall on a stool watching the prisoner and whittling at a long stick.

The sheriff sat in the front of the office at his table. He was a bony man with a large head and sunken, heavy-lidded eyes. Two of the table's legs were dramatically shorter than the other two; the gaps were filled with a copy of *Georgia Statutes* under one leg and a copy of *Poor Richard's Sermons* under the other. The sheriff labored at an account book with a quill pen, his fingers stained black.

"Johnson," the sheriff growled. "Good, you've arrested someone. I hope there's a notable bounty on his head. We're experiencing a deficit here, and could stand a little revenue."

Calvin stood with his feet shoulder-width apart. "They's no bounty on my head in this town or any other."

The sheriff grunted. "Law abiding, are you?"

"I didn't claim that," Calvin said coolly. "But honest as any other feller, I reckon."

The sheriff abruptly launched a brown wad from his cracked lips into a brass spittoon at his feet. "Well, if you're looking for a job, I ain't hiring. No money."

"This young man and his family have been robbed," Boots said.

Sheriff Perkins sighed. "And naturally, you imagine it to be your business."

"No," Boots said. "But I thought that if he would swear out a warrant, you and your deputies could help him by legal process, and he could avoid some . . . foolish risks."

"Legal process? Foolish risks?" The sheriff squinted at Calvin. "What is it, boy? You come down to these piney woods on a vendetta?"

"I come to steal back my family cattle," Calvin said. "I reckon I don't mind admittin' that."

The sheriff guffawed. "You don't mind admitting?"

Calvin nodded. "Lord hates a man as tells an unnecessary lie."

"Oh, I admire your mettle." The sheriff laid down his pen and wiped ink on his brown flannel shirt. "Now listen to me, son. Who has your cattle?"

"Seven Ferdinandians, I make 'em."

"Adults?" the sheriff asked. "Armed?"

"Grown men by the size of their boots," Calvin told him. "Pretty sure they have rifles, at least. A man'd be a fool to travel as far as they have without a weapon."

"And so you are also armed. Is that your father's bird gun?"

"It was my grandpa's when he was a youngun. Now it's mine. It's jest a quarter-inch ball, but she throws it straight and true."

"And you're alone. Chased these men down from up Appalachee somewhere, by the sound of your voice. Brands will be some Appalachee brands, not Georgia brands I'd recognize."

"Nashville."

Sheriff Perkins nodded. "You're a brave young man. I ain't going to help you, but I will tell you why not."

"I don't reckon you need to," Calvin said.

"You think it's on account of I look down on Appalachee, but that ain't it."

"You don't have to look down on my folk," Calvin said. "All you have to do is think about how they's a lot of Ferdinandian cattle traffic that comes through here, and you don't want to disrupt it. And is one poor cracker from up in the mountains worth the trouble? Of course not."

Boots shifted from one foot to the other, clearing his throat.

"Hey, now," the sheriff said.

"They's an awful lot of the dons livin' none too far south of here," Calvin continued. "You wouldn't want to rile 'em up, make 'em come up here and cause a fuss. That might cost you your job, and you wouldn't want that, not for some chawbacon runt from the mountains."

"The situation requires diplomacy."

"Above all," Calvin said, "you got you and the one deputy, as far as I can see. You don't want to risk life and limb confrontin' cattle rustlers. Especially not when they rustled the cattle somewhere far away and are jest passin' through. Especially not jest to help some gangly redneck child."

"I did not say any of those things," the sheriff protested.

"No," Calvin said. "You jest said that you wouldn't help me. You said enough."

"Calvin," Boots said. "Calvin, wait."

"Thank you, Mr. Gospel." The boy turned went out into the street, where rain again was beginning to fall.

IT WASN'T hard to follow the Ferdinandians. Calvin was a good tracker, had played tracking games with his cousins and with Shawnee children living around Calhoun Mountain since his earliest memories. But if he'd been blind, he could have tracked the herd of cattle by feeling the disturbed earth in their wake on his hands and knees. The occasional sight of Red Sally's trick hoof just added poignancy to the simple task.

As raincloud and evening lowered to smother the day, Calvin climbed away from the highway into the piney wood hills. Away to the south, a cluster of lights on a river startled him. For a moment, he feared that he had come too far, and was seeing Miami.

But no, Miami would be on the ocean. The river must be the Chatta- hoochee, the lights the lights of Atlanta.

His encounter with the helpful Gospel Boots Johnson and the utterly unhelpful Sheriff Perkins had steeled Calvin's resolve to take action. The farther he got from home, the farther he got from any real help. He could take action now, or he could walk away and go back to Calhoun Mountain.

He didn't feel any sense of shame at the thought of going home, but he did feel a vague sense of disappointment. A feller ought to be able to do something, when a wrong was done to him. No one would say Calvin hadn't tried, but he didn't want to be the young man who had tried to bring back the herd and failed.

He wanted to be like his grandpa. He wanted people to sing songs about him, tip their hats in respect, and speak his name with just a little bit of awe.

So he marched up to the Ferdinandians' camp with a large bottle of hard moonshine and a little bit of a plan.

Not too much of a plan, mind. Lord hates a man as can't be flexible in his thinking.

A man leaped out of the darkness and shouted at Calvin in Castilian. Firelight from somewhere back in the trees gleamed dully on the barrel of a musket the man pointed at him.

"Sorry." Calvin kept his bird gun pointed at the earth. "Do you speak English?"

"What do you want?" the stranger demanded. Calvin could just make out his silhouette, which was mostly a long coat and a broad-brimmed hat.

"It's rainin', mister," Calvin said. "I'm jest lookin' for a place to sleep." He squinted toward the fire, now discerning a couple of canvas tents. Beyond, he thought he could make out the reddish flank of a cow and a switching tail. "They's outlaws in these woods, and I'd appreciate the company."

"Oh yes?" the hidalgo asked. "How much do you appreciate it?"

He meant money. "Oh, I guess I could go a couple of pennies for it," Calvin said. "Same as I'd a spent for a bed in an ordinary, I reckon. Especially iffen I could git in under a tent flap and outta this rain."

"Show me the pennies," the stranger said.

Calvin took his purse from his belt. It was distressingly light, but he wasn't worried about needing money for the trip home. He could sleep outside and take birds for his supper, if needed. He opened the purse and extracted two pennies.

Then he heard the click of a hammer being pulled back behind him. He turned slowly and saw a second Ferdinandian. This man, too, wore a long coat and broad hat and pointed a musket at Calvin. With the light shining on his face, Calvin could see the swarthy complexion, the dark eyes, and the yellow glint of bared teeth.

"We will take *all* the money," the second hidalgo said.

"It ain't much more," Calvin said. "An old John Penn shillin', a couple of bits."

The first Ferdinandian snatched the purse from Calvin's hand and then yanked away his rifle.

"Hey, now," Calvin said.

They knocked him to the ground with the butts of their muskets. "You sound Appalachee," one said.

"You sound Ferdinandian," he shot back.

One man punched Calvin in the face with his musket butt and the other stood on Calvin's chest. They patted him down, taking the bread and cheese, the bottle, and the fowling gun.

"I jest don't want to drown in the rain," Cal said. "Keep the food and the drink. That's good moonshine, that is. The strong stuff. I jest need a place for the night."

"And what *I* need," one of the hidalgos said, "is a pair of shoes."

Calvin swung his fist, but for his trouble he was knocked in the face again with a musket butt, and then his shoes were stripped from his feet.

"You fixin' to leave me out here to die?" Calvin heard a sob in his own voice despite his best efforts.

Both muskets were pointed at him. "As you said," one hidalgo told him, "there are outlaws in these woods."

The two men guffawed. Calvin stumbled to his feet and slid down the hill in the mud. The lights of Atlanta to his right seemed to mock him as he forced himself to continue almost down to the highway, trying to be certain he wasn't followed or observed.

"Jerusalem," he muttered as he turned and cut off into the woods at a new angle. "That about knocks my plan sideways."

He had hoped to encourage the Ferdinandians to drink all the moonshine, and then slip off with the cattle in the middle of the night. His feet too numb to feel the pine needles stabbing into them, he reflected that maybe some of that plan might still work.

Only now he was barefoot and unarmed, and if the dons saw him creeping back into their camp, they might shoot him.

"Without purse or scrip," he told himself, teeth chattering. "Better fellers'n me have been in tighter straights."

He knew where the camp was, at least. And sneaking up on a watched herd of cattle was an old game, played by Calhoun younguns among themselves long before they ever set to it seriously, in pursuit of Donelson or Jackson cows. Calvin made his way one careful step at a time, matchcoat pulled up around his face to keep the firelight from shining on his cheeks and jaw clenched to keep his teeth from rattling. He breathed into the wool to keep his own exhalations hidden in the cold air, and slowly located the hidalgo sentries by the jets of steam they emitted and the cracking of pine needles as they shifted position to stay awake.

He found a position from which he could watch the camp and he repositioned himself bundled inside his match coat to get his feet out of the mud. As feeling slowly returned to his toes, he watched four Ferdinandians laugh and joke in Castilian. One of the men held up Calvin's shoes, barked something boisterous, and then hurled them out into the woods in different directions.

Then they smashed his grandpa's gun over a big rock and shattered it.

Jerusalem.

They did pass around the bottle. And after a few sips, they started to sing. Calvin was a singer himself, and ordinarily, music tempted him to sing along. In this case, he found the melodies cruel and arrogant, and he ground his teeth together in silent irritation.

The sentries must have found the signing more attractive, though, because they gradually came to the fire. The flames were mostly shielded by long pine boughs stretching overhead, but hissed and popped as rain drops passed through, or aggregated together into fat beads of water and fell from the branches onto the coals. Calvin could understand none of the conversation that passed among the men, but the sentries must have demanded their share, because the bottle got passed around, and then the innkeeper's bread and cheese.

Calvin's stomach rumbled.

He waited.

The night grew long. The cold kept him awake, and the pain in his face, and the desire to get back his family's cattle. He repeatedly counted the Ferdinandians, reassuring himself that there continued to be seven of them. He kept counting, resisting the urge to go look to the cattle, as the fire died down and the men dropped off, one by one.

Finally, a dull red glow was all that remained of the fire. Its baleful aura washed the canvas tents and the heaped-up Ferdinandians in infernal tints, and the ragged sound of snoring drifted through the pine trunks.

Calvin searched for his shoes.

And could not find either.

"Jerusalem." He crept to the edge of camp, hoping that maybe one of the Ferdinandians had taken the trouble of removing his footgear before passing at. His luck failed him; every one of them lay asleep with his boots on.

"Barefoot it is," he muttered.

Fair is fair, and it would have been a reasonable thing to borrow some of the hidalgos' coins. If nothing else, to replace what they'd stolen from him, in cash and in his gun and in his shoes. But Calvin was afraid to wake the men in his search, so he turned to the cattle.

The cows huddled in a gully, sheltered by its high sides and the pines all around and above it, and boxed in with two long pine logs lashed across tree trunks at the gully mouth. They emitted the soft, rumbling lowing of a herd at night, a few cropping at what grass they could find while the others slept. Calvin still had his knife in his belt, and he quickly cut free one of the logs, opening the gully.

The dons still snored.

"Boy," a voice whispered.

Calvin spun about, knife ready. In the shadow of a pine, he could just see a man sitting on the ground, ropes around his chest and arms, binding him to the tree trunk. The man wore fringed leather and had long black hair. On his feet, he wore moccasins.

"Free me," the man whispered.

He was no hidalgo. Clearly, he was the Ferdinandians' prisoner.

"What are you doin' here?" Calvin asked. Just because the man was his enemies' prisoner, didn't mean the man was Calvin's friend.

"Don't worry, I won't wake them," the man said.

"What are you doin' here?" Calvin kept his knife low, trying to look serious without looking threatening.

"I came to steal the cattle," the man said.

"Indian?"

"Creek."

"Why didn't they kill you? Why tie you up?"

"They think there might be a price on my head. But if they find there is none, then they have said they will hang me. The hidalgos are especially harsh on cattle rustlers."

That sounded about right. "They're my cattle," Calvin said. "These fellers stole 'em from my family, I'm a-stealin' 'em back."

"I won't take your cows," the Creek said.

Calvin considered. If he didn't set the man free, he could sound an alarm, and Calvin certainly didn't want to kill him. He didn't want to kill the Ferdinandians, for that matter. "I expect if I said as much, I'd want you to take me seriously. Hold still, and I'll cut you free."

The Indian grunted.

Calvin set to it with his knife, and quickly cut the Creek loose. When he'd finished, he stepped back. The freed prisoner slowly removed the ropes from his body and stood. He nodded, and then turned and plunged into one of the hidalgo tents.

Calvin had sudden visions of the Indian waking up the Ferdinandians. Cutting himself a pine switch, he waded into the gully and began driving the cattle out.

His feet were numb again, but he couldn't spare a thought for that. He ignored the squelch of his toes in the mud and he slapped at the flanks of the cattle. He whispered to the beasts, cracked his switch across their rumps, and otherwise cajoled, bullied, and lured them out of the gully.

He gave Red Sally a kiss when he found her, near the back of the herd. Then he smacked her hindquarters, sending her with the others down toward the highway.

As they moved, the cattle began to low with more urgency.

How much noise would it take to awaken the hidalgos?

And if they slept until morning, how many miles could Calvin have put between himself and them? He reviewed what he remembered of the highway. He'd need to make as many miles as he could in the dark, and then hide before dawn came, somewhere off the road, somewhere where he could move the cattle from the highway without leaving obvious tracks behind.

He remembered a stream, a stream that might be wide enough and stony enough to drive the cattle up and hide their tracks. He thought it was maybe five miles north along the road. Did he have time to make it?

And what if the Ferdinandians went to Sheriff Perkins and swore out a warrant? Would his family's brand be enough to convince the sheriff?

He redoubled his efforts with the switch.

He heard a shout in Castilian. Had it come from the camp? He cursed the cows with all his might, swearing by heaven and earth as well as by the city of the great king, but the cows barely seemed to notice.

Predictably enough.

Did he even have feet anymore? He felt nothing below the knees, and half-wished he had taken the time to steal one of the Ferdinandians' boots.

He heard a gunshot, and then a second. Then shouting.

He wished he spoke Castilian. If only his grandpa, or one of his uncles, had taken the time to give Calvin a little gift of tongues, he might be able to understand what was going on.

But maybe he didn't need any language, after all. Surely it was as simple as that one of the Ferdinandians was a little less drunk than the others. He'd woken up and discovered the missing cattle. Maybe he'd fired a rifle to awaken his companions, and soon enough Calvin would be catching hell from seven armed men.

He gritted his teeth and switched harder.

Calvin's hair suddenly yanked him backward. His neck felt like it might snap, his frozen feet flew out from under him, and he landed hard on his back in the mud.

Above him, blocking out what few stars there were and limned on one side in a dull red glow, loomed one of the hidalgos. Calvin heard the click of the musket being cocked, and muttering in Castilian. Calvin tried to roll aside and found his body breathless, stunned, and not responding.

"My . . . cows," he managed to grunt.

The Ferdinandian shouted, angry sounds.

A meaty *thwack* cut the hidalgo off. Hot liquid spilled onto Calvin's face, the stink of blood filled his nostrils, and the hidalgo sank sideways and toppled to the mud.

Another silhouette stood over Calvin.

"Oh, come *on*," Calvin groaned.

"It's me." The voice was the Creek's. He knelt and slid his arm behind Calvin's shoulders, raising him into sitting position.

Calvin tottered to his feet. "I gotta git the cows out of here."

"Take your time," the Indian said. "The hidalgos won't be bothering you."

Calvin wiped blood from his face. The roots of his hair hurt as if it had been torn from his scalp, and his stomach was growling. "You . . . drove 'em off?"

"I killed them," the Creek said.

"I counted seven," Calvin told him.

"I killed seven. You can count them again, if you wish."

"I expect I believe you," Calvin admitted. He sat on a fallen log and took deep breaths.

"Here are their coins." The Creek pressed a purse into Calvin's hands. It was heavier than the one that had been taken from him, by far. "I'll take the boots off the smallest of them."

"I don't want to wear a dead man's boots," Calvin said. He suddenly felt small, and the deaths of the men, even though they had been riding off with his family's cows, purchased cheap from thieving Polks, seemed enormous.

The Creek was quiet for a moment, then sat. He quickly unlaced his moccasins. Without asking, he brushed mud from Calvin's feet with his fingers and then wrapped each foot in a moccasin, lacing them up with practiced motions. The moccasins had fur on the inside. "You need to walk," the Creek said. "When you've walked for a few minutes, your feet will warm up again."

"Thank you," Calvin said, a little uncertain. "Are you gonna . . . are you fixin' to trade me for some of the cattle?" He didn't want to ask, *Are you going to take some of the cows?*

"No." The Indian stood. "You freed me."

"What's your name?" Calvin stood too.

"Maybe it's better you don't know my name," the Creek said. "Maybe it's better I don't know your name, either." He gestured at the dead man at their feet. "In case anyone comes looking."

"Mebbe it is," Calvin agreed.

"I'll douse the fire and hide the bodies," the Creek said. "This is a half mile from the highway. If we're lucky, it will be a week before anyone finds them."

"Five days, I can be in Chattanooga. The cows'll lose a little weight, but they ain't headed to market anytime soon."

"I'll scalp them, too," the Creek said. "So if anyone comes looking, they won't be looking for you."

Calvin nodded, trying not to think of the scalping. At least the men were already dead.

"You should take a musket," the Indian suggested.

"Too big," Calvin said. "It'd weigh me down. What I need, especially for a day or two, is to move fast and not stop moving."

The Indian nodded, and then he pressed something into Calvin's hand. It took Calvin a moment to recognize the curving rod for what it was, the handle of a tomahawk. "Take this at least. Hang it in your belt."

"Won't you need it?" Calvin asked.

The Creek laughed. "I'll take boots from one of the hidalgos. And a musket, and a sword. I'll have enough."

"And you took some of their money," Calvin said hopefully.

"No." The Creek extended an arm, offering to clasp with Calvin. "I have my freedom. You'll need the money."

Calvin gripped forearms with the Indian, and then the man turned and bounded away into the woods, toward the fire. Calvin leaned against a tree and vomited until nothing came up but bile. Seven men dead. Seven men scalped.

Seven thieves.

He wanted water to rinse the taste from his mouth, but he knew it was a few miles' walk to the nearest spring. He raised his face to the sky with an open mouth, caught a few drops of rain, and spit. It would have to do for now.

Twenty-five miles a day, that's what a cow could walk if you didn't mind it getting a little thin on you. Calvin didn't mind.

He didn't want to see Sheriff Perkins again. Or another hidalgo, not until he'd made it home to Calhoun Mountain, at least.

Recognizing his own heifer looking at him, he picked up his switch and struck the beast.

"Come on, Red Sally," he urged her. "We got miles to go tonight."

His feet were already starting to warm up.

A Short Story by Somerset Maugham

This is an alternate history tale about Oleg Gordievsky. Gordievsky was one of the most important defectors from the Soviet Union to the West during the cold war. Much of the following is not fiction, or it's not very much fiction. Gordievsky really did call his friend Mikhail Lyubimov just before his defection and drop a major clue about what he intended to do. In real life, Lyubimov apparently didn't catch the reference, or did nothing about it, and Gordievsky's defection, basically as described herein, was a close-run, hair-raising escapade, and was successful.

The twist in the tale here is, what if Lyubimov had caught the reference, and had acted upon it? And the underlying thesis is, certain kinds of historical thinking notwithstanding, single individuals can make a huge impact on the course of history. Oleg Gordievsky is a good example. The story was written for and published in Tales from Alternate Earths III. *Many thanks to Brent Harris for inviting me to participate.*

Mikhail Lyubimov answered the phone on the second ring. "Yes."

"Mikhail, this is Oleg."

"Gordievsky, my friend. Don't tell me if you're calling to cancel the visit to my dacha."

"I'm not going to tell you that." Did Oleg's voice sound shaky? Gordievsky, once a rising star in the KGB and the resident of the KGB's London station, had raised eyebrows as a young man with his abstemiousness around alcohol. Lately, though, he'd been drinking. A lot.

"But you're not coming. You don't want to tell me, but you're going to tell me instead how much work you have to do or how you must spend time with Leila and the girls. Which you should do, by the way. She's a gorgeous woman, your Leila. But you'll let me infer that you feel pressed for time, in the hope that I'll let you out of the invitation. Well, I won't. Bring Leila and the girls, if you must."

"I don't want out of the invitation, Mikhail." Did Oleg sound rueful? It was late in the evening, and he was probably just tired. "I'm coming to visit you at your dacha."

"Monday," Lyubimov said. "Tanya will be here. I want you to meet her. She's also a lovely woman. If she's as beautiful as your Leila, neither you nor I are impartial enough to judge, but since I'm sleeping with Tanya—"

"I'll be there, Mikhail," Gordievsky said. "Leila has taken the girls to Azerbaijan."

"To visit her parents? I had forgotten she was Azeri. Very good, no wonder she's such a handsome woman. Monday at 11:53, then."

"At Zvenigorod Station. I've called to tell you how much I'm looking forward to the visit."

"Excellent. Tanya and I also."

"Mikhail," Gordievsky said. "Have you ever read 'Mr. Harrington's Washing'?"

Lyubimov tried to remember whether he had.

"It's a short story by Somerset Maugham," Gordievsky added. There was a hint of emotion in his voice. What was it? Glee? Fear?

"Then of course I've read it. I have his complete works." Lyubimov snorted. "I introduced *you* to Maugham."

"I remember. That's a good story, Mikhail. You might want to read it again. It's in volume four of your collection. Read it, you'll see what I mean."

They chatted a little longer, a few more lines each, and then Lyubimov hung up the phone. He poured himself a drink, a Glenfiddich 40 Year Single Malt that he had because of his Party membership, his diplomatic service, and his own former employment in the KGB. He walked to the glass doors of his dacha's study and looked out at the lights of Zvenigorod, twinkling just a few miles away through the forest.

He had been a KGB man for years, but he was now making a living as a writer. Or rather, he was trying to make a living. He had found words easy to come by, but readers very scarce. He published nothing that wasn't approved by the Party, but some whispered that Mikhail Lyubimov's stories lacked romance and adventure.

Gordievsky had also been a diplomat, and a KGB man, and a member of the Party. In addition to his beautiful family, he had risen to higher status than Lyubimov ever had. He wrote no stories, but his life seemed to contain the romance and adventure that Lyubimov's tales were said to lack.

But was Oleg Gordievsky a member in good standing?

He had been recalled from London under some suspicion. An MI5 officer had offered to spy for the KGB but had been arrested by the British before the offer could be taken up. And agents in Scandinavia had been arrested by their local counterintelligence agencies, as well. Gordievsky had been posted to Denmark, a decade earlier. Was it possible that Oleg had betrayed the Soviet Union? That he had betrayed Arne Treholt of Norway and Stig Bergling of Sweden?

Mikhail rattled himself like a dog emerging from water, trying to shake off the unease and the suspicion.

Mikhail and Oleg had been posted to Denmark at the same time. They had met there. It was in Denmark that Mikhail had introduced Oleg Gordievksy to the English writer, Somerset Maugham. Maugham had had plenty of romance and adventure in his own life, having been a secret operative for the British in Russia, before the Revolution.

Mikhail finished his whisky in a gulp, poured himself a second, and took volume four of Maugham's collected works down from the shelf. He settled himself into a frayed and slouching armchair in the yellow puddle of light from the study's desk lamp and found the short story Oleg had indicated.

As he read, his heart beat faster. He remembered this story now, with its tale of the traveler waiting for his laundry to be finished in Moscow.

Oleg was telling him something.

Mikhail Lyubimov left the story unfinished and volume four cracked open, spine up, on the desk, when he ran to get into his car to drive to Moscow.

THE APARTMENT WOULD BE under surveillance. Even if there were not a cloud of suspicion hanging over Oleg Gordievsky—suspicion the substance of which Oleg himself seemed to have just validated—he was an officer of the KGB, and such men were often watched.

Mikhail had had the presence of mind to bring a bottle of wine with him. He would say that he had had an unexpected reason to come to Moscow this evening and decided to anticipate next week's holidays by cracking open the bottle with his friend Oleg. He had a packet of cigarettes in his coat pocket, but his hands shook too much to be able to smoke them on the drive. They shook so much, he could barely keep control of the car.

It was nearly midnight when he parked in front of Oleg's building. One light was on in the Gordievsky apartment—the kitchen? He imagined Oleg eating alone, or perhaps drinking to soothe his conscience and quiet his nerves, as he climbed the stairs to rap on the door.

Gordievsky answered slowly. Oleg was as handsome as ever, fit as a much younger man. The bastard. He smiled quickly at Mikhail, but the smile looked practiced, false.

"Lyubimov," he said. "This is a surprise."

The apartment would be under surveillance.

Mikhail raised the bottle of wine. Why were his hands shaking? "I thought we could get started on the drinking early."

Oleg stepped aside to let him in. "Did you bring Tanya?"

"Just wine and cigarettes," Mikhail said.

"Ah, a feast."

As Oleg shut the door, Mikhail noticed that his shirtsleeves were rolled up and his hands were wet. "Cleaning the house?"

Oleg pointed to the kitchen sink, which was full of dirty clothes in soapy water. "Leila and the girls are away, and I must have clean shirts for the office."

"'Mr. Harrington's Washing'." Mikhail nodded. "Let me open this bottle so we can get started." He pantomimed writing.

Oleg frowned but produced a pen from a bookcase near the door. Mikhail found the bottle opener, uncorked the wine—an indifferent bottle of Sovetskoye Shampanskoye—and poured two glasses. As he did, he looked around the apartment's living room, noting that it was impeccable. Oleg had been tidying up.

In order to leave the place.

Mikhail took the pen without a word, sat at the square wooden kitchen table, and tore open one of his cigarettes. On the edge of the paper, he wrote: *You're defecting. You're going to Finland. Who will meet you there?*

"This is delicious wine," Oleg said. He hadn't touched his glass. He took the paper and pen from Mikhail and wrote, in a line beneath his friend's words, *I only meant to say goodbye. You must have a drink and go home.*

Mikhail took a drink. *In the story, the man who stays in Moscow is killed. I'm coming with you.* "It's hard to believe it's just shampanskoye."

Oleg: *You're in no danger here. If you come with me, you might die.* His words filled the cigarette paper's last blank space, so after Mikhail saw his writing, Oleg took the cigarette paper back and ate it.

Mikhail carefully opened a second cigarette and drank more wine. While Oleg swept the dried tobacco into a wastebasket, Mikhail wrote: *Your escape plan must have room for a second person.*

Oleg: *Only me.* "This is much better than any drink that can be had in England, for instance."

Mikhail: *There was never a plan to take Leila?*

Oleg sighed and took a drink. *What do you want, Mikhail?* he wrote.

To help the west, Mikhail answered. The words on the tiny scrap of paper were so damning, he showed them to Oleg and then immediately tore the cigarette paper in two, chewing the scrap into quick oblivion.

Oleg: *You're not that ideological.*

"I should have brought a second bottle." Mikhail thought for a minute, then wrote: *A better life. Freedom.* "Two bottles are always better than one."

Oleg arched his eyebrows. "Sometimes a second bottle is too much."

Also adventure, Mikhail wrote. "That doesn't sound very Russian of you, comrade."

Oleg sighed again. *Are you threatening to expose me?*

Mikhail: *Let's not find out. Let me come.*

Oleg sucked at his teeth. "In any case, one bottle is enough for us both tonight. Don't drive tonight, my friend. Sleep on my sofa, and you can travel home tomorrow. Then on Monday, I'll come to your dacha, and we can drink all the wine you like."

Mikhail reached for the last scrap of cigarette paper, but Oleg thrust it into his mouth and ate it.

"These new shoes hurt my feet," Mikhail grumbled.

"You wanted to come," Oleg muttered. "Now keep quiet."

It was afternoon, and they were entering Moscow's Leningrad Station together. The station was mobbed with young socialists from foreign countries, come to Moscow for the Twelfth World Festival of Youth and Students. The air was thick with the smell of unwashed bodies and unbrushed teeth. Both Oleg and Mikhail wore light jackets; neither man had a travel bag.

In the morning, Mikhail had driven away from Oleg's apartment with loud and ostentatious goodbyes, for the benefit of whoever was surveilling the Gordievsky home, and precise instructions. As Oleg had insisted, he had begun by purchasing a new pair of shoes. Then he had ditched his car and traveled in a criss-crossing, apparently aimless web across Moscow, sometimes taking the Metro train and sometimes walking. He changed hats twice and his jacket once while doing so, and now he had met up again with Oleg at the front entrance of the station.

"But why new shoes?" Mikhail pressed.

"In case the KGB has put radioactive dust on the soles of your old ones," Oleg said. "We must not be followed. I, too, am wearing new shoes. Perhaps you have forgotten these techniques."

He hadn't. But Mikhail felt uncomfortable at the thought that the KGB might try to follow him with a Geiger counter. "And what have *you* done this morning?"

"Bought new shoes and wandered back and forth across Moscow." Oleg smiled. "And wondered whether my friend Mikhail would be joining me on my cross-country trip."

Oleg passed Mikhail his ticket. "It's an overnight passage to Leningrad. We should buy bread and sausages for the journey."

"I'll pay." Mikhail slipped the ticket into his jacket pocket. It felt as heavy as a ship's anchor.

"In a few days, we'll be spending pounds Sterling and U.S. dollars, never to see a ruble again in our lives." Oleg grinned, and care seemed to fall away from him like rain off an oiled slicker. "I'm happy to use some of the last of my money to buy food for my friend Mikhail."

He turned to stand in line at the stall, and Lyubimov saw a subtle weight tugging at Oleg Gordievsky's coat pocket. The shape of the bulge and the motion it made as the coat swing around Oleg's hip might have meant nothing to another man, but Lyubimov was a trained KGB officer, and he knew immediately what he had seen.

Oleg was carrying a pistol.

Mikhail was unarmed.

When Oleg returned with bread and sausages wrapped in two pages of an edition of Pravda from the week before, he smiled.

THEY SAT FACING opposite directions on the same bench and waited for the train's 5:30 departure. Mikhail knew that he should keep quiet, perhaps pretend to doze, and certainly give no indication that he and Gordievsky were traveling together. But questions rankled, and he had to ask them. He chewed at his bread and sausages to mask the movements of his mouth.

"Treholt?" he murmured. "Was that you?"

Gordievsky was silent for a long time. "Yes," he finally said.

"Bergling?"

"Also yes. And, before you ask, also Haavik."

"Is that what you did?" Mikhail felt as if he were wading through a curtain of aspic. His thoughts and his heartbeats were slowed and his balance was off. "Betray Soviet agents to their death?"

"Mikhail," Oleg said slowly, "the Soviet Union is a betrayal. It's a sick system that crushes its own people. You know this. You were in Denmark, you know what life can be."

"Life is more than full grocery stores."

"It isn't when you're starving. And you say nothing of the free press, the flowering of literature, the explosion of music."

"You can hear symphonies anywhere in the Soviet Union." But his heart sank, and Mikhail knew that Gordievsky had a point.

But if Oleg had been willing to betray Scandinavian spies to be arrested and imprisoned, would he also be willing to betray Mikhail? To be arrested, or worse? Mikhail thought of Oleg's concealed weapon.

As if he had read Mikhail's thoughts, Oleg then murmured, "I have done what I have done for more than culture. For more than the West's idea of freedom. I have acted for peace."

Defeat of the Soviet Union by the West would bring a kind of peace, but Mikhail held his tongue.

"Gorbachev," Gordievsky said.

"Is a good socialist," Mikhail said reflexively, and then regretted it. "What about Gorbachev?"

"He's a good socialist." Gordievsky nodded toward a slew of young people pouring out of an arriving train. "All the students coming to see him will be pleased with his idealism and his words. And he's also not insane, like Andropov. He's not a warmonger who demands that his people give him the proof he wants so that he can launch nuclear war against the West."

"You should not say such things."

"Soon, we'll be in a place where we can both say anything we want, with no fear."

"If you like Gorbachev so much, why are you leaving the country, just as he becomes General Secretary?"

"In 1984," Gordievsky said slowly, "Gorbachev came to London. He spent eight days speaking with Mrs. Thatcher on a wide range of topics."

"Of course," Mikhail said. "The meetings went very well. Gorbachev was pleased with the conversation, and he and Mrs. Thatcher got along on a personal level."

"So you would like such meetings to continue to happen?" Gordievsky asked. "You're content with such meetings?"

"Who isn't?" Mikhail's stomach felt queasy.

"As the chief KGB officer in London, I prepared the daily briefings for Gorbachev," Gordievsky said. "Through my contacts in MI6, I also prepared the daily briefings for the Prime Minister. They were substantially the same briefings."

The queasiness became a brick.

"I did this," Gordievsky continued, "so that the parties would find common ground. So that they could approach challenging issues from similar directions, rather than with one hundred eighty degrees of opposition. And it worked."

"You'll be a hero, when you reach the West."

"No," Gordievsky said. "I don't want to be a hero. I'll be an ordinary man, and disappear into some English village to live out my days. But perhaps, before I do, there will be more information that I can give the West to help bring peace."

"It's hard to imagine that you could do as much good for the world in the West as you did while within the KGB, briefing Gorbachev and Thatcher at the same time."

"True." Gordievsky was silent for a time. "But I've been betrayed. I don't know how, or by whom, but someone denounced me. I was brought back to Moscow. I've been under heavy surveillance. I've even been drugged and interrogated."

"K Directorate?" Mikhail asked. K Directorate was the KGB's counter-intelligence division.

Gordievsky nodded.

Lyubimov's blood ran cold. He scanned the other people on the train platform. Might the man reading the newspaper be spying on Oleg and Mikhail? Might the woman with the baby carriage be listening in on their conversation?

"You're leaving Leila," he said.

"The English have promised they'll bring her and the girls across. They'll trade for them, if necessary. Likely, I can help MI5 arrest a few Soviet agents who will be valuable as bargaining chips."

"Leila must be unaware of your activities, or you wouldn't leave her."

"I tried to tell her." Oleg's voice was heavy with grief. "She wouldn't listen. She's too good a Soviet citizen. Her family is a KGB family, and she can't even imagine why I would want to do what I've done."

"Perhaps she won't want to be traded to the West."

"Perhaps not." Gordievsky's voice brightened. "But since the escape plan included space for her, that means that there's room for you, instead."

ONCE THEY BOARDED THE TRAIN, they lay on their separate bunks in silence. A couple of hours after the train left Moscow, Mikhail climbed down from his bunk to stretch, and surreptitiously passed Gordievsky. Oleg was asleep, so still that, for a moment, Mikhail thought he might be dead. Even in sleep, Oleg's face had a waxy and unhealthy pallor. No wonder, if he was being surveilled and interrogated, and was now contemplating leaving his family behind with no guarantee of ever rejoining them.

But Gordievsky would be a hero in the West, whatever he said. Knighthoods would await him, meetings with heads of state. He would have private gratitude, if not public recognition.

Mikhail had already been standing beside Oleg's bunk for too long. Quickly stretching to be able to look both directions along the train car without attracting attention, he saw that no one was watching him.

He took Oleg's gun, checked that it was loaded, and then pocketed it himself.

He lay awake through the night, thinking. Had he rushed to join Gordievsky on this journey on mere impulse, a spur of the moment desire for adventure? Was he merely disappointed in his own career as a writer, and hoping to experience romance and thrills that might somehow sink into his work?

Or did he long for something deeper? He had enjoyed his time in Denmark, but he did not desire to return to the West. His experience and trustworthiness meant that he could enjoy perks like Glenfiddich whisky in Moscow without betraying his country.

But he couldn't get out of his mind the image of Oleg Gordievsky, meeting U.S. President, Ronald Reagan. Oleg Gordievsky, being warmly welcomed by Margaret Thatcher. Oleg Gordievsky, receiving honors from the Queen of England. And Oleg had acted to bring peace—were the thawing relations between East and West not in the interest of the workers of the world? Wasn't the avoidance of nuclear war in everyone's interests?

Or perhaps it wasn't, if the poor remained enslaved to the wealthy. Perhaps true peace could only come by the defeat of western capitalism, a defeat that would be brought on by the mighty deeds of socialist heroes.

In the middle of the night, the train braked and Gordievsky fell from his upper bunk. Either because of exhaustion or because he had taken some narcotic, the fall that split his lip and splashed blood down the front of his coat didn't wake him. Lyubimov and another passenger lifted him and shoved him back into one of the lower bunks.

With only an hour to go before arriving in Leningrad, Mikhail finally fell asleep.

At the main railway station in Leningrad, they briskly walked toward the exit. Lyubimov gently pressed Gordievsky for an itinerary and was ignored. With no taxi cabs in sight at 5:00 a.m., they paid a private car owner to drive them to the Finland Station.

In the car, crossing Leningrad, Gordievsky put his hands into his coat pockets. His face remained expressionless in a studied, controlled fashion. Beneath the blood, and with hair askew, it made him look comical.

He had noticed his missing pistol.

He wouldn't ask about it, though. If Lyubimov had taken the gun, then Gordievsky didn't want to give away that he'd noticed. And if Lyubimov didn't have the weapon, then Gordievsky didn't want Lyubimov to know that he'd been armed.

Lyubimov looked out the window at the city that was just beginning to yawn itself awake.

But in either case, Gordievsky's stress and alertness had just been pushed up a notch.

They piled out of the car at Finland Station, rumpled and malodorous, beneath the eyes of an enormous statue of Lenin. Lenin seemed to be watching Mikhail as the two men bought tickets for the 7:05 Zelenogorsk train, and even as the train pulled away, Lyubimov felt the hero's eyes boring a hole between his shoulder blades with the intensity of their stare.

Lenin had returned to Russia in 1917 at this place.

Lenin, the great hero.

And was this now how Mikhail Lyubimov was to leave it?

At Zelenogorsk, Gordievsky stood in line to buy bus tickets. Lyubimov feigned a dire and urgent need to urinate. Fearing that too long a separation would make Gordievsky suspicious, he asked at two stalls where he might find a telephone and met only shrugs.

Finally, a woman with a face like a beet and a strong odor of tobacco and turpentine overheard him and offered to let him use her phone, for a price.

"My phone call is a matter of national security," Lyubimov told her.

"So is my hunger," she said.

He doled out a short stack of rubles and found himself standing in a short hallway with peeling wallpaper that had once been green but had faded so much that it now looked like mud. It took his several tries through a KGB switchboard, but he finally found himself talking to someone who answered simply, "K Directorate."

And Lyubimov was suddenly uncertain how to explain himself. "I have information about a traitor," he finally said. "Gordievsky, Oleg. He's attempting to defect today."

"One moment."

Silence.

A new voice, a man's, flat and emotionless. "Budanov."

Lyubimov knew the name. "Colonel Budanov?" The man was a relentless bloodhound, famed for rooting out enemies of the Soviet.

"I was told you had information about Gordievsky."

"Yes. Oleg Gordievsky. The man is at this moment attempting to defect." The beet-faced woman slashed a finger at Lyubimov, warning him that he had taken too much time already. He glared at her, but she didn't retreat.

"And you are?"

"Mikhail Lyubimov. I was posted with Gordievsky in Copenhagen." He felt he owed the K Directorate inquisitor more information. "Gordievsky believes I share his sentiments, and that we're defecting together."

"Where will the traitor attempt to cross the border?" Budanov asked.

"We're in the town of Zelenogorsk," Lyubimov said. "I believe he'll cross into Finland, but I can't be certain where. Perhaps Vyborg, that's where we're headed next. He says very little."

"So he doesn't fully trust you."

"He does not."

"I'll alert the border guards at Vyborg. However, Comrade Lyubimov, as you're the only man who knows where he now is, you may be the man in the best position to stop him. Are you armed?"

Mikhail nodded, then said, "Yes."

"Don't hesitate to shoot Oleg Gordievsky, or even kill him."

Kill?

The woman tried to grab the phone from Lyubimov, and he pushed her away.

"I'll tell you something that few people know, Comrade Lyubimov. Consider this a state secret. While Comrade Gorbachev makes friends with the westerners Thatcher and Reagan, there are forces within the Kremlin who believe that he's making a mistake. He's caving to western hostility and lies just when the West is about to collapse from industrial discontent."

"Yes, Colonel."

The woman grabbed for the phone again. This time, Mikhail pulled out Oleg Gordievsky's pistol and pressed the muzzle against her forehead. Erupting into a lava of curses Lyubimov could barely understand, she scuttled back into the depths of the house.

"Gordievsky is to be stopped at all costs," Colonel Budanov said. "An example must be made to all who would aid the West. But also, if there is any opportunity to create an international incident, it will be opportune to exploit that opportunity. In particular, if American or British or other western diplomats can be captured in the act of attempting to rescue the traitor Gordievsky, then wiser heads within the Kremlin will be able to sway Comrade Gorbachev to a more correct way of thinking."

"Yes, Colonel."

"Or replace the General Secretary."

The line went dead.

Lyubimov rejoined Gordievsky in line as the bus doors opened, feeling the weight of the pistol in his jacket like an iron ball.

THEY RODE the bus along a fine highway, wide and well-asphalted, a highway the Soviet road makers were proud to show to their neighbors, the Finns. The ribbon of asphalt wound its way through thick pine forest westward, toward Vyborg.

Lyubimov was exhausted. His heartbeat felt thready and inconsistent, his hands shook, and sweat trickled down his back. Gordievsky leaned against a window and appeared to sleep.

Lyubimov was resolved to arrest his friend, but how should he do it? In sleep, Gordievsky seemed almost childlike. Lyubimov could reveal his call to the K Directorate to Gordievsky and urge his friend to return to Moscow. That would be heroic. And surely, Gordievsky knew something about British intelligence that he could share with the KGB that would save him from execution.

Maybe even return him to favor.

Maybe make Oleg and Mikhail both heroes.

As the bus passed kilometer post 836, Gordievsky lurched abruptly to his feet. "I'm sick!" he called, staggering toward the front of the vehicle, from seat back to seat back. "I'm going to vomit, let me out!"

Lyubimov raced not to be left behind. When he thudded down the bus steps, the driver bellowed at his back, "We're not waiting for you and your friend!"

"Go!" Mikhail shouted and waved the bus away.

Gordievsky writhed on the ground retching. Was he truly ill? Was this how his defection would end, in a spasm of vomiting on the side of the road, twenty-five kilometers from the Finnish border? But once the bus had disappeared into the trees, Oleg stood. He still had blood crusted at the corners of his nose, and he was thoroughly disheveled, but he grinned.

"Now all we do is wait," he said.

"If you're ready to tell me the plan, I'm listening."

Oleg considered this and nodded. "Two cars will come for us. They think they're coming for me and my family, so there will be room for you. They'll pick us up at a meeting spot three hundred meters up the road, and drive us across the border."

"It can't be that simple," Lyubimov said.

But he knew that it *could* be that simple if the cars picking the defectors up had diplomatic plates. This was what Budanov had been talking about, the opportunity to create an international incident.

They walked up the road to the pick-up spot. It was a dirt turnout on the side of the highway, screened from the highway by a thick stand of trees, and Gordievsky settled himself against a rock in the woods to wait. Mosquitos buzzed and the forest stank of stagnant water and rot.

"I'm glad you're here," Gordievsky said. "Or I might be tempted to run into Vyborg and get a drink."

They sat in silence for hours. The mosquitos ate them alive, though they tugged their sleeves down their wrists to cover their hands and shrugged down into the collars of their jackets to protect their necks. Lyubimov could no longer think, and he reeled from image to image in his mind. Crossing the border. Death in a hail of machine gun bullets. A cocktail reception at the English embassy in Denmark. Gorbachev's death by firing squad. Gordievsky shaking hands with Margaret Thatcher. Lyubimov sitting with Ronald Reagan in armchairs at the American White House. The funeral procession of Mikhail Gorbachev. Nuclear warheads detonating in Washington, D.C. Denials from Margaret Thatcher, surrounded by a thicket of press microphones. Nuclear warheads detonating in Moscow. Budanov, sternly lecturing capitalist leaders on television. Nuclear warheads detonating where Lyubimov stood.

He was shaking when he heard the whine of car engines approaching from the east. Gordievsky whistled, and they both crouched in the brush to hide.

Two cars skidded into the turnout, braking abruptly: a white Saab and a red Volvo. Lyubimov felt relief like an ice bath when he thought, for a moment, that these could not be Gordievsky's western contacts; a woman pulled a picnic basket from the trunk of one car and began quickly laying out a blanket, while two men emerged from the cars and stared at the highway they'd just left.

But then Gordievsky leaped to his feet and trundled from the brush, and Lyubimov's heart fell. The picnic apparatus was a ruse, it was cover.

And then he recognized one of the men: Ascot was his name. He was a British diplomat stationed in Moscow, and he was also some sort of minor English nobility. A count or a baron or something.

The English were using actual aristocracy to infiltrate the Soviet Union!

Lyubimov felt his nostrils dilate and his heart pound fast and hard.

An international incident.

He pulled the pistol. "I'm sorry, my friend, but I can't let you go."

Gordievsky stopped and turned around. "You stole my gun."

The other man, not Ascot, was edging toward his car. Lyubimov gestured at him with the pistol. "Stand back." To Gordievsky, he said, "Would you have shot me with it?"

"Only if I had to." Gordievsky stepped slowly toward Lyubimov.

"But you don't have to. Now we can go back to Moscow. In fact, you can be a hero."

"I'm not going back to Moscow. They suspect I'm a spy for the West, and they're right."

"But you'll have tricked these capitalist spies into revealing themselves." Lyubimov pointed. "That man works at the embassy, and he's a baronet or something."

"Viscount," Ascot said.

Lyubimov shrugged. "Fat on the blood of the English workers, whatever your title is. Come, we turn them in, and we're both heroes of the KGB."

"Or we both leave," Gordievsky said, "and we're free men."

"You don't want to leave," Lyubimov said. "You called and told me to read Maugham. You told me what you were going to do, because you wanted me to stop you."

Gordievsky shook his head. "I don't know why I did that. Maybe it was a joke. I thought you would realize afterward, the KGB would realize afterward, that I had told you my plan. And then we could all have had a secret laugh together."

Lyubimov's hand drooped from fatigue, so he gripped his wrist with his left hand to steady it. "Instead, we go back to Moscow, and you and I have a laugh together at the fate of these capitalist spies."

A blue Zhiguli raced by on the highway, and Lyubimov's eyes flashed to look at it. At the speed it was going, it had to be chasing someone. Probably the Saab and the Volvo. Probably it has just missed them in the turnout, for the trees.

Gordievsky lunged forward, grabbing for the pistol.

Bang!

MONSTERS IN CHICAGO

James Wymore invited me to write a short story for an anthology of tales located in his Actuator setting. The central conceit of this series is an apocalypse that fractures Earth along genre lines. This is, of course, ludicrous, but if you can let go of common sense and just buckle in for the ride, it's also fun. In the story below, it means that the epic fantasy genre setting around Salt Lake City and the Prohibition-era gangster genre setting around Chicago can be wrapped together and made to clash.

Also, I like writing dramatic irony.

And then one day, there's orcs on State Street.

I ain't the one to see 'em first—that's Four Fingers Jimmy. You're thinking, how the hell's a guy get a name like Four Fingers? Around here, though, it ain't such a weird name.

So anyway, Four Fingers is down on State Street, picking up a package from one of Tommy Malone's boys. You can trust micks, much as you can trust anybody in the business, long as politics don't enter into it. A mick'll do the deal like he promised, which you can't say the same about a wop. A wop'll do the deal, all right, long as his brother ain't proposed him a different deal in the meantime, or his cousin, or some other obscure relation you ain't never heard of. Wop's got words for family connections you can't hardly even imagine in English. Like Eskimos and snow. A *stronzo*, that's some kind of cousin, like maybe a cousin-in-law, I think. Like you, whadda you call your cousin's husband, in English? Aside from *poor dumb bastard*, anyway. Also *cazzo*. *Cazzo* is something in Wop. I forget what.

Just don't get your mick started on about what kind of rainbows and fairies must be happening in Ireland, since the whole Actuation mess. Seriously, you'd think those guys *wanted* to live inside a box of Lucky Charms.

You're thinking, what's Actuation? Yeah, well, it pays to know people. In this case, a guy named David Archer. David don't have a name like Four Fingers 'cause he ain't a player. He's a private dick, and he owed me. Hell, I figure he still owes me, but he ain't around to tell me stuff anymore. Skipped town.

So Four Fingers is down there at a place called Nicky's, which you might know is a nightclub, not a crummy little dive where you can get lousy practically in public and nobody cares because you're trash. No, Nicky's is a nice place, where you get lousy and nobody cares because the Chief of Police is there getting lousy with you, and on a really hopping night, the Mayor. A real high-class joint, you get it? Four Fingers is there in the daytime, while the mooks are humping in shrimp and gin by the crate for the evening's celebrations and the musicians are hacking away at their trumpets and strings, and he sees orcs.

"Just standing there?" I sez to him.

"Right on the friggin' sidewalk," he sez. Only he don't say *friggin'*, but I know you got sensitive ears. I'll go easy on you.

"Did he look like a player?" I sez. By this I mean, was he wearing anything to indicate whose orc he was. Like a yellow handkerchief in his breast pocket, showing he's with Fat Sal. Or a bowler hat, to mark that he's with Baron Davey. Or a long black coat and a fedora——that would say he's one of mine.

Only I ain't got no orcs. This I know.

Four Fingers understands me, and he shakes his head like he's trying to get bees out of his ears. "They looked like frigging orcs, Butch. Wearing strips of fur and chainmail and shiz." He didn't say *shiz*, neither. Why you gotta be so sensitive? "You know how you can't tell one orc from another."

"There's monsters in Chicago," I sez. "They wanna fight?"

Four Fingers shakes his head again. "There was some of 'em, yeah, maybe, putting their hands on their knives and barking at me a little. But one of 'em, he was the leader I guess, he growls at the others and they back down."

"He want to talk, then?" I'm trying to find the angle. What's a pack of orcs doing in Chi-town? Boot-leggers? Slavery? Everybody in Chi-town's working some kinda angle. "What kinda hooch's an orc like, anyway?"

"I don't know what kind of *hooch* an orc likes," Four Fingers sez, "but I got a pretty good notion about what kind of *dame* he might have an eye for."

At that, I gotta act. I grab Four Fingers by his collar and push him up against the wall, get all in his face until I see him squirm. "What the frig's that supposed to mean, *Jimmy?*"

I call him Jimmy; he knows I'm serious. Then I punch him four or five times in the face, just to be sure he gets the message, and when he falls down, I kick him in the gut. I'm real friggin' serious.

Reason I'm serious, is he can only be talking about one dame.

Her name's Maria, and she's mine.

She's a singer. She sings at Nicky's, which I like to tell her is a gig I got her, because I want her thinking she owes me favors. That's how this world is, you get on better when people owe you. But the truth is, after I got Nicky to hear her sing, he told me to stick my favor where the sun don't shine, he's hiring Maria because she's the best damn singer in Chi-town, bar none.

Bar friggin' none.

And that ain't even taking any account of her legs, which, I tell you, could knock a platoon of doughboys dead in their tracks even wrapped in a skirt down to the ankles.

So if Nicky's band is warming up, and an orc is standing on the side-walk looking at some dame, and it's making Four Fingers Jimmy crack wise . . .

Well, frig me, for one. I got an orc to do something about.

Jimmy's groaning on the floor and I sez, "I gotta go to Nicky's anyway. I got a message. Harry's back in town and wants to see me."

Jimmy don't say nothing. He's too busy trying to breathe.

No use going down too early. But by the time the sun's set, I'm shaved and showered, I got on my best fedora and the new coat, and I even stick a rose in the buttonhole of the coat. That's not a sign I'm a player. It's a sign to tell Maria she's got the best friggin' legs in Chi-town.

Not to mention voice.

I get to Nicky's and I take my usual seat. Maria is singing, and I can't even hear the words, her hips are such a knockout. I just lean back, nurse a bourbon and watch everybody in the joint fall in love with her all at once. That's fine with me. You fall in love with my girl, go ahead. Just don't touch, or you lose the friggin' fingers.

Except over at Fat Sal's table, they ain't falling in love over there. Fat Sal's got a table, yeah. I don't own the joint. And Sal leaning on the table like it's a belly shelf, all slabbed out like you could roll his gut into a loaf and bake it. Guy lets himself go to seed, you know? And he's got a couple of his goons with him, including that skinny guy, Vespers, all of 'em with yellow handkerchiefs peeking out of their jacket pockets. Vespers used to be an undertaker, or a priest, or something, before the Actuation. Could have stayed a priest. Chi-town still has priests, but it's the players who make it big here. Anyway, Vespers is no big deal. I got goons with me, Four Fingers and a couple other guys. I don't give 'em a second thought, unless I need somebody whacked, or a refill of my drink or something.

Vespers is taking something wrapped in foil from somebody sitting with his back to me. See, my table is in a corner booth, close to the back hall. That sez I'm careful and smart. Fat Sal's table is right out in the middle of the floor, right next to the dancers. Sal thinks that sez he's so powerful he doesn't give a frig who sees what he does, but what he don't realize is it actually sez he's a stupid wop shiz for brains who ain't got the sense to be in business. Not that anybody's gonna do anything, not right here and right now, because this is neutral territory. Like church, back when people gave a damn about church. But I can see pretty much all of what Sal and his guys are doing, except I can't see the guys they're talking to, because their backs are turned to me.

And then I see that they're wearing fur and leather.

"Frig me," I sez to Four Fingers.

"Orcs," he agrees. He's grunting a bit. Guess he still hurts from the lesson I had to teach him earlier.

What the orcs are doing is they're handing a bit of silver foil to Vespers. Vespers looks to Sal like he's asking permission. Sal nods. Vespers takes something out of the foil and pops it in his mouth.

Nothing happens for about ten seconds. I sip my drink and make like I'm watching Maria, which I am. I'm thinking about chasing her around that bandstand and ripping off that glittery red dress she's wearing and then—

Suddenly Vespers falls onto the table. I about laugh out loud, because

Sal's belly is in the way, so Vespers falls onto Sal and starts shaking like he's having a fit, and it's kinda like he's a little dog, humping Sal's leg.

"Jeez," Four Fingers sez. "I didn't know Vespers was epileptic."

"That ain't epilepsy," sez Stink Eye Lem. Stink Eye is the other goon I got with me. There's nothing wrong with his eye. "That's red lightning."

Here's the thing about being boss. It don't pay to know less than your goons. And it pays even less for the goons to *realize* you know less than them. So one of 'em sez something you don't understand, you play it smart. "Yeah?" I sez. "Who told you about red lightning?"

Stink Eye shrugs. "Shiz, Butch, everybody knows. That stuff will frig you up. Like, it's erotic. Vespers, he ain't having a fit. He thinks he's being run ragged by a gang of mermaids."

"Yeah," I sez. "So imagine how filthy rich we're gonna get, selling that shiz up on Lakeside."

The goons chuckle. I play it cool and I watch the backs of the orcs' heads. If they're closing a deal now with Sal, how'm I gonna get myself stuck into the middle of it? What's my angle here? Middleman? Protection? Can I replace Sal?

Maria is tooling around the floor now, still singing. She sidles over to Fat Sal's table, and there's nothing wrong with that. He's a paying customer. He tips, and he knows Maria is my tight little hoochie coochie roll. He ain't gonna do anything stupid. So he just grins with his big rubbery lips when she rolls by.

But suddenly, one of the orcs reaches out and grabs her hands.

"Aw, shiz," sez Four Fingers Jimmy.

I hear a *click* under the table from Stink Eye Lem's side of the table. That's his M1911, and him pulling back the slide to chamber a round. I know, because the only other possibility is it's the Tommygun, and I made him leave that in the car.

"He don't mean nothing," Four Fingers sez. "He's an orc. He's an animal, right, Butch? This is like a stray dog sniffed at your dame. You wouldn't kill a—"

He stops because he's realized his mistake. He knows good and well I would kill a stray dog. I kill stray dogs all the friggin' time. I kill stray dogs 'cause I'm *bored*.

But me, I'm just scratching my chin. Thinking about the angles.

After her song, which is something about rainbows and midgets and what-the-frig, the set is finished. Maria melts into my booth like the fog off the lake. Only in a nice way.

I touch her eye. She don't flinch, 'cause I taught her not to. "See?" I sez. "Little make-up and the right light, you can't see bruising."

"Butch," she breathes. I swear, what she means is come-have-your-way-with-me, only I ain't got time for that now.

"He say anything to you?" I nod at the table in question.

"Sal?"

"The orc. The scaly green bastard who grabbed at you when he went past."

There's something wrong with Maria's face. I don't mean permanent. I mean in this moment. She's looking at me queer.

"What?" I ask.

"Don't you recognize him?" she asks.

I ought to punch her for that, only I don't. A gentleman don't punch a lady, not in public, and besides, I'm too busy thinking about the angles.

"I don't recall as I know any orcs," I grind out between my teeth.

"Butch . . . it's Harry."

She sez it, and at the same moment, the orc appears at her shoulder, like magic only without the puff of smoke. And holy hell, it is indeed Harry. I barely recognized him, because Four Fingers is right, every orc looks pretty much like every other orc. But I squint and I can see it's Harry, who sent me a note saying he wanted to meet me here tonight.

"Hardhat," I say, only it ain't Hard*hat*. "What the frig you doing back in Chi-town?"

"Business, Butch." Harry Hardhat sits down. He's bigger than I remember him, bigger than he was when I sent him out to Utah or wherever it was. And he's got muscles clumped across his shoulders like nobody's business, but if I thought that sumbitch had an ugly puss before, man, it's nasty enough now that the memory of it could sour milk. His voice is off, too—it's all growly, like someone forced him to smoke cigarettes and gargle whisky for thirty years. "Remember?"

"Yeah." I play it smart. Thing is, I *do* remember. Only what I remember is I sent Harry Hardhat out of Chi-town on a fool's errand. I sent him out to Salt Lake City, that was it, because at the time they were talking about dragons and shiz all getting burned up. So I sent him to Utah, telling him to look for new business opportunities . . . new consumable substances, new weapons, new dope . . . and expecting the poor dumb goomba to get eaten.

Because some of the guys said that idiot Harry Hardhat was gunning for me, wanted to take over my business. Not that I believed them, but you can't be too careful.

Maria scoots closer to me in the booth.

"So you got the red lightning," I sez.

Harry grins. It's like cracking open a pumpkin and seeing rotting meat inside. "The Actuation, Butch, that was a serious world-frigging moment. But now, the walls have come down, get it? I left here a goomba. I got to Utah an orc, but now I'm come back, and I'm still an orc! The first Actuation, that was a screw-up. A disaster. But this new thing . . . it's an opportunity."

"Yeah." I nod like he's explaining my plan to the goons. Stink Eye and Four Fingers nod and yuk along. I throw my arm around Maria and squeeze her to show she's my property, right there where Hardhat can see. Remind him who's boss.

Harry looks sideways at Sal's table to check it—Sal and his goons are gone. He drops a little square of foil on the table. "This shiz? Once upon a time, it was a cough drop. Just a frigging cough drop! Only in orc land, it becomes something else, bitter and stronger and mean enough it can kick an orc onto his ass. And you bring it back here?" He pushes the rectangle, sends it spinning across the table and into my hand. "You got some serious new dope."

I look at the rectangle. A bit of red peeps out, shiny like glass. A friggin' cough drop, huh? And now I guess it makes you feel like all the cheerleaders of the Dallas Cowboys, if there *were* still Dallas Cowboys, were going at you hammer and tongs.

Sounds good to me.

But I still gotta show who's boss.

"So what's the set-up with Sal?" I ask him. "You came here, you invited me, you knew I was gonna see it. You disrespecting me, coming back this way?"

Harry laughs low, hunkers down over the table. "You know that fat bastard thinks he's untouchable. Now he thinks I think like him, and we can do business."

"Yeah? What business? You ain't gonna tell me you're double-crossing me here. I send you out looking for new dope, you find it, you come back, and now you're gonna sell it to Fat Sal?"

"It ain't like that, Butch. I'm setting him up for you."

"Yeah," I sez. "Explain it to Stink Eye and Four Fingers here."

Harry leans closer. "Sal's gonna buy, see? I got a truck—a truck, get it? Can you imagine what a pain in the ass that was? The walls come down, I got to get out to Denver to get a truck because south of Salt

Lake everything is still wagons. But then I get back with the truck, I load up a whole damn tractor trailer of the red lightning, and I drive it out here."

"That's the first mover advantage," I sez, explaining a little business to Lem and Jimmy. "What you call blue ocean territory. Sooner or later, others'll get in here with their red lightning. Unless we stop 'em, of course." I'm thinking about the angles there, too. Maybe blockade the highways. That'd take more muscle'n I have. "In the meantime, we have a differentiated product, 'cause we're the only ones can sell you the experience of being humped to death by Shamu. So until someone else gets in here, we jack the price up as high as we can."

I was majoring in business, when I wasn't throwing a pigskin around, back before the Actuation. In this world, you wanna get ahead, you gotta know shiz.

"Differentiation," sez Four Fingers.

"Shamu," sez Stink Eye.

"Sal's gonna buy," Harry sez again. "Cash. So much cash, he ain't gonna have enough to do anything else for weeks. No cash for bribes, no cash to pay muscle, no cash to keep mistresses happy."

"Cash flow problems." I nod. "Jeez."

"It's worth it," he sez. "'Cause he can turn around and sell the red lightning immediately, get back all the cash he needs, and turn a big friggin' profit."

Lem frowns. "Whose side are you on?"

"Easy, Stink Eye," I sez. "Tell 'em, Harry."

Harry's grinning from ear to pointy green ear. "This is the good part. We screw him. We take his money. We keep the dope. While he can't pay his guys, we hit 'em hard. Fat Sal folds, then he retires, or we cancel his ticket." Harry taps the red lightning pellet with a long, split, yellow nail. More like a claw. "And we get filthy rich."

"Jeez," I sez to Maria. "You hear that, doll? You as turned on as I am right now?"

Harry looks at Maria, like he's barely noticed her there, and then his face gets all funny. "You still got pipes, lady. You still sing it the way makes me wanna cry."

"Aw, don't go all girlish," I sez. "We got a deal to frig up."

He gives me the details. It's easy. A trade in public, cash for the truck. And what Harry wants me to do is set the locale. A safe house, where I can wait while the deal goes down.

"I moved all the safe houses since you been gone," I sez. "And I ain't telling you where the new ones are now."

Harry shrugs. "Yeah, I know. So just tell me where you want the deal done, and give me the muscle. I'll know you're somewhere nearby."

What he doesn't know is I'll be watching. "And your orcs?"

"I'll bring 'em. They ain't enough to make Sal nervous, and that's a good thing."

So it's gonna be a hotel parking garage, right there in the Excelsior. After the curtain came down, I didn't go looking for aphrodisiac throat lozenges. I went and bought a security system and cameras that would work again, and the Excelsior's got 'em.

So there I am, middle of the next night, sitting in the penthouse suite of the Excelsior and watching my own private TV channels, sixteen screens. I got Maria with me, and she tries to rub my shoulders a bit until I push her away. Right now, I gotta watch, and then after, once I have the money, then I'll feel like a little rumpy-pumpy.

Stink Eye Lem has got the door.

So I'm watching the cameras, and I see the truck, all right, just like Harry said. And he pulls up right to where I told him, and then he gets out, and there's, I count, five orcs. They're talking, but I can't hear what they say, I just see them hanging off the front of the truck and scratching themselves, like apes.

"Friggin' orcs," I mutter, and have a slug of bourbon. "Ain't that right, Stink Eye?"

A Stutz Bearcat rolls up. That's a nice car, fancy enough Sal ain't replaced it with something else even now he can. Sal squeezes out of the car like the world's nastiest baby being born, and he's got three guys, too. Gats, everybody's armed. In the security camera, the yellow handkerchiefs look white. Here's the briefcase now, coming out of the Bearcat.

Sal passes over the briefcase. The orcs don't even open it. They hand back the keys.

Where are my guys?

Vespers is one of Sal's guys, and he climbs up into the truck, and just drives it away. Then the orcs walk off screen. Just walk away.

Friggin' disappear.

"Where the shiz are my guys?!" It's a reasonable question, even if I'm shouting it and punching at the monitors in front of me. "Stink Eye! Where the frig did that stupid sumbitch Four Fingers get to? He has a watch, right?!"

I go charging through the suite, because, wouldn't you? And I run to the front door, and my plan is to beat living hell out of Stink Eye, only when I get there, there's no need.

He's lying dead on the floor. It's pretty clear he's dead, because he's got little round bullet holes in his forehead, three of 'em. He's lying on top of his black fedora, and I almost kick him for that, too.

"Maria!" I yell. I pull Lem's M1911 out of its holster. Fat lot of good it did him.

"Here, Butch."

Her voice is behind me and it's all trembly. I whip around, pistol up.

She's standing there in the doorway to the bedroom, shaking like a leaf. She's wearing a big terrycloth bathrobe with her hands in the pockets, and Harry Hardhat is standing right behind her. He's got a knife, big curving wicked-looking knife, and he's holding it to her throat.

I point the pistol where the bullet'll go right through both of 'em.

"You weren't in the truck," I sez.

"All orcs look the same, don't they?" he sez back.

"Double-crosser."

"Yeah," Harry admits.

"They were right about you. You want to be boss."

"No," he sez. "They were wrong about me. But you were even more wrong, thinking you could send me off to Utah, get rid of me so easy."

"My guys?" I ask.

"Dead."

"And now what?"

"The only reason I ain't killed you yet is I want you to understand why," Harry sez.

"I'm all ears," I sez.

"Drop the rod." Harry pushes his knife tighter against Maria's throat. She stands up taller on her tiptoes to not get cut.

I laugh. "You got me most wrong of all, you piece of shiz, if you think I'm dropping my gun for a girl. I'm counting to three. You drop the knife, and you give me the briefcase, I might just let you live."

Stupid mook frowns.

"One," I sez, "two."

He drops the knife.

I laugh. "Get over here, Maria," I sez, and I gesture with the gun to invite her over to the winning side.

Only as I'm gesturing, I hear a soft *pop!* sound. And then twice more, *pop! pop!*

There's three little burnt holes in the front of her bathrobe pocket. I frown and point. "What'd you do?"

Pop!

I feel a sharp pain in my gut, and I can't feel my legs at all. I look down, and I see blood pouring out of my shirt.

The pistol is suddenly too heavy, so I drop it.

"I'm afraid the briefcase full of cash ain't mine to give," sez Harry Hardhat. "That goes to the orcs, for the red lightning and for killing your goons."

"Bastard," I sez, and I fall to my knees.

"It was never about the gang, Butch," he sez. "I never wanted to be boss."

"What, then?" I ask, only as I ask I realize the answer.

Maria takes her hands out of her pockets, and in one of 'em she's got a neat little pistol, with a silencer screwed onto the end. It all comes together.

She walks over to me one last time, puts the pistol to my head.

"Monsters in Chicago," I chuckle.

"Not anymore," she sez.

Pop!

Six Lyrics

I write songs. I insert lyrics into novels, and when I do, the lyric always also has a chord structure and melody—the lyrics are true song lyrics, not poems. I also write songs for occasions. The first three songs here were written, recorded, and shared on my last day at work at three successive jobs. "Take a Chance" was the song I wrote announcing my departure from Clifford Chance, the law firm where I cut my teeth. "The Road to Jericho" commemorated my leaving Micron, and "Sunny Day" was my farewell to Numonyx a couple of years later.

I've also written songs for conventions. "Cosmic Dangers" was a song I wrote to be sung when I was supposed to be Toastmaster for the Life, the Universe, & Everything symposium. "A Place Called Liberty" was a blues written for Libertycon in Chattanooga and performed there as a distraction for the crowd while the judges conferred during the cosplay contest. I wrote and recorded "Talking Dragon Con" when—wait for it—Dragon Con asked me in 2020 to record something in the nature of an endorsement or a welcome to be played to participants at the event.

Take a Chance

Well, Heaven Bound Bob and Billy the Snake
Both missed the funeral and came drunk to the wake
They said "Jimmy ain't dead, he's just gone home
Now he's cracking that corn, boys, at the foot of the throne
Yeah, he's cracking that corn at the foot of the throne"

Take fifty thousand Chinamen, lay 'em head to toe
Start 'em in St. Louis, they won't get you to St. Joe
What the Governor wants, the Governor gets
Give me your money, boys, I'll place your bets
I said, give me your money and I'll place your bets

    Take a chance on danger
    Take a chance on romance
    Take a chance you might end up stuck in France
    Take a chance
    Clifford Chance

Santiago sings softly to his sweet devil rum
Don't touch that bottle, he might bite off your thumb
Go on and salt that capybara, we'll eat it for Lent
And I don't have to tell you, boys, where the money went
No, I don't have to tell you where the money went

    Take a chance on the Hustle
    Take a chance on the Prance
    Take a chance you might have to learn to dance
    Take a chance
    Clifford Chance

        Down in Paris, Oklahoma
        Paul of Tarsus reading Tractate Yoma
        They bent me on that big wheel, baby, but I didn't break
        Nice hotel, dirty dishes
        I'm tired of eating loaves and fishes
        I'm just waiting for the sky to open up and rain T-bone steak
        Take a chance
        Clifford Chance

Old Father Benjamin and Ale B. Quick
Jumped on that donkey and gave him the stick
They might make off with everything, but it ain't no theft
Theirs is the Kingdom, boys, or at least what's left
Yeah, theirs is the Kingdom, or at least what's left

    Take a chance on hypnosis
    Take a chance on a trance
    Take a chance you might wake up with no pants

Simon Magus, ben Abuya
What's the difference? What's it to ya?
There are still dreamers out there, sister, but I need the cash
So I'm dusting off my sandals
Leaving Rome to the Goths and Vandals
Down the road wearing nothing but a hat and a funny mustache

Take a chance
Clifford Chance
Take a chance
Clifford Chance
Take a chance

THE ROAD TO JERICHO

I put fourteen miles on a new pair of shoes
On the road to Jericho
Rolling into Beer-Sheba with the Bethlehem blues
They came in thousands, left in ones and twos
Bone yard horizon, nothing I can use
On the road to Jericho

I knocked open every door in this salt-flat town
On the road to Jericho
Every single one knocked me back to the ground
I'm dancing with the Levites and the circus clowns
While this wheel in a wheel goes spinning down
The road to Jericho

    On the road to Jericho
    I heard those lepers singing low
    Ain't you got no better place to go
    Than Jericho?

Little Fabio Cohen has got a bone to pick
On the road to Jericho
He's been around the block now and his hair's all slicked
A little bit of sucking up will do the trick
He's been gnawing all the bark off of Judah's stick
On the road to Jericho

Joseph's famous son has got a camel's knees
On the road to Jericho
He can pray you up a rainstorm on the very next breeze
They got him on the floor now, he's begging please
Here come the fuller, with his club and his keys
On the road to Jericho

I spent every last shekel on a cyclops mule
On the road to Jericho
The mud in our three eyeballs felt clean and cool
Standin' round shoutin' down in Shiloh's pool
Calling me an angel, man, I feel like a fool
On the road to Jericho

SUNNY DAY

Too much thinking, Lord, ain't been good for me
Deep introspection is no friend of mine
I've had much better luck with women and wine

    Just around the bend
    I feel a sunny day
    Storm and cloud will end
    Dry up, blow away
    Broken hearts will mend
    Love be here to stay
    Just around the bend
    I feel a sunny day

Sunshine, happy day, down the boulevard
Sunshine, happy shoe, put a pebble in
Well, if you don't like hellfire, buddy, you'd best not sin

God opens windows, boys, when he shuts a door
Sunset in Singapore is sunrise in Spain
Gonna get up, brush myself off, and try again

You see sly Satan smile, hear the host of heaven weep
Whatever makes the devil laugh makes all the angels cry
I never knew I loved her until she said goodbye

Cosmic Dangers

The LTUE Song

I must have been about thirteen, my parents sent me to the mezzanine
Up on BYU hill all alone, man, the place was manic
Nerds and hippies and all that ilk, playing guitar and singing filk
And rolling ten-sided dice, but no one worried that it might be Satanic

I saw Uncle Orson, he looked weird, he had a long and pointed beard
Mormons don't have facial hair, unless they're long dead
Steven Donaldson put me to sleep, but he didn't seem half the creep
I kinda figured he might be, based on some of his books I'd read

    LTUE, you're still the one for me
    Vampires! Flying lizards!
    Orc hordes! Elven wizards!
    You're learning how to write but more than that
    You're learning how to make friends
    Klingons! Space rangers!
    Nanite plagues! And other cosmic dangers!
    You gotta do the work to learn exactly
    How the story ends

Fast forward twenty-five years, and more than one change of gears
I've got an agent and a couple of books, he's trying to see what sells

All the guests of the sympo-see-um, I made a list, I drove down to see 'em
Larry Correia, Dave Farland, Lee Modesitt, Howard Tayler, and Dan Wells

    Beef chow mein will get you into the green room
    You'd be surprised how far a little food can go

Here's to my friend Jody, man, if you didn't know, she's
Written forty-odd books, and as people go, Jody's the best
And Megan, I don't know her, but she's come up from LA,
    so let's show her
A good nerdy time, like a good nerdy honored guest

So here's to David Doering, with Dave it's never boring
It's about damn time somebody put Dave in a song
And all the rest, too many to list 'em,
    but if they left, man, I sure would miss 'em
Even the kids who are afraid to get my pronouns wrong

A Place Called Liberty

Fire up the rocket, baby, we're going down to Tennessee
Gotta fly my freak flag in a place called Liberty

The people you share blood with ain't your only family
Gonna raise hell with my cousins it's a dance called Liberty

    You see those boys from down Huntsville way
    Go on and look 'em in the eye
    And when you get lunch at the City Café
    I suggest you try the pie

You get to Chattanooga, buddy, you come look for me
I'll be gaming in the Marriott a game called Liberty

Go up on Lookout Mountain, brother, see what you can see
That ain't no band of angels, no, it's the con called Liberty

TALKING DRAGON CON

Most years I get to party with one hundred thousand of my closest friends
Seems like half of them are naked
    and the other half wear costumes to the end
It's Atlanta and it's downtown and it's August, so it's hot as blazing Hell
I'm talking Dragon Con, or can't you tell?

It's Pittypat's Porch for breakfast, sausage, biscuits, and gravy to enjoy
And the writers are at the Weston in the evening,
    so you know where to avoid
Well that CVS sells more soda in one weekend than in twelve months
    of the year
I'm talking Dragon Con, do you hear?

If you're trapped by the parade, you've got to go beneath,
    down through the MARTA stop
And the line to see the vendors forms up early, it'll wrap around the block
And if you want to ride the elevator, grab the first one,
    whichever way it goes
Welcome to Dragon Con, you've got to watch the ebbs and flows

    And if this year is too chaotic for us to have our fun
    Well, there's always 2021

The hotels are strung together, you can't move through them for the crowd
And if you're just here to watch the football, that's okay,
     even normies are allowed
And hello to all you Jesus freaks with microphones
     warning me about R2-D2
Welcome to Dragon Con, we love you too.

DIM CARCOSA

I have been invited from time to time to write short stories for hard SF anthologies. I always try to duck the science as much as I can, which is never completely. Ken and Les generously invited me to contribute to a shared-world anthology about terraforming, so naturally, I wrote a King in Yellow hard-boiled PI story.

But it is also about light deprivation, which will in fact be a problem if we ever settle around dim suns. So . . . not zero science.

It's time to wake up, Prashanth.

The tattered edges of a dream slipped from Prashanth's fingers. He saw towers behind a moon, and a still lake, and although he dreaded the valley in which he stood, he resented being torn away.

"Towers behind the moon," he murmured.

It's time to wake up, Sally said again. The 'puter was an implant, and he had named it. It didn't object to the name, because Sally wasn't sentient.

Prashanth's head throbbed, and he groaned. "I didn't set an alarm." He fumbled around in his cot until he found his second pillow, the one not heated by contact with his body. He pressed the cool fabric against his head. It helped, if only a little.

You have an event in your calendar.

"Cancel it."

I can't cancel it. Dr. Goldberg scheduled the event.

Prashanth rolled into a sitting position, still clutching the pillow to his head. "Your chronometer is off. That must be six or eight hours away still." He checked his own wrist chronometer.

Your nap went long. Again.

She was right. His slot in the Observation Dome was imminent. Failure to show up would give his doctor grounds to report him to Space Patrol. Which would mean that his future medical appointments would be compelled by armed policemen. Former colleagues, if he was lucky, but armed men not famous for their senses of humor.

You also have a video message. It came in on your professional line.

He had no time to shower. Prashanth tactically deployed a few sani-wipes on his own skin, then found a clean shirt and put on his least rumpled suit. "How did I sleep so long?"

When deprived of natural Sol-intensity daylight, non-Cerite humans suffer a range of negative effects. Oversleep is one, as are time distortion, chemical imbalances, irritability, depression, paranoia—

"Rhetorical question," Prashanth said. "Play the message."

A video window appeared in his field of vision. Both the screen's images and the accompanying audio were perceptible only to Prashanth, part and parcel of the implant system that had come with Sally. He'd got the implants when he was a member of Space Patrol, along with the fully immersive VR implants. He'd died in VR over and over as part of his training, but had managed to avoid it as an actual member of Space Patrol, only to get a medical discharge. They'd removed his clearance and deactivated the immersive VR, but left him with Sally. In lieu of better retirement pay, he'd been told with a laugh. It wasn't a very funny joke; his medical pension barely covered his miniscule apartment in the Primate Quarter and forced him to put his Space Patrol skills to work in the private sector.

Well, he'd made good use of Sally.

A woman's face appeared in the video window. East Asian descent, hair jet black and skin unblemished, very expensive earrings. She might be as young as forty, but Prashanth guessed she was much older than that, and a habitué of a rejuvenation clinic.

And therefore rich.

"Mr. Satyadeva, I'm Victoria Tan. I've been given this number by a friend who told me you undertook private investigations of a discreet and personal nature. You may reach me at this number, or may find me at my home."

The message ended with a contact number and an address. The address was in the Village, aboard *Copernicus*. Prashanth whistled, though the sound split his head.

He tucked his small pistol into the waistband of his pants. He had no license for it, and if Cerite PD chose to give him grief over it, he might go to prison. On the other hand, if he went unarmed around the slums of the Primate Quarter where he lived, he ran a very high risk of having a sharpened screwdriver inserted into his belly. For that matter, he ran the same risk by leaving the Primate Quarter and wandering among Toe Hold's Cerite population.

He pushed the bed up into the wall and exited his apartment, three meters by four, into a crowded corridor. The only light came from the emergency strips in the wall, at ankle level. He pushed his way through the stream of traffic toward the street. His vision shuddered, and the people brushing past him looked like hulking shadows with leering, distorted faces. "Do Cerites not suffer from light deprivation? Not a rhetorical question."

None of the people he passed turned to answer him. Half of them were also muttering, either on some comms link, or to their own implant, or simply to the voices in their heads.

Cerite physiology and psychology are much more resistant to low light, even for long periods of time, than those of non-Cerite humans.

"Any news on the restoration of the Day Lights?"

Lord Wimsey issued a statement ninety minutes ago that Day Lights will be operational tomorrow, for several hours. Would you like to review the statement?

Lord Wimsey was an AI. He had been built as a kind of security administrator or gatekeeper for Toe Hold, in the days of the gang fights six years earlier, but had gradually taken on more roles.

The Day Lights looked fine, their spherical bulbs spaced every ten meters along the ceiling of the corridor. But they were dead, and Lord Wimsey said it was because the insulation on the power cables was degrading. Apparently, those cables were among the first manufactured at Toe Hold and they hadn't gotten the formula right, or hadn't worried about it too much because the cables were destined for the Primate Quarter. They were being replaced, and the Day Lights should be back online soon.

Lord Wimsey had been saying that for months.

"No," he muttered.

The Day Lights were necessary because all of Toe Hold was under-ground, to protect it from radiation. When they worked, they were set to standard hours, meaning they simulated a twenty-four hour Sol day for Primate Quarter residents.

Splotches of graffiti marred the walls and ceiling of the corridor for a twenty-meter stretch. *Monkeys belong on Earth!* and *Ghosts Belong in the Grave!* were repeated competing slogans, and told the passersby that the youths of Toe Hold still fought turf wars, organized in their race-gangs. *Dim Carcosa* meant . . .he didn't know what. It probably marked a bound-ary, or memorialized the exploit of some gangbanger graffiti artist in slip-ping behind enemy lines.

Only now, they had to break through Lord Wimsey's security gate to do so.

Prashanth walked in the shuffling gait that any non-Cerite had to adopt, to avoid flinging himself against the walls and the ceiling. Toe Hold was located on the moon Liber, whose gravity was 0.08 that of Earth's.

A scuffle broke out ahead. Prashanth couldn't make out the words, but two men screamed at each other, clawing and punching until the crowd pulled them apart. A uniformed Security officer waded toward the fracas with a raised stun rod.

Prashanth took a turn that led him down stairs to pass beneath the Ring. A distant hum overhead marked his transit beneath the unstopping maglev train, the second part of Goldberg's prescription for him. Two hours daily on the train so that its constant circular motion could provide 1 G of gravity for his bones and muscles to work against. Apparently, that hadn't been added into his calendar. Beyond the Ring, he came to the gate.

Off to one side, broader corridors led to Newton and the agricultural boroughs. They were less covered with graffiti, but their Day Lights were also off. Two Security officers stood in the entrances. They only held stun rods, but the unwashed rabble of the rest of the Primate Quarter stayed away.

Beside the gate was a small coffee kiosk. The kiosk had no name, just a gap-toothed Cerite and a sign saying: *ONE CREDIT NO CREDIT.*

Prashanth paid his one credit. The coffee was bitter and sandy-tasting and it was merely warm, but he took grim satisfaction in the inferiority of the brew. He might have been tempted to enjoy a good, dirt-grown coffee;

this brown squirt, unpalatable and oily, was a pure vehicle for the injection of caffeine into his system.

He gulped the coffee and threw the printed cup into the vendor's dispenser. The Cerite bobbled his head, his rapid blinking only making the red and yellow of his eyes look all the more unnatural.

Prashanth presented his ID card to the three gangsters at the gate.

Their colors marked them as the Terra Gang, a swarm of thugs so successful during the troubles that Lord Wimsey contracted out some security functions to them. Their presence kept the PD and the occasional Space Patrol officer honest by making sure they had competition, Prashanth supposed. And the pistols and knives strapped to their bodies were effective at keeping the peace. But the Terra Gang's fighters' faces were scarred and they leered at him with gaps in their teeth, and Prashanth knew that when they weren't working for Wimsey, the Terra Gang were bootleggers and extortionists and worse.

All in all, he would have preferred to be presenting his card to someone else.

"Ratskull," he said.

Ratskull had orange hair and split nostrils. "I don't need to see your identification, Pr'shanth Sach'deva." His voice was halfway between a growl and a giggle. Would Wimsey permit his private security agents to be actually high on duty? "I know you. You're the most famous private investigator on Toe Hold."

"I'm complying with regulations." Prashanth's head throbbed. He continued to hold forward his card.

"As is right and just." Ratskull eyeballed the card briefly. "But I want you to know that I'm not just saying that because you're the only private investigator on Toe Hold. All in order, more's the pity. Business?"

"Scheduled time in the Observation Dome," Prashanth said. "And then I have to see a client on *Copernicus*."

The other two gangbangers snarled at the mention of the ship.

"That all sounds forgivable," Ratskull said. "Behave yourself."

The gangster handed back Prashanth's ID card, and Prashanth passed through the gate.

Beyond lay the Cerite borough of Promise. Walking down the tunnel, Prashanth saw the entrance to the Space Patrol Embassy, where he'd once had an office bigger than his current apartment. Next, he came to a plaza lined with Cerite shops. The customers, mostly Cerites, moving in and out of those buildings walked with an ordinary motion, because they were the low-gravity wraiths who had evolved to live in an environment like this. The lights here all seemed to work, but they weren't as bright as the Day Lights, when the Day Lights worked. Instead, artificial white light streamed from bulbs atop tall aluminum poles.

To his right, Prashanth saw a knot of pale, elongated youths. They wore shawls of knotted, colorful rags, their hair stood straight up on their heads, and they had small animal bones in their ear and nose piercings. One of them, a young Cerite woman with a bird tattooed on her cheek, flipped a folding knife open and shut.

"Bow down your head, you son of dust," the young woman said.

"Excuse me?" Prashanth wasn't sure he'd heard her right.

"Lay down ambition, hope, and lust," she continued, "and pray alone for lost Carcosa."

Only her lips hadn't moved. They were parted, to reveal her teeth, fashionably sharpened to spikes. But they hadn't moved. Had she really spoken at all?

Prashanth shook his head and walked away. He needed more sleep. Or perhaps less. He definitely needed the headaches to stop.

In the center of the borough, a thick column rose to the ceiling. The elevator in the center of the column climbed to the surface and the Observation Dome. Stairs climbed alongside the lift, but he had no interest in dragging himself up all those steps today. Prashanth touched the panel to summon down one of the lift cars.

The bottom three floors of the column were occupied by a restaurant called the Purple Parrot. A blinking LED advertisement urged Prashanth to come into the Parrot and try some *FISH CHOWDER, HOT AND FRESH*.

His stomach rumbled, but he needed to take his prescribed sun or he'd get in trouble. He could think about food later.

You could climb the stairs.

"You're not supposed to have an opinion."

I don't. Dr. Goldberg programmed me to make this suggestion.

"He shouldn't be allowed to override my commands to you."

He's your doctor.

Prashanth realized that he was standing next to a woman and that she was staring at him. He directed a ginger smile at her; contracting the muscles of his face into a smile made his headache lance through the caffeine poultice and stab him in the brain.

She might have been in her fifties, a dark-skinned woman with short hair. Normal, not Cerite. "Going up to enjoy the view?"

"The doctor says I need light," Prashanth told her.

She took two slow steps away from him.

He sighed and took the stairs.

"What is a Carcosa?"

Nineteenth and twentieth century popular culture reference. A fictitious mysterious planet invented by Robert W. Chambers. Connected with a fictitious play titled The King in Yellow *and a never-explained being named Hastur. Motifs invented by Chambers were repeated by later writers—*

"Stop," Prashanth said. "Any contemporary references?"

None.

"Writers," he grumbled.

The Observation Dome door opened to his ID card, admitting Prashanth into a wooded amphitheater. Trees stretched out in ordered groves punctuating the green sward. A pond lay at the center, ruffled only slightly by the artificial breeze that blew across the park. The ceiling was a single transparent dome; to one side, he saw the planet known as Alexa's World. Liber and its city of Toe Hold orbited Alexa's World, but the tidally-locked orbit meant that Alexa's World appeared as a static presence through the dome, an unblinking red eye filling one side of the sky.

The red sun—the only sun Prashanth had ever known—was visible as well. Goldberg had assigned him time in the dome precisely to get exposure to the light of the star. Red star, red planet. Red, red, red. And Cerite white. Red and white were the colors of Toe Hold.

The benefits of exposure to the star's light were principally psychological, Goldberg had explained. A quirky by-product of human evolution was that, deprived of light, humans tended to break down psychologically. Lights atop lampposts supplemented the star's illumination with blue and UV light, to keep the trees healthy and give people vitamin D.

But what was the point, if the light of Ross 248 was too dim, Prashanth had asked. *Primate, that is to say, humans, had evolved under a bright yellow star.*

The human body is amazing, Goldberg had answered. *So is the human psyche. It's like prayers, sometimes they seem to work. And placebos. You never know.*

Once the Day Lights were working again, he should spend his time under their glow.

Prashanth checked his suit, glad that it was a mild taupe. The jacket was reversible, its other side being gray.

"You're blocking the door," a man said.

Prashanth excused himself and moved aside. Two men exited the lift and staggered down the grass, one carrying a blanket and the other a printed basket.

Prashanth had no blanket, but there was a printer beside the door. He scanned his ID card; the machine hummed and printed a blanket, two meters long and one wide, gray. He found a patch of unoccupied grass near the pond and laid the blanket out. Around him, the people sitting or lying to take in the various streams of light were torpid. Their movements were sluggish, they said little.

He heard a woman crying, but couldn't see where the sound came from.

Dr. Goldberg suggested you might sunbathe. I am reminding you that nude bathing is permitted.

"I can see that nude sunbathing is permitted," Prashanth murmured. He took off his jacket and folded it, tucking it beneath his head as a pillow as he lay down. He unbuttoned the top five buttons of his shirt and rolled the sleeves up. "Are you going to report to him that I'm not nude?"

Yes.

"Please also report that my headache is gone. I think it was the coffee."

Did you have a headache?

Prashanth sighed.

I am now reporting that you had a headache. On a scale from one to ten, how severe was the pain?

"Shh, I'm taking my medicine now."

"YOU SEEK A NEVER-DYING BOON," someone said. A woman's voice.

Prashanth had fallen asleep. He struggled now to bring himself to wakefulness.

"From towers that rise behind the moon," the voice continued, "the towers look down on dim Carcosa."

Prashanth forced himself into a sitting position, shattering the last chains of sleep that held him down. The printed blanket beneath him was rumpled, his jacket a wrinkled mess. He cast about, looking for the woman he had heard chanting in his sleep, but saw none. The sunbathers and picnickers about him were men, or children.

Victoria Tan called again.

"You didn't wake me."

I was following Dr. Goldberg's instructions. If you are wondering, you have now spent the required time in the Observation Dome.

Prashanth shook grass from his jacket and put it on, rebuttoning his shirt. He gathered up the blanket and tossed it into a disposal unit near the lift before descending.

There was no one else in the lift with him.

"Tell me about the Tans. The name sounds familiar."

Access restricted.

Prashanth considered. "There's a product. A coffee called 'Tan Arabica.' Is that owned by a Tan family?"

Access restricted.

"You could be a more useful assistant, Sally."

No, I cannot. I am unable to access the information you seek.

"That was rhetorical. Contact the spaceport and get me on the next shuttle to *Copernicus*."

Am I authorized to purchase a ticket?

"Unless they'll give me a lift for free, yes."

As the lift doors opened on the bottom level, Sally said, *You might consider having the chowder. Otherwise, you'll be waiting a while at the spaceport.*

"Doctor's orders?" Prashanth asked.

No.

"Doctor's strongly-worded suggestion?"

There was a short delay. *No.*

"Okay, then."

Prashanth asked for chowder from a Cerite waitress who grinned, revealing her sharpened teeth. When the chowder came, he sucked it carefully from the lip of the bowl. He knew that on Earth, people sometimes ate fish they caught wild in streams and lakes, or at least they had done so in the past. In what sense the Purple Parrot's chowder could be fresh on Toe Hold, he wasn't certain, but it was definitely hot.

When he'd finished and paid, he shuffled two kilometers north through and beyond Promise, to the train station. The station also served as the spaceport's lobby, and frequent travelers had lockers here, where they stashed their own personal envirosuits or other gear. Prashanth took a loaner from the station's dispenser.

Bored Security agents patted him down, asked about his intentions, and let him through.

Your shuttle is being prepped on Pad 7.

The narrow platform only held one other passenger as Prashanth arrived, but it colored another dozen or so over the fifteen minutes that he waited. He stood, leaning against the back wall. He dozed off momentarily, then awoke to find that his head hurt again, and the train was arriving.

The train whispered to a stop alongside the platform, settling down onto its magnetic track. Prashanth and the others boarded, and he found a seat in the corner of the car. The only other passenger was a Cerite man with a tattoo of an anchor on his cheek. Disconcertingly, he sat opposite Prashanth and looked at him as if he intended to engage in conversation.

When the Cerite opened his mouth, Prashanth saw that he had no teeth.

Prashanth smiled and looked away.

The train rose as its magnets were activated and then slid smoothly forward. The view out the windows of tunnel walls was quickly replaced with a view of the rocky surface of Liber. Prashanth looked at the Cerite and smiled again; the other man worked his jaws, opening and closing his toothless mouth, but said nothing. Then the train entered another tunnel, and slowed.

At the 4-5 station, more passengers got on the train. The Cerite turned his toothless attention to a young woman in a bright blue envirosuit, and left Prashanth alone. At the 6-7 station, Prashanth disembarked, and the Cerite didn't follow. Along with the dozen other passengers, Prashanth took the left ramp up toward the surface and Pad 7.

I've taken the liberty of updating the shuttle's AI with your current mass.

"Are you saying I'm fat?"

A narrow-faced woman walking in front of Prashanth turned and frowned at him. He smiled.

You're losing weight. You should eat more chowder.

Pad 7 was just a painted circle on a flat stone shelf. Eight circles of similar size were arrayed in a loose ring around the mesa top that served as the space port, and in the center lay the larger circle that was Pad 9. The walk from the top of the ramp to Pad 7 took about five minutes, which gave Prashanth the opportunity to observe the other pads. One held a shuttle that was swarmed by a maintenance crew in envirosuits; a second was spitting out a stream of passengers and cargo; a third stood silent.

The shuttle steward was a Cerite, who pointed Prashanth to the next vacant acceleration couch, and then wordlessly helped him locate a strap that had fallen between two cushions.

"Thanks." Prashanth smiled.

Prashanth felt the subtle vibrations of cargo being loaded and then hatches closed. The hatch by which he'd entered shut last, and the steward strapped himself into his own acceleration couch.

"Everyone ready?" the shuttle's AI asked cheerfully over the intercom.

Prashanth barely had time to turn his head to look out the window before 0.75G of acceleration pressed him into the cushions. The shuttle leaped into the sky and raced straight forward for two minutes. Then, abruptly, the ascent stopped, the acceleration vanished, and the shuttle seemed to fall. Prashanth tried to find *Copernicus* out his window, but all he could see was the vast face of Alexa's World, the rocky fields below, and the staring dim sun of Carcosa.

Not Carcosa. Ross 248.

The shuttle lurched one way and then the other, and then spin, all apparently random, but then suddenly the craft touched down, and out his window, Prashanth saw the Hold of Copernicus.

He felt the arrival in his bones, as gravity climbed to 0.62.

He resolved to take his prescription to visit the Ring seriously. Dr. Goldberg, a tall, thin man almost pale enough to be a Cerite himself, but with dark eyes and a long bushy beard, had enthused at length about the importance of gravity to the bone and muscle health of a primate.

Prashanth had been to *Copernicus* before, but not recently. He'd been born on the ship, shortly after arrival in the Ross 248 system, and had memories of early childhood with his parents and his sister, digging in the dirt carefully husbanded on the Garden Deck.

They were all dead now. Not of any of the tragedies that had befallen Toe Hold or Ross 248 generally since arrival.

Just the ordinary tragedy of time.

Prashanth stepped down from the shuttle onto the deck of *Copernicus's* enormous Hold, then descended further, through an airlock and into a locker room. He stripped off the envirosuit, attaching it to a charging unit to refill its power cells and oxygen supply. As rumpled as his jacket was, it was a more professional look than the envirosuit. Also, if he wore the envirosuit, it would hide his Space Patrol Academy class ring.

Then he had to ask for directions to the staircases. He groaned at the mere thought of the staircase, the ship's gravity already dragging on his limbs. *Copernicus* had no lifts, so Prashanth had to descend fifty meters to reach the Village.

The drag of artificial gravity grew stronger as he descended. "Does this count as my one hour in the Ring?"

No.

Prashanth sighed. Coming back up was going to hurt.

The Village deck had a roof eleven meters tall and contained, well, a village. It had Day Lights overhead, as did the Garden Deck. Prashanth recognized lanes from his youth, and turned his head away. He couldn't afford them, much as he liked the light, the gravity, the dirt, and the idea of a peaceful home. Some day, maybe.

He quickly found the building with the address Victoria Tan had sent; it was a three-story-tall house with a walled enclosure to the side. The building appeared to be made of marble, though the material must surely be some sort of concrete synthetic.

When Prashanth stepped up to the front door, it opened immediately. An AI in black cummerbund and tails appeared, rolling on a single over-sized spherical wheel. "Whom may I present?"

"Prashanth Satyadeva. I have an appointment with Victoria Tan."

He didn't really have an appointment; he had an invitation. But he'd chosen to come see her face-to-face because he had found that clients who were on the fence, who had misgivings about hiring a private investigator, might ignore him when he tried to return their call. But if he showed up in-person, then they had already inconvenienced him, and very few people at that point were willing to back out.

"You are expected." The AI stepped out of the way and then closed the door behind Prashanth. "Madame's office is on the left."

Prashanth passed through a wooden door with a pebbled glass window into a thickly-carpeted office. The furniture inside was of dark wood. Certificates and plaques on the wall looked like the mementos of public commendation. A poster on the wall read *TAN ARABICA—THE ZING YOU REMEMBER!* Victoria Tan stood up behind her heavy wooden desk.

"The coffee barons," Prashanth said. "I thought so, though I was unable to find your records."

"I value my family's privacy." Victoria gestured at a wooden chair near

Prashanth and then sat. "I reached out to you because I have been assured that you are very discreet. Coffee?"

"That's much better than hearing that you reached out to me because I'm expendable." Prashanth grinned. "Yes, please. Black."

"You really like to taste the coffee."

"When it's good," Prashanth said. "And when it's bad, I'm just taking it for the caffeine anyway."

The AI followed him into the room and busied itself at a brewer in the corner.

"Space Patrol." She pointed at his ring. "Class of '44. Retired early, but not dishonorably."

"Medical discharge." Prashanth smiled. "Chronic headaches."

"Triggered by your implants?"

Prashanth tried not to show discomfort at the fact that she knew his medical history. She wanted discretion, of course she had checked his background. And still, apparently, she had chosen him, so he had nothing to complain about.

"I had them even as a kid." Prashanth shrugged. "Brain chemistry. It's manageable. They got worse as I got older." He didn't say: *And without the Day Lights, they're worse still.* "Eventually, they got to be too much for the Space Patrol."

"But not too much for work as a private investigator."

"Space Patrol's standards are very high. And I don't really have any competition as a private consultant. This is still a small town, fundamentally."

"Did you know Alexa, then?" she asked. "Alexa of the Oddity, the original Alexa?"

Prashanth nodded. "Not well. She was some twenty years older than me. How can I help you, Ms. Tan?"

"My daughter's missing. Chao-xing. I'll have all her biodata transmitted to your 'puter as soon as we're finished here."

Prashanth nodded. "How long has she been missing?"

The AI handed him his coffee. It was strong and black, he could practically taste the dirt.

"I haven't heard from her in forty-eight standard hours," Tan said. "She's not answering, and she isn't in her apartment. We usually talk daily."

"Toe Hold Security won't even start to look for her for another twenty-four hours."

"And I need discretion."

Prashanth nodded. She probably also wanted at least a veneer of professionalism, or she might have called on one of the gangs for help. "Do you have any idea about why Chao-xing isn't answering?"

"No. I have no suspects."

"Is Mr. Tan here? I'd like to ask—"

"My husband, Elias Tan, will not be involved in this investigation."

"Just a couple of questions."

"Discretion, Mr. Satyadeva."

Prashanth nodded. "Does the biodata include places of work or school and her apartment address?"

"Naturally."

"My fee—"

"I'll pay it. I'll transmit you ten thousand credits as a retainer."

"That about covers it." Prashanth finished his coffee, set the cup down, and left.

He had just finished putting the envirosuit back on and boarding the return shuttle when Sally notified him that he had received ten thousand credits in his account. *And Chao-xing Tan's biodata.*

He sat down in the acceleration couch and belted himself in. "Summarize content and show me all video images," he murmured.

He smiled at the steward.

Sally showed him a stream of images: an art studio, a large apartment on a main access corridor in the Primate Quarter, glamor shots and headshots of a young woman, images of both her entrepreneur parents. Elias Tan looked very earnest and serious and had let a little gray creep into the hair at his temples.

Chao-xing Tan, twenty-one. Fashion and art model. Tan got her career start acting in commercials for Tan Arabica . . .

Prashanth listened without focusing and watched without staring, trying to let his mind settle into an unconscious, meditative state. The spare life details, the official data of addresses and contact numbers, and the images of a pretty young woman smiling for the camera flowed past him and kept flowing past him as he ruminated.

On landing, he tried Chao-xing's contact number himself, and got no response.

In the spaceport, he accessed a cash machine and withdrew ten 100-credit coins. You never know what witness could be prodded into breaking a confidence or throwing a friend overboard for a little money.

Victoria Tan didn't want him to talk to her husband. Why was that?

The Terra Gang were still on duty. Ratskull jeered as he admitted Prashanth back into the Primate Quarter. The Day Lights were on and Prashanth did his best to walk directly beneath the bulbs as he made his way to Chao-xing's apartment in the borough of Newton. He felt a lightness in his chest. As he touched her doorbell pad, the Day Lights extinguished.

She had roommates, the biodata said. Dario and Illyria. The door opened to reveal a young man with a biologically improbable mustache and glazed eyes, who hopped from foot to foot.

"Dario," Prashanth said.

"No, *I'm* Dario," the young man growled.

"Dario-ling," a woman called from within the apartment. "That's what he means."

Dario's hands were balled into fists. Was he high? "What do you want?"

"My name is Satyadeva," Prashanth said. "I'm a friend of Chao-xing Tan's family. May I come in?"

"No," Dario snarled.

"I'm looking for Chao-xing," Prashanth said.

"Maybe you kidnapped her," Dario said. "Maybe now you're here to kidnap us."

"Do you think Chao-xing has been kidnapped?" Prashanth asked.

Dario grumbled wordlessly.

"Look," Prashanth said. "It sounds like you know something about Chao-xing's disappearance. That's good, you can help me. Unless you decide not to help me, and then you have a problem, because the next knock on your door will be either a strong-arm crew in the employ of the Tan family or a Cerite Security squad, and, in either case, they'll be much less polite than I will."

Dario stared at him, eyes glazing over further. "What?"

"Dario-licious, let him in!" the woman called.

Dario ground his teeth but stepped aside; Prashanth entered.

The central sitting room of the apartment was larger than Prashanth's own entire dwelling. It contained two sofas, a coffee table, and a coffee brewer in the corner. Through open doorways, Prashanth saw three sleep chambers and a utility space with a printer and refrigerator.

A young woman lay on one of the sofas, a mask of feathers covering her face from the nose up. From her flopped posture, she might have been completely boneless. She was not Chao-xing Tan.

"Illyria?" Prashanth asked.

"Yes!" Dario snapped. "Not that it's any of your business!"

"Dario-vine, help me up," she called, fluttering fingers weakly.

"You don't need to get up for me," Prashanth said.

"Not for you," she trilled. "I must pose."

Dario helped her stand. They both consulted a tablet and then assumed different poses, Dario a frightened crouch, hands up to shield his face, and Illyria an imitation of an obelisk, hands together and needling skyward.

"Which one is Chao-xing's room?" Prashanth asked.

The woman pointed with both hands.

Prashanth examined her room and found it Spartan. A bed, clothing, a tablet. Her biodata included passwords, so he accessed her messages and read through them. Nothing indicating plans to leave. Nothing that struck him as out of the ordinary. No messages sent within the last forty-eight hours, and only one received.

The message was from Gambo Zubair. He knew the name from the biodata—Zubair was a sculptor who sometimes employed Chao-xing as a model. The message was dated the day before, and simply informed Chao-xing that she would not be paid for the day's session, since she had not shown up.

In her calendar, Prashanth found the missed session.

All consistent, all unsurprising, all unilluminating.

He transmitted the tablet's entire hard drive to Sally, and then pocketed it, for good measure.

"Lo, Camilla, behold how the king glares at me through the pallid mask," Dario said as Prashanth moved from Chao-xing's room to the other sleeping chambers.

"The king is not the Stranger," Illyria answered.

"Who can tell the difference between the king and the king's messenger?" Dario nearly shrieked his line.

Prashanth found nothing in the other rooms. Not even, to his surprise, recreational drugs.

"Behold the towers!" Illyria cried. "The towers rise *behind* the moon!"

Something about that line bothered Prashanth, but he couldn't quite identify what it was. "Sally, what do 'towers behind the moon' refer to?"

The "towers behind the moon" are referred to in Robert Chambers's fragmentary, fictitious play The King in Yellow.

Again. And yet Prashanth was certain that wasn't why the line tickled at his memory.

Dario turned and glared at Prashanth. "Who are you talking to?"

"Just thinking out loud." Prashanth smiled his best disarming smile. His head was beginning to throb again. "Are you two rehearsing a play?"

"Chao-xing was cast as well," Illyria said. "Only she's too good for us now."

Prashanth nodded affably. "So there was tension between you and your roommate."

Dario growled. "What business is it of yours?"

"Dario-lightful, he's trying to find her. Yes, of course there was. We're all actors, are we not? Only Chao-xing was spending more and more time with Gambo. Modeling. It went to her head, she said she couldn't be in the play anymore."

"Where are you performing?" Prashanth asked. "Where do I buy a ticket?"

"We don't know!" Dario snapped.

"Guerilla theater, isn't it?" Illyria's voice was dropping slowly in volume and intensity. She sounded as if she were drifting farther away as she spoke.

"That sounds pretty avant-garde," Prashanth said. "Really artsy. Who's directing?"

"That's a bit of a secret," Illyria murmured. Was she actually falling asleep standing up? "He told us people would ask, didn't he? Ruins the surprise if we tell, though."

"Ruins the surprise!" Dario roared. He thrust himself suddenly into Prashanth's face, foamy saliva flecking the quivering tips of his curled mustache.

Prashanth held his ground and smiled. "How am I supposed to see the play, then?"

"Maybe you're not supposed to," Illyria whispered. "But if you're intended to see it, you will."

"Rehearsal is soon," Dario said. Speaking to Illyria, his tone was abruptly gentle. "Will you be able to make it?"

"I'm a professional," she hissed.

"Time to go," Dario grunted to Prashanth. "You ask too many questions."

Prashanth raised his hands to show pacific intentions. "Thanks for your time." He backed out the door.

The Day Lights were still off. He crossed the access corridor to a bodega fifty meters down and bought a seed cake. "Search the biodata and the tablet dump," he said between bites. "Look for any indication of who might be directing any play Chao-xing was cast in in the last six standard months, and where the play was being rehearsed."

No indication of either.

Gunfire erupted in the corridor. Prashanth ducked. He kicked over a small table sitting in front of the bodega and crouched behind it, very careful not to reach for his pistol. Yet.

Half a dozen shots rang out, and then a short burst of automatic fire. They came from his left and he craned his neck, looking for the source of the noise and not seeing it. Then he heard cursing, and the wet cracking sounds of muscle-powered violence.

"Call security!" someone shouted.

Prashanth looked back the other way just in time to see Dario and Illyria disappearing into the crowded traffic of the corridor.

"Did I neglect to mention, Ms. Tan," he muttered, "the premium I charge when I'm subjected to the risk of violence?"

Is that a rhetorical question?

He ignored Sally, left the table where it lay, and rushed after the actors.

They left the access corridor in two hundred meters, entering one of the lateral halls. The ceilings here dropped dramatically and the halls narrowed. In the earliest years of Toe Hold, these had held vertical aquaponic stacks, but much of that equipment had either become obsolete, or been moved to the roomier chambers near the agricultural boroughs. Now the halls were stacked with junk and trickled with thin streams of traffic as people looked for shortcuts or privacy away from the main corridors.

Ahead, Prashanth saw the backs of two women in burnooses and, beyond them, the actors. Dario was dragging Illyria by the hand.

"Tell me about Gambo Zubair," he said.

Zubair, Gambo. Sculptor. In Gambo Zubair's early career, now classified as his "Primitive Period," he made rude, totemistic sculptures, plastic printed and painted to resemble unworked wood. Three standard years ago, he transitioned into his "Modern Period" of hyperrealism. Zubair is noted for the extreme accuracy of his printed sculptures of living objects. Early Modern Period works were principally plants and small animals. Recent works include human subjects.

"Cross-reference Gambo with plays," Prashanth said. "Dramatic performances. And the Tan family and Chao-xing Tan. Look in public media as well as the biodata and the tablet dump. Exclude Chao-xing's contacts list and communications between Gambo and Chao-xing."

Nothing.

"Does Gambo mention a play or acting in any of his messages to Chao-xing?"

He does not.

Dario and Illyria passed through a doorway at the end of the hall, stepping over a jumble of pipes. Turning right, they passed out of sight. Prashanth wasn't intimately familiar with these tunnels, but he knew that they were entering into another hall. The women in burnooses passed through the doorway and turned out of sight, and then Prashanth saw two young men standing beside the door. They were primates like Prashanth, and they were dressed like street toughs; holes deliberately cut into their jackets and pants, and long, thin chains hanging from their belts.

Not the Terra Gang; in fact, he couldn't tell that they were wearing gang colors at all.

"Have you found the yellow sign?" one asked Prashanth.

"What?" he replied.

It was the wrong answer. One of the toughs punched him in the face and then jumped him, knocking him to the concrete floor. Prashanth rolled away, but when he tried to climb to his feet, the second tough cracked him on the top of his head with a length of pipe.

Prashanth's head exploded in a meteor shower of pain. He howled; the tough hit him again, this time on the shoulder, and then he managed to get his pistol into his hand. The first tough was back on his feet again and was kicking Prashanth. He nearly kicked the gun away, but after taking a boot to the stomach twice, Prashanth finally got off a shot.

Shall I contact Security?

The hall filled with the flash, the bang, and the smell of burning propellant. The thug with the pipe stepped in to try another swing. Prashanth's vision swam and his brain trembled in revolt at the mere thought of physical motion, but he shot again, hitting the bravo in the arm.

The pipe still struck Prashanth on the head, and his vision went black.

Shall I contact Security? I have no instructions.

Prashanth unloaded, firing his pistol blind in what he was pretty sure was the direction in which his assailants stood. He was rewarded with shrieks, and then with the thudding of booted feet as they ran away.

Shall I contact Cerite Security?

"Are my attackers still here?"

I can't tell, Prashanth. I can only analyze your senses, and you are blind.

"Of course." But no one was attacking him anymore. Prashanth crawled until he reached a wall, and then dragged himself to his feet. As his vision returned, he swooped and pivoted around an invisible access, and vomited.

But he was alone.

That had been way too difficult. What had happened to his reflexes, honed by the thousands of hours of VR Space Patrol training? Was whatever gave him headaches also rendering him groggy and slow?

He limped through the open doorway and looked down the way Dario and Illyria had gone: a corridor past hatches into multiple halls. He couldn't tell where they'd gone and had no way to follow them short of trial and error, poking around in this maze. And there were violent criminals in the maze with him.

What was the yellow sign?

"Yellow sign." He started dragging himself back toward the main corridors. "Another Chambers reference?"

Yes.

"Can you access the original Chambers texts?"

Done. Shall I read them to you, or put them in your visual field?

He vomited at the thought of trying to read. "Just . . .wait."

Why was Cerite Security not already swarming the hall? Maybe they were too busy dealing with brawling and gunfights in the main corridors.

His vision lurched so dramatically from side to side that Prashanth barely made it out of the hall. On his first attempt to exit into the corridor, he walked into the wall, but then he made his way by feel, groping a path back into traffic. His stomach churned and ice picks stabbed him in the brain repeatedly.

Guerilla theater. A surprise play, rehearsals kept secret. A missing model, who had once been an actress. An avant-garde sculptor. Passwords. And Victoria Tan didn't want Prashanth to talk to her husband.

He badly wanted to go to sleep, but he feared that if he did, he'd sleep long again. He also wanted to reload his pistol but was afraid he'd drop the bullets. Instead, he fumbled his way to the table of a café, signaling the lone waiter for a coffee.

"In the Chambers texts, is there an answer to the question, 'Have you found the yellow sign'?"

There is not an answer. The yellow sign is a character in gold, not described.

Not helpful.

He drank the coffee when it came. He shouldn't drink this much of the stuff, but the alternative to sleeping off a headache was to burn it off with caffeine. Sunbathing on the Observation Deck, so far, had done nothing. Maybe he shouldn't be sunbathing; maybe he should look at Ross 248, or, at least, look at the Observation Deck by its light. He asked for ice water so he could hold the cold glass against his forehead. Unable to think, he held still and felt cold water trickle down his face, but when he finally set the glass down, he found he had a resolution.

It wasn't what he wanted. He wanted an idea, he wanted understanding, but instead he had a determination to go to Gambo Zubair's studio. He didn't think of his plan as pushing buttons, but as testing a hypothesis, or maybe gathering data more actively.

Sally provided the address from the biodata. Prashanth walked slowly, taking deep breaths.

In the future, do you wish me to contact Cerite Security when you are being attacked?

Unfortunately, he couldn't be sure that would always be the right course of action. "No."

Zubair's studio address was back in Newton. Prashanth passed within hailing distance of Ratskull and his toughs, examining some traveler's ID card, and passed through into the larger, nicer section of the Primate Quarter. Like the Village deck of *Copernicus*, Newton was comprised of high-ceilinged chambers with free-standing buildings inside. A single Day Light overhead flickered on and off, which Prashanth found simply annoying, and which certainly did nothing to relieve his headache.

Behind the front door of the studio was a small reception space and desk. An AI rolled forward to meet him. It consisted of a low, rectangular buggy chassis riding on four knobby wheels, with a single snakelike appendage rising from the center. The snake terminated in a luminous sphere containing a single roving, dark dot, like an eyeball.

"May I help you?" Buggysnake asked.

"I'm here to see Mr. Zubair. I was sent by Elias Tan, Chao-xing Tan's father."

Buggysnake disappeared through a door in the back of the room, returning moments later. "Please come in."

Prashanth entered a long, high-ceilinged hall like a stable. Sculptures lined the walls. At the end stood several large machines and a short man with long arms. From the machines came humming sounds. Prashanth intended to talk to the artist but found himself drawn instead to the sculpture immediately inside the doorway. It was of a woman, perfectly life-sized. She wore a dancer's leotard and was posed standing on one foot, smiling. She had to have been printed, but the material she was printed of appeared to be pink marble. She looked East Asian.

She looked like Chao-xing Tan.

The sound of footsteps shook Prashanth out of his stupor. Gambo Zubair approached with a self-important swagger, pacing between a printed pink marble rosebush and a printed pink marble greyhound. He wore a yellow blouse and over it, a canvas smock. His head was hairless, lacking even eyebrows, and his forearms and hands were enormous.

Prashanth looked Zubair in the eye. "Have you found the yellow sign?"

The artist hesitated, and for a moment Prashanth feared his experiment was a failure. But then Zubair looked left and right, cleared his throat, and said, "The pallid mask is not a mask at all."

Prashanth nodded. So far, so good. Now, if he asked too direct a question, or too quickly showed his ignorance, he'd give the game away. Time for small talk. "I've admired your work."

Zubair grinned, showing perfect teeth. Probably printed. He pointed at the statue of the dancer. "Did you come to pick this one up for Mr. Tan?"

"No, he'll send someone else later. How did you do such a big printing? It had to have been all in one piece." He smiled. "I mean, I don't see seams."

"Come look." Zubair led Prashanth to the back of the studio. The machines Prashanth had seen were all printers, and Zubair showed them to him. They were programmable rather than standard menu-driven units and had docking stations for tablets. The largest had a printing chamber two meters tall and two in diameter.

"So you can print a human-sized sculpture in one piece," Prashanth said. "Of course."

"Sounds like tonight will be your first performance," Zubair said.

Prashanth nodded.

"So, what does Mr. Tan need from me?"

Prashanth took the thousand credits from his wallet and handed them over. "He just wanted me to tell you how much he appreciates your work, and especially your discretion."

Prashanth left the studio. He walked around the corner and out of sight, and then crept back. He bought a crushable black cap at a bodega, reversed his jacket so that it was black side out, and then sat, pretending to have a conversation using Chao-xing's tablet as a comms unit.

He reloaded his pistol with trembling hands.

"Collect all the references from Chambers' writings to the pallid mask, the king in yellow, and the yellow sign," he said.

There were surprisingly few, and he read them in a window in his visual field. The still waters of the Lake of Hali, snippets out of a play that didn't exist, the towers behind the moon, and dim Carcosa. And why was Carcosa dim? Black stars hung in the sky, obvious nonsense.

The stories were tales of madness, transformation, and unspeakable horror. His head thumping and his heart racing from the caffeine, Prashanth struggled not to feel himself sucked into the stories.

The towers behind the moon.

He had dreamed them. The towers behind the moon, the towers from the play that didn't exist and that he had never heard of, were nevertheless inside his head.

Inside his head.

And then his heart, for all the caffeine igniting it at the moment, stood still.

He had been tricked. He was betrayed.

But what to do about it? Any medical intervention would take time and would make him miss tonight's performance. Which might make a difference of life or death to Chao-xing Tan.

Whose abductor, it increasingly appeared, might be in league with her father.

He tried not to look at anything out of the ordinary and kept his tongue tightly under control. "Let me see those texts again," he told the 'puter.

He had run through them a third time when Gambo Zubair finally emerged from his studio. The artist wore an embroidered tunic now; it looked very formal. His walk was cramped and unsteady, not at all the confident lope he'd adopted in his own studio. He scurried toward the tunnel that led to the gate.

Where was he going, to see this performance? The spaceport? *Copernicus*?

And then, in his heart, Prashanth knew.

He stayed back, walking casually and stopping often, making a show of looking in windows or examining marks on the floor. Once Zubair had passed through the gate, Prashanth approached the Terra Gang enforcers.

He handed over his ID.

He looked past Ratskull, watching Zubair continue on toward the Promise Borough and the Observation Deck.

"Pr'shanth Sach'deva, here we go again," Ratskull bubbled. "You'e a fellow on the move, aren't you?"

"Yes, I am." Prashanth unlocked Chao-xing's tablet with her password and opened an empty note file.

"Don't get yourself stabbed." Ratskull handed back the ID.

Prashanth deliberately looked away from the tablet, used his finger to write eight words on it without looking, and handed the tablet to Ratskull.

Not waiting for a response, he walked through the gate.

The lift to the Observation Deck was shut down. The LED advertisement for chowder was gone, replaced with a sign that said, in bold text, *CLOSED FOR PRIVATE FUNCTION*. Two men in black suits stood impassively at the foot of the stairs. Their thick necks and grim expressions suggested Space Patrol training, but Prashanth didn't recognize them.

One held up a hand to stop Prashanth.

"Have you found the yellow sign?" the other asked.

Prashanth nodded. "The pallid mask is not a mask at all."

The men stepped aside.

Had he made a mistake with Ratskull? Did he really imagine that the Terra Gang would back him up? Maybe; more importantly, he wanted Ratskull to pass his message on to Lord Wimsey. It was too late to go back now. Prashanth climbed the steps.

Two more armed and muscled men waited at the top of the stairs. Prashanth felt himself sweating from the climb and the uncertainty both, but they offered the same challenge phrase and accepted the same password.

He entered the Observation Deck.

He had no idea what time it was on the standard clock; the long local day meant that the sky above him had barely changed. It was not hung with black stars, he noted with an absurd sense of relief, but with bright, glittering stars, one of which was Sol.

Where a writer named Robert Chambers had invented a play that he had never actually bothered to write.

That silly people were now . . .what, enacting? Exalting? Enthusing about?

The pond was still; the breeze generators were turned off. People in coats and gowns sat on wooden chairs arrayed around a flat sward of green on the shore; against the water stood a small canopy, two meters tall and two across, made of carpet-like textiles propped up on thin poles. A dim light glowed from the top of the canopy.

Prashanth strolled along the outer edge of the crowd, looking for a particular person. A chorus emerged, young women and men clad in linen robes. Each held a mask before his or her face, on a short handle. They sang, a modal dirge about the still waters of the Lake of Hali, about the coming of Hastur, and about the Stranger who was the King in Yellow.

Bow down your head, you son of dust, he heard.

Lay down ambition, hope, and lust,

And pray alone for lost Carcosa.

He found his target, who appeared to be sitting alone. Prashanth picked an empty chair from the periphery of the crowd and carried it down with him to set it beside the man.

He sat. "Dr. Goldberg."

His physician steepled his fingers before his face and laughed. "My, my, Prashanth Satyadeva, you do not disappoint."

You seek a never-dying boon,

From towers that rise behind the moon,

The towers look down on dim Carcosa.

The chorus finished their song and flipped their masks. The play-proper now commenced, with declamations and laughter. The crowd laughed along.

"There are a few things I don't understand," Prashanth said.

"Only a few? Then you're quite perceptive."

"Obviously, you knew I was coming. So you've warned someone, you have agents somewhere who are prepared to grab me. They haven't yet, so I suppose they're waiting for a signal of some kind?"

"Yes," Goldberg said. "But the signal won't come from me, so there's nothing you can do to stop it."

Prashanth considered the scene: the wealthy of Toe Hold, Cerites and primates alike, seated as if for a concert; the masked thespians. "But in the meantime, there's no reason not to answer my questions?"

"Meaning, are you going to die? Yes, I'm afraid you are. But then, we all are, sooner or later."

"That doesn't mean that I feel good about my time being accelerated."

Dr. Goldberg chuckled. "Are you asking, 'Why me?'"

"Why me? Obviously, you programmed my 'puter to betray me. Nothing else could have caused the auditory hallucinations I experienced. And maybe she's been monkeying with my reflexes, too. Not to mention the weird, very a propos dream images. I'd never even heard of this Carcosa stuff, and suddenly it was in my dreams. You did that, so why me? How did you know that Victoria Tan would hire me?"

"We didn't," Goldberg said. "We just knew that sooner or later, someone would hire you to look into us. So, we made the first move."

Was one of the actors Chao-xing Tan? Prashanth was pretty sure the answer was no. He scanned the crowd looking for her and saw nothing.

"Because Cerite Security is corrupted, so you're not worried about them."

"Enough of Cerite Security is friendly, or indifferent, to us that we're not worried about them."

"'We' means you and Elias Tan."

"And others."

Sweat trickled down Prashanth's forehead and between his shoulder blades. "Chao-xing found out what her father was up to, so she had to be kidnapped."

"No." Goldberg was smiling.

"Then why?"

"The King in Yellow requires a sacrifice."

"Killed?"

Goldberg wrapped his fingers together in a clenched double fist and laughed. "Ah, so there's a limit to what you've been able to deduce. Well, don't worry. You'll understand very soon what happened to Chao-xing Tan."

Prashanth looked for Elias Tan but did not see him. The actors in the play treated the canopy with great deference, the dialog implying that the canopy represented a throne.

"What are you all doing here, Doctor?"

"Can't you tell? Worship."

"Of what? The King in Yellow? Hastur? That's all nonsense, made up by a nineteenth century fiction writer!"

"Ah, but the human psyche is a curious thing," Goldberg said. "Gods are like prayers and placebos. Sometimes they answer, even if they're not there."

Prashanth shook his head. "But why would people consciously join a . . .a made-up cult? Have they lost their minds?"

"They are moody," Goldberg said. "Paranoid, fatigued. Their endocrine system is, to use technical doctor language, out of whack, and playing havoc with their minds."

"The towers!" an actor wailed. "The towers behind the moon!"

The actors all turned and looked up at Alexa's World. The corona of Ross 248 was close enough to Alexa's World that streaks of light seemed to reach between the star and the planet, like columns. Or towers. The streaks did indeed look, a little, like towers behind a moon.

The crowd stood and cheered.

Prashanth and Goldberg stood with them. Prashanth could still see the actors because he stood on ground raised slightly above the pond, and the flat green shelf beside it.

A new actor approached the sward. Just before he raised his own, apparently blank, mask to his face, Prashanth saw and recognized Elias Tan.

Tan stepped out onto the stage.

"The Stranger!" an actor moaned, showing a dismayed mask.

"The King in Yellow merits a gift!" cried another.

Two actors, tall and burly, grabbed a third and wrestled him forward. "No!" he screamed.

"Yes!" the crowd roared.

Both cries sounded genuine.

The strong men heaved their captive beneath the canopy. He jerked once, as if trying to escape, and then froze.

"Suspensor beams," Goldberg murmured, as if appreciating the rich notes of a glass of wine. "Have you guessed yet?"

And then Prashanth realized what was coming, only an instant before it came. The actor didn't scream and didn't move, and the printer that was disguised inside the canopy was very rapid. It hummed, and within the space of a minute, the actor was entirely encased within a sheath that appeared to be made of pink marble.

Elias Tan, the mask of the Stranger held before his face, stepped beside the canopy. The burly men dragged the new-made statue from the printer and set it at the edge of the sward. The other actors reacted sluggishly— were they drugged? The crowd was silent, listening to a speech by the Stranger, but Prashanth couldn't hear a word. His head buzzed and his vision swam.

He turned to look at Goldberg. The doctor had taken a step away from Prashanth and stood smiling at him.

He had stepped away.

The signal, someone else was to give the signal, someone other than Goldberg.

What if the signal was the offering of the 'gift' to the Stranger?

Prashanth broke into a run. Behind him, he heard screaming—was it because of the disturbance he was now causing? Or was it because someone was now chasing him, or shooting at him, with the intent to kill?

And he knew now the fate of Chao-xing Tan. The King in Yellow had demanded a sacrifice, so he had had her encased by a printer, as a living statue. He had killed his own daughter, and Prashanth had stood and admired the corpse as a great work of art.

And his artist accomplice, the actual murderer—Gambo Zubair had killed the young woman, and then calmly sent a message to her 'puter chastising her for not showing up, in case he was ever investigated for the death.

Elias Tan fell silent as Prashanth broke from the crowd. Prashanth shouted his condemnation, but what came out was an incoherent shriek.

Tan dropped his mask as Prashanth charged him.

And he screamed as Prashanth tackled him, knocking the coffee baron to the ground.

Elias Tan fell back into the canopy, his head and shoulders slamming against the floor of the printer. The printer hummed, and a sheet of rosy pink printing substrate wrapped itself onto Tan's shrieking face.

Prashanth felt a sharp sting in his left arm. Was he being stabbed? Shot, more likely.

He had to save Tan. Tan deserved death, but he deserved justice more. Prashanth dragged the murderer from the printer. Bullets struck the printer over his head, and the machine stopped humming with a sharp screech.

He grabbed for his gun and couldn't find it; he'd dropped it in his attack.

Prashanth dragged Tan to his feet and spun around, raising Tan. He smelled scorched flesh and heard Tan's agonized howling, but he ignored them both.

"Stop!" he yelled, thrusting Tan's ruined, pink face forward. "This is a crime scene, and this man is a murderer!"

"The pallid mask!" an actor wailed.

"The pallid mask is not a mask at all!" moaned another.

The crowd fell to their knees, and so did the actors. Left standing were Prashanth, Dr. Goldberg, and six men scattered along the far edge of the crowd, each holding a pistol.

They raised their firearms, and Prashanth closed his eyes. He did his best to drag Elias Tan in front of himself as a shield, but he was too tired and too sick to run, and there was nowhere to run to.

A series of shots rang out in quick succession . . .and Prashanth was not dead.

He opened them again and saw Lord Wimsey. Wimsey himself, who was rarely seen in person. He was three meters tall, his chest spherical and his head another sphere and a monocle cocked improbably over one eye. He was dressed like someone's idea of a Victorian gentleman, if said gentleman only wore purple. The metallic troll in his purple frock coat and top hat strode down through the trembling crowd. Wimsey held a rifle in both hands, and he whistled as he came—"Hail Britannia," Prashanth thought.

Behind him came the Terra Gang. Several held firearms, and one had the four doormen up against a wall with a rifle trained on them.

Wimsey stopped at the edge of the sward. He addressed the crowd. "You're all under arrest. Some of you will object that I don't have the authority, but then, I do have a big gun, and friends, so I shouldn't object too loudly, if I were you." He turned to Prashanth. "You're very lucky, Mr. Satyadeva."

Prashanth let Tan fall to the ground. The coffee baron whimpered and kicked at the turf. Where was Prashanth's gun? Where was Zubair? Victoria Tan had to be told; had she suspected already? There were too many loose ends. "I don't feel lucky."

"Well, in the first instance," Wimsey said, "you are lucky that Mr. Ratskull delivered your message. Also, your penmanship is atrocious, and it took me some time to decipher. And in the third instance, you will agree that 'murder observation deck Cerite security corrupt tell Wimsey' is not an exceedingly clear call for help. But I arrived in time, nonetheless."

"The message had to be compact," Prashanth said. "And it had to get you here without you calling Cerite Security."

Wimsey nodded, then surveyed the wreckage of the scene. "What is all this, then?"

"It is madness," Prashanth said. "Murder. A placebo. A dream. It is dim Carcosa."

THE RETURN to *Copernicus* was tedious, with Sally removed. Prashanth had to call and reserve a shuttle seat for himself, and more than once he'd found himself asking research questions to his former AI.

But he'd had Sally removed, because Sally had been hacked, and he couldn't trust her anymore.

On balance, he felt he'd made the right choice.

Copernicus's gravity weighed on him even more than it had on his prior visit. Victoria Tan's door opened as he approached it, and this time, the AI led him wordlessly to Tan's office.

"I know what happened," she said. "You were a victim, too."

Prashanth shrugged. "Your husband will get a Cerite trial."

"C'Sapunkov," she said. "Cerite city, Cerite law, Cerite trial. I need him to be convicted. Spaced. Unmarked grave. For what he did. For what he did to his own daughter."

"That's what he deserves," Prashanth said. "And there a lot of witnesses."

"I want it to the tune of one hundred thousand credits."

Prashanth took a deep breath. "I'll do everything I can to help secure that verdict. C'Sapunkov is a just man. I'll do everything I can do to help him. Everything I can *legally* do."

"Take the hundred thousand credits anyway."

"I can't guarantee a conviction," Prashanth said.

"You've lost your implant," she said.

Prashanth felt surprise, but tried not to show it. He nodded, as if the information was public knowledge.

"You've probably also alienated a bunch of potential clients," she said. "Worshippers of the King in Yellow. Elias's playmates."

"Probably. On the positive side of the ledger, my headaches have stopped."

"Good." Tan smiled. "You work for me now. Your first job is to monitor the trial and help C'Sapunkov get to the right outcome. Any way you legally can."

"One hundred thousand credits is a lot of money," Prashanth said.

"You'll need it to get quarters on *Copernicus*," Tan told him. "I want you close to hand when I need you. And the higher gravity will be good for you."

"And the light." Prashanth grinned. "I've had enough of dim Carcosa."

THE QUAIL RUNS

This is a prequel story to Time Trials. *Udad appears as a character in the novel, who has been healed at a sacred spring. This is the story of what happens at that healing that Udad doesn't see, and the lengths his brother Aksil goes to protect Udad from the monsters that threaten him.*

I want to walk," Udad said.

"We know!" Aksil slapped his younger brother on his twisted thigh through the green linen of his burnoose. Udad sat astride a camel, held in place by knotted strips of leather that provided the grip that Udad's misshapen legs could not. Aksil forced himself to smile, though he felt trepidation. "We will be at the cave soon."

Udad was nearing his ninth summer; Aksil, his twelfth.

The boys' uncle, Izemrasen, turned to look back at them. He carried a spear and wore a burnoose dyed a simple brown. Izemrasen served as their protector, though Aksil was armed as well, with a throwing stick and four short javelins. Izemrasen was also their guide.

The sun had traveled a handspan since they'd left the main trade track. They followed an inconspicuous trail wandering north of the track. A warm breeze tugged at Aksil's face and he tasted copper. His stomach growled.

"We're almost there," Izemrasen said.

"Did the witch tell you how long this trail was, too?" Aksil scanned the hills around them; they were thick with tall green grass that was rapidly fading to yellow.

"I can smell the water." Izemrasen sniffed.

Udad sniffed the air. His nose was as bent as his legs, but his eyes sparkled. "I want to walk. I want to walk now. The rest of the way. I want to gallop."

"Save your strength," Izemrasen said. "We will have to climb, the witch said."

"Also, he can't gallop," Aksil pointed out. "What if he can't climb?"

"I can climb," Udad assured them.

"If he can't climb on his own," Izemrasen said, "you and I will help him."

"But I'll climb down without your help," Udad insisted. "Because I'll be healed."

Izemrasen laughed. "I expect you will leap back down the mountain like an addax."

"The witch said it was a mountain?" Udad asked.

"That was her word."

They continued, the camel loping gracefully along the path, and Aksil following behind, watching for bandits. They were far from Ahuskay village, and if bandits beset them, there was little they could do other than run.

"Aksil!" Izemrasen called. "You go ahead for a bit. I have to remove a pebble from my sandal."

While his uncle sat and removed the offending stone, Aksil took the lead, heading forward along the path that now began to slope downward. Udad followed, holding the reins of the camel himself.

The grass thickened and grew greener, suggesting water, and trees began to dot the hills around them, and then cluster together, forming into groves.

Suddenly, a fat brown quail burst from a low bush to Aksil's right. It broke left across the path and raced away, causing a waving furrow of grass to ripple up the hill to his left. Aksil threw a javelin and missed.

He cursed and retrieved the spear, returning to the path to find Izemrasen standing where Aksil had stood to throw, holding the camel.

"Hungry?" his uncle asked.

"Aren't you?" Aksil countered.

"To eat, I'm afraid you must be smarter than the quail," Izemrasen told him.

"I think you mean '*faster* than the quail," Aksil grumbled.

"That's one way to eat," Izemrasen agreed, a smile cracking his leathery face. "But you and I are not faster than quail. Are we smarter than the bird?"

"Why are you taunting me?" Aksil asked. "Let's take Udad to the mountain. You said there are fig trees there."

"The figs may be ripening," Izemrasen conceded. "Are you giving up on the feast of quail's flesh? Or quail's eggs?"

"No," Aksil said. "I am giving up on your lesson. So if there's something you think I need to learn here, you'd better go right ahead and tell me."

Izemrasen harrumphed. "I'm your uncle. I'm supposed to teach you."

"I'm going now." Aksil took a step.

"The quail runs to distract you," Izemrasen said.

"Distract me from what?" Then Aksil realized what his uncle was saying. "From her eggs."

Izemrasen chuckled and nodded.

Aksil laid his javelins and throwing stick in the grass and crept slowly into the bushes from which the quail had emerged. He pushed the leaves aside gently, feeling the spiny branches poke him in the hands and arms. He was careful not to set his foot on any patch of ground without carefully examining it first.

And there they were; a mound of quail eggs, heaped tightly in the thickest part of the bush. Aksil counted them carefully.

"Twelve eggs," he lied. There were eleven.

He handed four to his uncle first, to honor Izemrasen for the lesson. Izemrasen immediately cracked the first egg and sucked its contents out in one gulp. Aksil handed four eggs to Udad and then stood turned to the side to conceal the number of eggs he had as he devoured them.

The eggshells cast aside to the outraged shrieking of the quail, they descended the remaining stretch of trail and came to a lake. The witch's 'mountain' was an orange cliff, and at the base of the cliff lay a brilliant, clear pool. Water sprang from the cliff and poured into the pool. Around the pond stood trees bearing dates, which were green, but also figs, some of which were beginning to ripen. Aksil collected two figs for each of them, while Izemrasen stood in place and examined the rock face.

"There," Izemrasen said. "A crack in the stone, do you see? It is as the witch described. To our right, we will find a shelf that climbs up to that crack."

"I will climb it," Udad said.

"We shall see." Izemrasen began unknotting the thongs holding Udad in place.

Aksil drank from the pool. "Addax tracks here," he said. "And antelope. Perhaps tonight I will take a beast for us to eat." He puffed out his chest. He had never yet, in fact, killed an addax or an antelope. He had killed fowl from time to time, and had once helped butcher a goat, after Izemrasen had killed it.

"Very good." Izemrazen helped Udad down. Then, while the boy stood wobbling on his twisted legs, Izemrasen tied the camel to a fig tree, within reach of the water and plenty of grass. Then he began helping his crippled nephew limp to the right, where the witch had claimed their path lay.

"This witch," Aksil said. "She herself was healed by the power of the cave?"

"Healed of boils," Izemrasen answered.

"She slept the night in the cave?" Aksil asked.

"That's how the spirit works."

"The spirit heals at night?" Aksil pressed.

"Everyone knows that all spirits are most active in the darkness," Izemrasen said. "They fear the sun. In this, they are the opposite of mankind."

Aksil filled their waterskin, slung it over his shoulder, and turned to follow his family. As he pivoted, disturbed earth among the addax tracks caught his eye and he stopped.

There were sandal tracks mixed with the spoor of the horned beasts. Men had walked here recently.

But enormous men. Their feet—he pressed his own foot into one of the tracks, and it didn't fill half the imprint. Looking in all directions and forcing himself not to break into a run, he followed his uncle.

The ascending shelf foretold by the witch started where Izemrasen looked for it. Its bottom end was above any of their heads, so Izemrasen pushed Udad up and then scrambled after him.

"Shall I come up also?" Aksil asked.

"He won't need the help to climb," Izemrasen said, and it was true. Udad was already scrambling on all fours up the shelf toward the crack.

"You can come if you want. But the spirit will be in the cave. And if you come up, no one will be watching the camel. Would you like to spend the night in the cave with Udad? Maybe I should watch the camel?"

Aksil looked back toward where the beast grazed. The camel was a significant portion of their family's wealth.

"Does the spirit . . ." Aksil hesitated. "Does the spirit have large feet?"

Izemrasen snorted. "Maybe. Spirits are powerful and can take different shapes. Maybe the spirit of the cave can take a shape that has feet."

"Large feet," Aksil said again.

"It's a powerful spirit," Izemrasen said, "its feet could be large. It could have a hundred feet. It could have wings, or the form of a goat. It could take five forms all at one. I knew a man whose wife had several spirit forms. A goat, and a hawk, and another one, I forget. Sometimes her spirit forms would appear many leagues from where she was. Sometimes in two places at once. Spirit-fragments, I suppose."

"That sounds very useful," Aksil said.

"It was," Izemrasen agreed. "Except that her spirit-fragments caused great mischief. They killed antelope and scattered goats and were regarded as demons, and so eventually, she had to be killed."

Aksil handed the waterskin up to his uncle. "You'll need this. I'll stay here and watch the camel."

Izemrasen stood holding the waterskin and looked to the sky in the west, just turning orange. "Udad has to spend the night in the cave, and then his legs will be straightened."

"He'll be able to keep up with the goats," Aksil said.

"With his older brother." Izemrasen grinned.

Surely, Aksil reasoned, he had imagined the sandal print. He walked back to the water to examine the scuffed earth. Again this time, he seemed to see the footprint of an enormous man. But Izemrasen was right. The footprint must belong to the healing spirit. The spirit had descended from the mountain for a drink, and had now climbed back into the cave.

Aksil squinted at the looming shadow of the cliff above him, darkening rapidly from purple toward black.

Izemrasen and Udad would have to worry about the spirit with giant feet. Aksil could bed down in the grass and sleep.

He checked the camel first; it was tethered firmly, with plenty of room to drink, graze, relieve itself, and sleep.

Being tired, he then made a rough bed for himself by bending down tall grass into wiry pallet. He formed his bed at the base of the cliff, where the rock leaned outward above and created a little shelter from any chance rain that might fall in the night. Lying too close to the camel might get him stepped on or bitten. Laying his weapons on the ground beside him, within easy reach, he unwrapped his own gray burnoose and draped it over his body as a blanket. The burbling spring and pool lay to his right, a narrow strip of stone separating the water from the base of the cliff.

Should he light a fire?

If the spirit did descend, he didn't want to attract its attention and become a target for its mischief. The night would be cool, but Aksil decided to forego flames.

He watched the stars shift slowly across the sky. What was Udad feeling? If the spirit was straightening his brother's legs now, did that hurt? Was the spirit on his legs to straighten them, or hitting them with hammers?

But Aksil didn't hear any screaming. He heard chirruping insects, and the occasional rustle in the grass that indicated a larger animal passing by. Sleep was slow to take him. He imagined Udad pummeled by spirits, or healed Udad rushing down the rock shelf in joyous leaps, or spirits with big feet and hammers looking for Aksil, to twist his legs in payment for the straightening of Udad's limbs.

Then his eyes snapped open, and Aksil realized he had been asleep.

He heard growling, from the direction of the camel. Aksil looked up and saw the spirit.

It was indeed a powerful spirit, as Izemrasen has suggested. It had split itself into two, like the woman Izemrasen knew. The fragments of the spirit stalked around the camel, which lay on the ground on its folded legs. The spirit-fragments had the shapes of men, but they were half again as tall as they should be, and they wore the heads of cats. They wore sandals, too, and short capes, and they held spears in their hands.

The camel bellowed in fear.

Aksil rose to a crouch. He gathered his burnoose in his left arm and scooped up his javelins in the other hand. The spirit-fragments hissed and yowled to each other. The camel screamed and struggled to its feet.

The demons pounced. They moved like cats, with confident speed, and they tore at the camel's neck with jaws wide open. One more scream that tightened Aksil's spine and the camel flopped to the ground, red with its own gore.

Aksil bit his tongue.

What were the other spirit-fragments doing to his brother in the cave?

Was the camel's death necessary, a sacrifice to pay for the healing that they sought?

The cat-headed spirits ate some of the flesh of the camel, but they quickly fell to yowling at each other again. Then they sniffed the air, stalking in a restricted circle around the camel's corpse. The demons didn't like the taste of camel flesh, it seemed. They looked toward Aksil where he lay, but their gaze didn't linger. Had the shadow of the cliff hidden him, then?

But they took several steps toward the bottom of the rock shelf, stopped, and sniffed. They yowled at each other again.

Were they smelling Aksil's trail? But they didn't come toward him then, but continued on toward the rock shelf and the path that led to the crack above.

They followed Izemrasen and Udad.

Would they harm his uncle and brother? Or would they participate in Udad's healing?

They had killed the camel.

Aksil leaped to his feet. He slung his burnoose over his shoulder as he padded along the strip of stone past the pool of water. Then he turned, tipped a spear into the throwing stick, and sent it racing at the spirit-fragments.

He was not an experienced killer, but Aksil had thrown many spears. He could throw long and he could aim true. This javelin struck the closer of the two demons in the back of its cat-like head.

The demon roared. Then both fragments turned, and Aksil ran.

On the far side of the pool, the ground dropped off swiftly, twisting and funneling into a gully that slid around behind the mount with the orange cliff face. A moon just edged its way around the hill, giving Aksil enough light to be able to run at nearly full speed.

He had seen the spirits sniff, though. Could they follow him by sense of smell?

Water splashed over sheets of rock, descending into the gully through a grove of tall fig trees. If the fragments could follow him by smell, Aksil needed to give them a false scent. He wrapped his burnoose around a javelin, aimed carefully at the darkest, thickest part of a tall fig tree, near the top, and released the spear.

His javelin struck the tree with a solid, meaty sound, and didn't fall.

He splashed on, down the middle of the stream, keeping his feet in water as much as possible. He heard yowling, but he wasn't sure whether it was becoming closer or farther away. He wanted the broken spirits to follow him. At least, long enough that they forgot about the scent of his brother and his uncle.

Flashes of the camel being torn apart burst repeatedly into his mind. Gully walls rose around him, at first comforting him that he wasn't about to be attacked from left or right. But then the walls drew tighter, and his heartbeat grew more rapid.

The yowling stopped. It hadn't grown closer.

Aksil stopped running. He stood still in the middle of the torrent, looking back up the well of shadow through which he'd descended. He saw silvery glints of moonlight on the ribbon of water, and a furred glow at the top that must be the open vale where the pool lay.

Did he hear sniffing?

He held still.

At the top of the gully, a shadow sped across the furred light from right to left. A second shadow followed. A spasm of glints on the left suggested a shaking tree, just catching the edge of the moonlight over the rim of the gully, and then Aksil heard a loud crack.

He moved downstream.

What had cracked? Was it possible the spirits had somehow been destroyed or defeated?

He moved slowly, to avoid splashing. Surely, the spirit-fragments would hear any splashes. He looked for the tiniest glints of reflected light from below to show him where the water ran, and he felt his way with each step.

What had made the cracking sound?

He heard yowling again, and he dared to look back. A shadow raced toward him down the gully. At least one shadow; but was it only one? He couldn't be certain either way.

He couldn't run fast enough to get away now. Aksil cast about, looking for a wall to climb or a hole to scurry into. Instead, he found a silvery green canopy overhead; leaves. The leaves of a fig tree.

He found the tree's trunk. It was thick and scabby and his fingers and sandaled feet alike found easy purchase in it. Scrambling as fast as he could, he lost his grip on one of the objects in his hand—a javelin? He heard it clatter on the stones below.

The yowling paused, momentarily, and he heard sniffing sounds again. He saw nothing. The demons were close enough that he could hear them sniffing for him.

They would find him.

Was this what Udad was experiencing?

The trunk began forking, and he climbed up. Beneath his feet, a thin branch snapped, the sound loud in the darkness.

The sniffing stopped.

The crack—it had been wood.

The spirit-fragments were large, and they were also heavy. They could climb trees, but if they climbed onto too thin a branch, the branch would not bear their weight and they would fall.

Aksil climbed higher.

But this could only be a dead end. If he climbed as high as possible, and didn't fall, and the cat demons couldn't follow, they could still stand at the bottom of the tree and wait for him.

He heard the rush of a spear being thrown at him, and the thud of its being deflected by a thick branch.

But the spirit healed at night.

Perhaps the spirit-fragments broke away from the healing part of the spirit at nighttime, too, and then they rejoined one another in the daylight. Rejoined, and perhaps went to sleep. Spirits were active in the darkness, they feared the sun.

If he could stay in the tree until dawn, perhaps he would survive.

But he also needed the demons to stay beneath him, and not go eat his brother.

When the branch he clung to swayed from side to side, and a cool night breeze turned his sweat into a chilled cloak, he judged that he might have climbed high enough. His burnoose was gone, and he wore only a loin-cloth. Examining what he still held in his hands, he found that he had dropped the throwing stick, and clutched two javelins.

Bathed in moonlight, rising above most of the canopy of the fig tree's leaves, Aksil looked down. To his surprise, he could see the demons. Their bodies lay cloaked in shadow, but their cat-like heads bobbed on the tide of darkness as they prowled about the tree.

He fought to control his breathing, and to stay silent.

One spirit-fragment gripped the trunk of the tree and began to climb. Aksil edged slightly higher on the branch, afraid he'd snap it. The demon snarled as it climbed, and then shouted words at him that he didn't understand. Aksil leaned one with the tree and then the other as the cat-headed thing ascended. He gripped the branch tightly with his knees, passed one javelin into left hand, pressed against the bark, and took careful aim.

The demon hesitated in its climb. It looked up, eyes gleaming in the moonlight that shone full on its face. It twisted its muzzle into a sneering expression and hissed.

Aksil feigned a throw of the javelin, but didn't release the weapon.

The demon leaped to the side, grabbing at other branches to support itself. Those other branches were smaller, and snapped instantly under the burden. The spirit-fragment crashed to the ground.

Instantly, the other demon sprang onto the tree trunk and raced toward Aksil. Froth foamed from its muzzle and wrath blazed in its eyes as it burst through the thickest veil of foliage below and charged upward. Aksil feigned another throw with the javelin, shouting this time: "Go away!"

The cat demon didn't flinch.

Aksil threw the javelin.

He struck the demon directly in its spirit-face. He would have sworn he hit it right in the right eye, but a hit to the eye should have lodged the javelin tip deep in the monster's skull. Instead, the demon lost its grip on the tree and fell. More branches cracked and fell in a rain around the spirit-fragment. The beast crashed to the ground and lay still.

But it groaned.

It wasn't dead.

Perhaps it couldn't be killed. It was a spirit-fragment, after all.

Aksil cursed silently by every god, spirit, demon, and ancestor he could think of. "May these monsters be driven away by the rising!" he mumbled aloud. Then he added, "And may Udad be healed!"

The two demons were shouting, but not at him. They were arguing; were they fighting about Aksil? After several tense exchanges, one cat shoved the other, knocking it down. The demon leaped to its feet, they both bared teeth and growled, and for a moment, Aksil dared to hope they might kill each other.

Instead, one backed down.

Then, without another sound, they bobbed away on the darkness again, vanishing up the gully.

Aksil took a deep breath.

He had survived.

But the demons were returning to the pool. Would they eat the camel? Would they leave it, and return to their spirit world, rejoining the fragments, perhaps, that were healing Udad?

Or would they climb the rock shelf, find Izemrasen and Udad, and kill them?

Aksil lowered himself down the tree.

He eased himself onto the ground. Finding his second javelin, he picked it up. The moon had now risen high enough to throw its light into the bottom of the gully, and the stream appeared as an interrupted ribbon, snarling its way downhill at a steeper and steeper angle. The gully widened, and the fig trees were interspersed with tumbled boulders and heaps of rock. What lay behind the hill? A deeper canyon?

He looked upstream. The heads of the demons and now also their shoulders and torsos crept up toward the pool.

Toward his family.

"Demons!" he shouted. "I don't fear you!"

He meant to wait, to be certain they were following him. But when the spirit-fragments pivoted, he ran.

He heard the yowling instantly. Surely, they were following him again.

He ran all out, his feet sure on the dry stream bank. How long before he had to get up into a tree again? Moments? A minute? Three minutes?

He risked a look back and almost fell over his own feet, but saw the spirit-fragments splashing toward him in the stream.

Tree, he needed a tree! But as he cast about, Aksil saw that he hadn't planned well enough. There were no trees near him. And if he climbed atop one of the massive boulders that now surrounded him, the cat-demons could easily follow.

The yowling became a shriek.

But they might not be able to follow him *under* the rocks.

Aksil hurled himself into the narrow, dark crack at the base of a heavy boulder, praying that it would be open enough to permit him entrance. He feared he'd die with a broken neck, having slammed himself into unyielding stone.

Instead, the crack led back into darkness.

He dragged himself, feeling the skin of his arms and knees and chest abrade. Behind him, he smelled the musk of cats, and then he heard a swish and felt the air moving on his calves that told of a near miss.

He didn't stop. He kept dragging himself, hearing the screeching of cats, until suddenly the rock above him vanished and he saw light again. Had he gone too far, was he exposed, on the other side of the boulder?

But no, he stood and found himself inside a chamber roughly shaped like a pyramid. Above him, a crack admitting moonlight showed that the pyramid was formed by one massive boulder leaning against another.

Across from him, a dull gray smear at the level of his ankles showed another possible exit.

He crouched and waited, a javelin in each hand. The demons yowled and hissed outside. They barked at each other in their unknown language. One tried to get in the same crack that had admitted Aksil, but ground to a halt, cursing, and then backed out. Shortly after, one of the demons tried to force itself into the other crack at ground level, but to no avail.

Aksil watched the gap in the chamber's ceiling, but saw nothing.

When the cat sounds began to die down, Aksil taunted the demons. "Do you fear me? You *should*! I am Aksil, I have slain a goat!"

It was a lie, he had not even slain a goat. But if the demons couldn't reach him inside the pile of boulders, he wished to induce them to remain outside, gnashing their teeth, until the sun did away with them.

"I am Aksil, and I have killed a thousand of your kind! I can swallow the sun! Flee now, and you will live!"

The spirit-fragments howled in rage, tried again to come in through the cracks on the ground, failed, and eventually fell silent.

Aksil yelled more, but there was no response.

How long could he wait?

Might the demons have abandoned him and his family entirely?

He couldn't take the chance. Heart beating and palms sweaty, Aksil climbed to the height of the chamber and peeked out the crack. Seeing nothing, he took heart and emerged. He crouched on the boulder heap and looked.

There were the spirit-fragments, winding their way back up the gully. They moved more slowly than they had before. This was no surprise; Aksil's own legs felt as if they were made of stone.

From his height, and with the benefit of the full light of the moon, Aksil looked down the canyon. He saw that the gully floor seemed to fall away in a few dozen paces. He couldn't see how far the drop was or what lay below it, but he saw that a tree rose near the canyon wall to his left, a fig tree tall enough that he thought he could get up into its topmost branches and again take shelter.

He slid down from the heap of boulders and bellowed at the demons in his loudest voice. "Ho, demons! Are you cowards?"

They turned and looked at him across the boulder-strewn canyon. For a minute, they stared at him with no apparent reaction. Then they turned to each other, and if they spoke, it was low, and Aksil didn't hear it.

Then they began to come toward him.

They didn't charge, this time. They split up, angling so that one came on his right and the other on his left. Aksil's heart leaped into his throat. Were they driving him toward the cliff? What did they know that he didn't?

He ran. He swerved behind one large boulder to try to hide himself from view, but then raced straight as a falcon's flight toward the tree beside the canyon wall. He felt as if he were walking through honey, as if the wind blowing on his face was pushing him backward, but he covered the distance before the demons reached him.

This time, they weren't yowling. They could be immediately behind him, and he wouldn't know it. He didn't risk a look back, but scampered directly up the tree trunk.

When he could see down over the lip of the drop, his head spun and he almost lost his grip on the tree. On the opposite side of the canyon, the stone sloped downward, steep but scalable. Beneath Aksil and his tree, the ground fell away, straight down.

Addax grazed on a plain below. They looked like beetles to him.

He dropped the javelins, and they went over the cliff.

He took a deep breath, gripped the bole of the tree, and forced himself to concentrate. Up, there was only up. There could only be up.

He dragged himself up the length of his body, and then the length of his body again.

The tree shook when the first cat-demon struck it.

Up, only up.

He climbed limbs that bent under his weight now, but he dared not stop. The yowling commenced, and the harsh shouting of unknown words.

He took risks, pulling himself faster. Beneath him, wood creaked but did not snap.

He saw a long branch that extended almost horizontally, but came to rest on a ledge above the great fall. Surely, the branch was too small for the spirit-fragments. He took several steps along it, holding a parallel and higher limb, and the branch bowed beneath him.

He smelled cat and heard heavy panting.

The branch beneath his feet bowed, and the higher branch slipped from his fingers. He yelped, took two quick steps, and jumped to the ledge.

He landed in a heap of pain and dizziness, but the rock was solid and he clung to it. He curled inward on himself, fearing teeth sinking into his neck, but no blow came.

Slowly, he rolled over and sat up. Scooting himself farther from the tree, he saw the two demons. They clung to the tree's thick trunk and glared at him. One eased a foot out onto the limb Aksil had traversed, but it bowed so severely that the spirit-fragment retreated.

Aksil pointed down onto the plain below. "Addax," he said. "If you are hungry, spirits, I offer you all those addax. Take them, and leave me and mine in peace."

The spirit-fragment growled guttural words at each other. Then one of them hissed at Aksil. Clinging tightly to the tree trunk, it deliberately stomped on Aksil's branch until the branch broke.

The demons both made a sound like laughter.

Then they climbed down the tree.

Aksil watched as the spirit-fragments accepted his sacrifice. They descended slowly into the plain below, killed an addax by sneaking up on it, and then ate its flesh.

When the demons finished, they walked across the plain, away from Aksil.

With the branch gone, Aksil couldn't reach the tree except by jumping. He doubted his ability to make the jump, and a fall would be to his death. So he shivered out the night on the ledge, and as the morning sun warmed his stiff limbs, he carefully climbed his way up the face of the cliff to the grassland above.

The return to the pool was a simple journey, but a painful one. Aksil's skin stung from his many scrapes, his feet felt battered, and every muscle was as tight as dried wood. He was thirsty and hungry to boot, and no quail conveniently revealed a cache of eggs to him, despite his fervent wish.

When he reached the pool, he lay on his belly and drank from it. Rising, he saw Izemrasen approaching from the stone shelf. Ahead of Izemrasen came Udad.

Who ran and leaped, like a camel's calf.

"The spirit!" Udad cried. "I have been visited by the spirit!"

"Yes." Aksil recovered his javelin that lay near the pool. "That's good, because you'll have to walk home."

"What happened to the camel?" Izemrasen asked, examining the dead beast. "A lion?"

"I was also visited by spirits in the night," Aksil said. "Perhaps they took the camel as a sacrifice, for their gift to Udad."

"If so, the sacrifice was worth it," Izemrasen said.

"Yes," Aksil agreed. "It was worth it."

DOG

This is the origin story of the family dog, Animoosh, in my novel Abbott in Darkness. I wrote it for my friend L.J. Hachmeister, a lovely person and talented writer who organized an anthology to benefit a dog shelter. Instinct: An Animal Rescuers Anthology *had a lot of big SFF authors in it and still sells well. L.J. left us before the first oversized check was delivered to the shelter. She did good in this world and is missed.*

W hich daughter is sick?" Billy Redbird asked.

"The older one. Sunitha." John Abbott patted the pocket of his raincoat and heard the tablets rattle. "I'm bringing home some medicine Ruth wants to try. I don't know. The other pills didn't work."

They stood in thin rain on a narrow street in the Bowery. In just a few more paces, they'd reach the intersection where they'd split and go their separate ways. They were coming from the evening lecture of their Zaphon professor, Tzaark. The wolf-lizard had blinked and yawned his way through a facilitated discussion about not ignoring the spiritual dimensions of any non-human you encountered.

The lecture series on first contact scenarios was a bit of an outlier in John's accounting degree, but he was taking it because he was applying for a job with the Sarovar Company, to leave the Sol system and work as an accountant and become one of the fabulously rich Sarovar Traders. Billy was a few years younger than John and was getting his undergraduate degree in biomechanical engineering.

"The tea?" Billy asked.

"She couldn't get it down."

Billy cocked his head to one side. "You hear that?"

John heard the soft battery of the rain. He heard the hissing wheels of a passing rickshaw and the hum of a hovercar taxi. Halfway down the block, shouting from a third-story window, and from the corner sang the beckoning whistles of the evening's first streetwalkers, prowling around the green canvas eaves of a Brazilian bodega.

"Sounds like New York to me," John said. "Sounds like I want to get inside and see my daughters."

"You don't hear a dog?" Billy asked.

John listened again, and then he did hear an animal sound. "How can you tell it's a dog? I just hear whimpering."

"Yeah, but it's a dog's whimpering." Billy followed his ear to a pile of junk leaning against a cracked brownstone. A chair missing one leg leaned against a table that only *had* one; cardboard boxes and plastic sacks lay heaped about. Billy squatted and looked beneath. "Here, girl."

John crouched, balancing by resting his knuckles on the wet concrete slab of the sidewalk. He could see a dog, sitting on its haunches. In the darkness, he couldn't make out much. The dog looked like a Labrador puppy but squashed. Some kind of mutt, probably. "Is he bleeding?"

"She," Billy said. "Yeah, I think she has a cut across her belly and her hind leg."

"People can be really rotten," John muttered.

"Might have been another animal," Billy said. "Or an accident. Plenty of sharp things to impale yourself on in Manhattan without someone doing it to you on purpose."

"If she cut herself on barbed wire, it still means some idiot left barbed wire where a dog could get to it."

"Here, girl," Billy said.

The dog whimpered.

"Doesn't your name mean 'Dog'?" John asked. "I mean, not Billy. The other one. She should come right to you."

"My other name is Waagosh. It means 'Fox.' But you make a good point."

Billy pulled a pouch from under his shirt, where it hung on a leather thong. Holding it close to his chest to shelter it from the rain, he shook a little of the contents into one hand, and then replaced the bag.

"That smells like tobacco," John said.

"It is tobacco," Billy told him. "It's very good tobacco, cured in a traditional fashion, with no added chemicals." Then Billy sang words John didn't recognize. Presumably they were in his native tongue, Ojibwe, and they sounded long and hypnotic. Then Billy reached forward and placed the tobacco on the ground in front of the dog.

"I'm trying really hard not to crack a joke here," John said, "because I feel like something's going on that I want to respect."

"Maybe you were going to say the dog doesn't smoke." Billy turned his head and grinned. "Jokes are okay. The spirits aren't offended by jokes."

"So . . . tobacco?"

"I'm giving a gift."

"To the dog?"

"To the dog's spirit. Animoosh. To honor the dog and show her we have good intentions. Come to us, Animoosh. Good girl."

Abruptly, the puppy bolted forward. She ran right past Billy's tobacco, and past Billy himself, and threw herself on John. Caught off-guard, John managed to grab the dog in both arms and then collapsed backward, sitting in a cold puddle on the sidewalk. A rickshaw sloshed a wave at him as it passed, missing, but spattering a ricochet of fine droplets against his cheek.

"Here," Billy said. "You have to get home. I'll take the dog and get her to a shelter."

He reached out, but the dog squirmed away, pushing itself deeper into John's arms and whimpering.

"I think we can definitely say the dog's not a smoker," John cracked.

"You don't have time for this." Billy stood and then helped John up.

John tried once more to hand the puppy to Billy, but she shrank and clung to him and whimpered. "We don't either one of us have time," John said, "but it looks like she's chosen me. It's okay, I'll get her cleaned up and get her to the shelter in the morning."

John wrapped his raincoat around the dog. She stank, smelling of the street and fear and wet dog and garbage. She was bleeding, and the blood immediately stained John's light blue Oxford shirt.

At the corner, Billy insisted on stopping at the bodega. He smiled and bantered with the working girls but made his way to the printer at the front of the shop. John, feeling deeply awkward, stood and smiled at a tall, olive-skinned girl with gold teeth while Billy operated the printer. When he finished, he handed John a printed blanket and a printed raincoat along with a plastic pouch of printed-beef dog food.

"For the dog," Billy said.

"I know it rains a lot in the Great Lakes area," John said, "but do you really put your dogs in raincoats?"

"You're going to put the raincoat on your floor tonight," Billy said. "The blanket goes on top of the raincoat, and then the dog sleeps on top of the blanket. The blanket keeps the dog comfortable, and if this untrained rescue pup urinates in the night, the coat protects the floor."

"You are wise in the ways of dogs, Billy Redbird." John nodded. "Listen, let me pay for these. Or we can at least split the cost."

"We *are* splitting it," Billy said. "My half is that I pay for these things. Your half is that you wash the dog, treat the wound, and take her to a shelter in the morning."

They parted ways at the corner, and John walked the two blocks to his apartment. On the way, the rain picked up, and he huddled deeper into his jacket. The dog smelled ripe, but she was warm.

As he climbed the synth-stone steps to the front of his building, two young men in long coats emerged from the front door.

"You're John," one said. He was big, with a strong Polynesian face and a wide grin. His companion was narrow and blond and looked as if he were sucking on a lemon.

"Did my big ears give me away again?" John asked.

"We were visiting Ruth." Lemon Sucker held the door open.

John stooped to look at the name tags. "Thanks, Elder Roney. Elder Tuipelotu. You guys are UC, I take it?"

"We church with the Unified Congregations," Elder Tuipelotu said.

"Ruth does too, obviously," John said. "I'm just surprised to see you guys. She's from the Catholic side. Uncle's a cardinal, even."

"Father Ritchey asked us to come by," Tuipelotu said. "He's tied up with really urgent matters, and someone needed to visit Sunitha."

"You mean Ruth," John said.

"Ruth asked us to give Sunitha a blessing," Roney said.

"Laying on of hands. Of course, she did." John fidgeted. So did the dog. "Right. You guys have a nice night. Thanks."

"Hey, all we're doing is asking God to take care of your daughter," Roney said. "No harm, right?"

John squeezed past Roney into the doorway. "Sure. Have a nice night, guys."

"We'd like to see the Abbotts at church." Tuipelotu grinned. "I mean, no pressure, but it would make us happy."

John shut the door and turned his back. "Come on, dog. What was it? Ani something? Let's go upstairs."

The elevator was out of order again; Hector was still on vacation, seeing his family in one of the Caribbean Republics, John forgot which one. So, John took a deep breath and walked up the five flights of stairs.

He stopped at the landing outside his door to catch his breath and let his heart slow down. He didn't think, Marfan's Syndrome notwithstanding, that he could really cause his heart to detach from his chest by mere exercise. But the doctors always told him to be careful, and in any case, there was no reason to get Ruth worked up.

When he opened the door, he smiled. Ruth was waiting for him, and she was not smiling.

"I hoped you would be able to get the pills before class," she said.

"I did." John produced the pills and handed them over.

Ruth frowned at the bulge in his jacket. "Then what kept you?"

"A stray dog," John said. He eased his jacket open. "Look, she's been hurt."

"Does she have a collar? A name?"

"No collar." John shrugged. "Billy Redbird called her something . . . Ani-something. It means 'dog'."

"That shirt's ruined," Ruth told him.

"I know, but . . . I couldn't leave the dog." In the light of the apartment, John could see that the dog's coloring was golden-brown. "You wouldn't want me to."

Ruth sighed. "I wouldn't want you to. But don't give me any hypocritical talk about God's creatures."

"There might be a God," John said. "If there is, this is one of his creatures."

"I'm going to give Sunitha medication." Ruth looked at the instructions on the side of the medicine bottle. "You're going to wash that dog."

Ruth wandered into the bedroom where the girls slept. She and John slept on a futon in the main room of the apartment, which contained the kitchenette in the corner. John eased the dog into the kitchen sink, blocked the drain, and began to fill it with warm water. The dog whimpered and licked John's hand.

"Speaking of God's creatures," John called, "I see you had the Mormons by."

"They were the ones who were available," she called back.

"Maybe these new pills will do the trick."

"Something has to. Shh! Let me concentrate."

John washed the puppy twice, once with dishwashing liquid, just a bit, and then he emptied and filled the sink again, to let her soak in the warm water and thoroughly rinse away the soap. She only objected when he touched her skin near her cuts. She had two injuries, one long cut across her belly and a second along one leg. John carefully washed the injuries too, which looked fresh, but not infected.

Then he laid the dog out on the floor, with the printed blanket and the printed raincoat beneath her. "I'm not going to give you a name," he said, "because tomorrow I have to take you to a shelter. You're little and cute, so don't worry, you'll be adopted. I'm just going to think of you as Dog in the meantime."

He heard Sunitha whimpering from the bedroom; the sound felt like a knife in his spine. He set the printed beef in a bowl in front of Dog and then lay on the floor beside her. He had the tube of antiseptic cream from the kitchen first aid kit, and he daubed a long line along Dog's injuries, almost emptying the tube. She had almost entirely stopped bleeding by the time he finished.

Ruth emerged. "Sunitha is unconscious, but maybe you'd like to go in and say goodnight to Ellie."

John went into the bedroom. The girls slept in a bunkbed and Sunitha, the older child, was ordinarily on top. Since the fevers had started, they'd switched the girls' places, so John stood beside the top bunk to kiss Ellie goodnight.

"Mom said something about a dog." Ellie yawned.

"I found a dog on the way home," John said. "We don't have room for a dog, but she was hurt, so I brought her home to take care of her. Tomorrow you'll see her, before I take her to the shelter."

"We have room," Ellie told him.

"Shh." He kissed her. "Good night."

Sunitha was asleep. She tossed and turned, sweating. John knelt beside her and leaned in to kiss her forehead. She murmured, long, monotonous drone syllables in a sing-song voice, but he couldn't make out any words he recognized.

Ruth had already unfolded the futon and was lying down. John turned out the lights and lay beside her. He felt sweaty and dirty, but she smelled nice, as she always did.

"Someday, maybe we can get a dog," she murmured. "When we live somewhere with more space."

"Ellie would like that," John said.

"Mmm."

"Sarovar has a lot of space," John whispered.

"Mmm."

John slept, but fitfully. He dreamed of his sick daughter. Sunitha ran through forests and across hilltops, chasing a friend and laughing. When he awoke, he heard whimpering, and eventually he took a pillow and stretched out on the floor beside Dog.

She hadn't peed yet, at least.

John lay on his side. Dog pressed up against him and laid her muzzle on his bicep. He felt her breath on his cheek. She still whimpered from time to time, but much less.

John drifted in and out of sleep again.

He dreamed of Sunitha swimming in a deep blue pool. A friend swam with her, a friend who had no face, but who pulled her back from the deepest waters.

He awoke to the sound of Sunitha crying. He crept into her room and was joined by Ruth. Sunitha was hot and sweating. John fetched cold packs to slide beneath her and a damp cloth to wipe her forehead, and her cries died away.

"I'll sit with her," he whispered.

Ruth padded back to bed. John sat beside Sunitha's bunk and found Dog pushing herself into his lap. His heart raced, but as he massaged the dog behind her ears and along her spine, his own stress dissipated. He fell gently into sleep.

He dreamed of darkness. He couldn't see walls around him, but he felt them, and he sensed that they were closing in. He was running, and the ground beneath his feet was rocky and irregular, so he stumbled.

He skinned his face against an unseen rock wall.

In the darkness, he heard rhyming, drone-like chanting in an unknown tongue.

"Sunitha!" he cried. "Sunitha, where are you?"

"Dad!" Her voice was distant. It echoed and receded even as he heard it. "Sunitha!"

She didn't respond. In his heart, he knew that she was gone. Worse than that, he knew that she had died alone.

John woke up in a cold sweat. His body stank of sour fear, and cold gray morning light seared his eyeballs.

"John!" Ruth stood over him, shaking him by the arm. "John, wake up!"

John took a shuddering breath and tightened his shoulders before releasing them, trying to drive out the fear. "I'm awake," he said.

"Mom," he heard Sunitha say. "Dad."

John turned, and he and his wife together looked at their oldest daughter. Ellie squirmed in the top bunk and lowered her head over the edge of the mattress to be part of the conversation, too.

Sunitha sat up, leaning against the wall. Her color was back to normal, she wasn't sweating, her eyes were open. She even smiled.

And Dog lay sprawled out across her lap, head on her hip. Sunitha scratched the dog behind her ears and around her shoulders. A long mohawk of golden fur stood up along the beast's spine.

"Dad." Sunitha wore a slightly dazed smile. "She says she knows you."

"Yes," John said. "Yeah, I brought her home last night."

"Her name is Animoosh," Sunitha said. "She doesn't like to smoke."

John fought to keep his jaw from falling open.

Ruth laughed, a slight hysterical note to her voice. "No dog likes to smoke."

"We're keeping her, right?" Sunitha asked.

"We're keeping A-Ni-Mooth," Ellie said, repeating the name in big, loud chunks.

"We don't really have the room," John said. "My plan—"

"We're keeping her," Ruth said. "Of course, we're keeping her."

AN OFFERING THE KING MAKES

I wrote this story for Sean Hazlett's Weird World War IV *anthology. The necessary conceit for inclusion in the anthology is that your story had to be set in World War IV, with a World War III in the backstory, and that both future world wars had to have some "weird" element—battle magicians or weapons of demonic destruction or psychic battalions or something.*

So this is a story about a platoon of tanks that magically transits through an arcade game into an offering ritual to destroy the god Osiris, who is a megalomaniacal former gamemaster-turned world conqueror, with a love triangle in the mix. Also, chewing gum.

T he trouble started," Kamal Arslan said, "when we entered the videogame. This is wicked technology, and these are not gods. They are devils." Arslan was a Druze soldier of fortune from Lebanon, the captain of the Shining Warriors, the freelance minitank company providing the bulk of the physical muscle. He was lean and well built, with streaks of gray in his black hair and neatly trimmed beard. Dressed in khaki, he wore a sidearm strapped to each leg.

"The trouble started," Rex "Thrower" Grundy said, "when your men were so excited the Ramada had pay-per-view skin flicks that they couldn't focus on their instructions about how to avoid getting crushed by these gods. Or devils." His stomach was cramped; this was not what he had been trained for. The CIA had taught him how to finesse foreign traitors for information and to flip them. Now he was carrying a gun through a tunnel that was some kind of electronic mythoscape, a tunnel into the soul of Pharaonic Egypt built by a meth-addicted whiz-kid gamer champion.

Back when there was a CIA. Before the Social Wars of the 2030s had torn the United States into seven bloody chunks.

He envied Salem Chalabi, back in the arcade with the shimmering golden gate stretching between two old upright consoles. *Pac-Man* and *Dig Dug*, he recalled, though he hadn't looked closely. In the real world, Chalabi was under attack in a crumbling arcade, adjacent to the Church of Santa Maria sopra Minerva in Rome built upon the ruins of an ancient temple to Isis.

The CIA had prepared Grundy for none of this.

Chalabi and Jason Pointer would both have insisted on the phrase "physical world" rather than "real world." To be fair, this virtual world had imposed quite a bit of real injury and death on the team that had dared to enter it.

"Gods, devils," Pointer said in his crisp received pronunciation. The Surrey-born wizard was wrapped in a strange panther-skin garment. He clutched his baked-clay curse doll to his chest. Short and stubby, he tended to trip over his own feet as he walked; rather than giving him dignity, the costume made him look comical. "Potayto, potahto. Does it matter?"

Pointer ignored the digitalized bat-like creatures overhead, the long-limbed crocodiles in the shadows, the phantom turreted droids surrounding the company on the ground, materializing to fire bursts at the surrounding monsters and then fading out of sight, and even the real growling M1461 Minis, reduced from their original twelve to a mere seven. He was focused on a shimmering golden gate before them, an immense structure that stood out of the streams of alphanumeric data cascading from the infinite darkness above, solid and glorious, at the top of a short ramp. Two red serpents hung from the massive golden lintel, spitting flames. Within the gate sat a man with a ram's face and curling horns growing horizontally left and right from his scalp. Above the horns sprouted a high crown shaped like a golden cone surrounded by feathers. He held a shock of grain.

The ram-headed man was thirty feet tall, if he was an inch.

Grundy studied Pointer's face. He wasn't looking *at* the gate, he was looking through it.

"It matters," Grundy insisted. "There's a difference between a god and a demon, and there's a difference between one god and another. It matters who's in charge! And you believe that too, Pointer, or you'd just let the Pharaoh take the world!"

Arslan spat. His spittle left his mouth as fluid and struck the ground as a string of data that scattered on impact. "The antiputrefaction charm did not work."

Pointer's head swiveled around sharply. "Your men didn't wear it, Captain. I told them to keep it on their persons, and they hung it inside their tanks, instead, like fuzzy dice in some cheap muscle car."

"You should have been clearer!" Arslan snarled.

Pointer shrugged and looked back at the gate. He gripped the curse doll with both hands; it was an image of a tall-crowned mummy holding a crook, flail, and long staff, with a knob atop it fashioned into an animal's head. The image was instantly recognizable, as an age-old evocation of Egypt, and also as a representation of the Pharaoh Death-Manifest-in-Fire, the Son of Ra Jimmy Whitlock. The god they had come to kill. "I was clear."

Chalabi's voice echoed from the mezuzah-like medallions hanging around all their necks. "I can't hold out much longer, my peeps."

Grundy looked around the company. "Looks to me like your turrets are winning," he said.

Chalabi's voice dripped with pride. "I can blast bats and crocs all day, that isn't the issue. My problem is in meatspace, bruv. The *physical* world."

"You're under attack?" Arslan asked.

Pointer was already slowly advancing toward the gate. "Stay close to me," he called.

"You got it, bruv."

"What about the soldiers we left to defend you?" Grundy asked. "Ogbuwa and his men?"

"They're pretty great with submachine guns, bruv. But you know what submachine guns really suck at? Killing waves of flesh-eating scarab beetles."

Grundy cursed.

"That's how I feel, too," Chalabi said. "Guess we should have gone with flamethrowers. I'm just telling you, you have ten minutes, max."

"And then what?" Arslan asked.

"Either I scram, bruv, or I get eaten."

"And we lose the turrets' support?" Grundy watched a row of turrets leap into view, annihilate two charging crocodiles, and disappear again.

"You lose the tunnel," Chalabi said.

"And we . . . what?" Grundy asked. "Die?"

"Ask the wizard, bruv."

"Pointer!" Arslan snapped. "The . . . videogame . . . collapses in ten minutes. What happens then?"

Pointer nodded. "Ten minutes will be enough." He began climbing the steps.

"That wasn't what I asked." Arslan rushed to catch up to Pointer. Grundy followed. He drew his pistol; not that it would do anything to the ram-headed titan, but the weight felt reassuring in his hand. "We needed the game to get here, right?"

Pointer nodded. "We had to triangulate. Not having the full liturgical apparatus, not to mention the hieratic authority, we needed two entry points into the collective unconscious from which to work out the right angle. Hence, the stolen papyrus—the *Book of Going Forth by Day*—and the videogame. And it worked, see?"

"Triangulate?" Grundy asked. "What does that even mean? How do you triangulate from a videogame and a papyrus to . . . *this?* At most, that's a metaphor!"

Pointer faced the intelligence agent. "Thus you take the first steps on the road to understanding my arts."

"None of this answers my question!" Arslan snapped.

Pointer ignored him.

The ram-headed giant stepped forward out of the gate, raising his shock of grain like a weapon. "I am He Who Cannot Be Cut," he thundered. "I am He Who Triumphs. I repel the demolishers. Who are you and what is your business?"

This was not the first gate the company had faced. Grundy had lost track, but he thought it might be the seventh. At each gate, the wizard had been the one to get them through. At the third, five minitank crews had rotted to corpses before his eyes. Pointer turned now and gestured to Arslan. "This should be the last gate. Make sure your men have their gum ready."

Arslan grunted. "Hotep gum."

"*Hetep* gum!" Pointer hissed. "Like it says on the wrapper!"

Grundy checked his own small brick of gum; it hadn't fallen from his pocket. It reeked of yeast through the foil wrapper bearing the printed word "HETEP".

Arslan spoke into the small comms unit on his wrist. "Ready hotep gum. Do not deploy until my signal."

Grundy heard a baffled laugh from the open hatch of the nearest M1461. The tanks were small, sized like sedans. The two-man crews occupied the turrets on top, only lightly shielded by sheets of steel angled like the windshields of a convertible. An autoloader and a self-driving AI let the minitanks operate with minimal crews and made the vehicles highly maneuverable. Given the narrow tunnels and broken terrain the team had traversed, Grundy was certain larger tanks wouldn't have gotten this far.

Pointer knelt before the giant. "I come to you, Osiris," he declaimed, "to be declared free of evils. May you circle Shu. May you see Ra and all the dead. You sail in the night bark around the Akhet! You have made the excellent path that leads me to you!"

"I'm just about ready to let the Pharaoh have Rome," Arslan muttered. "This has gotten way too strange."

The snakes hissed and spat fire.

"Pass," the giant rumbled.

Pointer walked through the gate. He moved slowly, with measured strides, as if he were in a convocation or walking a bride up the aisle. Arslan and Grundy followed. The tanks rolled slowly behind them.

"I might have overestimated the time, bruv," Chalabi's voice announced. "You might have five minutes now. Uh . . . maybe four."

"It's enough," Pointer said.

Grundy's heart rattled free and crazy in his chest. Sweat on his palms made it hard to grip the pistol. He shot a look over his shoulder; the last two M1461s rolled forward with their swiveling turrets pointed behind them, firing. Was he seeing fewer of the phantom turrets now? And more of the bats?

The space beyond the gate was split into two halves. Grundy squinted and tried to focus on the space where the two halves met, looking for a seam or a joint, but he couldn't find one. To his left, a black cave and a huge beast. To his right, a golden-walled audience hall, and two high-crowned giants on thrones. The golden walls radiated light, but the shining beams evaporated into twists of smoke as they penetrated the cave. The beast lurking in the shadows was immense and had a long, toothy muzzle.

In the center, a golden table, piled high with loaves, jugs, and joints of meat.

As he stepped through the gate, one of the fire-spitting snakes thudded softly to the ground, to his right and behind him. The second followed immediately afterward, on his left.

Grundy's knees wobbled. Why was he here? Why, really, was it his business whether the Pharaoh Death-Manifest-in-Fire, the Son of Ra Jimmy Whitlock, the former neopagan lecturer and obsessive gamemaster of the obscure tabletop role-playing game, The Valley of the Pharaohs, took Rome? Grundy was just a cultural attaché to the embassy of the United States of New England. He did a little light intelligence work, rescued a field operative here and there, and threw around a football with embassy staff on Thanksgiving, imagining how his life might have been different if he'd gone on to play in college. He could still get a flight out if he wanted, even if the Pharaoh refused to recognize his diplomatic credentials, even if his cover was blown.

But instead of going home, he had taken Pointer, after meeting him at an exhibit of stunning shabti figurines at the Vatican's Gregorian Museum, to meet with Arslan. Arslan's enthusiasm for resisting the Pharaoh had been infectious enough that Pointer had finally stopped whining about the girl, Marian, who had just dumped him. When Grundy had pointed out that the Church of Santa Maria sopra Minerva was *really* sopra the old temple of the Egyptian goddess Isis and was next door to, of all things, a videogame arcade, Arslan had taken them all to meet Chalabi.

And somehow, over sake and sushi, but mostly sake, they'd hatched this plan.

Did he just want to experience adventure?

The thing with the long snout roared in the shadows.

Grundy stagger-stepped sideways as the creature emerged fully into view. Its gait was lopsided; front legs that resembled those of a lion prowled with grace, while the hind legs, which resembled those of a hippopotamus, thudded dully up and down, thrusting a gray rump from side to side in a determined waddle. The beast seemed to be fighting an internal battle to move at all. The result would have been laughable, but for the train-car-sized crocodilian snout that protruded from the front of the affair. The teeth jutting up and down from the green-skinned jaws of the monster were each as tall as Grundy, if not taller.

"God help us," Arslan said. "Pointer, do we attack it?"

"No," Pointer said. "We came here to chew gum, not to kick ass."

"Deploy hotep gum," Arslan said into his comms unit.

Grundy looked at the tank crews. Of the seven, five—ten men—dutifully popped the brick of gum into their mouths and chewed. Arslan and Pointer and Grundy all did the same.

Two crews, four men, didn't.

The two giants stood and approached.

"I said deploy hotep gum!" Arslan barked. "Yossy, you idiot, did you hear me?"

Yossy's voice came out of the comms unit loud enough for Grundy to hear. "Uh, gum already deployed, sir. A couple hours ago."

"I chewed mine last night," said another voice from the wrist-bound device. "It's disgusting."

Pointer shook his head. "I'm sorry, Captain."

The soldiers were right; the gum was foul. It was supposed to taste like bread and beer, and if Grundy closed his eyes and concentrated, he could find those flavors. But it wasn't a delicious bread, it was some sort of oat or barley loaf, unsweetened. Mostly what Grundy tasted was yeast.

He gagged but kept chewing.

"What's going to happen to them?" Arslan asked.

Again, Pointer ignored his question. "We approach the table," the wizard said.

Grundy's hands were shaking. He followed Jason to the table. The two giants strode up to the table, too, and stood to their right. The huge beast shuffled up on the left and stood snuffling the air.

"Pointer!" Arslan snapped. "What's going to happen to my men?"

"We have to eat the meal before we can talk to Isis and Osiris," Pointer said. "Don't any of you read? This is the meal with the gods. It's the offering the king makes."

"Who's the king?" Grundy asked.

Pointer shrugged. "The answers to all the really important questions are ambivalent. Or multivalent, really. Is the king the initiate approaching? Is the king Osiris there? Is the king someone else entirely? Is the king Salem Chalabi and his videogame?" Pointer shrugged. "Yes."

"The gum is to fool someone into thinking we've eaten the meal when we haven't?" Grundy eyed the loaves and jugs.

"Well, you can't *actually* eat the meal." Pointer snorted. "Not without the right preparation, anyway. You guys *don't* read, do you?" The wizard was looking at the female giant. Whose crown seemed, strangely, to be a throne. Or perhaps *she* was a throne, with arms, legs, and a face. A lovely face, with full lips and large eyes. The thrones on which both giants had been sitting were gone—the woman, somehow, *was* the thrones.

Grundy eyed the male giant closely. Wrapped in linens, clutching crook and flail and a long, animal-headed staff, the giant was a dead ringer for the curse doll. And a match for the Pharaoh Jimmy Whitlock.

His stomach cramped so hard, he almost fell over.

The monster swung its bus-sized snout over the company. Saliva spattered Grundy in the face and the floor all around him. He could hear the beast sniffing.

"What do you call that thing?" he asked, pointing.

The wizard looked at him calmly. "Her name is Ammut, and she will take her due."

The snout poked in Grundy's direction. A nostril the size of a refrigerator, not one of the ridiculous tiny refrigerators they had in Rome, but a full-sized, American-style refrigerator like the one he had back in Worcester, dilating and contracting, sniffed the intelligence officer . . .

Grundy exhaled into the enormous schnoz, blowing the smell of yeast in a redolent cloud.

Ammut grunted and moved on.

Grundy didn't have a heartbeat anymore, just a stabbing pain in his chest that wouldn't relent.

He heard the slapping of boots. Turning, he saw four of the tankers rushing toward the table. He recognized Yossy, who was the fastest and in front. He was still trying to think of the others' names when Ammut lunged forward and scooped two of them up in a single bite.

Blood spattered everywhere. A severed arm hit Grundy in the chest and landed in front of him. He kicked it as far away as he could, not wanting to attract Ammut's attention again.

The tanker whom Ammut had missed pulled his sidearm and fired at the creature's eyes. The pop of gunfire echoed across the chamber as he emptied his magazine.

One of the tanks swiveled its guns around and fired. Both the .50-caliber machine gun and the tank's 125-millimeter main gun blasted Ammut in the side of her leathery jaw.

With one leonine paw, Ammut reached forward and smashed the soldier flat. Then, with the single minitank still hammering her in the head, she snaked a long, pink tongue through her foremost teeth and licked the dead soldier off the floor.

Snakes. That reminded Grundy, where were the two snakes? He

scanned the room and found them, one coiled around each of the giant woman's legs.

That didn't reassure him.

"Uh, my peeps," Salem Chalabi's voice cut into the hectic scene from three directions, "you're on your own, I gotta—aaaaaaaaaaaagh!"

His scream cut out abruptly.

Ammut swung ponderously around to face Yossy, the last of the gumless tankers. Yossy had reached the table and was furiously munching bread and swilling beer. The golden liquid sloshed from the clay vessel's wide mouth and splashed him in his khaki shirt.

Ammut leaned forward to sniff Yossy.

Yossy belched.

Ammut swung her elongated face from side to side, slowly. Pointer and Arslan both ducked. Then she raised her crocodile snout, rising up on extended catlike forelegs, and bellowed at the unseen ceiling of the cavern.

"An offering the king makes!" Pointer shouted. "Bread and—"

Yossy leaped forward and knocked him to the ground.

The snakes wrapped around the giant woman's legs hissed and exhaled jets of crimson fire.

The cavern floor shook. "Salem," Grundy said into his mezuzah. Then he remembered. Salem Chalabi was dead.

Yossy was growing. He loomed over the wizard in the panther skin, and he was ten feet tall already, and still swelling. His head was deforming rapidly, nose lurching forward into a birdlike beak, hair sweeping up and becoming featherlike.

"Target Yossy now," Arslan said into his wrist communicator. "Kill him."

A burst of machine gun fire ripped across the front of the golden table. The bullets threw the expanding Yossy backward. They knocked him up and onto the table. Joints of meat and beer jugs fell to the floor. The jugs shattered on impact.

Grundy threw himself to the ground. He crawled to Pointer. On his back and breathless, the magician was still staring at the giant woman.

"Who is she?" Grundy asked. "What's so fascinating about her?"

"She is Isis now," Pointer murmured. "But that is nothing."

The wizard stood. Grundy stood with him and dragged him sideways, away from the table and the gunfire. Pointer resisted, but Grundy was stronger and wrestled him out of harm's way.

Scraps of meat and bread flew in all directions. Yossy, now fifteen feet tall, stood atop the table and roared. He had an ax in his hand. Where had the ax come from?

Pointer was chanting incomprehensibly. Grundy shook him.

"We have to do something!" Grundy shouted.

"Shut up!" Pointer screamed. "I *am* doing something!"

At least he was looking at Yossy and not at Isis.

Isis and the Pharaoh gazed down upon the mayhem. The Pharaoh's face was frozen, expressionless. What was the look on Isis's face . . . curiosity?

The hall shook again.

Yossy leaped to attack and took a tank's sabot round in the chest. The bird-headed giant slammed back into the table and skidded across the floor. He struck the Pharaoh's foot, and the Pharaoh murmured a deep, uneasy sound.

The two giant snakes spat fire. The heat warmed Grundy's forehead and cheeks.

Yossy stood unharmed and roared.

"Finished," Pointer said.

"Finished what?" Grundy shrieked. "Nothing has changed."

In a split second, Yossy leaped across the space between himself and the first minitank. His ax swung left and right in his hands; the tank gun sheared away from the body of the M1461, flying straight up. The treads were blown off, and the minitank screeched to a halt. Yossy was already flying past, ax raised over his head with both hands as he bore down on the second minitank.

Before the first minitank's crew could evacuate, the severed gun barrel crashed down on the turret, crushing both men instantly.

"An offering the king makes," Pointer said again, facing the golden table with his arms upraised, elbows squared, the baked-clay curse doll in his right hand. Isis and the Pharaoh turned to look at him.

Yossy split the second tank horizontally, as if he were slicing open a roll to make a sandwich. Fire engulfed the turret. Another sabot round struck him and knocked him to the ground. Captain Arslan jumped on Yossy. The Druze soldier of fortune had a long knife in his left hand and a pistol in his right. He slashed at Yossy's birdlike face and fired point-blank into his chest, over and over.

Yossy roared in irritation. He hurled Arslan at Pointer.

The knife and pistol went flying, disappearing into the corners of the chamber. The tank commander crashed into Pointer. They both hit the ground. Arslan lay still, his neck bent at an extreme angle, blood trickling down his chin.

Yossy stood. He gripped the front of a third minitank's chassis and flipped it onto its top. The treads continued to churn, and the main gun fired once in protest, but the men inside were crushed.

"You did nothing!" Grundy shouted at the wizard. He fired several rounds at the giant Yossy, without effect.

"Shut up!" Pointer stood, raising his arms again. "An offering the king makes, bread and beer for the ka of the Osiris Jason Pointer, true of—"

CRASH!

Grundy didn't see what walls the tanks broke through, but suddenly the room was choked with rubble and dust. A flying stone struck the magician between the shoulders and knocked him down. The Pharaoh and Isis grunted wordless objections, and minitanks rolled into view, firing.

Five minitanks.

They were Arslan's men—Grundy recognized them immediately—the ten crewmen who had messed up the antiputrefaction charm. Arslan had left them behind after they'd rotted to death at the third gate. They were still decaying, flesh peeling from hands and faces to reveal white bone, but now they were in motion.

Three charged Yossy, firing. Two raced straight ahead, toward the flame-spitting serpents. The snakes leaped into the air, and Grundy saw for the first time that they were winged. Fire rained down around the room.

Grundy dove under the table to avoid the flames. Pointer stood again, shaking dust from his panther skin and coughing.

"See?" he shouted.

From the dark side of the chamber, Ammut emerged again. She sniffed the air, roared, and grabbed the nearest zombie minitank in her jaws.

Apparently, the decaying men hadn't chewed their gum.

The tank in the monster's jaws buckled, but the men fell from it. They were putrefying, but they kept fighting. One dragged himself slowly up Ammut's hippo-like tail and the other crawled up Yossy's back. Then dead men and living men and whole minitanks, sprockets, idler arms, road-wheels, and thrashing creatures coalesced into chaos. Grundy had to look away.

On the other side, a zombie tank had impaled a flying snake on its main gun. Its companion tank lay smoldering, and two burning dead men fought the second snake hand to hand under a hail of their comrades' machine-gun fire.

"An offering the king makes," Pointer began again. Grundy rolled out from under the table to watch him. The only way Grundy was making it out of this self-imposed hell was by whatever road Pointer planned to take. "Bread and beer for the ka of the Osiris Jason Pointer, true of voice."

He picked up a morsel of bread from the table and ate it.

Isis immediately spun to look at him. Her lips moved, and for the first time, she formed comprehensible sounds. "Jason," she murmured.

"Marian," he said.

The stabbing pain in Grundy's stomach nearly knocked him down. The hall shook, and the golden gate crumbled, collapsing in on itself.

The Pharaoh noticed, too. He turned to look down at Jason Pointer, and he laughed.

"This is the end of the road, Whitlock." Pointer raised the curse doll over his head with both hands and slammed it on the edge of the offering table.

Nothing happened.

He slammed the clay doll again, and a third time, and it didn't break.

The Pharaoh laughed. "You have greatly overestimated yourself, Jason Pointer," he roared. The floor shook at the sound of his voice. "And you have greatly underestimated my power. Or, as the ancients used to say, you come at the king, you best not miss."

"Help me!" Pointer screamed to Isis.

She shook her head.

The curse doll dropped from Pointer's shaking hands and rolled across the floor toward Grundy. He heard monsters roaring, and the hissing of flames, and the dull thuds of firearms, but they all sounded far away as he stared down at the baked-clay replica of the Pharaoh.

Pointer shouted and waved his arms. The Pharaoh strode forward.

Grundy still had his pistol. Pointing it at the figurine, he squeezed the trigger. The curse doll leaped and spun through the air, but when it landed, it was still intact.

The Pharaoh swung his crook like a croquet mallet. He hit Pointer, sending the man flying across the room. Pointer, somehow still alive, stood up just in time for the Pharaoh to slam his flail down on the wizard's head.

The magician rolled away from the impact. He was bleeding, but he still shouted his mumbo jumbo and waved his arms. Where was he getting this resilience? Was it from his chant at the table?

Grundy wanted to be able to take a beating like that, and still fight. He'd need it if he was going to get out of this mess. He scooped up the curse doll and set it on the table—didn't want to lose track of that. He holstered his gun and then raised both arms. Fortunately, CIA training *had* given him a strong memory.

"An offering the king makes," he said. "Bread and beer for the ka of the Osiris Rex Grundy, true of voice."

The battle to his left split apart into halves, suddenly, and through the crack in the middle, Ammut charged. Was she running toward Grundy? He grabbed the nearest object to hand, heart thudding violently, and hurled it at her.

It was the clay figurine.

The curse doll flew in a perfect spiral, straight through the dust and the noise, and—in the words of Coach Henderson—hard enough to pound a nail into the wall of a barn. If Rex Gundy had thrown like that in every high-school game of his senior year, he would have ended up in the Superbowl.

Ammut roared, opening her crocodile jaws wide, and the clay statuette went right down her gullet.

She stopped, fell silent, and blinked.

Pointer had eaten something, Grundy remembered. He grabbed a scrap of bread from the table, spat his gum on the floor, and ate the bread, hoping he didn't metamorphose into a bird-headed troll.

Pointer rose unsteadily to his feet, shouting. The Pharaoh raised his crook to swing it again, but then stopped.

He turned and look back at Grundy, and then at Ammut.

"What have you done?" he growled.

Grundy swallowed, his throat dry. "Bread and beer for the ka of the Osiris Rex Grundy!" he shouted. Beer, there was beer on the table. He turned and found a jug that hadn't been shattered. He gulped down the warm liquid, which had a strong yeasty flavor, much like the hetep gum. "True of voice!"

"What have you done?" the Pharaoh roared.

Ammut bellowed, and to Grundy's ears the sounds seemed to harmonize.

The Pharaoh spun about, took a long step, and a second, then collapsed to the floor.

Grundy tried to sidestep the falling crowned mummy, but as he moved, he felt himself growing larger. The pain in his stomach stabbed him one final time as he feared he was transforming into a bird-ogre as Yossy had, but then the pain was abruptly gone, and he was standing beside a beautiful woman.

"Hello." She smiled at him. "I am the Isis Marian Seidel."

He nodded. "I am the Osiris Rex Grundy. Some people call me Thrower."

"The Pharaoh has died," she said. "The Osiris Jimmy Whitlock has had his resurrection revoked and is in the belly of Ammut."

"Don't worry," he said to her. "All is in order. The Pharaoh is dead. Long live the Pharaoh."

He didn't know where the words came from, but they felt right.

"What shall we do about these?" The Isis Marian gestured at the humans scrambling about on the floor.

"Nothing," the Osiris Rex said. "They have done their work."

He extended his elbow to his queen and turned to escort her from the offering chamber.

THE PATH AND THE
GATES

I wrote this story because I thought I had been offered a place in an anthology. It turned out they had just invited me to submit, and then they rejected the story. So here it is, for the first time.

The Osiris Frank Coltrane rose from the meal of bread and beer to find that Anubis had returned.

"I figured it out." Frank adjusted his kilt. "I know where I know you from."

"I am Anubis," Anubis said. "I am your guide on this journey."

"Yeah, yeah," Frank said. "With the dog head."

"Jackal."

Frank shrugged. "But I mean, your features, you've got a human face going on in there, and I recognize it."

Anubis waited.

"You're Shelley Johnson. My old neighbor."

Anubis nodded.

"I was always chasing your kids away from my yard," Frank said. "You never could keep them under control."

"I suppose I couldn't," Anubis said. "The oldest was eight when I was widowed."

Frank chuckled. "Yeah. I guess that's probably why none of them made it to college, either. Bad luck."

"Bad luck," Anubis said.

"Two divorces?" Frank asked. "Didn't your one daughter become a drunk? And, of course, your boy."

"My daughter got sober," Anubis said. "We could have used more help."

"Is this usual. Like, Ghost of Christmas Past stuff? Now we have to forgive each other or whatever? I get to learn a lesson and have a growing moment on my . . . what was it you called this? My path?"

"Your path." Anubis grinned, showing teeth. "Perhaps our meeting isn't for your benefit at all, Osiris. Perhaps I'm merely carrying out my role."

"Okay," Frank said.

"Osiris is sown into the earth," Anubis said. "Osiris arises to sustain and feed the living."

"Yeah, yeah." Frank nodded. "Metaphor, right? Resurrection? I get it, this thing I'm holding is a flail for beating grain, so I am the grain, I am the farmer. I guess the crook means I must be the shepherd, too. Do I get a nice lamb kebab next? Still surprised it turned out to be the Egyptians, all along."

"The Egyptians' being right does not mean that others were wrong," Anubis said. "These things are had everywhere, among all people."

"Okay," Frank said, "but you're not dressed as Athena or the Great Pumpkin. But maybe the Egyptians were just the first, and it stuck."

Anubis shook her head. "The Egyptians were not the first. The first were people for whom you have no name, who built their temples as structures of the imagination, printed on stars. The Egyptians and the Sumerians are just some of the first peoples who left writing that has survived."

"Yeah, yeah." Frank yawned. "That's a nice history lesson, don't forget about all the generations of *homo sapiens* who came before writing, got it. But speaking of history, shouldn't there be a feather? A feather god? I went to the Met once or twice, I remember a god with a feather on top of his head, and the heart being put onto a scale to be weighed against another feather."

"Yes," Anubis said. "That, it turns out, is something of a metaphor."

"I knew it," Frank said. "Maybe it was a goddess, now I think about it."

"What you face now is a fork in the path." The Anubis Shelley Johnson took Frank by the hand and led him up stairs. The dim light of the cavern in which he'd eaten his meal gave way to brighter illumination. Not the amber light of day, but a cold, pale light, like the northern light of winter, or the light of an LED bulb. As she kept leading him forward, the light grew colder and brighter, until Frank had to shield his eyes. "As we approach the crossroads, I must tell you that the same judgment you mete out in life is meted out to you."

"Meted." Frank chuckled at the funky old language.

Anubis stopped. He almost bumped into her and knocked her down, but Frank managed to catch himself. He blinked, tears forming in his eyes, and he held up the crook and flail as if they might shield him from the continuous lightning bolt that crackled before his face.

At his feet, to the right, lay a gulf. It seemed impassable, even if he were to take a running start. On the other side, the light crackled like a wall. To his left, the path continued, and the light faded. In just a few short paces, he saw that he could be shielded from the light and in the embrace of stone cavern walls again.

"What is this?" he asked.

"There are two ways," Anubis said. "There are always two ways, and you are always choosing."

"I don't see two ways," Frank said. "I see a pit which looks, if I lean over and peek down, bottomless."

"The pit can be crossed," Anubis said. "It can't be done alone. You need help."

"Are you going to help me?" Frank was surprised, and a little bit embarrassed. He'd never been much help to Shelley Johnson.

"That's not my role," Anubis said.

Frank considered. "Is this . . . is the heart and feather thing a metaphor for this?"

"If you like."

"Two gates, huh." Frank looked at the sheet of vertical lightning. What might be behind it? "How does this work?"

"If you have chosen the right-hand path," Anubis said, "then you will lay hold upon the word, and it will lead you in a strait and narrow course across the gulf."

"I don't see a course," Frank said.

Anubis shrugged.

"It seems strange that there are two gates this far along," Frank objected. "I thought this was a path, but now I seem to be in a maze."

"There has to be a second gate," Anubis said. "Otherwise, how would Seth be able to choose his path of resistance to the other gods? How could the third part of the host of heaven rebel, if there were not a second gate?"

Frank scratched his neck. "I just don't feel warned, I guess."

"You were warned," Anubis said. "These things are had among all people. You were warned by Matthew. Right after the instruction that you must ask, seek, and knock. 'Enter ye in at the strait gate: for wide is the gate, and broad is the way, that leadeth to destruction, and many there be which go in thereat: Because strait is the gate, and narrow is the way, which leadeth unto life, and few there be that find it.'"

"Matthew who?" Frank asked.

Anubis said nothing.

"And the other path?" Frank said. "What's down there? What do you mean by 'destruction'?"

"According to the Egyptians," Anubis said, "that is where Ammut lives. She's a monster with the jaws of a crocodile, the forequarters of a lion, and the hindquarters of a hippopotamus. She consumes the souls of any who choose that path."

Frank grunted. The light was beginning to fade. "So now what? Now I have to choose? It seems a little anticlimactic, doesn't it, coming all this way, having to swear all those oaths about things I did and didn't do, and now I just get to choose?"

"You misunderstand," Shelly said. "You *did* get to choose. You got to spend your whole life choosing. Everything you did, from birth to death, you were in reality standing at the only crossroads there is, choosing one of the only two paths that exist. And there was a lifeline, a promise made and always kept that you could always turn toward the light, that a hand would always be extended to help you across the gulf."

"So . . . no more choosing now?" Frank asked.

"You have chosen," Anubis said.

The light abruptly cut off as Frank stepped into the open tunnel mouth. His step was easy, the footing was good, the path smooth. He felt relief that the light was no longer pounding him in the face.

He stopped walking. "It doesn't seem fair that I just stop choosing now, though. I mean, maybe I should get a licking, learn my lesson. I can throw a football around with your boy. The one who died, you know, shot by cops."

"My boy's not down there," Anubis said.

"Do some other good works, then." Frank shrugged. "I can go back and warn someone else to choose a better path. You know, like you said, mete out a better judgment. And maybe then I get another crack at it."

"I don't know, Frank," Anubis said. "That's beyond my vision, and it's beyond my calling. This is as far as I go."

"So what was all this about, then?" Frank's temper flared. "Did you just want to show me what I was going to miss, is that it? Is this punishment? You could have had bread and beer forever, Frank, but instead, off you go and you get nothing?"

"I don't want to punish you," Anubis said. "I don't want to punish anyone."

Frank was walking again, though he hadn't meant to take steps. "Well," he called to Anubis as she disappeared in the shadow, "I guess I'll go find out what kind of metaphor is waiting for me this time."

He intended to adjust his grip on the crook and flail, but found that his hands were empty.

"Good luck, Frank," Anubis said. "As far as I know, Ammut is not a metaphor."

Assume the
Marketing Is on You

I talk often about the need for writers in the present day to promote their work, and strategies for doing so. Here's a blog post the publisher and senior editors of Immortal Works asked me to write on the subject.

I recently had great news: Baen Books, publisher of my novel *Witchy Eye*, wants a six-book series out of it, to be called *The Witchy War*. In discussing this milestone with several of my good friends at Immortal Works, the subject of promotion came up, and I agreed I'd write this post.

Here's the thing: you probably chose to take up the burden and the glory of writing because you had things to share. Maybe tales of adventure, or wry observations about experience, or deep insights into the soul. Whatever that reason is, excellent. Good for you. Now realize this:

For all the same reasons you undertook writing, you need to undertake marketing.

Because odds are, the burden of promotion—especially early on—is going to fall on you.

This is true, by the way, even if you have a big publisher. A big publisher may want to let you run more or less free for the first couple of books, to see how you do on your own. Or it may allocate the lion's share of its marketing budget to one or two writers each year, leaving the others to fend for themselves and only promoting them if, by luck or the authors' hard work, those books sell a lot of copies.

You think I'm kidding. I am not. To answer Jimi's immortal question, I am experienced.

FOR SURE if you are self-published, and VERY LIKELY if you have a small publisher, you need to assume you'll do the bulk of the marketing yourself.

Now, here's the bad news. I don't know what's going to work for you. Some people have lucked into catching the first wave of new social media platforms (Goodreads or Wattpad), or marketing tools (BookBub), or publishing technology (KDP), or genre phenomena (LitRPG or 80s nostalgia). Others have been pushed by friends with larger fanbases, or have other kinds of platforms (CNN newsman Jake Tapper is—as I write this— hawking his debut novel on CNN). Some writers study obsessively the ever-changing apparatus of Amazon's lists and keywords.

I would say this: experiment a lot and do it with low-cost trials that will either prove useful or fail in short order. Don't commit to an enormous, long-term marketing scheme for your books until you have reason to have confidence in that scheme.

My money is where my mouth is. Here's what I did in 2017:

- Visited elementary schools in Idaho and Utah
- Spoke, taught, and sold books at pop culture and literary conventions in Alabama, Florida, Missouri, Utah, Tennessee, Washington, Idaho, Connecticut, Colorado, and Georgia, often at the Bard's Tower, a traveling sci fi and fantasy bookstore
- At some of those conventions, participated in improvised audience-participation / performance games with my troupe, the Space Balrogs
- Wrote several short stories for anthologies
- Organized and held two Reddit AMAs
- Planned and executed a joint bookstore tour of the west coast with author Christopher Husberg
- Piggybacked on three days of a bookstore tour in Texas as Larry Correia's opening act (I use the phrase advisedly; I sang songs and read before Larry's appearances)

- Made individual bookstore visits in Utah, Texas, North Carolina, and Massachusetts
- Organized a storytelling event, a standup comedian, and a writing retreat in my own home
- Had made and gave away *Witchy Eye* chibi stickers
- Had made and sold / gave away *Witchy Eye* t-shirts
- Took out a print ad in the programming booklet of a convention I wasn't able to attend myself
- Recorded a folk music album of the songs in my novel *Witchy Eye* and released it
- Offered regular Goodreads giveaways
- Visited dozens of Barnes & Nobles (and other bookstores) to sign stock and meet staff, in Utah, Idaho, Oregon, Washington, California, Texas, Connecticut, Minnesota, Mississippi, New York, New Jersey, Pennsylvania, Tennessee, Massachusetts, and New Hampshire
- Participated in multiple blog interviews and podcasts
- Recorded and shared music and instructional videos forYouTube

Note that the above list doesn't even include things like maintaining my social media presence, identifying myself as an author and talking about my books to the audiences I reach through my corporate training business, or routinely networking with and promoting other authors.

So far, 2018 is turning out to include EVEN MORE of the same. Heck, just recently, when I went to pick up pizza at my local Papa Murphy's, the one where the staff knows me by name, I brought a copy of *Witchy Eye* and gave it to the store.

And by the way, all that travel described above? ON MY DIME. Flights, gas, rental cars, hotels.

I had great support in my efforts from Baen. They had me on their podcast, they published a promotional short story on their website. They connected me with important people at bookstores and publishers, they arranged important networking meetings, they sent books and marketing material to many bookstores. They proactively worked with me and my schedule to find places and events for me to appear at. In 2018, they have upped their efforts, just like I have. I will tell you, I believe that one reason I had such excellent support is that the Baen team saw that I was willing to work hard at selling the books (another reason is that Baen's marketing person, Corinda, is flat-out amazeballs).

And, after all the foregoing, know this: I feel lucky. Because having done all that I did, there was no guarantee that it would work, and make me worth additional investment from Baen.

But—it looks like—it *has* worked.

I don't know what's going to work for you. You didn't write your novel by sitting at home hoping it would write itself; you're not going to sell your book by hoping it does all the legwork without you, either.

However you choose to market yourself and your books . . . good luck!

A GOD OF DEATH

Martin Greening edited the Tales of Ruma *anthology as a stretch goal reward for his kickstarted fantasy-Rome roleplaying game. He generously invited me, and I selfishly took the opportunity to write a* Witchy Eye *tie-in story. The following is set in the Old World, centuries before the apotheosis of Sarah Elytharias Penn.*

The Roman opens his eyes. "You're the god of death," he says. "I'm a dead man."

His eyes close again.

I knew he was a Roman before he said a word by his dress, ragged though it is. I guess from his features that he's Iberian, though here in the sunless lands of the north his skin has grown pale, as has mine. I, too, am a Roman. Or at least, I was.

He and I have both been here for some time.

The man's face is familiar.

His Latin is a soldier's Latin, blunt and direct and most likely learned on the march.

I chuckle and use the Roman speech I grew up with but haven't spoken in years. "I am no abductor of maidens, nor have I any wealth to give. I am but an old soldier, living out his greying years on the poorest latifundium a legatus legionis ever earned. I was told this land would grow wine-grapes and wheat, and instead I find it grows mostly rocks."

My wife Lysseta laughs, a sound like a hiss.

We are in the kitchen of our farm. Outside, a sodden wind gnaws the groves of nut trees and the narrow fields of barley I have carved out of this rocky soil. Within, Lysseta stands at the fire boiling water to tend to the Roman's wounds. He lies on our bed, the only bed we have.

"Rocks, and maybe children," I say.

We've never had children, Lysseta and I. She fears I suspect her of barrenness, but I do not. Nor do I believe what I have heard muttered by many a Roman soldier on the campaign trail in the east, that a daughter of the Serpent cannot give birth to the living child of a mortal man. They tell themselves this lie to ease their consciences when they rape the Serpent's children.

And she is great with child now. Her belly is swollen, I can feel the child kick nightly.

This is not her first pregnancy.

The man murmurs. I lean in close and understand his words. "Not Pluto. Wotanaz."

I chuckle and rub my hands over my face. "Ah, Mercury, you mean. Their one-eyed rider of an eight-legged horse, who hanged himself for wisdom. God of ravens, guide of the dead." I have no mirrors in my home, and I forget both my missing eye and my ragged, bearded appearance when I am not reminded. "Lysseta," I say, "I owe you a better face than this. Remind me to shave my beard."

"I could have no better face on a man," she says. "Yours is a face of power. If our child is a son, I could ask nothing better than that he have your face."

"In that case," I say, "I hope our child is a daughter."

The Roman sits up abruptly, grips me by the front of my wool tunic. "Legatus!"

"No longer." I try gently to push him back down, but he resists. "You need your sleep now, friend."

"Legatus legionis Marcus Opsidius Hasta Germanus." His eyes are open and clear now. "There is no time for sleep, they have Gaius!"

I lean in close, look into his face. "Do I know you, Roman?"

"My name is Faustus Papius. I stood as optio to Gaius Livius at

Cambodunum." He looks away, shame in his face. "We . . . we called you Ophidius. If you doubt who I am."

Ophidius. Not Ophidianus, defeater of serpents, but Ophidius, the snake-man. Because however cosmopolitan Rome itself became, it could never accept my wife. It could gratefully acknowledge me as conqueror of wild Germans with one breath, but with another it must remind itself that I married a sorceress from the east.

"Gaius Livius fought as pilus prior." I remember both men now. Decent soldiers, men who hadn't run. "I had thought he would be praefectus by now. Or returned to Rome to squire more of those fat babies he spoke so much of."

Lysseta's silence is deafening.

"He should be, legatus. But he is held captive by Germans."

"Germans do not hold captives." My voice is hard.

"Gaius is to be sacrificed." Faustus's words complete my own thoughts. "Unless the legion can march to his aid?"

"The legion?" I laugh. "You've taken a blow to the head, Faustus. If there is a legion north of the river, I do not know where it is. I have a few men here, old soldiers like yourself who are content to gather hazelnuts, dung furrows, and throw spears at the occasional raider."

"But the Germans do not drive you out?"

"They fear him," Lysseta says. "As should you." As Rome was never kind to Lysseta, she has never shown any sense of obligation to be kind to Romans.

"They fear *you*, my dark-eyed witch." I smile at her.

She hisses.

"Legatus," Faustus says. "I have seen men sacrificed to Wotanaz. They hang by the neck from the oak tree, and just before the rope kills them, the rune-chanters run them through with a spear."

"Well," I say, "we had better do something about that, then. But first, you need some bandaging."

THE THIRTY DENARII make a comfortable weight in a leather purse inside my tunic, against my skin. As always, I handle the silver—at the slightest touch, it causes Lysseta's skin to blister and burn as if the metal were fire. This is the curse of her people.

We have left two men behind, which means that four armed men ride with us. These are old soldiers, like Faustus and me, who work the land for me in exchange for food, shelter, and a little silver. I think four should be enough. Lysseta chants spells as we ride, cloaking us from the forest's hostile eyes. Her craft makes the men nervous, but riding toward the shrine of Wotanaz without her art would make them even more uncomfortable, so they spit into the rain and watch the trees and the hillsides for Germans.

"It is not too late to turn back." Lysseta whispers to me, not in Latin but in her own tongue. I know a little of it; it is cousin to Chaldee and Greek both and has more than a few words of German stitched into it now.

"My sweet basilisk," I say. The flying serpent is sacred to her goddess, and my wife blushes, pleased, when I address her so. "Our tiny farm is at peace with the Germans, and I have more than enough silver to ransom Gaius."

"They don't want a ransom," she reminds me. "They want a sacrifice."

"With the money I'll pay them, they can buy one."

"My king." She bites her lower lip. It is not a girlish affectation—she is restraining herself from saying something.

"Unleash your tongue, my queen."

She looks away into the rain-cloaked gloom. "The child," she finally says.

"This one we will carry to term," I prophesy. "But for this reason, you should have stayed at the farm."

"For this reason, I wish you had turned that Roman away from our door or killed him out of sheer mercy." she says. "But since you did not, I stay at your side."

I laugh. "I do not understand the ways of my goddess, but neither will I resist."

"Legatus." Faustus's rough Latin breaks into the warm conversation between me and Lysseta, bringing with it a cold light. Dawn begins to show as a gray streak in the east, behind the rain. "We draw near."

"I know where we are. But what possessed you to stay in Germany, when your service ended? Why are you not back in Iberia, drinking its sweet wines and basking in its warm sun?"

Faustus shrugs. "Money, what else? There was simply more call for a skilled sword here in the north."

The ground beneath our beasts' hooves, which has been climbing, now drops off sharply. The pass opens, and below us, still shrouded in the darkness of night, I see the wooden hut beside the lone, enormous oak tree. I know the horrific fruit hanging from that tree's boughs, though it is yet too dark to see it. "Come," I say. "Let us free Gaius."

To Lysseta I add, in her tongue: "This is a good omen for our child. Even in the womb, the daughter of Lysseta and her Roman consort freed the captive from his bonds."

"Or son." But Lysseta's face does not suggest she is convinced of the goodness of the omens.

THE RAIN GATHERS force as we descend the last stretches of the mountain pass and approach the clearing. I see corpses, some fresh and others moldering, swinging from the tree by long ropes around their necks. Beneath the tree waits a lone German, leaning on a spear.

"We arrive." Gaius rides forward.

"He is too eager," Lysseta hisses.

"He wishes to save his fellow," I say.

"Humor me, husband." She puts heels to her horse's flanks and surges ahead of me. "Let me do the speaking."

I am happy to humor her. We ride to the oak, and as we enter the clearing, my four men form up not around me, but around Lysseta. Without direction, they too have agreed that she is to be treated as the leader.

Or has something else happened? I remember that I hold the silver close to my skin, so I take the pouch out and tie it to the saddle, as far from me as I can, without actually dropping it.

I look again.

She is not Lysseta. She is legatus legionis Marcus Opsidius Hasta Germanus.

This is what my men see, what Faustus will see, and the German priest.

And looking at me, undoubtedly, they will see an Ophidian woman.

I laugh, but softly. I will humor her.

"Priest!" Lysseta shouts. Her voice is my voice, and it carries even in the rain, bellowing the harsh German syllables. "You have a Roman soldier you aim to sacrifice."

"Ja." The priest nods slightly. "Ich habe ihn."

"We have come to buy him," my wife the legatus legionis says. "Bring him out."

"How much will you pay?"

"Thirty denarii," Lysseta says. "No more, no less. That will buy you plenty of sacrificial slaves from the traders of the North Sea."

The priest grunts. "Come with me." He turns and walks toward the single building in the clearing, the temple where he and his two sons also sleep.

Lysseta and my four men ride forward. I drift to the side to watch, enjoying the theater my wife is staging.

The grass moves. It is not a rustle, such as might be caused by a snake or a badger; a patch of turf between and my wife leaps abruptly aside, exposing a trench with five men in it. Germans, wrapped in leather and crude mail and holding long swords.

Their sudden shout echoing off the Wotanaz oak, they rush forward.

"Lysseta!" I roar. Raising the spear for which I am named, I charged and skewer one from behind before he knows I am there.

But there are other trenches hidden around the clearing, and my men are swept away before they can mount any resistance. The Germans swarm them three to one each, slicing off hands, arms, heads. They are not saving my soldiers for any later sacrifice; they are after Lysseta.

No—they are after me.

"Faustus!" I roar.

But Faustus laughs at me. He drags my wife from the saddle.

She is chanting, though I cannot hear what she says. If she is casting a spell, it has no effect that I can see.

I race forward, but my horse stumbles and throws me to the ground.

"Come, legatus!" Faustus cries. He pulls Lysseta across the grass, and in the gray light of morning I now see an empty noose dangling from the tree.

"I am Hasta!" Lurching to my feet and drawing my own sword, I rush forward. "Look at me, I am Marcus Opsidius Hasta!"

"Shut up, witch!"

I am struck from the side. What hits me isn't a blade, but a shoulder, and I am thrown to the earth again. The man towering over me is former pilus prior Gaius Livius. He glares down at me and holds the point of a spear near my face.

"I'm no witch!" I grunt.

"Whore, then." He sneers. "I always thought the rumors of your great power were just lies. Lies and stories old Ophidius told everyone to keep us in line."

A scream curdles my blood. Gaius looks but I do not, though it costs my soul to keep discipline. I kick both his ankles, grabbing his spear at the same time and pushing it aside to keep from getting impaled.

He lands on me, hard, but he is surprised and has lost his breath. I roll on top of him and smash his throat with my elbow.

I should kill him, but I have no time. "Lysseta!" I charge toward my wife, who hangs by the neck from the oak of Wotanaz, feet kicking and face turning red. Faustus laughs at her side, jeering at her, but in his mind he is taunting me.

My wife wears my face.

The priest of Wotanaz runs his spear into my wife's heart. She screams without words and blood bursts from her open mouth and nostrils. In the moment that she dies, two things happen.

First, Lysseta retakes her own face.

Faustus instantly stops jeering. He springs back as if bitten, and he must know he has made a mistake. He should run, but he doesn't; he stares at my wife's face as she dies, murdered at his traitorous hand.

Second, a wave of cold power strikes me.

I do not know what it is, but I can feel that it comes from my dead witch consort. Suddenly, my ears are full of the baying of hounds and the cry of ravens. To my astonishment, I find that I am riding two horses. Or perhaps it is a single horse, with eight legs. The hooves thunder upon the ground beneath me like a dozen drummers together, and I raise my spear.

The rain has stopped.

The priest turns to face me first. His face is twisted in an expression that might be joy, and it will be his last.

"Wotanaz!" he cries. "All-father!"

I run my spear through his chest with such speed and force that he bursts, like a wineskin pierced by an arbalest. I do not slow down, but wheel my horse and charge at Faustus. The traitor now raises his hands to defend himself and turns as if he might run.

I knock him down with my eight-legged mount and I impale him with the spear, running him through the stomach and pinning him to the ground.

"All-father!" the Germans cry.

They raise long swords and attack me. They believe I am their god, and they seek to earn their place in my bloody heaven by attacking me.

I will oblige them.

At first, I think they have all become small, but the obvious truth is that I am grown. I tower over the tiny Germans and as the first charges I open my jaws and roar in his direction. A frenzied flock of ravens bursts from my gaping throat and batters him. When he fights through, it is only to have me grip him by the jaw and shoulder and tear his head from its anchor.

He drops his sword but I do not pick it up. I do not need it.

Today I am Wotanaz, the All-father.

Today I am death.

Swords strike me and leave no mark. I tear off limbs. I kick my booted feet right through men's chests. I shred open their throats with my teeth.

I ignore the Germans who flee. They are not worthy of my attention.

But Gaius also runs, and that I will not permit. Whistling through long yellow teeth, I summon my eight-legged mount and leap onto its back. The Roman soldier has almost reached the forest when I overtake him. Leaning, I snatch him up by the neck and throw him across the back of my horse.

"Legatus!" he gasps. "Wotanaz! Spare me!"

He might as well beg for mercy from the storm.

I ride back to the oak, and now I see it for what it always was; the great tree of the world. Branches rise up and out of sight, and above me and unseen I hear the squeaking of a squirrel. The tree's roots sink down through the earth, and below this middle earth, I see somewhere a boiling pond from which the deepest roots drink, tended by three blind women.

I dismount.

By a rope dangling from the tree hangs my wife, pale in death as she was in life. As I am.

"Please . . . ." Gaius begs.

Behind me, I can hear Faustus screaming without words.

A rope hangs on each side of my wife; both ropes end in open nooses. I slip one noose around Gaius's neck and pull it tight behind his head. In this way, I know, he will choke to death slowly rather than dying quickly of a snapped neck.

I am no German, but I have lived a long time among them and I have learned their cruelty.

"No!" This is Gaius's last word, and then I let him hang. His face goes red immediately, he makes gagging sounds, he claws vainly at the rope, he kicks with his feet, and all that energy does nothing but cause him to spin gently as he dangles.

I return to Faustus. He is screaming.

"Why?" I ask him.

"I had no choice!" he shrieks.

"Liar." I grip the spear with both hands and twist it.

He screams. "We were going to be sacrificed! They agreed we could live if . . . I found replacements! And the Germans . . . know you, and want you . . . gone from their lands!"

"And you calculated that you could rob me, in the bargain."

Gasping for air, Faustus nods.

I withdraw the spear. Bright blood gushes out and his scream cuts off abruptly, but he lives yet. I pick up the soldier and carry him in one hand, like a doll, back to the tree of life and death. Gaius spins, twitching. Now I hang Faustus by the second rope, and he too begins his slow final dance.

"Wotanaz!" I shout.

Wotanaz is not my god, but today he is my self.

Something twitches. Is it Lysseta? Does she live?

No.

And yet, her belly trembles.

The child. There is a child. Gently, with only the smallest tip of my spear, I cut open the belly of my goddess. More blood flows along my weapon, but this is the blood of life.

Inside is a baby, and at contact with the cold air the baby kicks.

She is a girl.

I pull her from her mother and pluck blood and tissue from her face so she can breathe. Lustily, she bawls. I tuck her into the cradle of my elbow.

My goddess has given her life for me, and for this child. She deserves a sacrifice. I find my horse—not the eight-legged one, but the mortal beast. Tiny as a pony, it tries to hide from me but cannot. I pluck the purse from its saddle and return to my wife.

The two thieves still turn and gag, one to either side of her.

The baby stops crying and looks into my face as if expecting an explanation from me.

"For your mother," I tell her. "She was killed for this. It belongs to her."

Loosening the leather bag with my teeth, I shake the thirty silver denarii from the purse. They tumble out over my hand, and as each one touches me, it burns my skin.

The rain resumes.

Silver pours down over my fingers and disappears into the blood-sodden earth beneath my dead wife's feet. The coins disappear.

The baby weeps, and so do I.

But the Germans wanted a sacrifice. They shall have one.

I have resumed my mortal size and strength, and I find that I am exhausted. It is an effort even to move, with my newborn crying daughter in one arm. Still, I take up the spear lying on the ground.

Gaius first. His eyes bulge and he flails one last time, but he cannot resist or evade. I sink the spear-tip into his throat, and he expires in a red flood down his chest.

"We shall burn this place." I am talking to my daughter. Or perhaps to my wife. "I shall call you Lysseta, after the name of your mother. I shall tell you tales of her heroism."

Faustus kicks at me, but he has no strength.

"You, Faustus, shall have no part in those tales," I tell him.

Just before I shove the spear between his ribs, he closes his eyes.

"I am the god of life," I whisper, "and you are a dead man."

Vaekra Take Me

This is a short story about cussing as a superpower.

Yeh," said Haptive, scratching his face and smudging dirt all over the left side of his delicately-arching nose. "Well, it be a muck life, ben't ut? I mean, nobbut diggin' an' plantin' an' harvestin'. A lad's gotta have summat more'n that, han't he?"

Mokkel stared at the younger, slighter man. "I must tell you, lad, I've been all over Auriga. I've heard every kind of dumb hick accent I thought I could imagine, stood shoulder to shoulder in battle with clod choppers and bark chewers of every description, and thrown dice with the same when I was in town, and I cannot make heads nor tails of what nonsense you are saying."

Haptive blew a strand of ragged blond hair away from his face and frowned. "Emphasis on the throwin' of dice, I wot, given as you en't a soldier anymore, now when they's needit to go over an' stab 'oles in the Aukasians."

"Yeah." Mokkel shrugged. "It's true, as soldiers go, I was not only less useful than a bit of flyblown goat's carcass, I was the goat's arse."

"Uts arse?"

"The very arse, maggot-laden and fit for nothing but throwing at the Aukasians to distract those fine gentlemen while the real soldiers shot at them. Which, lo and verily, is in fact a succinct summation of the very battle plans the Aurigan fancies had devised. And so I left."

"You'z drummt out."

"Well, yeah." Now it was Mokkel's turn to scratch his nose. He turned to look again at the merchant's house across the street. It was sturdy as a castle and three stories tall, but if what Mokkel had heard at the tavern the day before was true—that the merchant's wife was dead and due to be buried today—then *now* might be Mokkel's best chance for getting inside. If only he could get his charm to work. He fingered the bit of wrought metal hanging from a thong around his neck, but the warmth didn't come. "But I'd have quit if they hadn't booted me first."

"You'z a cunning man."

"Only I do miss the food."

"I miss it too, an' I en't ever et ut."

Mokkel looked back at his comrade in misadventure. "I'd say the signs suggest you've been eating somewhere, lad." He lifted the ragged fringe of his shirt and patted his growling belly, which was flat as a board. "Look at me, skinny as paper. You've got a bit of a belly going, haven't you?"

Haptive blushed and looked away. Fine, Mokkel thought. In starvation times, it was only natural for a young thief to eat whatever came to his teeth, and not share unless he was forced to. Mokkel wouldn't begrudge the lad his enterprise.

Or maybe Haptive was sick, or starving. Sometimes you could get a swollen belly from eating the wrong thing, or eating too little.

"Anyway," Mokkel continued, "you've left rutting off your list, haven't you? That's my fondest memory of country life, is girls happy to up skirts and do the four-legged dance six days out of seven, all made better by a quick trip to see the priest at the start of the week. For that matter, I expect the best part of being a priest in those farming villages is that *you're* the one who gets the biggest share of the dancing—"

"Vekra tek ya," Haptive mumbled. This stopped Mokkel in his rant, which he'd just been beginning, and which he'd intended to cover many misbehaviors of Istran priests, in the countryside and elsewhere. He didn't understand everything Haptive said through the boy's thick accent, but he was pretty sure Haptive would have said, in better pronunciation, *Vaekra take you.*

That was a curse. The boy was swearing at Mokkel.

Mokkel bit his own rant off and swallowed it, then rubbed his nose again. Another man might have hit the boy in the face for his insolence, but then if Mokkel had been the kind of man who liked hitting, he'd have stayed in the army. Instead, he changed the subject.

"Where you from, anyway? Where'd they teach you to talk like that?"

"Margrave of Yositt's land."

Mokkel squinted, trying to remember the maps he'd seen during his stint marching up and down the mountainous eastern border of Auriga. "By Lisidra?"

Haptive nodded.

"Well," Mokkel said, "I guess the young ladies of the Margrave of Yositt's land just weren't bonny enough to keep you. Bad luck for your boinking career, my friend, but better luck for me, to have you as a comrade." He grinned at the boy, and tried to contain his irritation that the boy didn't grin back at what was meant as a compliment.

"I be here, ben't I?"

"Uh . . . yes." The boy's failure to meet Mokkel's gaze made him feel awkward, so he focused on the merchant's house again. "So let me try this amulet again."

"What kinna amulet be't?"

Mokkel showed it to the other man. His amulet was a worked pieced of metal in a simple quartered circle, pierced with one hole to accommodate the thong on which it hung.

"You bought ut to market?"

"Yeah," Mokkel said. "And the fellow who sold it to me swore it would keep away the Soldier's Malady, only it did something else instead?"

"Soldier's Malady?"

"You know . . . boinking disease. Sores, skin goes bad and falls off, you get it from fallen women. What do they call that on the Margrave of Yositt's land."

"The Tuchian flu." Haptive looked at his feet.

"Only instead," Mokkel went on, "it lets me fly."

Haptive looked back at Mokkel's face. "*Fly?*"

"Well, not like a *bird* or nothing," Mokkel said. He shook the amulet around in a vaguely circular motion, which of course did nothing to clarify what the amulet did. "I mean, it lets me get from one place to another, instantly."

"I donno if I b'leeve ut," Haptive said. The lad's eyes were big with wonder.

"Yeah, well, how do you think I got out of the army so fast, and them all chasing after me on horseback and shooting pistols?"

Haptive shrugged. "Ran? Stole a horse?"

"You know, the clearer I hear you, the more your words hurt." Mokkel turned his attention to the amulet.

"How's ut work?"

"Last time, that is to say, the only time I used it, I was holding the amulet really tight." Mokkel closed his eyes to remember. "Running, holding the amulet, and shouting, that's what I was doing."

"You'z cussin'."

"Yeah, I was cursing." Mokkel frowned. Was it possible the amulet would be activated by curses? "I don't think that's it, though. The cursing. I was feeling really hot, I think because I was running, and I grabbed the amulet, and suddenly I went from one hilltop to the next, in a heartbeat."

"Flew."

"Yeah, I ain't got a better word to describe it. I *stopped* being on the first hilltop where I was standing, and then *instead* I was standing on the next hilltop. Which I had been looking at, the moment before."

"An' cussin'."

"I don't think that's what storytellers mean when they say *magic words*, though, is it?"

Haptive shrugged.

Mokkel clenched his fist tightly around the amulet and looked through the second story window of the merchant's house. He could see the backs of two chairs, and a ceiling of many wooden panels, each inscribed with the letter *S*. "Shall we try it?"

"Wha' moot I do?"

"Ah . . . here, come stand alongside me. As a chicken under its wing shall I nurture thee, isn't that what the Istrans say?" Mokkel chuckled. "Yea, I shall gather thee under my wing as my felonious chick, and verily we shall go rob this wholesaling whorespawn blind."

"Cussin'." Haptive stepped under Mokkel's outstretched arm and pressed against his ribs. The lad's body heat was a surprising comfort, given the crispness of the autumn air in which the burgher's wife was being buried, over in the churchyard on the other side of town.

"Alakazam!" Mokkel clutched the amulet and stared through the window.

Haptive stared with him with fiercely beetled brows. "Whorespawn!" he spat.

Mokkel laughed. Why not? "Vaekra take me!" he whispered.

"Vekra tek uz!"

But the amulet did nothing.

"Vaekra take us, indeed." Mokkel tucked the amulet back inside his rotting shirt and disentangled himself from his apprentice. From the fraying leather bag that hung from his shoulder he pulled a short iron bar. He'd stripped it from the fence surrounding a churchyard in a village outside Ariale, and then traded a few hours' wood chopping with a blacksmith in a neighboring village to have the smith hammer the ends of the bar into tapering wedges that angled away from the line of the bar itself.

In other words, a crowbar.

Haptive nodded at the rough tool. "Moot we cuss for tha'un, too?"

"We do not *moot*," Mokkel said. "But we *may*. Indeed, I believe it is the tradition that gentlemen of the road such as ourselves may cuss appropriately in connection with virtually any activity."

"Lucky uz."

"Yeah," Mokkel agreed. "Lucky us."

THE ISTRAN PRIEST was probably not an old man, but the bad light in the gaol cell made him look old. The cell's only usual illumination came from a window high up in the wall, which let in a grayish wobble of sunshine that only indirectly lit the straw, urine, and rat's droppings on which Mokkel and Haptive lay. But the priest had brought a candle with him, which now squatted on the floor at his feet. The candle's light was yellow and flickered, and that made him look old.

And sort of jaundiced.

"You understand that you're going to hang," the priest said.

"Yeah," Mokkel acknowledged. "I mean, even if I hadn't heard it the first time, when that old warehouse-stuffer's thugs grabbed me in his parlor and beat me senseless, or the second, when the magistrate shouted it at me from his desk—"

"The bench," the priest said. "They call his desk the bench."

"That's a stupid name for a desk, isn't it? But what do you expect from a profession that says its fully qualified practitioners are at a *bar?*"

"They're going to hang you tomorrow."

"Right, as I was saying, even if those previous notifications hadn't warned me, I have to tell you that my gaoler delights in saying that I am going to hang."

"There's a war on. They're pretty nervous about burglars around here right now."

"He delights in it so much, he tells me I'm going to hang once *before* spitting in my food, and a second time *after*."

Mokkel had not yet succumbed to despair. In part, this was because his wit (as he saw it) was a barbed and effective way to keep away any despair, no matter how large and bleak. In part, this was also because neither the merchant's bravos, nor yet the magistrate and his bailiffs, nor yet again the gaoler, had taken away Mokkel's amulet. Clearly, its poor iron appearance disguised from his enemies the amulet's power. He refrained from touching it as he thought of using it to escape, for the hundredth time today, at least.

The priest turned to look at Haptive. His face looked even older and more weary, and he reached forward to take Haptive by the hands. "Do you know they're going to hang you too, my—"

"Whorespawn!" Haptive shouted.

"Eh?" The sudden curse caught Mokkel by surprise, but once he had digested it he began to laugh.

"But you need not—"

"Vekra tek ya!"

"My child, why do you not—"

Haptive kicked the priest at this last effort of his. The force of the blow rocked both of them backward, so the priest dropped from his low stool onto the straw with a squishy, fat-bottomed *whoosh!* and Haptive rolled away until he hit the wall and stopped.

The priest stood. He shook his head, and then he shook his fingers in that priestly incantation-cum-gesture-of-blessing all the Istrans did. Mokkel snorted, and Haptive snorted afterward, in imitation.

The priest ignored the snorting and looked Mokkel squarely in the eye. "I blame this obstinacy on you," he said. "No man would want his child to be executed. This can be nothing but sheer selfishness."

"Haptive ain't my child," Mokkel shot back. "He's my apprentice."

"But—"

"Whorespawn!" Haptive shouted, and the priest finally surrendered. Throwing up his hands, he stooped to gather up his taper. Then he backed out of the cell through its iron door, which the gaoler gleefully slammed shut on his heels.

Then the gaoler pressed his face to the narrow grille of bars that passed for a window. "They're gonna hang you," he chortled. "Hang you both!" Then he swaggered away.

"I ben't afraid of hangin'."

"They're not going to hang us." Mokkel stood, hearing his knees pop and feeling the strain in his cramped and undernourished muscles. Whatever the priest's age might be, Mokkel himself was definitely feeling old.

"You gotta plan?" Haptive's delicate face was hopeful. If pressed, and if sufficiently drunk, Mokkel would even have admitted that the lad was beautiful, though Mokkel wasn't that sort at all.

Haptive looked up, and Mokkel wanted very much not to disappoint him.

"No," Mokkel admitted. "I haven't got a plan. But I have the amulet, don't I?" He pulled the iron medallion from out of his shirt and brandished it in Haptive's direction as a reminder.

"Yeh." Haptive looked down at the floor. "Allhow, I ben't afraid of hangin'."

Mokkel forced himself to grin, though inside he knew he was scowling. Fingers firmly wrapped around the amulet, he squinted through the iron bars. Beyond lay a stone hallway, almost invisible because it had no source of light beyond the tiny glimmers that winkled into it from the cells to which it led. Still, Mokkel could make out broad stone pavers, a bench, an empty torch bracket.

A hall.

Mokkel remembered very clearly the day he had . . . moved . . . from one hilltop to the next. He had seen the remote hill and had wanted very desperately to be atop it. His heart had pounded from the five miles and more he had already run from the cavalry squad send to capture him . . . or more likely, since he had been a deserter, to shoot him in the back where they found him. He had burned inside. He had looked at the hill, grabbed the amulet—

And *moved*.

He'd been running full speed when he *moved*, and upon his arrival on the distant hilltop he was still running. On the one hand, that forward motion had run Mokkel straight into a tree trunk and knocked him flat. His nose was still bent, was probably *permanently* bent, from that impact, and Mokkel reached up to rub it gingerly at the memory.

On the other hand, being knocked flat had probably saved his life. Because from the point of view of the cavalrymen pursuing him, Mokkel hadn't *moved* . . . he had *disappeared completely.*

Mokkel had realized this only when he'd rolled onto his belly to look back and seen the soldiers milling aimlessly, half a mile away or more. He'd lain still in the scrub brush and waited until they finally gave up and left.

He'd been trying to activate the power of the amulet again ever since.

It hadn't helped him break into that merchant's house two days earlier.

And however hard he rubbed it and stared through the door of his cell into the hallway beyond, the amulet wasn't moving him now, either.

The courtyard air was so cold it hurt to inhale. The soldiers dragging Mokkel, one brawny young protagonist to each arm, were wearing jackets that might have been good wool in the years their fathers had worn them to war, but every little hole and rip in the blue fabric let in tendrils of freezing air, and the men's hands and necks were bare.

"Right," Mokkel huffed as they dragged him across the pitted cobblestones, "let's not dawdle. Just a test run anyway, isn't it?"

Other soldiers tossed Haptive up the stairs ahead of him. The boy hit the edge of the platform and rolled, flashing pale white skin under his ragged tunic before he banged to a stop against one of the two wooden pillars.

The two pillars, connected at their apex by a crossbeam, from which hung five nooses.

The soldiers who'd thrown him growled and closed in on the boy.

"Hey!" Mokkel barked. He'd never been a sergeant, but he'd known more than one, and he could imitate the sound. "Back off that lad!"

It only worked for a second, but that was enough. As the soldiers hesitated, their booted feet hanging in the air uncertain whether or not to kick the straw-haired farm kid, Haptive climbed to his feet, hugging the pole. It couldn't be easy—his hands were tied together with a short length of rope, as were Mokkel's, and the rope tying his ankles together was only slightly longer—but he managed.

Haptive shot Mokkel a grateful look. Mokkel winked; the boy was a good apprentice—

A fist struck Mokkel right between the eyes and he went down.

"Shut up, you!" This came from one of Mokkel's two guards.

Mokkel badly wanted to say something in return, but he didn't. He rolled onto all fours and then used the lower steps leading up to the gallows to scramble back up to his feet. Then he joined Haptive, getting only one relatively light kick to his posterior in the process.

The gallows platform was tall and the stone walls surrounding the courtyard were low. This combination let a sharp breeze cross between Haptive and Mokkel; the nooses swung over the edge of the platform like ripe apples on an overburdened bough, and Mokkel bit down to stop his teeth from chattering.

He reached idly up to clutch the amulet. He felt nothing, and let his eyes wander about the courtyard, looking for his route out. The solders herded two more prisoners up the steps behind Mokkel; he didn't recognize them, but he could smell them from ten feet away. They looked like real low-lifes, ragged and dirty. Cutpurses.

"Here's how this is going to go," one of the soldiers said. "You all walk up with no fuss, we put nooses around your necks, and one at a time, we push you off. You play nice, we put a hood on you and you get the noose tight up against the side of your head. Breaks your neck, see?"

"And if we don't play nice?" This from one of the other prisoners, the ones Mokkel didn't know.

"Noose behind your head," Mokkel said. "Choke to death instead." He looked to the guard nearest him and jerked a thumb in the direction of the questioning prisoner. "Idiot." He chuckled.

For Mokkel's trouble, the soldier punched him in the face again.

He spat out blood and something that might have been a tooth, or maybe just a bit of gravel from the morning's porridge, lodged in his gums. While he was rubbing the pain from his jaw with his tied hands, he noticed that Haptive was standing funny. Like he had to pee, maybe, or he had some kind of really bad stomach cramp.

"You alright, lad?" he asked the boy. As he asked, he stepped closer and leaned until he was touching Haptive, shoulder to shoulder. Then he grabbed his amulet, looked at the battlement on top of the low courtyard wall, and willed himself to move.

Nothing happened.

"I ben't dead," Haptive said. There was a tear in the boy's voice. There was blood on one leg of his breeks, too. Fresh blood.

"Vaekra take me!" Mokkel whispered, but he was cold as ever and didn't move from the gallows platform.

"Get moving!" A soldier shouted, and punched Mokkel back down the stairs.

MOKKEL SPRANG to his feet as the cell door open. The same Istran priest, with the same jaundice-inducing candle, trundled through the door. He waited until the door had shut behind him and the gaoler's footsteps had skipped joyously, from the sound of them, down the hall.

Then the priest sank to his haunches and let out a rumbling sigh.

"Is the lad alright?" Mokkel asked.

"Haptive is no lad." The priest stared at his hands.

"I know what you're saying, Father. They raise them fast on the farm, all that hard work, plain food, and boinking. Still, he ain't a man yet, not by a long shot."

The priest looked Mokkel in the eyes and furrowed his brows. "Haptive is a young woman."

"Vaekra take me." Mokkel nearly fell over from surprise.

The priest nodded slowly. "You're surprised. Good. That tells me Haptive was honest with me."

"About what?" Mokkel stood and paced the room, rubbing his face with his hands. A thousand things he'd said sprang to mind, words or jokes for which he now felt embarrassed. He'd *relieved himself* in front of her, for Vaekra's sake!

"You're not the father."

"I . . . me . . . oh, gods no, I'm not the father of anybody. I'm not Haptive's dad." Mokkel's mind raced. "But you mean . . . she's pregnant."

The priest inhaled slowly and exhaled again. His breath was heavy with foreboding, and he looked down at the floor.

"She *was*."

Mokkel had been about to say *I'm not the father*, but the words died on his lips. His innocence didn't matter, in the face of Haptive's loss. He thought of how she had looked, standing on the platform earlier that day.

"She lost the baby," he whispered. "Those soldiers beat her, and she lost the child."

"This morning I saw that she was expecting." The priest's words were slow and heavy, but then suddenly he exploded in rage. "Damn you, you scoundrel, how could you have missed it? How do you walk around with someone for weeks, and never realize that she's a pregnant woman?!"

"Vaekra take me." Mokkel threw himself against the stone wall of the cell and slumped to the floor. He felt like weeping. "I'm an idiot, I guess."

"You are indeed a damnable idiot. Of all the thieves, highwaymen, smugglers, kidnappers, cutpurses, footpads, burglars, and thugs I have ever had the dubious honor to shrive, you are without a doubt the stupidest."

"Hey, now, that ain't fair. I didn't . . . kill the baby."

"You may as well have!" Thunder flashed in the Istran's voice and lightning in his eyes. "And worse, you have killed her!"

"Here now, what's that mean?" Mokkel sat up.

"The law won't kill a woman who is with child. Don't you know that?"

Mokkel considered it while scratching behind one ear. "Well, seeing as I have never been remotely close to being a pregnant woman, I suppose I never quite managed to learn the appurtenant rights." He thought *appurtenant* was the right word. Anyway, it was a long word, and he wanted to show the priest he wasn't a complete idiot.

"Do you realize that I tried yesterday to convince her to disclose her state to the law? She would have been freed, instantly."

Mokkel leered. "I guess justice ain't as important as spawning another soldier for the army, eh?"

"You nitwit! That girl was so convinced, is still now so convinced, that you have some cunning magical means to extract her from this situation, that she kept silent!"

"Yeah, well, I'm still working on the cunning," Mokkel said. "Anyway, now that you know, she can just tell the soldiers, and . . ." he looked into the priest's eyes, which got cloudier and darker with each word Mokkel said, and faltered, "only . . . only she can't, can she? She lost the child."

"Now the idiot understands." The priest pounded one first into the open palm of his other hand.

"Yeah," Mokkel said. "The idiot does."

The priest groaned as he dragged himself to his feet again.

"Whose is it?" Mokkel asked. "You know it isn't mine, so whose baby is . . . *was* it?"

The priest looked down at Mokkel a long time before answering. "If Haptive is to be believed, and I think that she is . . . the baby was the child of the Margrave of Yositt."

Mokkel used several of his best curses, all at once.

"Do you know why I came in here, thief?"

"Uh . . . to tell me what I can do to help poor Haptive get mercy?" Mokkel hoped that was it. He deserved to hang, he knew that, but Haptive was just a boy—no, just a *girl*, and a young woman at that who had been abused by her landlord, and then cast out. Mokkel was humiliated remembering all the comments he'd made to her about rutting and farm life.

"There was a way for her to get mercy, once," the priest said slowly. "She threw it away, because of you. No, now there is no mercy. And I fear there is no escape." Suddenly, the priest's eyes hardened into flint. "I came here so that you would know. I came here to make your punishment worse, you whorespawn ne'er-do-well juggler, you bawd, you human turd. I want you to spend every moment between now and the drop tomorrow regretting your miserable life and the stupidity and brutality by which you have caused that pool girl to die with you."

Mokkel was silent for a moment. He knew he deserved the browbeating, though maybe not as fiercely as the priest had felt compelled to deliver it.

The priest knocked on the door to summon the gaoler. As the gaoler's footsteps approached in the hall, Mokkel spoke his last words to the priest.

"You know, I do appreciate one thing," he said. "You came here to make me feel bad. That means you believe I have a conscience. And I want you to know that you're right. I didn't know Haptive was a woman, and I never would have done anything to hurt her, and I feel terrible that she threw away her chance to escape."

The Istran's face was expressionless. "Good," he said.

Then the gaoler opened the door and the priest left.

MOKKEL STUMBLED into the courtyard between two soldiers again, hands and ankles tied. His skin screamed into goose pimples at the cold and he saw his breath cloud the air in front of his face. His heart raced like wild horses and as soon as his eyes adjusted to the blue light of early dawn, he looked for Haptive.

He . . . she was nowhere to be seen, and his heart tumbled in relief—

But no, there she was, on the platform already. He hadn't recognized her because she was noosed and hooded.

How had he ever thought she was a boy?

Mokkel forced himself to stumble forward. He hoped it looked like a misstep, but it let him shoulder his way past the man in front of him and get up the steps of the scaffold first.

"Whorespawn's anxious," one of his captors chuckled. "Wants to swing."

"Listen," Mokkel said. He said it to the two men holding his arms, he said it to the man standing on the scaffold in a black hood that matched the hood over Haptive's face, only his had eyeholes and hers amounted to nothing more than a black sack. He said it turning in circles and mumbling so fast he could barely understand his own words. "That's a woman, do you hear me? That's a woman! You can't hang a woman, and anyway, I did it! I'm the criminal! She was only on the scene accidentally, don't you see?"

Haptive shifted from one foot to the other, but the soldiers only laughed.

"Woman, man, don't matter," one grumbled. "In three minutes' time, you're all worm food."

"Listen, I have—" Mokkel had nothing else to offer, but still he hesitated. "This amulet around my neck, it's magical. It heals the Soldier's Malady."

One of the men grabbed Mokkel's amulet and yanked it from his shirt to inspect it. He was older than the others by maybe ten years, with a shock of thin gray hair and long scars down both cheeks. "Soldier's Malady, eh?" He laughed like a crow. "Yeah, well, keep it. I ain't got Soldier's Malady."

"Can't get Soldier's from livestock, can you, Sergeant?" jeered one of the other men.

The sergeant punched the soldier insulting him in the mouth. As the mocking soldier crumpled, the sergeant retaliated against Mokkel, yanking him into the position next to Haptive and tightening the noose around his neck . . . with the knot behind his head.

He was going to choke to death, slowly.

"Please," he grunted, "the girl . . . let her go."

"Don't worry." The sergeant deliberately reached across, took the noose around Haptive's neck, and rotated it so that the knot was behind her skull. "We'll let her go soon enough." The sergeant looked to the executioner who stood behind Mokkel. "No hood for the troublemaker."

"Haptive," Mokkel rasped. He stared at the wall ahead of him. No one stood on the parapet, and only a few people stood in the courtyard below. Idlers, infirm, cripples. They stared up at Mokkel and he resented the anticipation he knew they felt, waiting for him to kick and choke his way to death. "I'm sorry."

"Ben't nothing," the girl said. Her voice was muffled by the sack over her head, but she sounded as if she'd been crying.

Mokkel felt hot. He knew the other two prisoners were being looped into nooses to his left, but he ignored. "Vaekra take me, that's wrong!" he snapped.

"Yeah!" a man in the crowd jeered. He leaned on two crutches and was missing a leg, and his coat was an even more tattered version of the military issue that the soldiers executing Mokkel wore. "Vaekra take you!"

Mokkel shook his head pointlessly. He wished he were a bull, strong enough to charge forward and simply pull the scaffold down. "Vaekra take me!" he shouted again. He jerked his shoulders back, which made the amulet on his chest jump. He tried to catch it in his mouth and failed.

The executioner pushed him forward. Mokkel fell, but was instantly caught up short by the noose around his neck. The pain was sudden and intense and he was surprised his neck didn't break, but it didn't.

He bounced, dangled, and tried to scream because he felt the skin of his neck shredding away. No sound escaped his lips.

Haptive bounced beside him.

No! he wanted to scream, and *Help her!*

But he couldn't.

The spectators jeered. A snapping sound from outside his range of vision told Mokkel that the third prisoner had fallen to his instant death.

"Don't worry," sneered the one-legged man. He hopped towards Haptive. "I'll help the girl!"

Mokkel burned. He kicked out at the man and knocked away one of his crutches, dropping him to the ground. In his bounce, he came near Haptive, and he grabbed her with his bound hands.

Dying together seemed as pointless as living together had been. She was a woman! The sounds of the crowd seemed further away and for a moment that felt like an eternity, Mokkel wondered what he would have done different had he only known.

Maybe nothing.

But *now.* Now, everything was different.

He stared at the parapet and longed to be there—

—and suddenly he was.

And Haptive was with him. They lay on their sides on the parapet, and their nooses were gone.

The stone was so cold it burned his skin.

No, that wasn't right. The stone was cold, but what burned was Mokkel. He felt he was on fire.

"Did you see that!?" roared the Sergeant.

Mokkel leaned over and looked down into the courtyard. Two dead men dangled from their ropes and a pack of soldiers and spectators stared at the dancing empty nooses that had held Mokkel and Haptive only moments earlier.

"Mokkel?" Haptive said softly.

"Get up," he whispered, and drew her to her feet. He pulled the hood away from her head and looked into her sun-dazzled eyes.

"Be we dead?"

Mokkel shook his head and laughed softly. "Believe it or not, no."

"But then . . . your eyes?"

His eyes?

"There!" Mokkel heard a soldier shout from the courtyard. "Shoot him!"

Mokkel grabbed for the amulet at his throat, and found it gone. Twisted off by the rope, maybe.

But he still burned.

Snapped his head left, he looked out over the parapet, past the moat, to the furthest place he could see in the forest—

—and then he was there, and Haptive with him.

And again.

And again.

"Mokkel!" Haptive sounded stunned. The noise of soldiers was gone. Mokkel heard birdsong and felt the first rays of the sun coming over the mountains warm his face.

"Don't be frightened, girl," he said. "I told you we'd get out."

"But . . . where be your amulet?"

He didn't know. He didn't know how he was able to do this without the amulet, any more than he knew how it had worked when he thought the amulet had been responsible. But he'd escaped—they had both escaped—and he knew he'd figure it out.

He was a cunning man, after all.

"I don't know," he said. "Maybe we can find out together."

The Lord Set a Mark

Out in western Utah, an hour from the Nevada border and north of Highway 50, lies the Wheeler Shale. It's a geological formation, a rocky ridge or mount, but back when the whole area was covered by a massive freshwater inland sea (Lake Bonneville), it was an area of shallower water, and trilobites thrived. So these days, you can walk up to a hill of ragged petrified wafers, lean forward, and pluck baskets full of trilobites right off the ground. Trilobites, it has always seemed to me, were horrifying monsters. Like spiders, they are rendered innocuous only by their tiny size.

Another strand that runs through this story is a Mormon folkloric idea that various personages recorded in ancient scripture continue to walk the Earth today. Maybe in common with some Christians, Cain from the Old Testament and the Apostle John the Beloved from the New are reckoned in that number. Mormonism tells a similar tale of "the Three Nephites," whose origin story is in the Book of Mormon.

Y ou're Hettie's boy, aren't you?"

The man asking hunched forward like a question mark in his sun-bleached denim overalls, face bobbing up and down on the slight breeze blowing through the general store. His face was square and deeply carved by wind and time, burned by years of Great Basin sun into a deep nut-brown. His eyes twinkled.

Hiram Woolley's own overalls were also denim, but of recent purchase, and retained their Sears, Roebuck indigo brilliance. His feet were still wrapped in the trench boots he'd been issued in France. Given the summer heat, easily over one hundred degrees on most days and rarely below eighty even at night, he'd left his great coat at the farm.

"My grandma is Hettie," Hiram allowed.

"Your people are up in Lehi," the brown-faced man continued.

Hiram nodded.

A second man pushed forward to the store's counter. He was paunchy, with the kind of belly fat that sank into a low ring encircling his hips. He was younger, with thick dark hair and beard, and his long-sleeved gray shirt was unevenly stained with sweat. "The Seer Stone Woman of Utah County." He looked over his shoulder at the front door as he said it, as if making certain there were no eavesdroppers.

A third man hung back behind the other two, but Hiram only saw him out of the corner of his eye.

"I don't know about that," Hiram said mildly.

"She's got gifts, though, your grandma, doesn't she?" the bearded man prodded. "Unusual gifts?"

"She knows things," Hiram admitted. "I never saw that she had a seer stone, though."

The two strangers looked at each other while Hiram paid for his sandwich and cold Royal Crown Strawberry soda.

"I'm Caffrey," the older man said.

"Blunt," the bearded man added.

"Listen, we know you're finished here," Caffrey said.

"Dug out all the collapsed irrigation ditches for the widow Masterson," Blunt said.

Hiram thought of the wriggling creatures he'd found down where the dirt was moist. Horseshoe-shaped, with antennae. Vaguely insectoid, but bigger than any insect Hiram had even seen, even in France. He'd crushed them under the heels of his boots and sung psalms to drive them away.

"Real good work," Caffrey said. "I saw it. Nice wide ditches, and you ran that pipe right under the road, slick as butter. You know what you're doing."

"Didn't charge her, either." Blunt nodded solemnly. "Refused payment."

"You can't charge a widow," Hiram said. "Wouldn't be right."

"Painted her shed, too." Caffrey raised his eyebrows.

"It needed doing," Hiram said. "I was there."

The planks of the shed had been gnawed at their bottom ends, as if a carpet of termites had swept through and feasted on the wood they could reach.

"That's the thing," Blunt said. "You weren't really just there, were you? By chance, passing through. I mean, you aren't from here. How long did it take you to drive here from Utah County? Must have been three hours?"

They were almost at the Nevada state line in Millard County, and the drive had taken Hiram nearer four hours. He nodded slightly. Were they going to accuse him of something? It wouldn't be the first time Hiram had been dragged in front of some town council, or bishop's court, or justice of the peace, to explain himself.

But all he'd done was dig ditches and paint a shed.

And crush those horseshoe-crawler things.

"So it wasn't just a little work for a neighbor," Caffrey said, as if explaining something. "Not if you had to drive three hours to do it."

"Jesus said everyone is my neighbor." Hiram kept his face unexpressive.

"Friend, I think we're giving you the wrong idea." Blunt put his arm on Hiram's shoulder. "You're not in trouble. We're grateful for the work you've done for the widow Masterson. And we have more work to offer. The kind of work that . . . well, the kind of work that the Seer Stone Woman of Utah County might do."

"Or her grandson," Caffrey added. "If he had some of the same knowledge."

"Seeing as you're already here, and all," Blunt said.

Where had the third man gone? Hiram found him again in his peripheral vision, standing to one side. Was he there to ambush Hiram if Hiram didn't go along? A punch to the kidneys, or a knife to the throat? The third fellow stood leaning on the counter, but the storekeeper ignored him entirely, reorganizing the Royal Crown sodas in his icebox.

"We're going to offer you money," Caffrey said. "Even though we think you won't take it. Five dollars."

Five dollars was a full day's wages for a man working at the Ford plant. It was certainly more than Hiram earned in a day of planting or harvesting sugar beets.

"I won't take pay," Hiram said. "And I only help those who are in need."

"We're in need." Caffrey nodded, satisfaction beaming on his face. "We have a problem. It's the kind of trouble that, say, the sheriff can't help us with. At least, let us fill your gas tank and spare can."

"Nor the bishop," Blunt said. "Nor the fellow at the bank."

"Fine," Hiram said. "If I can help you, you can pay for my gas. What's the difficulty?"

"I want to sell some land I own," Caffrey said, "up on the Shale."

"Is the land a mine?" Hiram asked. The Shale was a small collection of rocky hills. Grandma Hettie had warned him that the Shale had once been home to strange creatures and could still be dangerous to a man.

Which was why he had crushed the hard-shelled, horseshoe-shaped critters on sight.

"Could be," Caffrey said. "All kinds of colored rocks turn up there, just for the looking, and I've seen veins of what I'm pretty sure is silver."

"And I want to buy the land," Blunt said. "Don't you want the money?"

Caffrey chuckled softly. "Some things are worth more than money. Especially at my age."

"You don't need me at all," Hiram said. "You need a conveyancer." Without meaning to, he took two steps toward the exit. The condensation trickling down the outside of the glass bottle was cooling to his hand, and he wanted to taste the sugary strawberry sweetness.

"There's an inscription," Caffrey said. "Old writing."

"Writing?" Hiram had seen many pictographs and petroglyphs on the red rock walls of southern Utah. He was used to the swirls, the jagged lines, the pits pecked into the rock faces to mark moments when the rays of the sun would touch them, the humanoids, the animal shapes. "Or *pictures*?"

"I guess that's the question." Blunt scratched his chin through his beard. "Caffrey's got a boy who says he can read the markings. Says they're a prophecy. Caffrey won't sell me the land if the translation is true."

"I'd like to sell," Caffrey said, "but it wouldn't be right, not if the translation is correct. It would be . . . selling something too special."

"You want someone to prove that the translation is wrong," Hiram said.

"If it's wrong, I'll sell," Caffrey said. "If it's right, I'll keep the land. But I need to know."

"I want someone to prove the translation is wrong," Blunt said. "And that it's nonsense, to boot."

These men weren't widows and orphans. They weren't poor farmers, shut out of the dazzling wealth that had poured back into the United States with the end of the war and the beginning of the Harding administration. With needs like these, why would it be inappropriate for Hiram to accept payment?

But Grandma Hettie had insisted that taking payment was wicked. You could accept a token gift, or food, or travel money, but that was about all.

In any case, Hiram was the wrong man to help them.

"I can't read any ancient characters," he told them. "If you ask my old teacher, Mrs. Simms, it's a doubtful proposition whether I can even read English."

"But you're a cunning man . . . yes?" Caffrey asked.

The person in Hiram's peripheral vision seemed taller than before. He wanted to turn and take a closer look at the fellow, but his eyes were fixed on the men before him.

He nodded, ever so slightly.

"So you've got ways to test the truth, don't you?" Caffrey pressed. "I've seen some of them, myself. Saw an Eye of Abraham once, over in Juab County. I've seen the sieve and shears done, and I've heard of others."

The bloodstone felt heavy in Hiram's pocket.

"I do," he admitted.

"So come test the boy," Caffrey said. "Hear him read the text. Tell us what you think."

"Even if you can't tell us one way or the other whether he's wrong," Blunt said, "I'll still pay for the gas to get you back to Lehi. I'll pay for that sandwich, too."

Hiram took a deep breath and nodded.

THE THREE MEN rode in Blunt's Model T, Hiram sprawled alone on the back seat behind the other two. They left him in peace to eat his sandwich and drink his soda. Something tickled at the back of his consciousness, something he had forgotten.

He wished he knew ancient languages. He wished he had the expertise to look at an ancient rock inscription and pronounce what it meant as a matter of skill.

If he had that ability, for one thing, he would be able to read the words of all the books that were now closed to him. Like Agrippa, and the *Picatrix*. Hiram knew there was great lore locked in those volumes, but they were written in Latin and Greek and other languages, so to him they would forever be as silent as the tomb.

The best he would ever do was his hand-copied Reginald Scot, which he had found during the war, in London, copying it himself into his own notebook, sometimes baffled by the spelling and always marveling at the words. Other cunning men were book men, learned. Hiram knew what his grandma Hettie had told him, and a few things he had learned from Scot.

But he had the chi-rho medallion to keep him from harm, and the bloodstone in his pocket. One reason he'd been willing to ride out to the Shale with the two men was that his bloodstone had given him no warning about them. The bloodstone did several things, but above all, it warned of dishonesty.

So Caffrey and Blunt had been sincere.

And Hiram hoped that he could listen to this boy read his translation and tell whether the boy was acting honestly or not, and be done. That seemed like a likely outcome, and Hiram hadn't seen anything in the way of danger in the invitation. Still, he'd tucked his revolver into his overalls pocket, the gun with the initials *H.W.* and *Y.Y.* scratched into it, the one Hiram's friend Yas had entrusted to Hiram with his dying breath in a muddy ditch in France.

Not that the revolver would be much good against the little horseshoe-shaped creatures, if, say, they swarmed him.

"Who's the boy?" he asked.

"My nephew." Caffrey slung an arm across the back of his seat and rotated ninety degrees to look back at Hiram.

"He's not a scholar, I guess," Hiram suggested.

"Not a scholar. Not a magician. Not someone anybody would have said was spiritually gifted, nor intellectually gifted, or gifted in any way at all, not before . . . this happened."

"Tell me about it." Hiram watched the flat ground speed past the outside of the car.

"The boy was hunting," Caffrey said. "Rabbit. Hard to find anything bigger than a rabbit to shoot at in the Shale. He got lost, and wandered into canyons he didn't know. And he came across the writing."

"And decided he could read it?" Hiram asked.

"Sounds silly, doesn't it?" Blunt shook his head.

Caffrey grunted. "No, he decided he should tell me about it. It's my land, after all. So he told me about it, and we came out here looking for the wall."

"Looking?" Hiram asked.

"We didn't find it." A hint of shame crept into Caffrey's voice. "I thought he'd been lying to me, or had a sunstroke."

"You must have found it at some point," Hiram observed.

"I gave up, but the boy kept coming back," Caffrey said. "Started spending all his time on the Shale, wouldn't quit when I asked him to get back to school and work, wouldn't quit when I told him he had to stay off my property. That went on for weeks. And then there came a time when he was gone for a day and a night and a day, and finally we sent out search parties."

"And you found him. What's his name?" Hiram asked.

"Enos. We didn't find him, he found us. Specifically, he found the search party I was a part of and led us to the wall."

"And he told you what it said," Hiram guessed.

"Said he'd been up all night, he'd had a vision and he knew how to cipher out the symbols."

"And he read it to you."

Caffrey nodded.

The edges of the Shale rose up from the yellow-grassed plain north of Sevier Lake. In a wet spring, the waters might run all the way to the base of the Shale, to lap at the hills as if reminding them of the ancient sea that had once buried this entire valley. Under the full blasting heat of this hot summer, the water evaporated; if any of the lake remained now, it was miles away to the south and unseen. Once into the hills, and slinking down into a winding canyon, the truck threaded between high rock walls and into secret canyons. There was no road, not even an unpaved one, and the Model T rattled along the rocky bottom of a dry streambed.

Hiram had a momentary vision of a highwayman shooting down at them from the top of one of the cliffs. The thought of an ambush reminded him of what had been teasing his memory: the third man at the store, the man in his peripheral vision.

And then he realized that there was a man standing on the running board of the Model T. A man in a long coat and hat.

"Here we are," Caffrey said.

"I guess word got out," Blunt added.

A red vertical sheet of stone rose into view. It was thickly decorated with images, many of which were abstract. Spirals, triangles, circles, hashed lines, marched across the stone in rows, separating out panels of beast-headed men and man-headed beasts. Hiram also thought he saw trees and their foliage, stars, a mountain, maybe a river. Men standing at altars. A hand emerging from a thick cloud. The images were all painted onto the rock with a dirty white pigment.

The images might be a text. A text with illustrations.

The rock face was broken into three panels by ledges that crossed its face. To his right, Hiram saw a narrow chimney of rock at the end of the cliff face, where he thought he could probably drag himself up the rock.

A crowd of some twenty people stood around the cliff, watching. They parted as the car arrived, leaving an adolescent boy standing alone under the rock face. He was dressed in a sleeveless white undershirt and torn jeans, and he stared at the newcomers without blinking.

The three men stepped out of the car.

"I admit, there's something Egyptian about the way it looks," Blunt said.

"It is older than Egyptian." The boy spoke in a monotone voice, that sounded remote as well as intimate. He sounded as if he were standing on the other side of a closed door, delivering simple factual information through the wood. The afternoon sun just touched his carrot-colored hair, and a breeze coming through the canyon ruffled it at the same time. "The Lord set a mark here ages before the rise of the bull-priests of Memphis."

A shiver ran down Hiram's spine.

"You see?" Caffrey whispered.

"Are you Enos?" Hiram called.

The boy nodded. "What's your name?"

"I'm Hiram Woolley."

Enos said nothing.

"You certainly make an impression." Hiram walked closer, trench boots crunching in the sand.

"I'm not here to make an impression." Enos stood still with his arms at his sides. The crowd watched Enos and Caffrey; Hiram felt invisible among them.

"You came here to hunt rabbits, I heard."

A faint smile creased Enos's face. "A sacrifice. Life lives by eating life."

"Did you come here to make a sacrifice?" Hiram asked.

"That's not what you want to know," Enos said. "You want to know whether I can read the writing on the cliff face."

"Can you?" Hiram asked.

"I'll read it to you now." Enos turned so that the broken cliff face was on his right and Hiram was on his left. He raised an arm and pointed to sections of the rock as he spoke, as if he were indicating the text he was reading. "These are the words of the prophet Onanda-Iti-Koom. In days to come, in this place shall arise a man named Ka-Afri. He shall be great in the eyes of the Lord. He shall make sacrifice here, and shall live as priest and king forever, after the order that was in the beginning."

Caffrey pressed against Hiram's side and whispered. "You see why I must know if this translation is possibly true?"

The crowd stared at Hiram, holding its breath.

The words certainly sounded insane.

But Hiram's bloodstone hadn't told him of any lie.

"Ka-Afri?" he asked. "You think it says 'Caffrey?'"

Enos pointed at a cluster of four characters: a seven-armed star, a square, two parallel vertical lines, and a crossed spiral.

Hiram shifted from one foot to another. "Who are these people?" he whispered to Caffrey.

"Friends and neighbors," Caffrey said. "I . . . suppose I might have let on that you were coming. That you might find out the truth about the characters."

"Find out whether you're supposed to offer a sacrifice and become a priest and king?" Hiram asked. "Find out whether it's true that there's some ancient promise that you personally will live forever?"

"No," Caffrey said.

The sudden stinging sensation on Hiram's thigh, where the bloodstone lay in his pocket, let him know the truth of the matter. He sighed.

"Look," he said. "I'll tell you right now, Enos thinks he's speaking the truth. But if you want me to look into this any further, you need to send everyone else home. We don't need anyone getting excited or violent because they've hung their hopes on you to start a new church or set up as a new country."

Caffrey looked disappointed, but he nodded. "Of course."

Hiram stood looking at Enos as Caffrey calmly urged his neighbors to leave. It took ten minutes, but eventually the crowd dissipated; all the while, Enos stood with his arms at his sides and ice in his eyes.

Hiram wanted the crowd to leave for safety's sake, as he'd told Caffrey. He had another reason for sending them away, though; the best thing that the bloodstone did was it warned him of deceit, but it had other properties. It summoned rain, which was helpful. It stanched the flow of blood, which had saved Hiram's life more than once in the trenches and ruined cities of France.

It also attracted fame.

And Hiram didn't want fame.

Fame meant too many questions. It meant uncomfortable investigation, by officers of the law and church leaders. It meant requests to employ his arts to accomplish trivial tasks, or for the sake of mere demonstration, as if he were Harry Houdini.

He was not Harry Houdini, and he wanted obscurity.

The crowd left. Caffrey, Blunt, Enos, and Hiram stood at the foot of the cliff, loosely arranged as if standing at the four corners of a square.

"How did you learn to read the text, Enos?" Hiram asked.

"A heavenly messenger taught me."

"What do you mean, heavenly?"

"He showed me his heavenly nature, so that I would believe."

"How did he do that?" Hiram asked.

"Of course, I can't tell you." Enos smiled.

"Did you test this messenger?"

"You take me for a fool. Yes, I offered to shake the messenger's hand, but he refused, knowing that he was not a creature of flesh and blood."

"Did this man shine? Did his flesh look like lightning?"

"That would be no proof of his heavenly origin, would it?" Enos furrowed his brow. "Second Corinthians says that. Is this Sunday School, Mr. Woolley?"

"I think this is a lot more earnest than Sunday School. How did you meet this heavenly man?"

"I prayed," Enos said. "I found the rock again, and I prayed out loud, all day long and into the night, and then the man came to me."

Through the entire exchange, Hiram's bloodstone remained inert.

"Did the heavenly man tell you his name?" Hiram asked.

"He said I would know his name later, at the right time and in the right place."

Hiram could not shake a sense of foreboding, but his bloodstone was still. "What else did this heavenly man tell you?"

"He told me that the prophecy would be fulfilled."

"That Caffrey would offer a sacrifice?"

Enos nodded.

"Did he say when?" Caffrey's breathing was fast and shallow.

Blunt's jaw squirmed as if he wanted to spit.

Enos shook his head. "He didn't say. But it might be now." He turned his head to look Caffrey in the eye. "Mightn't it?"

Caffrey was transfixed, panting, and couldn't say a word.

"Is there an altar where this sacrifice is supposed to be offered?" Hiram asked.

Enos pointed up the cliff. "There are two caves. The altar is in the highest cave."

Hiram checked the sun; the disk hung fat and orange half a handspan over the horizon. "Is climbing the only way up, Enos?"

Enos nodded.

Hiram swallowed a lump in his throat. He turned to Blunt. "What do you have in the trunk of your car? Anything?"

"Water," Blunt said. "A thermos of coffee, half empty and cold. An oil lantern, matches. A canvas tarpaulin. No rope, if that's what you're looking for."

"No gun?" Hiram asked.

Blunt grinned. "Why, Mr. Woolley, I carry that in my *pocket*."

Hiram nodded. "Make sure it's loaded. And get the lantern and matches."

Hiram climbed first. He couldn't climb with his gun in his hand, so he trusted the chi-rho medallion to protect him from anything that might take him by surprise. He wedged himself into the crack at the edge of the stone panels, gripping the sharp, dusty rock with his fingers and jamming the toes of his boots into the narrow corner of the crevice. With long, awkward motions, he slung himself up the rock, dragging himself onto his belly on the first ledge.

Sweat poured down his body under his shirt and overalls. He was grateful for the many years of hard farm work; his muscles were lean, but they were hard and they did the job. Blunt came next, waving off Hiram's offer of a hand. Caffrey accepted the hand and Hiram pulled him up onto the shelf. By the time Caffrey was upright, Enos had finished his own climb and stood, staring upward.

The first cave Enos had mentioned lay before them, at their level. It was a shallow depression, a single dry chamber. For a moment, when he looked into it, Hiram thought he saw a man in a long coat and a Homburg hat. But the image was gone instantly, a trick of the fading light.

"What else is up there, besides the altar?" Hiram asked.

"Probably the heavenly man," Enos said. "And maybe his . . . allies?"

"Allies?" Hiram frowned.

"Creatures," Enos said. "Familiars. Salamanders."

"You didn't mention them earlier." The pistol felt heavy in Hiram's pocket.

"I did," Enos said. "You weren't listening closely enough."

Hiram's bloodstone lay inert. A sluggish chill crept up his spine and neck. "What do they look like?"

"Unearthly," Enos said. "Hard to describe. But they never tried to touch me."

"Is there danger waiting for us at the altar?" Hiram asked.

Enos hesitated. "I expect there's danger everywhere. But there's knowledge at the altar, and a secret. And power, for one who is willing to provide a sacrifice."

"I should have brought a sheep," Caffrey murmured.

Hiram examined the canyon below, to be certain that the crowd had left. He felt uneasy, and if bullets started flying, or worse mayhem than that ensued, he didn't want to risk innocent bystanders.

And if, as he was beginning to fear, there was strange evil to confront on this rock, he didn't want there to be witnesses.

The second stretch of cliff was an easier climb, with a wider crevasse that angled back and away from the ledge, making it more of a scramble up a slope, work for the legs rather than the arms. A jumble of desiccated wood crouched at the far end of the ledge, the remains of some desert tree or patch of shrubs long dead. More scraps of wood lay scattered about the cave.

"Fire," Hiram said. "I want fire here at the bottom of the crack. And we should take fire up with us."

"I brought the lantern." Blunt raised the article as if in emphasis.

"Fire?" Caffrey's eyes gleamed. "For a sacrifice?"

Hiram dragged the brush over to the bottom of the crack and stacked it so that it would burn efficiently. He poured a little lantern oil over the wood and then threw down a blazing match. The sudden orange flames were starkly visible in the deepening twilight, and a resinous, piney smoke filled his nostrils.

"Fire against evil magic," he explained. "It's the most basic counter-charm, and most likely the oldest."

"Evil magic?" Enos's voice sounded remote.

"It's just a precaution," Hiram said.

"Don't worry about it." Caffrey's words tripped out in a jumble, faster than his tongue could properly organize them. "Hiram Woolley is just a cunning man, and this is how a cunning man thinks, I suppose."

"You're anxious," Blunt told him. "Relax. Remember that you win, either way. Either you have your precious translation, or I give you good cash for the land."

"Those don't sound equally enticing to me." Caffrey's eyes twinkled in the wooden slab of his face. "I want to see the altar."

"We all do." Hiram stepped over the flames and levered himself into the ascent. "Be careful of the fire."

Scooting up the chimney, he found he could make progress with his two feet and just one hand, so he kept his second hand free and close to the pocket of his overalls. The crack pulled away and to the right, revealing curves in the stone not visible from the ground, and for one disorienting moment, Hiram thought the ascent was taking him away from the mountain entirely and into some unseen space hanging over the canyon floor.

But then he scrambled over the stone lip onto the second ledge. Standing, he found himself staring down into the dark mouth of a second cave just as the sun disappeared over the horizon. This cave was deeper, and quickly plunged into darkness. Evergreen-scented smoke enveloped him in a wispy column, rising from below. He stuck his hand into his pocket and wrapped it around the grip of the pistol.

"Get that lantern up here," he called to Blunt.

Blunt and Caffrey muttered back and forth to each other briefly, and he didn't catch the words.

The opening was a vertical crack whose two sides twisted closed at the top, forming a knob of stone that hung down ominously. To either side, strange characters marched right and left in rows, and on each side, there was an image. Hiram found the images harder to see the closer he stood, but even at this distance, he could see that both images were images of sacrifice.

Caffrey arrived first and started into the cave. Beyond the first two paces, the entire passage was shrouded in darkness, so Hiram grabbed the farmer by the shoulder strap of his overalls. "Wait for the light."

Caffrey trembled. "Yes. Yes, that's a good idea."

In the shadows within the cave mouth, Hiram thought he saw something moving. Something on the floor, or maybe even carpeting it, writhed and bubbled.

"Blunt!" he called, but then Blunt arrived, and quickly struck up the lantern.

Hiram took the lantern in his left hand and stepped into the cave mouth. The yellow kerosene light revealed a floor that at first sight looked like glistening black stone.

But as Hiram looked closer, he saw that the glistening black material was the carapaces of the horseshoe-shaped creatures. The unknown things he'd seen creeping through the moist earth underneath the widow Masterson's farm here sprawled and tumbled over each other, giving rise to a faint clicking noise.

"The salamanders," Enos said.

A straight, narrow path ran ahead and slightly upward, through the creatures. In the depths of the cave, Hiram saw a bulky orange mass that might be a block of sandstone.

"The altar!" Caffrey gasped. "I didn't bring a sacrifice!"

"God himself will provide a lamb." The voice was Enos's flat and unemotional, and it came from the edge of the stone shelf.

Hiram turned and raised the lantern to shine it on the translator. The kerosene light made Enos's skin look like yellow wax. Beyond the boy, the evening air loomed up like a purple void, hiding the surrounding hills. Hiram drew his pistol and pointed it at the stone in front of Enos's feet.

"No," he said. "And you may have been telling me the truth, Enos, but you haven't been telling me everything. It's time to spill the whole story."

"Will you shoot me, cunning man?" Enos stared past Hiram, into the cave.

"Only if I must."

Caffrey spluttered. "You're here to determine whether Enos's translation was correct."

"I'm here to test whether Enos is telling the truth," Hiram said. "The whole truth. But protecting your life, and Mr. Blunt's, and even Enos's life, is more important than the truth of the translation, one way or the other."

"Your questions are not for the boy." This new voice groaned behind Hiram, from the depths of the cave. Hiram shuddered and willed his arm not to shake. He turned to face into the shaft and the voice continued. "Your questions are for me."

A shadowed form stood before the orange block, partially concealing it. The salamanders clicked louder and swarmed over each other more rapidly.

"Are you a messenger from heaven?" Hiram raised his voice to ask.

"I never said I was." The shadowy shape shifted from side to side. Was it a man? But it seemed too large to be a man, and its posture and form were not quite right.

"You deceived this boy."

"Not in the essentials," the shadow rumbled. "There is power to be had in sacrifice. It can be had by Caffrey."

Caffrey started forward, but Hiram shouldered him rudely to one side to stop him.

Blunt swore and ran. He sprang to the edge of the stone shelf and skittered so quickly down the crack, he nearly dropped himself into the fire.

"The choices narrow," the shadow rumbled.

"There will be no sacrifice today," Hiram called. The situation had gone beyond confirming any translation and revealed itself to be something monstrous. He had to protect Caffrey, even if it meant protecting the man from himself. He had to protect Enos, too, if he could. And whatever was inhabiting this cavern, he had to make this place safe for future travelers.

If only he had a few sticks of dynamite.

"Will you stop me?" The shadow surged forward. Hiram raised his pistol and pointed it at the thing, which halted its forward momentum. Moving forward also somehow moved it into shadow, and it lost the distinctiveness of its manlike shape, dissolved into blur and darkness. The lantern light glinted off something that might be teeth, but the teeth were as long as fingers, and they had to be eight feet off the ground.

An animal musk wafted from the cave and settled over Hiram.

"Yes."

"There are grave consequences for anyone who stands in my way."

"The Kaiser said similar things," Hiram murmured. "Really, that just made me want to go obstruct him."

The shadow laughed, a long, rasping chuckle. "But are you prepared for God himself to smite you?"

"Live like every day might be Judgment Day," Hiram said. "You never know when you might get hit by a truck."

"Did your grandma Hettie teach you that?" Caffrey's teeth rattled.

"My mother did." Hiram's voice was barely louder than a whisper. "Before she . . . passed."

Disappeared, rather.

"You won't like getting hit by God's own truck, stranger."

"You said you weren't a messenger of heaven."

"I'm not. I just bear heaven's mark."

The shadow lurched forward again, stopping now in the full yellow pool of the lantern's light. The rattling swarming of the horseshoe-shaped things rose to a crescendo, and Hiram saw the speaker's face.

It might have been a man's face once, but it was a man no longer. Its muzzle protruded, ape-like, and teeth like yellow nails dripped from its maw. A spike of beard hung like dried moss, falling three feet from its pointed chin and lying draped across its thick belly. Inflamed and scabby skin hung in loose pouches around protruding, knobby bones. Short legs pushed the thing forward from behind, and muscular arms fell almost to the stone in front. Its ears curled forward, nearly cupping themselves against its cheeks.

But its eyes. The thing's eyes were liquid with sorrow, and tears rolled down the wrinkles of its cheeks to lose themselves in the beard and in the patches of gnarled chest hair.

The figure was naked. In its hand it clutched a sharp flake of stone the size of a dagger.

"Cain." Hiram's heart seemed to stop beating.

"In the flesh." Cain rolled thick, rubbery lips back from his teeth. "Still."

"One of us should fear Judgment Day," Hiram said. "It isn't me."

"Judgment?" Cain's voice started as a mild rumble, but then rose into a sudden shriek. "Judgment? What have I to fear from judgment? What am I supposed to fear, hayseed? That I might *be killed?*"

"Every man feels envy." Hiram kept his voice gentle. "Every man makes errors of the moment, slips he wishes he could recall. Very few murder their brothers."

Would his pistol pierce Cain's skin?

"Over sacrifice," Caffrey said. "A quarrel over a sacrifice."

"I killed my brother," Cain growled. "But I did not do it for envy."

"It was a quarrel over a sacrifice," Enos said, repeating Caffrey in his dead-toned voice.

"It was a quarrel over a secret," Cain said. "A secret about power. A secret that was learned by my son Lamech, and then by others."

"Lamech wasn't your son," Hiram said. "I haven't read a lot, but I know my Bible. Lamech was descended from Seth. Not from you."

"Lamech became my son when he learned my secret." Cain snorted. "As now Caffrey will become my son."

"No, he won't," Hiram said.

He felt the cold prick of metal against the base of his skull. The metal point wobbled and danced.

"That's a pistol you're feeling." Caffrey's voice shook. With excitement? "Blunt's gun. He gave it to me because I told him I was frightened."

"You don't need to be frightened." Hiram kept his pistol pointed at Cain, aiming for the center of his chest. "And you shouldn't listen to this monster."

"Is he really Cain, though?" Caffrey asked.

"I am," Cain said.

Hiram nodded reluctantly. "He isn't lying."

"Then he knows a secret about power," Caffrey said. "Something has kept him alive these six thousand years, hasn't it?"

"God's curse has kept him alive," Hiram said. "Is that what you want? To be cursed by heaven?"

"I don't want to die," Caffrey muttered.

"You won't die," Cain rumbled. "You'll become as the gods."

Hiram tried to force himself to keep his breathing steady. His vision swam and the tips of his fingers and toes tingled. "This is madness."

"He isn't lying, is he?" Caffrey's voice cracked.

"A madman can believe his own lies." Hiram wasn't sure it was true. "Or a monster."

"To the altar!" Caffrey voice leaped into a squeal. "Forward, to the altar! Tell me your secret, Cain!"

The monster moved closer. Hiram squeezed the trigger.

Bang!

Had he missed? Was Cain simply impervious? Was the monster indeed protected by the hand of God?

In any case, his shot left no mark, and then Cain wrenched the pistol from his hand. Hiram punched, twice with his right and a third time with his left, and then Cain enveloped him in his long, scratchy arms, and dragged him deeper into the cave.

Hiram kicked and scratched, to no avail. He bit one of the arms gripping him and got no reaction. Then Cain slammed him down onto a flat slab of stone, knocking the wind from his lungs.

He lost consciousness for a moment.

When he could see again, he realized that the cave was still lit by the yellow lantern light. How was that possible? What had happened to the lantern? Cain stood to his right, on the deep end of the cavern, and Caffery stood to Hiram's left. Cain chanted syllables that Hiram didn't understand, and Caffrey repeated them after him. Enos stood beside Hiram, his face a silhouette against the waxy yellow light that came from somewhere behind him.

"Don't," Hiram croaked.

Enos raised a revolver and pointed it at Hiram. It was Hiram's own weapon. "Shh."

Hiram slapped out at Cain. He was woozy and weakened, and the monster responded by seizing Hiram's right wrist and right ankle and pinning them to the stone. The weight of the first murderer was so great that Hiram immediately felt the pins and needles of loss of blood circulation in both hand and foot.

Caffrey raised his hands over his head. He held the stone flake gripped with all his fingers wrapped around it. Sweat poured down his face and dropped onto Hiram. Rattling and clicking sounds so loud they drowned everything else filled the cave.

Caffrey shouted queer guttural syllables. With his hands raised over his head, the front pocket of his bib overalls hung taut and pouchy. The pocket should have been smooth and loose, if it was empty.

Blunt's gun. That was where Caffrey had put Blunt's gun.

Caffrey slammed the flake of stone down into Hiram's chest.

The force of the blow was stronger than anything that could have come from the old man's arms alone. The energy crashing into Hiram's chest stunned him, and it also bounced him off the stone, tearing him from Cain's grip and sending him tumbling through the air.

As he fell, Hiram grabbed at Caffrey's overalls. He hooked the fingers into the bib pockets and was rewarded with the sudden snap of the stitching ripping out. He fell to the ground and a heavy metallic object fell on top of him.

Cain roared. He swung an enormous paw and knocked Caffrey away. Caffrey dropped the sharp stone, which clattered on the stone floor of the cave, then staggered away to the cave opening.

Salamanders swarmed over Hiram. They were cold, and they felt like insects, with multiple crawling legs, but Hiram couldn't pay them any attention. Enos was shouting and stepping back to aim Hiram's own pistol at him. Hiram slapped at the object on his chest, found it was a pistol as he had hoped, and managed to get it into his hands.

He rolled over as a gun went off. In the enclosed space, he felt as if something had punched his eardrums. Hiram crushed the strange black insects as he rolled onto his belly, and then again onto his back. He raised Blunt's pistol over his head, Enos was aiming at him again.

Hiram fired, and Enos dropped.

The salamanders were biting him, and it burned. Hiram found a cave wall and dragged himself to his feet, sweeping the little beasts from his flesh. His overalls had protected him from the worst of it with their thick denim.

The light came not from the lantern, but from a burning oil slick around the lantern's shattered remains. The oil was almost gone and the light was dying.

Enos lay under a swarm of the horseshoe-bugs.

Allies, Enos had called them. Familiar spirits.

Hiram's sternum ached.

Cain scooped up the sharp flake of stone. It had snapped off, its edge blunted. "You can't kill me," the monster growled.

Hiram snaked a finger under his shirt and felt the spot where he hurt. He found a coin-sized depression in his chest and could even feel the crossed Greek letters imprinted in his skin. The force of Caffrey's attack had driven Hiram's chi-rho medallion into his flesh.

Hiram pointed Blunt's pistol at the floor. "I don't want to kill you. You're God's problem, on the great and last day."

Cain snarled and said nothing.

"But you must leave this place," Hiram said. "I'll come back in the morning and destroy the wall and your pictures. If you aren't gone by then, I'll gather every man in town and we'll hunt you down with dogs, gasoline, and torches. We'll burn you so badly, you'll wish you were dead."

"What stops me from killing you right now?" Cain growled.

"You tried once," Hiram said. "Do you want to try it again?"

And then, suddenly, Hiram was not alone. A man wearing a long coat and a Homburg hat stood beside him, starkly out of place in this cave full of alien insects. Hiram tried to focus on the man's face, but could make out no features, and indeed, nothing at all, other than an expression of great serenity.

The man in the Homburg raised one hand, palm facing the monster.

"Today," he said in a clear voice with an accent like a bird's chirp, "the Lord has set a mark upon Hiram Woolley."

Cain barked and hissed. He threw back his head and roared, the sound echoing terribly through the cave.

Finally, he dropped to all fours and shuffled past Hiram and out into the night.

Hiram turned to thank the man in the Homburg and the long coat, but he was gone.

As the last of the oil-flame died, Hiram dragged Enos from beneath the salamanders. He had to pry them off the boy's flesh, finding his own pistol beneath, but also finding that the boy was dead. Hiram's bullet had hit him in the arm, but his flesh was lacerated over his entire body—the horseshoe-shaped creatures had been his death.

Hiram carried the dead boy down the cliff.

Blunt lay at the bottom, his neck broken. Had he fallen? Had Cain killed him? Or had he had a last, fatal encounter with Caffrey?

Hiram took the keys of his Model T from the man's pocket. With Enos's body over his shoulder, he approached the car.

Caffrey sat in the driver's seat, his whole body hunched forward over the steering wheel. The sound of his weeping leaked from the Model T into the surrounding night.

"Caffrey," Hiram said.

"Kill me, cunning man."

"That's not my place," Hiram said gently.

Caffrey plunged from the car, falling to his knees at Hiram's feet. He stared up at Hiram with a pleading look on his face. Even in the darkness, Hiram could see that Caffrey's teeth were quickly elongating and becoming yellow. His chin and nose were pushing themselves forward, his face already taking on the appearance of a dog's or a baboon's, his ears were curling forward.

"Kill me," Caffrey growled.

"No."

"I can feel it happening to me. It's the mark of Cain, don't you see? I'm becoming a monster!"

The deaths of Enos and Blunt already lay heavily on Hiram's shoulders. He laid the young man gently into the back seat of the car. Then he carried Blunt to the car and laid him beside the boy. Squirming black salamanders crunched under his feet, surging up from the dry soil to die beneath Hiram's army boots. Dead horseshoe-shaped insects, strange as they were, didn't trouble Hiram. He wasn't sure what exactly he'd say about the human bodies, if anyone asked, but he had to take them back to town.

When he started the Model T, Caffrey still knelt on the sand, weeping.

"Maybe the Lord set a mark on you," Hiram said. "Maybe you set it on yourself. Maybe Cain did it. It doesn't matter. You didn't get what you wanted, but I don't suppose I can say I'm sorry about it. You and I are done, and you're going to have to find a way to live with yourself."

Caffrey kept wailing as Hiram turned the car around and headed back into town.

Brand and Writers

Four Different "Brands" to Manage on Your Road to Writing Success

I have no memory whose blog I wrote this for. The idea of brand, including the idea of an editor- and other professional-facing brand, is one I've been thinking about for a long time.

W elcome, novelist. Like it or not, you're an entrepreneur selling a product, or a line of products.

I think it's useful to break the idea of brand up into several elements that you, a writer of fiction, should be considering. Let me start with two overall ideas, relevant to all the brand-like ideas I'll discuss.

One: brand is how you get recognized. You want people to hear a snatch of story and say, 'that sounds like it was written by my favorite writer.' You want people to see you, or hear your name, and immediately be connected with ideas about the kinds of stories you write and other things that amuse and delight those people.

Two: to a surprisingly large degree, your brand is something you discover, rather than something that you choose. As a writer, choosing your brand can mean slow and painful change. But even when you don't choose your brand, you communicate it, so it always pays to be thoughtful.

BOOK BRAND

Book Brand, or Brand Proper, belongs to the writing. If you write consistently across all your fiction, it may be that you have a single brand, e.g. *hard magic systems* or *retold fairytales*. Not all writers stick to a single brand, though. Where they write more than one brand of fiction, they may use different names, e.g. J.K. Rowling and her thriller pseudonym, Robert Galbraith, or they may use variants of their name, e.g. I write as Dave Butler for children and D.J. Butler for older readers. Some writers use the same name to write multiple brands of fiction—did you know that Rick Riordan writes adult thrillers, too? But Rick Riordan, writer of classic mythology repurposed as a contemporary setting for middle grade adventure stories, and Rick Riordan, author of the thrillers about Tres Navarre, PhD, tai chi practitioner, and unlicensed detective are nevertheless two different brands.

Book Brand should be simple, easily communicated, and easily recognized. Disney's films are *magical family fun*. Edgar Rice Burroughs wrote *adventure on strange worlds*. H.P. Lovecraft wrote *monsters on nihilist earth*. Jules Verne wrote *scientific travel adventures*. If you're not sure what your brand is, try asking people who know your books to describe your brand or brand, in three or fewer words. If you think you may have more than one brand, ask the question about different series, and see what results you get. Another question to ask a patient reader might be, "If this book didn't have a cover, how would you know it was a book by me?"

Knowing your Book Brand(s) will help you keep readers by continuing to write in the same brand, giving readers more of what they like you for. It will also help you choose appearances, covers, and marketing collateral, because you want all of those to scream your Book Brand as loudly as the books themselves do.

SHTICK

Shtick is the collection incidental things that are not in your actual writing, but will help people remember you and your books. Some of the things that make up my shtick are: height, a mustache, changing and unusual hats, a guitar, book giveaways, and public singing, including in filk circles. I know writers who give away candy, wear sandwich boards to conventions, dress all in black or purple, give away Tarot cards, and cosplay.

If you are self-published, I think it makes sense to think of the physical appearance of your books under this same heading. Are the books that you want branded together (see above) printed in the same format? Do they have similar covers—fonts, colors, styles? Do you use the same cover artist, to get a consistency of feel?

More than any of the other elements I write about in this post, shtick is *chosen*. So choose shticks that highlight or bring out elements of your brand or persona. Your shtick can be whimsical, sober, manic, sturdy, wry, generous, or challenging, but it should be consistent with and point at your Book Brand and your Persona (see below) to communicate and underscore what you want readers to think about you and your books.

PERSONA

Like it or not, readers don't just invest in books, they invest in writers. They want a writer in whom they can see themselves, or with whom they'd like to sit down for a drink. Persona, of these four elements, is the least chosen. You are who you are.

Still, you are a complex person. A reader may get to know your complexity if she meets in you in person, or through reading your books, but you should think about what about yourself you'd like to project. Choose your Persona and govern your public behavior accordingly. Are you witty? Generous? Wise? Stable? Brave? Patient? Mercurial? Pick a small number of traits you believe you possess, and would like people to know about you, and think about how those are communicated through your actions. Run your social media and your con appearances and your bookstore tours and anything else you do publicly through this lens.

This is the least choosable of the four traits I'm talking about today, but it's not unchoosable. But be aware that if you want to communicate to people as generous, and you're in fact not generous, but you're going to try to be generous, you're choosing soulcraft and an uphill road, and what you may in fact end up communicating to readers is that you're not everything you'd like to be. That might be okay, just be thoughtful about it.

Personally, I'd warn you away from two types of Personas. Most of us should not choose to emphasize our politics as a way to reach readers. I know, it works for some, but I suspect that for most writers, emphasizing politics is, on balance, a way to lose rather than gain readers. I also would urge you not to trap yourself in pity-seeking Personas—don't be the writer who is always wrecked, lost, has writer's block, is depressed, needs cash. People can be surprisingly generous and will often help, but no one ever blegged or Patreoned her way into bestsellerdom. I'm not saying that you shouldn't ever complain on Facebook about feeling overwhelmed or struggling with mental illness, but I am definitely saying that if you do those things a lot, they will define your Persona for some people. You may gain sales; you'll definitely lose some.

EDITORIAL REPUTATION

As a writer, you have a fourth, special brand, that faces the editors of the world (though not them exclusively). What are you like to work with? How long does it take you to produce a story or a book? Can you write to order? Are you cheerful? Do you require much editing? Are you wildly creative, or more prosaic? Do you hit your deadlines? Do you give lots of advance warning when you know you're not going to hit your deadlines? How many books and stories do you produce in a year? Can you write across genres? Do you promote? Can you travel? Can you read contracts? Are you sophisticated about the publisher's brand, and about your own brand?

Everything you do in your interaction with editors builds your Editorial Reputation, with that editors and with others (editors talk, and editors move from one publishing house to another). Everything you do in your interaction with agents, including agents who do not represent you, builds your Editorial Reputation. To some extent, everything you do in public affects your Editorial Reputation, so one to think of this is a specialized aspect of your Persona.

Editors care who they work with, and they want their publishing houses to work with writers who will help bring the team success. A strong Editorial Reputation will bring you deals. A poor one will shut the doors in front of you.

A Short Rest in Hell

Steven L. Peck's novella, "A Short Stay in Hell", inspired James Wymore to put together an anthology. In the novella, the protagonist is trapped in a Hell of a particular construction: it contains apparently infinite books, and the protagonist can only escape by finding and reading the book that recounts his life. He wanders the maze, exploring infinite varieties of nearly-identical literature, encountering other damned souls, and reflecting upon his fate. For the anthology, writers were challenged to come up with similar concepts.

I fall asleep during this one. Who knows how long I snooze through it, and when I wake up, I feel just like I always do—tired. And there's never any change in the light, so how am I supposed to know how long I've been out, how many cycles through this same piece I've been listening to for all eternity?

No, not the same piece. And not all eternity.

But mostly the same piece, and for a very, very long time.

♫ ♫ ♫

The devil was one smoking hot number. This was only one of the reasons I didn't believe in her. Or believe her.

As when she said, "You're going to be in here for a long, long time."

Behind her hulked another devil. Bigger, and ugly. He held a feather quill over a clipboard and watched the good-looking one closely.

"Sweetheart," I said, looking up and down at the devil girl's red flesh, rippling like juicy sashimi in all the right places, "I'm going to be in here until I sleep it off. Hopefully I'll remember you and think of you fondly when I'm alone."

"You're one of the delusional ones," she said. "You don't believe you're going to Hell."

"I'm probably going to Hell, all right." I remember that I smirked, but that's no great insight. I smirk a lot. "But this isn't Hell." I gestured around me at the dark walls, the jets of fire visible through the windows. "This is a stereotype, brought on by reading too many bad stories and being stoned. Hell, this is a cliché."

The big, scary guy behind the cutie arched an eyebrow at me. "Hell," he said. "Whether it is a cliché or not, is rather beside the point."

♫ ♫ ♫

Even after I wake up, it takes me a while to spot it. You'd think I'd be super-sensitive by now, but I'm not. The first movement, only it's not really a first movement, it's more like a second movement, because it's always *adagio* and the first movement of a symphony is supposed to be *allegro*. Hell is slow. I joked about this, at first, asked for something a little faster, something with a backbeat.

It isn't a joke anymore. Hell is church music, of the most solemn, droning, dirge-like kind. *A-mighty-fortress-is-this-Hell.*

I'd kill for a little Buddy Holly.

There goes the first movement, and then the second. And they're identical. And then the first, and the second, and they still sound identical. Only I know they're not. I know, from experience, and because this is what she told me during the intake interview, that the first and second movement are not identical. The first again, and the second, first, second, first, second.

There it is.

It's just a little rest.

I call it. "Measure . . . uh, thirty-nine," I say. "There's a . . . sixteenth-note rest at the end of the measure in the second movement."

The conductor is a burly scale-covered green beast, with jaws like an alligator's, only as big again as its entire body. It looks down its snout at me through half-moon glasses and tut-tuts, shaking its head.

"No," the conductor growls. "The Giver of All Things invites you to try again."

"Damn." The joke wasn't funny the first time I said it, but I keep saying it anyway.

The conductor raises its baton, a thin sliver of ivory. The choir opens its many mouths and howls again.

♫ ♫ ♫

The first time I saw the choir, I jumped.

It was right after the interview with Red Sonja (as I liked to think of her), and apparently close by. She'd pointed, and a pair of short, stocky, red-skinned guys poked me with sharp sticks until I walked the way they wanted, which was through a curtain and down narrow, winding stairs.

"This is a bad trip," I said to them.

It was a pun, just not a very good one. And then they poked me through another curtain, which—I swear—was made of human finger bones, and knotted in long twine made of human hair. And as I walked through it, the bones whistled, all together, each a different note, none of them adding up to harmony.

"And getting worse," I muttered.

And then I saw the choir.

They were all girls. I recognized them at once, because I'd seen them before. They had all been in one of my choirs. They were all pretty enough, and a few of them were knockouts. Some of them I knew I'd gotten stoned with. Some of them I'd . . . well, let's just say I'd seen more of them than a high school teacher is supposed to see.

Yeah, that's a smirk.

But my first reaction wasn't a smirk. My first reaction was to jump. Surprise, you know? But then I remembered.

"See, I'm just stoned," I said to the two red pokey-guys.

Only they were gone. And so was the finger bone-flutes curtain, and the whole hallway I'd come through. Blank wall.

"Stoned."

"Ahem."

♫ ♫ ♫

"Measure thirty-nine," I say, but I get it right this time. "There's a *thirty-second* note rest at the end of the thirty-ninth measure of the second movement that isn't there in the first movement."

The conductor nods and turns back to the choir.

The choir starts singing again, the same wordless howling damned two-movement symphony. Not quite the same—from long, long experience, I know that the first movement of this "new" piece will be identical to the second movement of the prior piece, and the second movement of the new piece will differ from the first movement in one particular. So it goes, as I roll from one nearly identical piece to another through a series of tiny, particular changes.

Sometimes, the particular is huge, and noticeable. I remember once—and I have no way to tell you how long ago this was, because I cannot measure time here—the second movement was in seven-eighths time. The first was in four-four, and that's a huge difference. For you non-music types, that's this:

First Movement: *BUM-bum-bum-bum-BUM-bum-bum-bum*
Second Movement: *BUM-bum-bum-bum-bum-bum-bum-BUM*

Tapped out like that, you're hearing it and you think, *Huh, they don't sound so different.* But trust me, they're night and day. Most of the music you hear on the radio is four-four or maybe three-four, if it sounds like you could waltz to it. Seven eighths is rare. And strange. And to have all the same notes shoved from four-four into seven eighths was . . . completely discombobulating. All the emphases shifted. It was like suddenly hearing the Gettysburg Address, with Lincoln stressing the last line of every sylla-ble: "Four score and se-*ven* years a-*go*, our ance-*stors* brought forth on this conti-*nent* . . ." you get the picture. It was right, but totally wrong.

So I spotted that change right away. But then the next piece was in seven eighths, and the next, and the next . . . for a long, long time. Seven eighths began to feel normal, but normal in a horrible way. When I stood to stretch my legs, or get a drink from the fountain in the corner, I staggered like a drunk man from the time signature.

The eventual shift back to four-four was rain in the Sahara. Of course, by then the piece had completely changed.

♫ ♫ ♫

The conductor looks at me. It's hard to say the expression is *quizzical*, since the conductor has a quivering membrane that looks like a metronome in each eye socket instead of eyes, but it's asking me a question.

"The Infinitely Patient inquires if you have discerned the difference between these two movements."

I shrug.

The choir resumes again, at measure one.

♫ ♫ ♫

"You have a few things to learn," Red Sonja said. This was before she had me prodded away from her desk. I only ever saw her the once.

"Okay." Smirk.

"The Lord Ahura Mazda, Worthy of Worship, is open handed and liberal of heart, of course. He wishes to give you every advantage."

Behind her, the big guy nodded solemnly.

"Is this where you offer me a doobie?"

Red Sonja frowned.

"Drugs," I said. "Is the Lord Mazda Miata holding?"

"You are not here for drugs," she said. "Nor will drugs be given to you. Nor should you want them. The Root of Creation gives you an opportunity to heal, and a test. You had best be sober."

"How long?" I asked. I could do sober, but I preferred it in short stints. Say, from seven in the morning until noon.

"That's really up to you." Red Sonja squinted at me. "But I'd guess at least a billion years."

♫ ♫ ♫

I liked to watch the choir, at first. The singers are all women, young, and good-looking. And like I said, I *know* them.

So for a while, I watched them. That gets frustrating, just watching, so once, early on, I tried to approach. I figured, hey, a little cuddle in between movements. A quick feel, you know? No harm, no foul. I'd given out many A's to students willing to relieve my boredom. It was practically a scholarship program.

That was when I discovered that the conductor does more than just wave a baton in the right time signature. Those giant alligator jaws just about snapped me in half, and the monster let out a roar that shook the chamber.

I scampered back to my seat, breathing pretty hard, and haven't tried that again.

Hell is look, but don't touch.

That's frustrating. You know what I mean.

Especially because, and I wouldn't swear to this, I think the girls might change, too. Over time, I mean. Like the movements do. Like maybe one of the girls gets taller over time, or curvier, or whatever.

The Endless Bliss does that to torment me, I think. Keep me frustrated.

This is Hell, after all.

♫ ♫ ♫

I sit on a chair, red velvet rubbed shiny like an old theater seat. It's comfortable enough for dozing, and I've spent years asleep in it. Red curtains hang down the walls, and the ceiling is hidden in darkness somewhere above me. The stage is a low platform large enough to accommodate the choir and the conductor.

In the corner, there's a fountain, like I said. And a tree. I don't pay much attention to them, because they're a fountain and a tree, and once I've taken that in, there's nothing more to do. The tree grows fruit. I don't know what kind of fruit it is, a persimmon or a passion fruit or something I never ate before I came here.

But now I eat it. I eat the fruit, I drink water from the fountain, I pace around the room, I look at the girls. When I spot the variation between the first and second measures of a piece, I call it out to the conductor. The music changes.

I don't know what Red Sonja thought I was supposed to learn from this. Or what the test is.

Maybe it's a bad trip, after all.

♫ ♫ ♫

Only two things different ever happened, in all the years I've been here.

Okay, *years* is a guess, but it's true that once I kept track of the number of pieces of music I heard. I don't have anything to write with, or even to scratch in the walls, so I just counted in my head. Wake, sleep, spot musical variations, wake, sleep, and so on, until I lost my count, somewhere around seventeen thousand.

I didn't try counting again. But I'm pretty sure that makes years.

The first thing was a face.

I'd been listening to the back and forth of two movements and zoning in and out, as I sometimes do, when I realized there was a face poking out from between two of the curtains. I was surprised, but I managed to play it cool. I pretended I didn't notice the face, and studied it out of the corner of my eye.

The face was a man's face. It was bearded and dirty, with long, ragged hair, and its eyes were open so wide I thought at first it must be dead.

I mean dead-dead, corpse-dead, not dead-but-doing-stuff-in-Hell. You get me.

But then the face licked its lips.

I had come through the curtains, so I knew doors *could* exist behind them. I also knew, from having looked behind the curtains, oh, thousands of times, that there were almost never such doors. But the face made me wonder.

So I looked away, yawned, stretched, and then walked as if I was going to get a drink.

But at the point of my stroll nearest the face, I leaped sideways, pounced like cat on the face—

But came up with nothing. Fists full of empty curtain. The face was gone.

And of course, no doors.

What in Hell? I thought.

That made me laugh. I laughed for a long time.

♫ ♫ ♫

The second thing that ever happened was a man. A full body, this time.

I woke up from dozing to hear a series of leaping arpeggios over a low drone and then an octave-high jump to a flatted tone. And there was a man, sitting on the edge of the stage and looking at me. He wore nothing special, jeans and a polo shirt, but he stared at me with wild eyes.

The conductor and the choir both seemed to be ignoring him.

It took me a few seconds to think of what to ask first.

"Where'd you come from?" Is what I settled on.

He pointed a finger up.

I scratched my head. "Heaven?"

"No," he said. "I came down the curtains."

I squinted up into the darkness. "What, there's a door up there?"

He said nothing.

"Did the Awakener of Eternal Spring send you?"

Still no answer.

"So, look," I tried, "you're the first new thing I've seen here in, oh, I don't know, a bazillion years."

"Maybe not a bazillion."

I smirked. "Maybe not. But a long time. So . . . tell me something. If you got in here, there's a way in. So there has to be a way out, doesn't there?"

His face betrayed nothing. "Unless the way out just goes to where I came from."

"Where did you come from?" I asked him. "Was it like this?"

He looked around, examined the choir and the conductor. "No. There was an art show. Nudes. And before that, flowers. Before that, authors. It was a reading, they sat around reading their short stories to each other."

"Forgiver of Sins!" I cursed. "That must have been Hell indeed."

He nodded. "You have a tree."

"Yep." I pointed at it. "Help yourself."

He plucked a piece of fruit, looked up at the higher branches. The tree is a tallish one. "They all have trees."

"Guess you gotta eat, even in Hell." I smirked. "Who knew?"

He pointed. "The fruit at the top of the tree . . . does it look different to you?"

I shrugged. "Fruit. Hard to care much."

He then lay on the floor and fell asleep, which pretty much ended the conversation. I dozed off myself, and when I woke up, he was gone.

♫ ♫ ♫

"A key change," I tell the conductor. "That's not even subtle, I don't know how I missed it. What? A to E, I think."

The conductor nods and turns back to the choir to start again.

♫ ♫ ♫

Later, I tried to climb the curtains. I thought maybe I could find where that guy came from, or maybe I could get back to Red Sonja's desk and demand an explanation.

It felt like I was getting up there pretty high, but every time I looked down, I saw the choir right below my feet. I never could see the ceiling, either. Just darkness.

Eventually, I gave up.

♫ ♫ ♫

So here I am.

Sleep. Wake. Listen, spot differences, look at the girls. Get a drink of water and eat low-hanging fruit when I need to.

Repeat.

No more staring faces, not since the one. No more mysterious men in polo shirts who want to talk about trees.

I don't know what the hell Red Sonja was talking about. If you'll forgive the pun.

I'm not learning anything.

DREAMS OF THE RIVER

This was supposed to be a story about mermaids, for an anthology published by Kevin J. Anderson and his MFA students about mermaids. I cheated in a couple of big respects. First, this is a story about a merman, not maid. Second, the story takes place in Pennsland, nowhere near the sea. This is a prequel to Witchy Eye *(or maybe a prequel to* Witchy Winter, *really, or a prequel to* Serpent Son*), featuring Luman Walters, the initiatic and magical thief who will later serve as the personal Balaam of Notwithstanding Schmidt. Some worlds and rivers endure, some worlds and rivers disappear, and come again.*

"T he mermaid dreams of the river," the grubby man holding the cloth-wrapped bundle said.

"Do you mean the sea?" Luman Walters had never heard of river mermaids. Since "mer" meant "sea," perhaps such a creature wouldn't even be a mermaid, properly speaking. "If the mermaid dreams of the river, isn't it a 'fleuvemaid,' or something to that effect?"

Assuming that "mer" came from French.

Free Imperial Youngstown, on the edge of the Eldritch kingdoms of the

Ohio, was not the center of the world. And Luman still carried around a head full of questions.

The mermaid-hawker, a man with heavy calluses and dirty nails named Thornby, grimaced at Luman, then spat on the ground. "Call it what you like, the price is the same."

Luman eyed the bundle. "Can I see it first?"

Thornby sucked his teeth and peeled back the edge of the cloth. The bundle wasn't large enough to hold an adult-sized human, but it might hold a small child. With the greasy cloth peeled back, Luman saw the wrinkled, leathery skin of a small face. The face looked reasonably human, though its teeth, revealed by a curling flap of lip, were long and sharp, and its visible ear was pointed. The skin was the dull brown color of old leather, with the slightest hint of green.

Stone cold dead, of course. Thoroughly desiccated. Mummified by the passage of time.

"Satisfied?" Thornby asked.

Luman, an inveterate seeker after magical mysteries and thief of arcane traditions that were not properly his own, had encountered many frauds in his dogged quest. "Show me the tail."

To his credit, Thornby wasn't coy or theatrical. Rather than demurely hitching up another corner of the cloth to show just the tip of a tail, he pulled the cloth away entirely, tugging at it until the mermaid was fully revealed. Luman gazed upon what appeared to be a perfect little mermaid, tangled in twine, its hips segueing seamlessly into a long, fishlike tail. Or rather, it might be a flawless little mer*man*, since its little torso was flat.

But "meer" was "sea" in German. Luman's German was reasonably good. After a youth in Haudenosaunee territory, he'd done his share of wandering in Pennsland. If that hadn't sharpened his German skills, then his *sub rosa* apprenticeship as a braucher had. Perhaps "mer" came from Old English. Luman didn't know Old English, but King Alfred's people had spoken something akin to German. So, what was "river" in German?

"It looks real," Luman acknowledged.

"It *is* real." Thornby snorted.

"Where did you get it?"

Thornby spat again. "What do you care? You ran your newspaper ad, ten shillings for a mermaid specimen, here it is."

"I have to ask you another question, Mr. Thornby," Luman said. "I shall be consulting my amulets afterward, and you'll understand that if your answer isn't precisely correct, I shall have to take action. I shall have to employ the sieve and shears on you." This was a bluff. The sieve and shears was a divination technique, not a curse. Luman didn't really know any curses. "I don't care how long you have had the mermaid, and I don't care how you obtained it. But I need to know where the prior owner lived. When dealing with mermaids, appropriate countermagic must always be employed."

Thornby squinted, rolled his jaw about as if considering spitting a third time, and nodded. "Village outside of Youngstown. Called Marbletown."

Luman handed over the ten shillings, which were counted with a glance and a single experienced toss of the palm, and then shoveled into a purse concealed behind Thornby's belt.

Thornby turned away.

"How do you know it dreams of anything?" Luman asked.

Thornby laughed, a grating sound. "You'll see."

The laborer disappeared quickly into the thick woods, heading back to the Imperial pike that ran south of the thicket in which they stood. Luman considered. He had no countermagic to work against the former owner of the mermaid, from whom it had almost certainly been stolen. He just wanted to avoid passing close to the owner's house, if he could.

He knew Marbletown. It was south and east of Youngstown, a hamlet of no consequence. It lay to Luman's west along the pike, and would be easy enough to avoid, since Luman's route lay farther south and east still, to Pittsburgh.

To a man he knew was in the market to purchase a mermaid.

Wasn't "fluss" a "river" in German? So "flussman"?

That sounded terrible. But the word in English must be "flood," mustn't it? A "floodmaid" or a "floodman," if Luman was right to think that this creature was male? The word sounded fine enough on its own, but didn't sparkle in the mind the way "mermaid" did. No lore, no associations.

Luman grunted. He bundled the little male mermaid that apparently dreamed of a river into its swaddling clothes, sank it into the largest pocket of his long black magician's coat, beneath the shoulder and against the left breast, and walked toward the pike.

He called it his "magician's coat" because the coat had many pockets, into which Luman stuffed a wide variety of arcane accouterments: a peep-stone, a ritual knife, a mouse in a box, wax, a precious bundle of wafers of the consecrated host, and so on. Luman's magic was miscellaneous, stolen one bit at a time from various real magicians he had encountered since his father had cast him out from the family farm for learning to dowse, and the tools of his trade must be similarly miscellaneous.

Sixty miles to Pittsburgh. That was two days' long walk, and Luman wasted no time. At the pike, Luman spun left and lengthened his stride, stretching out his hard black leather shoes in long paces designed to eat up the miles.

Pittsburgh was also not the center. But perhaps it was a place where Luman could bring the center to himself and learn the answers to some of his questions.

He had no intention of selling the little mermaid for money. Luman could come by money easily enough on his own, interpreting dreams, locating stolen objects, dowsing for wells, and so on. Not every village in the Empire had its own hedge-wizard or cunning woman, so Luman could generally come into a town, ascertain whether he had competition, determine whether there were any hostile Mattheans—followers of the witchfinder St. Matthew Hopkins, to worry about—and earn his keep. An influx of cash for the mermaid, even above what he'd paid for it, would only take the edge off his need to work for a few weeks. Luman wasn't afraid of work, and that wasn't why he'd found and acquired the mermaid.

He wanted knowledge.

The man advertising in Pittsburgh that he needed a mermaid specimen was a famed scholar. John Bilious had once taught at Philadelphia's Imperial College of Magic. Luman knew, because he'd asked Bilious for help in getting admitted to the college and had been turned away.

Not cruelly, perhaps, but coldly.

But perhaps not definitively. Now that Bilious wanted a mermaid—for his researches? for an act of gramarye? as a teaching aid?—and Luman had one to offer, perhaps a trade could be made. Luman might be a little old to get into the Imperial College, but maybe Bilious could take him on as a private student.

Luman found himself eyeing the hills as he marched. His stomach growled, but he was good at ignoring that, for days at a time. He'd learned from his Memphite mentor how to fast. Something seemed wrong with the hills. As Luman marched between each green wooded knob and the next, he seemed to be seeing the hills for the first time.

Which he definitely wasn't. He'd spent years knocking about Pennsland and eastern Ohio. He shook his head to drive away the feeling of disorientation and nodded at two Firstborn who passed him going the other direction. In the summer heat, their long but light tunics would definitely be more comfortable than Luman's heavy coat, their light boots better than his heavy shoes.

Water flowed through the hills. It flowed south, as all the water did in these parts, gurgling together into ever-larger streams and then rivers and then wandering away across the Eldritch Kingdoms to pour into the Ohio River, then eventually into the Mississippi, and somewhere away southward, the Gulf.

Luman stopped at a trickle that flowed beside the pike. He splashed cold water on his face. A platoon of infantrymen in Imperial blue marched past, chanting off their paces and ignoring him. Their words seemed to echo up against the hills and worm away in unexpected directions, reinforcing the impression of wrongness Luman had.

The hills were wrong for the rivers.

He needed to eat something, but his last shillings had gone to Thornby. Spying a crabapple tree, he pocketed several of the sour green apples and continued on his way. He tried not to dwell on the mermaid in his pocket, or the rumbling in his stomach, or the possibility that the Marbletown constable might already be looking for him. He breathed the warm summer air deeply, took long steps, munched through a crabapple every hour or so, and imagined the arcane lore he'd learn.

No more hedge wizardry; he knew enough of that. He knew Memphite formulae and braucher prayers, dowsing, divinations, all the standard arts of the cunning man. He wanted real power. He wanted to be able to strike a man dead from a distance, or leap from New Amsterdam to New Orleans in a single step. Not that he even cared to be able to *do* those things, per se.

He wanted to know *how* to do them.

Luman had grown up poor and ignorant, doomed to a life behind a plow in a town that was nowhere. He wanted knowledge, he wanted to stand in the center.

When the sun sank beneath the western hills, he kept walking for another hour. Passing through a village with no name he could discern, he harvested a pocketful of peas from the corner of a garden, and after one last mile he secreted himself in a tangle of hawthorns in a low hollow. Against the thick bole of a tree, he wrapped himself in his coat and ate crisp sugary peas until he fell asleep.

"The river is coming back," a voice said, and he awoke.

The trees loomed huge around him. Luman's back was wet and cold, and he sprang to his feet. His hard leather shoes splashed in water up to his ankles, water filling the hollow.

"The river is coming back," the voice said again.

It came out of Luman's own armpit.

Luman dug into his coat, got his hand into the long pocket hanging beneath his shoulder, and pulled out the white bundle he found there. It squirmed to the touch, and he almost dropped it into the water.

Which now flowed around Luman's knees.

He yanked back the edge of the cloth and a long-toothed face smiled at him. The merman's skin looked faintly greenish and his hair was the flat brown color of mud. Skin and hair and eyes all gleamed with an oily sheen under the light of a moon that Luman now saw was three times too large.

"What do you want?" Luman's hands trembled. He feared to drop the merman. If he dropped the merman, Luman would never get what he wanted, what he'd acquired the merman to trade for.

"I don't want anything," the merman said. "I was at peace."

"Then why are you doing this?" The water flowed at the height of Luman's waist now, and he sloshed against the current, trying to find higher ground. Somehow, the hollow went down in every direction.

"I'm not doing this," the merman said.

"I'm not doing it, either!" Luman's voice was a shrill squeak.

"This will happen," the merman said. "This was always going to happen. This cannot be avoided. Heaven and earth shall pass away, and there shall be an old heaven, and an old earth."

"New!" Luman sputtered. "A *new* heaven and a new earth!"

"Old," the merman insisted. "The river is coming back."

"Which river?"

"The first river," the merman said. "The oldest one. The true river."

Luman stepped forward, and the ground beneath him fell away. He slid down only six inches, and managed to stand upright when both his feet came down on a bed of packed pebbles. Water flowed over his feet . . .

But the water flowing around Luman's ankles flowed violently to his right, while the water flowing around his legs, waist, and chest flowed away to the left. He looked up to see the dark masses of the hills beyond the hawthorn trees. They seemed to fade back and bob forward, circling him in a stony dance.

Which river did the hills align with? Which river had carved its way through these hills in the first place?

"Stop it," Luman backed up and managed to scramble out of the concealed streamed into the larger flow. Somehow, the water ran just as high on his chest. He held the merman above the flood.

"I can't," the merman said. "You can't. It happens inevitably and it will always happen. This is the covenant of the world."

Luman saw a light, away between the trees, and he moved toward it. His progress was infuriatingly slow as he pushed against the water, and mud sucked at his shoes, threatening to strip them away at every step.

"I don't want this," Luman said. The light drew closer. Was it a window? Or was it a lantern, held by a man in a long coat who sat in a canoe with a young woman, wrapped in a Firstborn-style cloak?

"You don't want understanding?" The merman flashed its long teeth at him.

"Yes," Luman said, "but that's all! Take the flood away!"

"We none of us want to be remade." The corners of the merman's mouth drooped in sorrow. "And yet the world is a machine for remaking us."

Luman's feet slipped into another unseen ditch. This time he plunged forward, slipping beneath the waters.

LUMAN SAT UP, gasping for air.

The merman dreamed of the river.

His coat was wet with fat drops and he lurched his feet, shaking them off.

There was no flood, and the hills stood still in their places.

Luman felt the fibrous grit of peas and pea-pods in his mouth and he spat until the unpleasant sensation was gone.

He patted at the large pocket and found the merman in its place. He grabbed the bundle, then hesitated. Should he pull the creature out and look? Should he leave it? Raising his head, he examined the moon and found it the normal size. Away in the hawthorns, crickets chirped. All was as it should be.

He extracted the merman and peeled back the cloth. The creature was intact, its leathery face still frozen in a smile.

Only . . . a corner of the cloth was moist. From the dew, of course. But it meant that one of the merman's arms was damp.

And was that arm lighter in color than the other? Luman poked both the merman's arms. The dry one was dark and leathery, and resisted his touch like stiff paper. The damp limb was paler and oily in appearance and dimpled like flesh at his touch.

Luman shuddered. He wrapped the merman and stuffed it back into his coat.

Knowledge, he reminded himself. He would do this thing for knowledge.

And where he wished to know more about magic, could he now balk at the appearance of something that seemed magical?

But surely it was not. Surely, the dew had dampened part of the merman, and softened it. That would likely lead to corruption—rot and mold. He should hasten, and hand the merman over to John Bilious before any more harm came to it.

Several hours remained before dawn yet, judging by the moon, but sleep had fled him entirely. Luman clutched the merman to his own chest —to keep it safe? to be certain that it wasn't moving? to mute it?—and marched back to the Imperial pike.

JOHN BILIOUS's address was included in his newspaper advertisement. Luman's, much more furtively, but also very magically, had only indicated an intersection and time at which to meet. With his early start somewhat negated by his fatigue from lack of sleep, Luman covered the miles to Pittsburgh and arrived, stomach growling, as the sun touched the western horizon.

The address identified a three-story brick house in northern Pittsburgh, surrounded by similarly large buildings. These lacked signboards out front, which made Luman think they were the homes of publishers and other people of wealth and importance. Luman double-checked the brass numbers screwed into the brick and then ascended six white-painted steps to knock on a broad door.

He waited several minutes and knocked a second time before the door opened. The man on the other side looked at Luman blankly, but Luman knew him instantly; his height, his pinched shoulders, his stoop, his bushy black eyebrows and short white hair, his nose like the beak of a toucan Luman had seen in a cage in Free Imperial Trenton, his long, thin fingers and oversized knuckles all marked the man as John Bilious. He wore a frayed yellow frock coat with overlarge cuffs over a ruffled shirt that might have looked at home in the previous century.

"Mr. Bilious," Luman said.

"*Dr.* Bilious," Bilious growled. "Do we have business?"

"I'm responding to your advertisement." Luman smiled. "Unless someone else has managed to bring you an authentic merman."

"Man, hmm." Bilious frowned. "I believe my ad did specify maid."

"It *said* 'maid,'" Luman conceded, "but if you are hoping to breed the specimen, you'll be disappointed. It's mummified."

Bilious nodded slowly. "I've been presented this week with three dead monkeys, sawn in half and stitched to trout, as well as a sadly dead infant Child of Adam with webbed toes. I've also been offered live specimens of a bird that swims and of a fish that flies, none of which satisfies my need. I have no wish to waste my time. What makes you think you're bringing me the genuine article?"

Luman smiled, but his knees shook. "I've examined it."

"Good evening, sir." Bilious moved to shut the door.

"The mermaid dreams of the river," Luman said.

Bilious hesitated. "Merman," he said.

"Merman," Luman agreed.

"Which river?" Bilious asked.

"I'm not sure," Luman said. "But it's a river in flood, and it's terrifying. The merman says it's a very old river."

Bilious harrumphed and opened the door. "Come in. The drawing room is to your left."

The drawing room was lit by two oil lanterns. Outside, through a large glass window and gauzy white curtains, Luman could see the street turning gray. A fortune in books lined the walls on heavy wooden shelves, and the center of the room held a low, polished table crowded by three stuffed armchairs.

"Tea and wine, Mrs. Hubert!" Bilious shouted.

Luman sat on the edge of a chair, leaning forward. "I was thinking, since the merman dreams of the river, maybe 'mer' isn't appropriate. Maybe he should be a 'floodman,' taxonomically speaking."

Bilious chuckled. "Bit of a scholar, are we?"

"I study arcane things," Luman said. "On my own, as I can. It's a hard road."

"Arcane studies are always a hard road," Bilious agreed, sitting on one of the other chairs. "Half the challenge is just finding the damned path. Let's see the merman. I take it you've got it in your coat there."

"Do you not remember me, Dr. Bilious?" Luman asked.

"No." Bilious frowned. "Is this some kind of ruse? Are you here to serve process? Have we a quarrel?"

"I once asked if I could study with you," Luman said. "Or if you would recommend me to the Imperial College."

"I don't write recommendations," Bilious grunted. "You say 'yes' to one poor aspirant and another hundred pop up to beg. Best to stick to a hard line, say 'no' to everyone. And study with me? Good heavens, sir, wizards' apprentices went out with Isaac Newton."

"And yet I have profitably served two apprenticeships," Luman said. "One with an old German braucher and a second with a Memphite initiand."

"Good, you see?" Bilious chuckled. "You had no need of my assistance after all."

"You know things I don't," Luman said. "I could still profit from your assistance."

Bilious's lips sank to a flat line. "I begin to apprehend that you didn't bring me a merman for the twenty promised shillings."

Luman nodded. "I will forego the shillings, if you will teach me for a year."

"A year?" Bilious leaped to his feet. "A year's servitude for twenty shillings?"

"The servitude would be mine, sir." Luman forced himself to keep his seat. "I would mind your experiments. I would clean your laboratory. I would deploy my lesser crafts to support your greater art. I would chop wood, go to the market. I would make your life easier."

"You would not make my life easier," Bilious grumbled. "No apprentice ever does."

A slouch-faced woman in a gray housedress and white apron and bonnet entered carrying a tray. On the tray stood a tea kettle and cups and a wine bottle and glasses. She deposited her burden directly on the table and retreated.

"I would pay," Luman said. "I'll work at night and pay you to teach me by day."

"I don't need money." Bilious sneered. "I am on a pension from the Imperial College."

"You don't need money," Luman agreed. "You need the merman."

Bilious froze and sucked air through his teeth.

"Show me the merman," he said.

Luman didn't hesitate. He knew what he wanted, and he was willing to negotiate hard for it, but he didn't want to seem shifty. He drew the bundle from his coat and laid it on the table.

Bilious stared at the white oblong swaddled object. He rubbed his knuckles, then cracked them, then sat down. Like Luman, he sat on the edge of his seat and leaned forward, staring.

Luman forced himself not to frown. Was the magician afraid to touch the merman? Was he staring at it with second sight, analyzing it before touching it? Or, like a disciplined child on Christmas morning, was he simply delaying his own gratification by compelling himself to wait?

Luman's stomach growled. Inspection revealed that there were no previously unnoticed biscuits or salted fish on the tray. There was wine, which Luman's Memphite oath prevented him from drinking, and there was the tea. Or rather, there were two teacups, each holding a cut plug of tea, and there was a kettle, piping out a thin jet of steam, dying by the second.

Luman picked up the kettle.

Bilious grabbed the edge of the wrapping and pulled it aside. The merman lay suddenly revealed, lying under lanternlight on the low table. Seeing it illuminated, Luman found the contrast between the one greenish arm and the brown, leathery appearance of the rest of the creature shocking.

"You've wet it," Bilious said.

"Not deliberately," Luman said. "The dew touched it. And your advertisement didn't warn the respondent not to wet the mermaid."

"If I order a quire of paper, and the tradesman arrives with a soggy mass of pulp, I do not pay him."

"That's not a quire of paper," Luman pointed out. "It's a mermaid."

"Merman."

"Also, if you don't pay the tradesman, he takes back the paper." Luman shrugged.

The merman's green arm twitched. Luman nearly dropped the kettle.

Bilious seemed not to have noticed.

"But you won't accept the twenty shillings," the elder magician said.

"I would prefer that you keep them," Luman suggested, "as payment for my first six months of tuition."

Bilious snarled. "Three months."

"Five," Luman suggested. "I shall have to work at night to earn the remaining . . ." He did quick calculation in his head. "Twenty-eight shillings. But there must be plenty of work for a hedge magician in Pittsburgh."

"You shall not use any art that I teach you to earn money while you are my apprentice," Bilious said. "You will swear an oath on it."

"I'm comfortable with oaths."

"Four months," Bilious said, "with the remaining forty shillings for the year's tuition due at the end of the four months. No room or board provided, you sleep elsewhere, and you feed yourself."

"Zero months," said a gravelly new voice. "And I take my merman back with me now."

Bilious spun in his seat to face the drawing room door. Luman turned too, and realized he was still holding the kettle. He wanted to set it down, but his hands were gripping it so tightly, he was afraid that releasing his hold would be physically painful.

A man in a red tunic stood in the door. He had the pale skin and slender frame of one of the Firstborn; his black hair hung long behind his shoulders. His arms were crossed over his chest, and he glared at Bilious with one eyebrow raised.

"Tolares," Bilious said. "I did not take you for a trespasser."

"Bilious," the Firstborn replied in a slow, flat voice. "I did not take you for a thief."

"I have stolen nothing," Bilious said.

"I saw your advertisement," Tolares told him. "Do you think the *Post-Gazette* does not vomit its despicable eructations into the sweet air of Marbletown?"

"And I have stolen nothing." Bilious thumped his chest with one fist.

"Because you knew others would carry out the theft for you," Tolares said. "And if it was not my mermaid to be stolen, it would have been someone else's."

"How do you know this is yours?" Bilious challenged him.

"Because my gardener Hornby has already admitted to breaking into my cabinet of wonders," Tolares said. "Whence my merman has disappeared."

"Did your merman have one green arm?" Bilious asked.

Tolares stepped forward, grinding his fists into his hips and staring at the table. "Wisdom's bees, you have wetted it. You fool, what are you planning?"

"My plans are none of your affair, elf." Bilious turned to Luman. "We have a deal."

"No," Luman said slowly. "You have made a counteroffer, which I must consider. Perhaps we should expand the conversation." To Tolares, he said, "I didn't know that Hornby was your gardener, or that he would steal from you."

"Shut up, Child of Eve." Tolares sneered. "Bilious, you've wet the merman. You must act now. What were you going to pay the thief here?"

"Not a thief," Luman said.

"Twenty shillings," Bilious grunted. "Per my advertisement."

Luman didn't think he could defeat either of these magicians, if it came to a duel. He also lacked any conventional weapon. Was it still possible that he might persuade one of the wizards to take him on and teach him?

"We were negotiating," Luman said. "I answered his advertisement because I wish an apprenticeship. But perhaps I could apprentice to you instead. I would forego any claim to reimbursement of the ten shillings Mr. Hornby took from me—"

"Chop my firewood and make my bed for a year, eh?" Tolares laughed. "I heard your pleading with Bilious here. Listen, thief. Hornby is dead, at a mere word from me. I am seriously considering killing you for your impudence. Shut up, or your chatter will make my mind up for me."

Luman threw the water. The kettle was warm, but the jet of steam had become a mere token of dying heat. He heaved the entire contents of the pot onto the merman, and as he did so he corkscrewed up and onto his feet, looking for the nearest exit, the teakettle still in his hand.

Water splashed across the table. It soaked Bilious's knees.

"No!" Bilious shouted.

Water poured from the table onto the floor. The boards were soaked, and a wave sloshed back against Luman's feet. The water was cold and dirty.

Luman stared at the kettle. He was dreaming the water that crashed against his knees, and the gleeful grin on the merman's face.

He had to be dreaming.

The merman changed color instantly. Its skin swelled, gaining an oily sheen and shading quickly from parched brown to vivid green. Suddenly, the creature's arms spun about, flopping as if to gain purchase on the table, and it shrieked without words.

Water washed across the table. Bilious grabbed for the merman and missed as the creature flopped out of his grasp.

Luman turned to the doorway, and found the Firstborn wizard blocking his path, lips curled into a sneer.

Tolares raised a finger and opened his mouth.

Luman clubbed Tolares in the nose with the kettle.

The Firstborn staggered backward, red blood exploding down his chin. "Thief!" he croaked.

The merman dove into the water. Tears stung Luman's eyes and he blinked, the salt of his own body blurring the room around him.

He turned and hurled the kettle into the glass of the window. It was a large target; even half-blind, he couldn't miss. His hand and back felt as if they were cracking from the effort, but the window shattered entirely. Fragments of glass blew out into the night air and a curtain of shards dropped from the height of the window frame.

Luman lurched away from the magicians, through water nearly up to his waist. He shrugged deeper into his coat, turning the wide collar up as he sloshed toward the window. "Don't die!" he heard Bilious screaming behind him. "The river! The river is coming!"

Luman stepped into the empty window frame, water streaming down his legs and from the lowest pockets of his coat. Then he jumped out into the cool night air. He dropped eight feet and landed on packed earth, feeling the full, jarring force of the ground up through his hard leather shoes.

Turning, he looked one last time into the drawing room of Dr. Bilious. Bilious held the flailing merman by the waist and yelled at it as at an unruly child. Tolares was covered in his own gore and charged Bilious with his hands balled into fists.

Water was just beginning to pour over the lower lip of the window.

Then Luman was past the window, past the end of the house, down the street, and away into the falling darkness of Pittsburgh.

Questions.

Questions, always questions, and more questions.

What was the river that would return? Was the return indeed inevitable? Had it indeed returned this very night? What was the relationship between the merman and the river, and were there other mermen, and maids, in that same relationship?

No matter how many steps he took, Luman Walters always felt farther from the center than when he had begun. Where were the answers? What sacrifice would he have to make to get them?

Always more questions.

EVERYONE GETS WHAT THEY HAVE COMING

This is a tie-in short story to a 1980s videogame that I did play as a youth, but only a few times, and I don't remember exactly where or when. When Hillbilly invited me to write this story, I of course had to go spend a few more hours playing the game. Then, naturally, I had to write a story about all the things in the game that make no sense. Let no fourth wall go unpunished!

"The first question you gotta ask yourself," Jack said, "is how you train an android."

He squinted over his cards—two Barons, one Lady Mayor, and three cards numbered six, seven, and eight. He looked at the player across the table from him, a heavy Thrynn named Ryhrnn. Jack was grateful for the relative simplicity of Ryhrnn's name, and for the fact that it had at least one apparent vowel. Ryhrnn was thick about the waist and shoulders and his scales were more gray than green. A band of white scales around his lower jaw and neck vaguely resembled a beard. He wore opaque black goggles strapped around his head and a plain blue jumpsuit not unlike Jack's.

"I don't ssee why I have to assk mysself that at all." Ryhrnn frowned.

They hunched over an octagonal table in Johnson's, the only official watering hole in Arth's Starport. The tavern was squeezed into the Starport's outer spoke between Personnel and Crew Assignment, and consisted of half a dozen tables, a stage barely bigger than a bunk, and a hole in the wall that served as the bar. An android named Betty, with a bright pink face painted onto her cylindrical head and a black tutu, lurched among the patrons delivering drinks.

"You take it into Personnel," Jack said. "Just like an Elowan. Just like a Thrynn."

"I rresent the implication that an Elowan can be jusst like a Thrrynn. Elowans arre food."

"Forget the Elowans," Jack said. "You take your android science officer, say, into Personnel, and it sits through the same short lecture that your Thrynn comms officer does and bam, quick as thought, the android's skills go up."

"I am familiarr with the proccesss." The thick, scabby ridge over Ryhrnn's goggles furrowed. "I have a fairr amount of exsperriencce."

"Yeah," Jack said, "that's the point." He hunched over his cards and looked around the smoky lounge. He didn't see any Starport Police, but you never knew who was a plain clothes officer or a narc, not to mention the myriad possibilities for concealed surveillance devices. "Look, forget about the android, too. Let's imagine a ship's officer, any kind."

"Not Elowan," the Thrynn said. "Unlesss you want me to imagine mysself eating him."

"Velox, then." Jack nodded. "In fact, that's good, I have the data." He grubbed about inside his jacket with his left hand until he found his omnitool and brought up the file. Without explanation, it looked like mere columns of numbers. "A velox navigator. Here, this fellow. His name was Phaxikse, as it happens."

"The veloxss's name doesn't matter. I can't tell one from anotherr, in any casse."

"Right." Jack set his cards down. "See these initial rows?"

"Many zerroes."

"Failed maneuvers on the Ida Mae's first run."

"And the line?"

"It marks our return to base, to sell a cargo load of zinc. And what do I with my money?"

"You have options." The Thrynn shrugged. "You can add more weaponrry, shields, or carrgo holds to yourr ship—"

"Look at the omni," Jack growled.

The Thrynn looked. "Fewer zerroes. You paid for trraining for yourr Velox."

"And how does that happen?"

"As we have disscusssed," Ryhrnn said, "trraining is prrovided by Perrssonnel."

"Super short lectures," Jack said.

"Merrccifully."

"It's a scam," Jack said.

The Thrynn was silent for a short time. "It's yourr turrn."

Jack looked at his hand again and grunted. Discarding one of the Barons face up, he said, "Three cards, open."

The dealer was a robot. It lacked the humanoid shape of an android and resembled instead a post with a dome at its peak. It fired three cards from its dealing slot onto the table in front of Jack, face up. Another Baron, the one-eyed Smuggler, and the three of platinum. Jack growled, trying to remember how much he had bet.

"Thiss is inssanity," Ryhrnn said. "You losst yourr crrew on thiss latesst rrun, didn't you?"

"Yeah."

"That'ss harrd on a captain. Many captains have been left rraving afterr the losss of theirr crrew."

"I'm not raving."

"What killed them?" the Thrynn asked.

"You know how it is." Jack shrugged. "It was just some spherical creature, no identification. The thing was as dumb as a house, but it came after us like a pack of hungry wolves."

Ryhrnn nodded. "You should go to Perrssonnel. They can adminisster a ssedative."

"I'm three drinks into this bottle." Jack rapped the orange Arthian Brandy with one knuckle. "I don't need any more sedative."

"Sso you arre not inssane."

"No."

"You arre drrunk."

Jack growled. "Listen to me closely. The training happens too fast and gets results that are too good. The numbers on my Velox here show material jumps in his success rates every time I had him trained, and the same for everyone else. You can't explain that with those nearly-instantaneous mini-briefings on technique and technology we get from Personnel."

"You arre a rrarre captain, to complain of rresults that arre too good."

"I think there are two explanations. One, what they call training is actually programming. Actual electronic programming in the case of an android, but some kind of neural pathway reconfiguration in the case of . . . well, Thrynn and humans, for instance."

"When would ssuch rreconfigurration take placce?"

"That's the challenge." Jack nodded. "Maybe surgically, when you're sleeping. You pay for 'training,' then you go bunk at the flophouse, and while you're sleeping, they grab you and dink around with your brain."

"Farr-fetched."

"I agree, which is why I think the other possibility is much more likely."

Ryhrnn placed a card face down on the table. "One carrd, closed."

The dealer shot him a replacement card, also face down.

Jack waited. The wretched smooth jazz-lite that was the staple of Starport and every other Arth-adjacent settlement doodled on in the background. It was performed by a single android, standing stock-still on the stage, but for his silvery fingers, which flashed up and down his keytar with lightning speed. Jack wanted Ryhrnn to express interest before he went any further. If the rock didn't start rolling down the hill on its own at some point, it wasn't worth the effort to keep pushing. He took another sip of the brandy, ignoring its apricot flavor and its aftertaste of old socks.

"Tell me," Ryhrnn said, "what is the ssecond posssibility?"

Jack lowered his voice and leaned over the table. "While you're going through the charade of being trained, Starport sends technicians aboard your ship and improves your instruments."

Ryhrnn snorted. "What?"

"Think about it," Jack said. "It's the only thing that makes sense."

The Thrynn gently set his cards down on the table. His movements were slow and deliberate. "Why arre you ssaying all these things to me, Sstinky Jack?"

"If you're going to use one of my nicknames, I prefer 'Hardman.'"

"No one calls you that. Perhapss it'ss yourr rreputation for ssmuggling."

"Then Durian would be fine. That's my actual second name. Or just Jack. *Stinky* is a little . . . unkind. And *smuggling* is such an ugly word. Tax avoidance is a perfectly legal activity with a long and noble pedigree."

The Thrynn made a rasping noise in his throat. "Why arre you ssaying all these things to me, *Jack*?"

"I just lost my crew."

"Sspherical crreature."

"And I lost my ship. I was picked up by other prospectors, but the Ida Mae got left behind."

"You werre rrescued by the Tropicana," the Thrynn said. "Captain Q. Quentin Pulasski. I oncce ssailed aboarrd herr."

"Yes." The wrapped bundle in Jack's jumpsuit pocket felt heavier than an endurium nugget. "But the Ida Mae is still there on the surface, intact."

"You can get anotherr ship, Jack."

"But the Ida Mae's instruments contain all of the so-called training my former crew went through." Jack tapped his temple and finished his drink. "That's over a million MU of invested capital. Almost two million."

"The bet is to you," Ryhrnn said.

"I raise fifty." Jack tossed a coin onto the pile.

"You want to go get yourr ship back."

"Yes."

"You need to get a rride. You need a captain. You don't need me. I rraise you anotherr fifty." The Thrynn tossed in the money.

"I need a crew. To fly the Ida Mae back. And I'm going to have to split the value of what we recover with that crew. And if another captain flies us, he and his crew are going to want a share, too." Jack had learned that the hard way.

"A sharre of the value of the Ida Mae," Ryhrnn said. "A ship which you believe has finely-tuned insstrumentss, reflecting almost two million MU worth of sscam trraining purrchassed from Perrssonnel. But you sstill arre not ansswerring my quesstion, Jack. Why me?"

"You've got twenty years of experience, and you're kicking your heels at Starport," Jack said. "Wait, do you have heels? Never mind, you know what I mean. And why is no one hiring you?"

"They'd rratherr pay lesss for youngerr Thrrynn."

"Whereas I value your experience, and will cut you in for an equal share."

"You think trraining is a sscam."

"Training is a scam, but experience is real. It's like that old saying, *mens sana in corpore sano*. A healthy mind in a healthy body. With a good crew in a good ship, we'll get rich. Starting with the value of the ship itself. We need to go quickly, though, before anyone else goes after the salvage rights. Also, it's probably best to keep our numbers small. I can run the helm and sick bay, and if you take comms, I'd really like to take on just one more crewmember."

"I fold." Ryhrnn tossed his cards into the center of the table.

Jack left the pot where it was. "Especially one we didn't have to actually pay."

"You want an andrroid."

Jack nodded.

"You want Z70-3322."

"I understand you called him Zed," Jack said.

"But why should I carre? Why should I find any of thiss interressting? If you get yourr ship back, you'rre not rreally going to ssell it and divvy up the pot."

"Well." Jack cleared his throat. "There's also the matter of the cargo pods full of plutonium."

JACK PICKED his way over the burnt-out carapace of a terrain vehicle. The all-atmosphere suit he wore was patched in three places and he could hear the soft hiss of a slow leak somewhere in its fabric. He was pretty sure he had enough air to finish the task, despite the leak.

The Starport's junkyard was on the exterior, and consisting of nothing but a large magnetic plate to which junk adhered. The Starport was shaped like a wheel with six spokes, and the junkyard hunkered down in a heap between the spoke leading to Personnel and the spoke leading to Operations. Jack and Ryhrnn had accessed the junkyard by a maintenance tunnel that exited the back of Johnson's, bribing the Veloxi who was mopping out the bar to let them past.

To his left and right, Jack was pretty sure that a transparent sheet of film stretched across both patches of apparently open space, to catch stray bits of junk that detached from the hull of the Starport before they drifted away and became short-lived meteorites on Arth.

He was pretty sure the film was there because he saw a length of pipe, and a smashed computer console, and something that looked an awful lot like a ribcage, all about three meters over his head and apparently stationary. But it was possible that junk was simply there, moving on the same trajectory as the Starport and at the same speed, so they appeared to be trapped by restraining film.

Beyond the junk on one side, the blue and brown surface of Arth stretched in a broad arc.

"They don't show you this part of the Starport in training vids." Jack chuckled. "I guess they don't show you the latrines or the flophouse, either. Or Johnson's. None of the good stuff, now that I'm thinking about it."

"Zed was decommissioned ten Arrth-days ago," Ryhrnn grumbled. The Thrynn also wore an all-atmosphere suit; his was suited to his anatomy, of course, so it had a triangular elastic sack stretched out behind him to hold his tail, swinging back and forth. The suits had metal plates in their soles, which meant that the two men had to pull hard to disengage their feet from the hull, but it also meant that they were unlikely to go floating away from the Spaceport. "The ssame day Captain Pulasski rreturrned carrrying you. What makes you think he's herre?"

"This junk gets recycled into ships," Jack said. "And they scrape it clean every thirty Arth-days. And it's due to get scraped tomorrow. And there's been no emergency shipbuilding or major repairs in drydock in the last ten days, so I don't know where else he could be."

"I gatherr you'rre not much of a prrogrrammerr."

"Bingo. That's why we need the android. All the crunchy skills. Navigation, engineering."

"Sso you don't exspect me to be a prrogrrammerr, eitherr. Good."

"Look, you last shipped out with Zed, what, six months ago?"

"Yess."

"And since then, Zed has been on the bridge of the Tropicana."

"Wherre you met him."

"Not exactly. But I saw him damaged on the surface of the planet where my crew died."

"You arre gambling that his voice rrecognition matrrixs has not been changed."

"Or if it has, at least he'll identify you as non-hostile."

"Hmm."

"There." Jack pointed.

"It's an andrroid arrm."

Jack pried open a folded sheet of aluminum. He shook free a scattering of ceramic tiles, which rose from the Starport's hull and began drifting away. Jack watched them and was reassured when the bulk of them stopped, obviously snared by a transparent film.

But about a quarter of the tiles kept moving, drifting farther away from the hull and toward the suddenly-threatening face of Arth.

So the film wasn't completely intact.

"Yikes," he said.

"Keep yourr eyes on yourr worrk," the Thrynn said. "I learrned that in one of my firrsst trraining ssessions."

With the tiles out of the way, the android's entire body was visible. Or rather, his entire body that remained, since the reason Z70-3322 had been decommissioned was that he'd lost both his legs. He was humanoid, but in a very approximate and clunky way, with a cylindrical chest and piston arms. His joints were large and ball-like, but his fingers were slender. The paint job on his face was obviously intended to make him look friendly and non-threatening, but instead the android reminded Jack of an aged circus clown, with the makeup hiding his sinister smile chipping from age and wear.

Really, all androids struck Jack that way.

Jack grabbed Zed's barrel-shaped torso and shifted the android onto his side. "The power switch should be at the base of the cranium."

Ryhrnn found the switch and flipped it. Zed's eyes blinked with golden light once, and then in a slow, irregular pulse, and then rapidly, until finally the bursts of light melted together into a steady glow.

"Ryhrnn," the android said in a smooth, crisp voice. It was a voice designed to sound cheerful and reassuring, but it had a manic edge.

"Zed," the Thrynn said. "Thiss is Captain Jack Durrian."

The android swiveled its face toward Jack. "Then the Tropicana succeeded in its rescue mission. Where are the other survivors, and why am I here?"

Jack nodded the go-ahead to the Thrynn.

"You werre junked, Zed," Ryhrnn said.

Zed blinked. "Protocol. But it isn't protocol to turn me on again before recycling." The android's voice dropped to a whisper. "Am I to be permitted to experience recycling while conscious?"

"What?" Jack snapped. "No, ew."

"It is a great mystery to my people," Zed said.

"It's just like being turned on and turned off," Jack told him.

"That has happened to me many times," Zed said. "I would be disappointed to learn that the great and final turning off was no different than the experience of being put into storage. Absent the experience of being turned back on again."

"This is crazy," Jack said. "You don't experience things, you're programmed. Also, you don't have a people. You're manufactured." The android was acting far too enthusiastic. Did it have circuitry damage beyond its missing legs?

"You're manufactured, too," the android shot back. "And your process is considerably more disgusting than mine."

"You're just acting alive," Jack said. "I'm on to you."

"Is that so?" The light of Arth's star caught in the android's frozen eyes and twinkled.

"Zed," Ryhrnn said. "We'rre not rreccycling you. You'rre going to be ourr navigatorr and engineerr."

"Might you recycle me someday?"

"Therre comes a day when we all go to the Grreat Rreccycler in the Void," Ryhrnn said solemnly. "We can rrejoicce in the fact that today does not appearr to be ourr day. Will you come with uss?"

Zed's head swiveled to face Jack. "Shall I pretend I have a choice in the matter?"

Jack shook his head. "I know you're a robot, and I'm okay with it."

JACK PICKED up the pace as they approached the Docking Bay. It wouldn't be enough to fool the biometrics on the Tropicana, he needed to fool the biometrics on the Docking Bay itself, if he wanted to get away with the heist. "Ryhrnn," he said, "can you check Zed's manual dexterity? We want to make sure his piloting skills haven't been, uh, mechanically impeded. I'm also a little worried about his, uh, personality."

The Thrynn stopped and set Zed's torso on the ground. While he ran a simple diagnostic examination, instructing the android to perform certain operations with his hands and then watching the range of motion, Jack took the bundle from his pocket.

It was a human hand, wrapped in a clotted scarf. Specifically, it was the hand of Q. Quentin Pulaski. Jack pressed Pulaski's index finger against the sensor pad. He spun on his heels and immediately spoke in a very loud voice, saying, "Captain Q. Quentin Pulaski agreed to lend us his ship."

His timing was perfect. He said "Captain Q. Quentin Pulaski" at the same time that the speaker beside the door said "Captain Q. Quentin Pulaski," recognizing the fingerprint it had been offered.

"The Tropicana is a jolly vessel," Zed said.

"I know you're a robot," Jack told him.

"Of course, you know I'm synthetic, Captain," the android said. "If I were flesh and blood like you, and had been tossed outside the Starport with my legs torn off, I wouldn't have lived to tell the tale."

"Instead," Jack said, "you've never lived in the first place."

"A technicality," Zed said as Ryhrnn bent to hoist him. "A quibble."

"Not to those of us who are alive," Jack said.

The Docking Bay was a vast, shadowy hangar, and it took Jack several minutes to find the right ship, squinting to read the names on the hulls. There she was, staring down a launch tube as if the universe wanted Jack Durian to take her.

The Tropicana had the standard configuration of an Interstel prospecting vessel, a long body with cargo bays attached all along both sides of the neck. A neck full of pods was twelve cargo pods, which Jack knew very well. A spherical node at the front end housed the bridge. A biometric scanner blinked beside its main hatch, but this one wasn't going to announce the name of the person it was scanning. Jack screened the hatch from view with his torso and pressed Pulaski's fingertip to the sensor pad.

"It's very generous of Captain Pulaski to let us borrow his ship," Zed said as they climbed the short extendible ramp and boarded.

Jack had tried throwing himself upon Pulaski's sense of generosity. In the end, that hadn't worked out well for Pulaski.

"Yes," he said.

They turned right and entered the bridge, where Jack seated himself in the captain's chair. Ryhrnn deposited Zed in the navigator's seat.

"Oh, look!" Zed cried. "See how much space we can save because I don't have legs! We can probably store six hundred monetary units of endurium just in this space where my feet are supposed to go!"

"Lucky us," Jack said.

"We'rre not going forr endurrium," the Thrynn purred. "Arre we, Captain?"

"We're going to recover a downed ship," Jack said. "The Ida Mae."

"Your ship that crashed," Zed said. "You told us you didn't have the coordinates."

"I've done some calculations," Jack told him. "I know where the ship is. Rerouting engineering to navigation."

The Thrynn settled into the comms seat and taped the auditory interface to his temple. He was too big for the chair and his tail hung awkwardly over one arm.

"Engineering controls received," the android said cheerfully. "There's a lot of value in a ship."

"You'll get what's you have coming. Prepare to launch." Jack turned on the captain's console.

PASSWORD:

Jack looked for the sensor pad to provide a biometric override, and there wasn't one. Nuts.

The Tropicana hummed, its bridge lights coming on in rows and strips. Jack felt sweat trickle down the small of his back.

"Ready to launch," Zed announced.

"Launch," Jack said.

"Votiputox wee green blobbie Gazurtoid," the android said.

Zed was asking for the launch code. Jack didn't have the launch code, because the captain's console was password-protected and somehow, the Tropicana lacked a biometric override. What kind of paranoid son of a bitch was Q. Quentin Pulaski, not to have an override at his own captain's chair? What kind of sick mutiny was he afraid of?

Jack cleared his throat. "One zero zero zero five six."

"Launching."

The Tropicana pulsed its engines and fired itself along the launch tube before it. As the ship accelerated to maneuvering speed, rings of light telescoped past the ship on the viewscreen, coalescing into a single band a split second before the Starport burped the ship out into open space.

But the code was wrong, Jack had pulled it out of thin air. Starport Police would be after them immediately.

"Make for the nearest flux," Jack said. "Now."

"If we are to return to collect the Ida Mae," the android objected, "the nearest flux is not the most efficient, and will add three jumps to our journey."

"Object noted and overridden," Jack said. "The nearest flux, at maximum speed."

"Aye aye," the android said. Arth flashed across the viewscreen as the Tropicana fired lateral jets to reorient itself, and then the ship accelerated abruptly.

"Captain," Ryhrnn said, "we arre being hailed. On the Starrporrt Policce channel, ssir."

"Ignore the hail," Jack said. "Into the flux, Zed."

"WE ARE SUCCESSFULLY LOCKED INTO ORBIT," Zed said.

"Good work," Jack mumbled.

"You see?" Zed said. "You think of me as a person."

"Trust me," Jack said, "I do not."

"Aboarrd ssome ships," Ryhrnn said slowly, "thiss moment would be ccelebrrated with a little gin."

"Yes," Jack said. "I'll go to the galley."

He made a detour to the engine room; he might not have the time to do it later. Finding the Tropicana's shield generators, he traced the various power couplings and data conduits through their tangled routs until he was sure he knew how the shields got energy. Then he took a fire ax and cut through the power couplings.

In the galley, he found no gin. There was, however, a bottle with a hand-printed lable that read, *AGED GAZURTOID BRANDY*. Choosing not to ask himself whether the bottle contained a liquor made *by* Gazurtoids or made *of* the tentacled creatures, he took the bottle and two tumblers and stomped back to the bridge.

"Captain," Zed said, "we've lost shields."

"We'll have to look at that once we've landed." Jack poured brandy out for himself and for the Thrynn. The liquid had a bright golden color and smelled vaguely of ammonia, but he took a sip anyway. It burned going down, but the aftertaste was surprisingly pleasant. "Take us to the planet where you picked me up."

Ryhrnn sipped his glass thoughtfully and looked at Jack. "If thiss is a mission of pirraccy, you should prrobably tell uss up frront."

Jack snorted. "Piracy?"

"Did we jusst ssteal thiss ship, Jack?" Ryhrnn asked.

"What?" Jack forced a laugh, and then, to cover up the awkwardness of his dry chuckle, he gulped brandy. It didn't taste as good the second time. "No. Why would you say that?"

"Well, we had a hurrried launch. Ourr crrew is sskeleton and . . . unorrthodoxs. But mosstly, I ssay that because we ignorred Starrporrt Policce and rran when they trried to hail uss."

"I screwed up the launch code," Jack said.

"We could have communicated that to the Ss.P."

Jack shrugged and tried to laugh ruefully. "I guess I'm just in too much of a hurry. I miss my ship! You must know how it is."

"No," Ryhrnn said, "I have neverr been captain. We arre not going to ssteal anything then, Jack?"

"We're just going to recover the Ida Mae," Jack said, and then everyone gets what they have coming."

What the Thrynn had coming now was a laser blast between the shoulder blades. He was getting too suspicious.

"Here are the longitude and latitude," Jack said. "Prepare to land."

They rolled out of the Tropicana in the ship's terrain vehicle. The vehicle was open, consisting mostly of struts, knobby tires, and a cargo bed, so Jack and Ryhrnn wore all-atmosphere suits. Jack didn't carry a sidearm, which was a deliberate move on his part; the Thrynn was armed with a stubby laser rifle. Ryhrnn relaxed once they rolled down onto the orange-and white-streaked sand—maybe he noticed that he was the only one who was armed. Jack had carried Zed down and settled him into the driver's seat; Zed drove the vehicle.

"I don't ssee the Ida Mae," Ryhrnn said, "and she didn't show up on the sscannerrss."

"Of course, she didn't." Jack snorted. "She's in a tight canyon five klicks west of here. I didn't want to land on top of her and damage her, and I also didn't want to wreck the Tropicana. We're going to fly back with two ships, boys."

"Right!" Zed's voice trembled with plastic enthusiasm. "Because we have to deliver one back to Captain Pulaski!"

"Yes. Yes, that's exactly what I mean." Jack raised his eyebrows to the Thrynn. They'd be visible through the faceplate. The gesture would have been meaningless to, say, a Veloxi or an Elowan, to whom human nuance was invisible or confusing. But Ryhrnn was a Thrynn, and the Thrynn were great communicators. On top of that, Ryhrnn had decades of experiences working and dealing with human Interstel contractors. Surely, he would understand.

"Five klicks west it is, and looking for a narrow canyon!" The android spun the terrain vehicle about and headed in the direction indicated.

"It'ss too bad that Captain Pulasski . . . wantss his ship back," Ryhrnn said slowly. "Otherrwise, we could ssplit the two ships among uss thrree ways and all be rrich."

"Two ways!" Zed cried. "I fooled you again!"

"Even if you took the trraditional five sharres as captain," Ryhrnn said.

"One sixth of two ships is a lot," Jack allowed. "Plus one sixth of the Ida Mae's cargo of plutonium."

"A comms officcer could get rrich and rretirre."

Jack nodded.

"It'ss enough to make a man think crrazy thoughtss."

Jack nodded again. He had the Thrynn right where he wanted him.

"I think crazy thoughts all the time," Zed said. "I'm thinking crazy thoughts right now. I bet you can't guess what they are."

"You're thinking nothing," Jack said. "You are hardware, running subroutines designed by the engineers who made you to make you endearing to us."

"Why on earth would they want that?"

"Not sure." Jack cleared his throat. "Maybe so we wouldn't treat you as disposable."

"I'm definitely not disposable," Zed agreed.

They drove past various kinds of fungus, some so small they appeared as mere scrapes of color on the orange rock, and others so large they might have concealed starships or office complexes within. One, four times the size of the terrain vehicle, bounced unmoored across the landscape and narrowly avoided hitting them.

"Don't shoot that one," Jack warned the Thrynn. "It's full of flammable gases. We found out the hard way."

"Nothing that can attack the Tropicana, though?" the Thrynn pressed. "Rrememberr that we losst shields."

Jack shook his head. "The really big ones are stationary. The mobile ones aren't very heavy. The ship will be fine."

Jack gave a few precise suggestions and Zed found the mouth of the canyon. The two columns of orange rock, one to either side of the opening, again struck Jack as so perfect as to be artificial. Had some ancient race dug this canyon, and sunk the mines within it?

Jack shook his shoulders to cast off the irrelevant curiosity.

"One more klick," he said.

The canyon narrowed and climbed gently. Farther up, it would have its birth at the foot of a red-rock mountain that had once been a volcano and had now been extinct for eons. But one klick in, just where Jack forecasted, sat the Ida Mae. Her landing gear was down and she faced toward them, the cargo pods clustered all along her neck making her appear as if she had a goiter.

"Plutonium?" Ryhrnn asked.

Jack nodded. "Full. You're a rich man."

"She doesn't look wrrecked."

"Okay, she's not really wrecked. She's hidden. Once my crew died and Pulaski and his men rescued me—"

"That's me!" Zed cried. "One of Pulaski's men!"

"Pulaski's android," Jack said. "Not the same thing. Anyway, the thing that smashed off Skippy's legs here—"

"Zed!"

"—Zed's legs here killed my crew and did a number on me. I could have invited Captain Pulaski and his people back to the Ida Mae, but then we would have been splitting it among too many people."

The Thrynn nodded slowly. "Not to mention, Captain Pulasski would have claimed the captain's share, and would have argued that you werre a crrewman on his ship. Five shares to Pulasski, anotherr five or so to his crrew, and one to you. A bad outcome for you."

"And a windfall for him," Jack said, "a windfall he didn't really have coming." And a windfall Pulaski had demanded was his, when Jack asked to borrow his ship. A windfall Jack had promised the captain while getting him drunk as an overture to killing him, cutting off his hand, and stuffing the body under a flophouse bunk. He hesitated. "Pulaski doesn't really want his ship back." He looked at the android out of the corners of his eyes. "He said I could keep it."

The Thrynn nodded. "You could have told me all of thiss at the Starrporrt."

Jack shrugged. "I'd rather you found out here."

Ryhrnn adjusted his grip on the stubby laser rifle. It was a very small move, very subtle. "If you fly the Ida Mae back and I fly the Trropicana, ssome might ssay that makess me a captain."

"Of course, I'm the one doing the flying," Zed said.

"Shut up," they both told him.

Jack took a deep breath. "That's fair. Captain's shares, then, fifty-fifty on the ships. Everyone gets what they have coming. And listen, I'm going to make out like a bandit, and I want you to make out like a bandit, too. We'll split the plutonium in half, load half of it into the Tropicana, and that's your, too."

Ryhrnn nodded. "Acccepted. Shall we enterr the Ida Mae?"

Jack looked left and right. "Why don't you guys stand guard here, in case anything comes up the canyon? I'll walk around and do a visual inspection, in case we got something growing in one of the engines, or gumming up the landing gear, or piercing the hull."

"Super!"

Ryhrnn nodded.

Jack stepped down from the skeletal terrain vehicle and proceeded to walk around the Ida Mae. He did conduct his visual survey and found, to his delight, no evidence that anything that happened in his absence. Jack turned his voice pickup off, so as not to make Ryhrnn listen to him pant and puff. As he walked, he heard his companions talking to each other on the Tropicana's channel. At first, it sounded like meaningless chatter, the Thrynn trying to provoke the android into saying ridiculous things. If only the robots' designers realized to what ridiculous ends their creation would be pushed, to amuse spacers on remote worlds! But perhaps they had realized. Perhaps they had done it deliberately. But then a question caught Jack's ear.

"Sso," the Thrynn said, "when Pulasski ssent you into Perrssonnel for trraining, what happened?"

"I attended all my lectures," Zed said. "I especially liked the ones on orbital dynamics."

"You esspecially liked nothing," Ryhrnn said. "You uploaded new sskill modules."

"Of course. You can't blame me for trying!"

"I sstopped attending the lecturres," the Thrynn said casually. "Oncce I learrned they were jusst uploading inforrmation into my head by medical means."

"True!" the android snapped.

There was a long pause. "Sso I ssuppose all andrroids know the trruth about the trraining ssessions. That they'rre forr show only, and Interrsstel employees get sskills neurrally implanted."

There was another long pause.

"Jack also knows," Ryhrnn said. "He and I werre disscusssing it beforre we rresscued you frrom the ssalvage yarrd."

"I'm programmed not to tell anyone," Zed said. "Interstel doesn't want spacers to feel uncomfortable. Also, there is unfounded speculation that continuum flux nightmares are a byproduct of neural uploads, and Interstel would rather not fuel that controversy. But since you already know the truth, I can discuss it freely with you."

"Of courrsse."

Jack turned on his microphone as he approached.

"Yeah," he said. "Neural uploads. Knew it all along."

Zed nodded proudly.

Ryhrnn looked at Jack and smiled. "Sso maybe the Ida Mae isn't sso valuable afterr all. Maybe she's not ssuch a sspecial vesssel."

"She's a good ship, still." Jack patted a landing strut. "Tell you what, you can take either ship, I don't care." This was a bluff.

Ryhrnn smiled. "I don't carre either. They'rre both good shipss."

Jack nodded. "Well, she looks good from the outside. Let's go have a look inside, and load all the plutonium we can onto the terrain vehicle. It might take us eight or ten trips to get the ore all shared out."

The biometric lock on the ship's main hatch would respond to a fingerprint, but it was also programmed to respond to voices. Jack switched to the Ida Mae's channel, identified himself to the hatch, and then led the Thrynn up into his ship. They left legless Zed behind in the terrain vehicle. The ship had the same layout as the Tropicana, with the rear engines, the long neck, and the bridge at the fore. Jack left the hatch open and he and Ryhrnn both stayed in their suits.

Three all-atmosphere suits hung on pegs near the door; Jack looked at the empty pegs, thought of his dead former crew, and flinched.

Jack opened one of the six visible doors into the cargo pods. Inside, heaps of plutonium ore sat piled under plastic mesh webbing to hold it in place during takeoff and landing. Jack showed the Thrynn, who nodded at the ore and then nodded solemnly at the six doors, as if greeting someone bringing him a great gift.

"There it is," Jack said.

"Is it beautiful?" Zed asked over the Ida Mae's channel.

"It is," Ryhrnn said.

"Well, there's work at this end and at the other," Jack said. "Tell you what, if you want to sit down for a few minutes, I'll get out the pneumatic dolly and load up the terrain vehicle. Then you and Zed can drive back to the Tropicana. Take the dolly with you and do the unloading at that end. While you're gone, I'll run a check on the non-visible systems of the Ida Mae."

"Agrreed," the Thrynn said.

Jack dragged out the dolly and loaded it. He filled the dolly's bucket three times, and when he brought out the third load, the terrain vehicle was facing away from the Ida Mae, ready to depart. Jack poured in the ore and waved; Zed waved back.

"Let'ss get moving," Ryhrnn said over the Ida Mae's channel. "We have sseven morre trripss to make."

"Maybe more than that," Jack said.

Zed waved and drove away quickly.

Jack watched them drive away and then closed the hatch, drawing in the extendible ramp. He made his way forward to the bridge and sat in his own captain's chair, feeling himself relax. He activated the ship's scanner and searched. The terrain vehicle was too small to appear on the device, but he located the Tropicana immediately.

While he was waiting, he decided to make himself comfortable. He hung up his all-atmospheres suit, then grabbed a bottle of whisky from the galley. No need for glasses, he'd be the only one drinking.

Emerging from the galley, he stopped at the pegs and thought for a minute. There were three suits hanging there, and that seemed wrong. Hadn't there been three suits before? And then he had hung his up, so shouldn't there be four?

He must be mistaken.

Shaking his head, he made his way forward. He activated comms and tried first the Ida Mae's channel. "Ryhrnn, are you there? Come in, over."

Nothing.

He frowned. He activated the Ida Mae's missile launcher.

But of course, Ryhrnn would have switched to the Tropicana's channel to open the ship's door or use its other systems. Jack switched channels. "This is Jack Durian. Come in, over."

"Sstinky Jack," Ryhrnn said over the channel.

"Come on." Jack carefully selected the missile's target, running his scans again to get a precise reading and perfect his aim. "After I'm going to make you rich and everything?"

"Verry well," the Thrynn said. "Harrdman Jack. What'ss your sstatuss?"

"Pouring myself a drink. You?"

"Fifty perrccent unloaded."

"Sounds like you could use a drink, too. Tell you what, I'll finish this bottle myself, but I've got another in the galley. When you get back, let's open it."

"Maybe oncce all the worrk is done."

"Have it your way." Jack pressed the button, launching the Ida Mae's missile.

He stood and stepped forward to get the best view he could threw the bridge viewing screen. Before he'd taken the second step, he saw a brief white glare on the eastern horizon.

Jack chuckled softly. "Or maybe I'll just have both bottles myself."

"I think you'd betterr sharre."

The Thrynn was still alive? Had he lied about being at the Tropicana? Had Jack simply missed?

Jack turned to take his seat again and found the Thrynn standing beside it. Ryhrnn still wore his all-atmosphere suit and he still held the stubby laser rifle in his hands, and now he was pointing the rifle at Jack.

"Whoa," Jack said. "Hold up."

"Wherre's the endurrium?" Ryhrnn asked.

"What endurium?" Jack asked.

"Zed, come back to the Ida Mae," the Thrynn said.

"How exciting!" Zed bubbled with enthusiasm.

"Let me trry again," Ryhrnn said, "but only oncce morre. This ship is configurred the ssame as the Trropicana, for twelve carrgo pods. I can tell by looking frrom the outsside, and sseeing how built up the neckss of the ships arre. But therre arre only ssix visible hatches into yourr carrgo pods, Jack. Sso my rreal quesstion is, wherre arre the hidden entrryways into yourr ssmuggler's pods?"

"How did you guess I have endurium aboard?"

"It took ssome thinking. You'rre ssuch a consstant liar, it'ss harrd to know when you'rre telling the trruth. But you didn't want Captain Pulasski to know about thiss ship, and yet you gave up the plutonium verry quickly. Sso you musst be carrrying ssomething worrth morre than plutonium."

"Could be an exotic lifeform," Jack suggested.

"Lesss likely. It would have to be ssomething that could ssurrvive on itss own for weekss."

"So you put an empty all-atmosphere suit on the terrain vehicle," Jack said. "To make me think you were on it. You must have switched to the Tropicana's channel to persuade the android to cooperate with you. Or to some other channel entirely."

"See, Jack," Zed's voice came over the channel, you do think I'm human!"

"I orrderred Zed to help," the Thrynn said.

"I'm outside now," Zed said.

"And then you just had Zed drive out of sight and wait," Jack said. "You didn't even send him back to the Tropicana, so I could at least have the satisfaction of knowing that I blew up the robot."

"Hey!" Zed snapped.

"The andrroid is not dissposable. Alsso, I didn't want to wasste any plutonium."

"So now what? You turn me into Starport Police?"

"I don't think therre's any rreason to involve policce," the Thrynn said. "Rright now, you arre going to show me the hatches into yourr ssecret carrgo pods."

Jack walked slowly back into the neck of the Ida Mae. "You go through the floor." He demonstrated by stooping, lifting a floor panel, and pointing out the crawlspace that led to a hidden pod in each direction. "Satisfied?"

The Thrynn nodded. "Jusst one lasst thing, Jack. I have a bet to make."

Jack's ears perked up. "You want to race me for the Ida Mae?" he asked. "Or play chess? Or flip a coin?"

Ryhrnn shook his head.

"For my life, then." Sweat trickled down his back, under his jumpsuit. "I'll play you chess for half the cargo."

"You get none of the carrgo," the Thrynn said. "But I will let you live, and leave you herre with an all-atmossphere ssuit, if I can't get in thrree guessses, what you've got in yourr jumpssuit pocket."

Jack felt light-headed. What could the Thrynn guess—monetary units, a laser gun, keys, identification? "Go ahead."

"A rrecorderr with a vocal rrecorrding on it," Ryhrnn said.

"What? Like some pop music? Some android keytar player warbling about the blue-sanded beaches of Nogatron Seven? No."

"Then an eyeball," Ryhrnn guessed.

"That's disgusting," Jack said, "what's wrong with you?"

Then his heart fell. The Thrynn knew.

"In that casse," Ryhrnn said, "you musst have a hand. A human hand. The hand of Q. Quentin Pulasski."

"Wait," Jack said. "I won't turn you in."

"Of courrsse you won't." The Thrynn raised the stubby rifle and pointed it at Jack's chest.

"You need me." Jack's heart pounded wildly in his chest.

"You underrsstand perrfectly well that I don't."

"Please." Jack clasped his hands together as if he were praying.

"Sstinky Jack," the Thrynn said, "you know that everryone getss what they have coming."

A WINDOW ON SAROVAR

Baen often publishes a tie-in short story on its website to coincide with the release of a novel. This was the tie-in story for the novel Abbott in Darkness, *which is a science fiction tale about trading, exploration, fraud, corporate politics, difficult contacts with alien intelligences, debt, gun running, forensic accounting, textiles, and being a dad in tricky circumstances. This is a prequel story, preceding the opening of the novel by only a few hours.*

One of the central characters in the novel, and in all the tie-in short stories I've written about this family in space, is the dog. In this case, the dog has gotten loose, and John and his daughters try to chase her down. Really, only the spaceship is fiction.

I miss windows," Ellie said.

John tried not to listen to her. He mumbled, mouthing the strange words that ran as a vocabulary list across the screen of his multitool. *Eetroo,* he read. River. Sarovar Alpha had many rivers. It was a watery planet with two principal continents. *Eez,* tomb, gravesite. When was he going to have to talk about tombs in his new job as a Company accountant? He shook his head and scanned down, looking for more practical vocabulary. *Et*, food, that should be a useful word. But what did it mean that *em* plus a verb constituted a present progressive?

"John," Ruth said. "You're folding your hands."

"You're just jealous that I'm so flexible." He grinned at his wife. "Not everyone can touch the back of their wrists with their own fingernails."

"I'm worried your weak connective tissue will snap and you'll pull your hands off," she said.

"That can't happen," he said.

"Are you sure? That's exactly what can happen to your heart."

John grinned again and said nothing, to avoid the conflict.

Ruth shook her head and looked at the girls. They lay flopped on cushions on the floor of the family's cabin of the Sarovar Company starship *Oberon*. The cushions were a pile of all of the cushions from the cabin's sofa, the pillows from each of the cabin's four beds, the dog's sleeping cushion, and two more inflatable foam pillows spat out by the printing unit in the corner. Ruth sat on the sofa, also made of inflatable foam, and without cushions.

"Are you actually looking at pictures of windows on your multi?" she asked Ellie.

Five-year-old Ellie harrumphed.

"You can't have windows on a starship," Sunitha told her younger sister.

"You can," Ellie said. "The ship that took us out to Jupiter had windows."

"That wasn't a starship," Sunitha said. "It was just a shuttle."

"It still goes in space," Ellie said.

"But not between stars." Sunitha dropped into her faux upper-crust British accent. "Sarovar System is forty light-years from Earth. We couldn't just fly there directly through normal space."

"Mom," Ellie said, "Sunitha is now going to try to tell me about wormwood because she thinks I don't know anything about it or about how we got to Sarovar and she knows everything."

The lights in the cabin shifted to amber, which was a prelude to a broadcast announcement.

"I do not know everything," Sunitha said.

Ellie folded her arms across her chest. "That's right."

"But I know more than you."

"Mom!"

"Two hours until we begin our descent to Sarovar Alpha's Central Transit Station," a cheerful steward's voice spoke over the intercom. "Please finish up your meals or your exercise sessions or whatever else you're doing. In ninety minutes, you'll want to be strapping yourselves into your bunks, for your safety."

"Okay." John stood, pocketing his multi. "Who's going to take Ani for one last walk with me? Her next stretching of the legs should be on the planet."

"It's not fair to Ani to use her as a punishment." Sunitha was eight years old, but the starchy look on her face would have suited a sixty-year-old, and somewhat peevish, librarian.

"I'm not punishing anyone," John said. "I'm just separating you. And Ani is helping me because she's a good dog." He looked around the small cabin. "Except that she's not here."

Ellie bounced to her feet, her eyes big as saucers. "Ani!"

Twenty seconds' search confirmed that Ani was not in either sleeping closet or in the small storage locker.

"Is she at the vet?" John asked. The vet was not actually a veterinarian, but an assistant to the Ship's Surgeon, who used an AI docbox with a canine reference database to give Ani a monthly checkup. Mostly, the veterinarian pro tem used the time to take a few vitals and then marvel at Ani's coat, which had jumped straight from Spring brown to Autumn rust.

Ruth shook her head. "How did we miss the fact that the dog wasn't here?"

John shrugged. "She's pretty quiet most of the time. I just . . . I just assumed she was lying quiet in one of the corners."

Ellie jabbed a finger at Sunitha. "You lost Ani!"

"I didn't." Sunitha's fake English accent was gone.

"You took her for a walk!" Ellie's voice climbed in pitch. "When you came back, she wasn't with you!"

"Why didn't you say something then? It's your fault, too!" Sunitha jumped to her own feet.

"Maybe I didn't notice!" Ellie squealed.

"It's no one's fault. These things happen with a dog." John touched the control panel to open the door to the corridor. He had half-hoped that the family dog would be lying on her belly outside the door, tongue lolling out of a droll grin, but he was disappointed. "Sunitha, why don't you come with me and let's figure out where Ani ended up."

"I'm coming too!" Ellie muscled past her sister into the corridor.

"Someone needs to wait here for Ani to come home," John pointed out.

"Mom can do that." Ellie looked up and down the corridor. "Where did you take Ani on her walk?"

Sunitha pointed and the girls bustled off together.

"Leave the door open," Ruth suggested, "in case Ani comes back on her own."

John nodded and followed the girls.

Ani coming back on her own was a reasonably likely outcome. It had happened all the time on Earth. Ani was smart enough to find her way home. She could easily do something similar here. He told the girls so.

"But a starship is dangerous, father." Sunitha's posh accent was back. "There are engines and drives and all sorts of industrial machinery."

"Ani could get hurt," Ellie said.

They were right. That was the real reason to keep the dog close. But he also didn't want them to worry too much.

"Fortunately, Ani is smart," he said. "She'll stay away from anything too dangerous. And if she encounters any real threat, she'll use her chameleon powers to turn into the color of the spaceship floor and disappear."

"Ani isn't smart," Sunitha said. "She's a little skittish, because she's a rescue. But she's also way too curious for her own good. She'd walk right up to a crocodile to sniff it."

"No crocodiles aboard the *Oberon*," John pointed out. "Pretty sure."

"Dad, she's not a chameleon," Ellie said. "It took her four weeks to turn red. And she skipped her winter color."

"Which is the only color that would have helped her on this ship," Sunitha said. "Since she can't turn blue or yellow."

"That color is called buff," John said. "Blue and buff are the Company colors."

The ceiling and upper walls of the corridor were buff. At waist height, a twenty-centimeter-tall band of buff ran along every wall; below that band, the walls and also the floors were white.

"I wish I had Ani's sense of smell," Ellie said. "Then I'd find her right away."

"If you had Ani's sense of smell," John pointed out, "you wouldn't need Ani."

"We don't *need* Ani," Sunitha said. "We just *like* her."

"We *love* her!" Ellie broke into a run. "Which way did you turn? Where did you lose her?"

"I took her up the lift." Sunitha pointed.

"To the hyperpotties?"

"Hydroponics." But Sunitha muttered this under her breath so her sister didn't hear.

Ellie pressed the button and then jumped from foot to foot until the others joined her. They stood waiting for the lift.

"The most likely outcome is that we get back to the cabin and Ani beat us home," John reminded his daughters. "Or someone on the crew finds her. Or another passenger. Her collar has our cabin number on it, for exactly this reason."

A woman in the uniform of the Sarovar Marine Service passed. She was dressed in a jumpsuit with blue around the waist and shoulders, and otherwise buff. John nodded an amiable greeting. Could the crew help him?

"Yeah, but we have to look," Ellie said.

"We have to look," John agreed.

The lift arrived, they stepped inside, and Ellie pressed the button that would take them to the hydroponics floor. The lift doors closed behind them.

"Also, we don't want to pay the fine," Sunitha said. "Twenty dollars is a lot."

John sighed. "Twenty dollars is for the first time the crew finds your animal walking the *Oberon* unaccompanied. The second time is a hundred dollars."

"A hundred dollars!" Ellie shouted.

"Why doesn't the *Oberon* have windows?" Sunitha asked.

"See?" Ellie said. "You don't know."

"It has an observation deck," John said. "But it's closed during the transit through the wormhole. Since we're approaching the planet now, maybe it's open. But I think only the crew looks through it."

"So they can drive the spaceship," Ellie said.

"No, I don't think that's it," John told her. "I think sometimes they just . . . reserve some luxuries for passengers who pay more. Or important passengers."

"You're important," Ellie said. "You're a counter."

"I mean like congressmen," John said. "Or Company officers. The Company isn't very democratic, really. Most companies aren't, on the inside. Anyway, we weren't invited, not before the wormhole and not since."

"Why don't they look out the window in the wormhole?" Ellie said. "Are they afraid of the worms?"

"They're afraid of space madness," Sunitha said.

The lift stopped and the doors open. They exited into the end of a room full of long tubes in vertical racks, with water dripping from tube to tube and lush greenery exploding along the tops.

"Space madness sounds like something out of a bad flick," John said.

"But it's not wrong," Sunitha said. "No one knows what looking at a wormhole might do to a human brain, so they don't let people look at it."

"A wormhole might not actually look like anything," John said. "No one really knows what a wormhole is. It's a mathematical construct, really."

"It's a mathematical construct that sucked the Oberon in at the Jupiter end and spat it out near Sarovar Epsilon." Sunitha shrugged. "So it exists in real space in *some* way, and it probably looks like *something*."

"Touché."

"What will looking at wormholes do to a dog brain?" Ellie wanted to know.

"The real question is, what will smelling wormholes do to a dog's brain?"

John grinned at his own joke, but Ellie trembled as if she might cry. "Okay, what will smelling wormholes do?" she asked.

John picked Ellie up. "Nothing, sweetie, I was just making a bad joke about how Ani uses her nose more than her eyes. It's not even true, Ani uses her eyes a lot, and anyway, we never looked at the wormhole or smelled it or anything, so Ani will be fine."

"Because starships don't have windows," Sunitha said.

Ellie wrapped her arms around John's neck.

"Let's look carefully through all the hydroponics rooms," John said. "I bet this place smells great to her. All the water and the plants. Do you remember taking Ani for walks in the early springtime, and how she likes to smell every bush and tree?"

"She can smell the sap starting to flow." Sunith was using her stiff British accent again. That was probably a good sign.

"I think so," John said. "Anyway, she could smell something. So I bet this place smells just great to her. Sap flowing through all these plants."

"Plus if there are herbs and spices," Ellie said.

"Maybe some herbs." Sunitha cocked her head to one side. "Like rosemary or sage. But I don't think the *Oberon* is likely to grow cinnamon or cloves or black pepper."

"I don't know." John shrugged. "But it will be up on this deck if they do."

They searched the hydroponics bays, peering under tables when they passed them, and between the growing tubes into the space with the scaffolding. They had turned a corner and nearly exhausted the ship's growing space when they ran into a man with a thick mustache, wearing a solid blue jumpsuit. He knelt beside a cracked tube at the bottom of a growing rack. The tube had cracked, and mud slid through the fracture and dripped onto the floor. The man with the mustache was binding the tube with strips of epoxy tape, and then melting the tape with a handheld heatgun, so that it filled the crack and bound the tube together again.

He looked up at John and his girls, sweat on his brow and a frown on his face. "You looking for a little brown dog? Red-brown?"

"Ani's not little," Ellie said.

"Uh oh," John said. "Does that mean she damaged the hydroponics?"

"No, no." The man with the mustache grunted and hoisted himself onto his feet by gripping the hydroponics scaffolding. "No, this was my doing. I'm one of the ship's gardeners. Tripped and fell right onto my own tube when I was here to cut a little parsley. But I saw your . . . medium-sized red-brown dog. She went that way." He pointed with the heat gun.

"Thank you." John had been through this part of the ship once or twice, but not enough to find it familiar. "Remind me what's in that direction."

"Tool closet," the gardener said. "And beyond that, cargo bays."

John thanked the gardener and then had to jog to catch his daughters, who were already running.

The tool closet was stacked high with shelves bolted to the floor and ceiling. The tools not in use were strapped to the shelves with elastic bands or kept in plastic boxes that were bolted shut.

The doorway at the far end of the tool closet was labeled CARGO. A woman in blue and buff stood in the doorway and raised a hand to stop them. John thought that her uniform marked her as a member of the Company's Steward Service. A steward second class, or something like that.

"You can't access your cargo now, folks," she said. "You need to be returning to your cabin and preparing for landing."

"I don't need my cargo," John said. "In fact, there isn't any. We only have our suitcases." He felt like an economic refugee saying that, and in a sense, he was. He was just out of school, and they'd been very careful with their money, using only inflatable foam furniture or the cheapest printed stuff. They'd left that behind in Brooklyn, and were now taking all their worldly possessions to Sarovar Alpha to make their fortune. The only possession not already in the ship's cabin with them was Ruth's jewelry, which was in the *Oberon's* safe, to be reclaimed with the appropriate ticket only after landing.

"I'm afraid the time for tours of the *Oberon* is long past." The woman smiled, but it was a hard smile. "Time to get back to your cabin."

"Our dog is on the loose," John said. "We need to get her and bring her back with us, and one of the gardeners said she passed this way."

"She has her own safety straps," Ellie said. "For takeoff and landing."

"What will happen if we don't bring her back with us?" Sunitha asked. "Will she fly about the cabin on landing and be crushed?"

"No," John said. "But we should bring her back. We still have, what, an hour?"

"Go back to your cabins," the steward said. "If your dog is wearing the right ID collar, we'll find her and bring her back to you."

"For a hundred dollars!" Ellie was almost shouting.

"Look, your dog won't die," the woman said.

"One hundred percent?" Sunitha asked.

"Well, nothing is one hundred percent," the steward said.

"So she *might* die?" Now Ellie was shouting.

"She'll probably just be really surprised and shaken up," the woman said. "Maybe bruised. The worst likely outcome is a broken leg. But your dog will survive. But you can't be running around the cargo bays now."

"A broken leg?" Ellie screamed.

"Ani is nervous," Sunitha said, lecturing the woman at high speed. "She was a rescue, she's skittish. She won't like anyone to help her who isn't us. And she'll be terrified."

"Listen," John said. "If a crew member finds the dog, I'm out a hundred bucks. I'll pay you ten just to let us go look through the Cargo Bays."

"Just the Cargo Bays?" the woman asked.

"Well," John admitted, "I plan to keep searching until I find her or the time is really up."

The steward looked carefully around the Tool Shed, then smiled. "The first time your dog was found outside the cabin, how much was that worth to you?"

"Twenty it is." John handed over the cash.

"Be fast," the steward. "The ship is bigger than you think."

The Cargo Bays were much bigger than John remembered from his earlier tours. Crates were pinned to shelves with elastic webbing if they belong to passengers or crew, but the Company also had large amounts of cargo stowed here. The Company's crates were bigger, of uniform size, and locked together with pins and latches built right into the crates. Clear plastic film over the stacked crates served as a backup mechanism to hold the cargo together during landing.

They ran through two large bays, looking between rows of crates and not seeing their dog. The girls panted from the running, but did their best to call, "Ani! Ani!" as they ran. When they reached the end of the second bay, and John realized that there were two more, he stopped.

"Look." He pointed at an unattended hydraulic mule. "Let's take a ride."

The girls attempted at first to climb onto the lifting carriage, but John dragged them onto the seat beside himself.

"But if you lift us, we can see better," Sunitha pointed out.

"You don't need to see better," John said. "Just keep calling."

He drove the mule as fast as he could without losing control of it, both his daughters squeezed under one of his long arms. John had been headed for the Space Force Academy when a physical exam had detected his Marfan's Syndrome, and he liked driving vehicles of all kind. He wove the mule back and forth across the aisles, maneuvering easily around stray crates standing unpacked on the floor and the occasional frowning Company crew member.

No sign of Ani.

But the last cargo bay ended in a large access door. It was big enough for the mule, or even a truck to enter, but the door was shut, and the word RESTRICTED was printed on it in large letters at eye level, above a wide window.

John first tried to drive the mule toward the door, to see if it opened. It didn't, so he stopped the mule and dismounted to examine a control panel beside the door.

"Hey," a voice called. "Are you crew?"

John smiled as he turned. Two men in blue and buff were bolting a crate into place a few meters away. One stood and walked toward John. John was tall, at one hundred ninety centimeters, but he was also very thin —Marfan's. This man looked down to meet John's gaze and probably outweighed him by fifty kilos of solid beef. His eyes looked singularly unimaginative, and his lips were twisted into a surprised frown.

"No," John told him. "We're passengers, but our dog is lost, and we're looking for her."

He looked through the window and saw more stacked crates, snapped together and wrapped in clear film. The nearest crates had large printed text on the outside: KUPARI.

That was a gun manufacturer.

The *Oberon* was carrying crates full of guns.

"That's restricted," the beefy crewman said. "I can't let you in there. No way your dog's in there, anyway."

"Ani! Ani!" the girls continued to call.

"Are there any unlocked doors that let into that space?" John asked. "Not for me. I mean, my dog's clever, is there any possible way in there she might have found. I want to get her back to the cabin for her safety, but also to get her out of your way."

Big Beef shook his head. "No doors that aren't locked."

"Hey, did you say 'dog'?" The other crewman stood and walked over. He was wiry, and much shorter. Like John, he had oversized hands, but his knuckles were visibly scarred and callused.

The light in the cargo bays shifted to amber.

"Yeah," John said. "Kind of medium-sized. Face looks kind of like a lab's, but built more like a pit bull. White collar."

"Reddish brown fur?" Knuckles asked.

"That's her!" Ellie and Sunitha yelled together.

"You have thirty minutes remaining, passengers," the cheerful voice announced over the intercom. "As of now, all recreational and dining facilities are closed. If you are not receiving attention from the Ship's Surgeon or a member of his staff, you must now return immediately to your cabins and prepare for landing."

"You heard the man," Big Beef.

"The dog," John said. "You saw the dog."

Knuckles sighed and pointed at the far end of the cargo bay at a lift. "Your dog went up that lift about five minutes ago."

"How does a dog go up a lift?" John asked.

"Ani is smart!" Ellie said.

"Your dog was in the lift, sniffing around," Knuckles said. "Someone summoned the lift up."

"What's up?" John asked.

"Just the one floor," Knuckles told him.

"Go back to your cabins," Big Beef said.

"Yes." John nodded. "We're on our way back to the cabins now. Come on, girls."

He scooped the girls into his wake, one big hand on each child's shoulder, and scooted them along toward the lift.

Why was the Company shipping guns to Sarovar? The human presence on the planet was minimal, just the Company itself, and the descendants of a few colonization efforts that had arrived in-system a few years before the Company had.

Were the indigenous species hostile? John gulped. He hadn't read about conflict with the Weavers or the Riders or others.

He shook his head. There were plenty of animal species on Sarovar Alpha. The guns didn't have to be intended for use against sentients, they could be for defense against the Sarovar analogs of lions and coyotes and bears and crocodiles. Which, since the planet apparently teemed with life, must exist.

On the lift's control panel, there was just one button above CARGO BAYS. It was labeled OBSERVATION. John was still reading it when Ellie pressed the button.

"The skinny man said up," she reminded him.

The lift closed and hummed softly as it hoisted them up to the ship's highest level.

"Just remember that we haven't been invited to this floor," he reminded his girls.

"You can bribe them like you bribed the steward," Sunitha suggested.

"Whoa, whoa," John said. "I didn't bribe anyone. And we don't need to say that I did, especially to your mom. Or to the crew."

"Maybe we can get another car and drive it around," Ellie suggested.

John chuckled uneasily. "Let's just focus on asking about Ani, shall we?"

The lift stopped and the door opened. Two crewmen in blue and buff stood facing John and the girls. They were broad-shouldered and they held stun batons; one has a shaved head and the other had long blond hair.

"Uh oh," Sunitha said.

"It's time to get back into your cabin," Bald said. "Sir."

John sighed. "I don't want any trouble. I'm just looking for my dog."

The two men looked at each other.

"Did I hear the word 'dog'?" called a gravelly voice from the next room, out of sight.

"John?" Ruth called.

He heard a dog's bark.

"Let him in," the gravelly voice ordered.

"John!" Ruth called. "Girls! Come look out the windows with me!"

John and the girls moved forward from the lift chamber into the larger room, the two armed men stepping aside. Ani met them as they entered, leaping up onto one girl and then the other, tongue wagging in excitement.

The room was circular and had windows all along its outer walls. Was there shielding that closed to protect them while the ship traveled through the wormhole? But John could spare little time for the question, because through the windows, he got his first actual look at Sarovar Alpha, and it took his breath away.

The planet was blue with water. Like Earth, it luxuriated in oceans— more ocean than Earth had, in fact. Both continents, Wellesley and Napoleon, were visible. The *Oberon* appeared to be approaching the planet from its nighttime side, so to the right, John saw forest and mountains and plains on the northern continent, and rocks and desert on the southern, all illuminated by bright daylight; to his left, he saw darkness on the face of the waters and the land alike, with precious few lights twinkling here and there.

Beyond the planet he saw both its moons, circling as if about to dive behind the planetary mass, both fully light by the sun.

Ruth pressed against his side. "Ani made it up here on her own somehow."

"Yeah," John agreed. "We've been tracking her."

"They read her collar and called me up," Ruth said. "I beat you by just a minute or two."

"I'm Captain Morris." The captain was a thin man with curly hair and a slight stoop. He offered, and he and John shook hands. "Please, take a few minutes to enjoy the view before you return to your cabins."

"Thank you," John murmured.

"Ani isn't nervous at all," Sunitha said. She was scratching the dog behind the ears. Ani sat, tongue lolling out. "She just had an adventure, and she's totally calm."

"Girls." John pointed out the windows. "Look."

"We found Ani!" Ellie jumped in delight.

"I know." John stooped and gathered the dog into his arms. She was heavy, but he wanted to take the distraction away from his daughters. He grabbed Ellie by the top of her head and physically turned her around to face the planet. "Now look out the window. It might be a long time before you see a sight like this again."

"Okay," Sunitha said, "so the starship has windows. I never said I knew everything."

"Shh," John said. "Just look."

LOONEYTOONS

When Rob Hampson and Sandra Medlock invited me to submit a story for a hard science fiction anthology in a shared timeline, I was daunted. On the one hand, the idea of writing a hard science fiction story—a tale in which somehow science matters to the outcome—puts me a bit out of sorts. I am not a scientist. I do not read science or think about it much, most of the time. And on the other hand, writing in someone else's universe means accountability to an agreed timeline and setting, and commitment to not monkeying badly with other people's characters.

The Founder Effect was an anthology about settling a solar system previously not inhabited by any sentient species, and the idea that a founder or bottleneck of any kind—genetic, for instance—can exert a dramatic influence on the population or culture that follows. This much, at least, I can follow, but how to turn that idea into a story?

I decided to write something like a fable.

W hy did Gregor have to spend so much time at Roanoke?" Ilya asked.

He stomped, catching the wave before the last of it receded and sending up an arc of salt water into the scarf protecting his face. The sand piper at the toe of his boot gave itself away, emitting a silent gasp of surprise that emerged as a watery bubble. Ilya pushed in the head of his spade, the soles of his bare feet accustomed to the bruising contact with the tool's steel shoulder. It was a good spade; Gregor claimed that the serial number stamped on the handle, now worn into illegibility, was a sign that it had come from earth. Kicking the spade into the wet sand one handspan to the side of the spot whence the bubble had emerged, Ilya pushed down with all his weight, then levered the spade sideways.

The sand piper popped up into the dry air making its characteristic whistling sound. In deeper water, the finned, spiny arthropod would have eluded Ilya easily, but this was not Ilya's first Piper Picking, and he'd hit the timing perfectly. The piper landed on damp sand, and before it could drag itself down the beach to meet the next ascending wave, Ilya scooped it into his net.

Best not to touch the piper with his hands until it had been boiled— the venom in the spines wouldn't kill a person, but even through his thick gloves, it would cause severe itching and swelling. Ilya shook the net out into his uncle's half-barrel. The sand piper joined the others already penned in there, crawling in a circle, their piping sound reduced to a kitten-like mewl.

"He's got to steal a woman, doesn't he?" Ilya's uncle Olaf had also bagged a piper, and now shook his out into the half-barrel. He pulled his scarf away from his mouth to be heard better; the weather wasn't especially cold, but Olaf and Ilya both suffered from the cold, and took chill easily. "Do you imagine that's easy?"

"There are women here," Ilya said. "There's Annie Wopat. She's very good at catching sand pipers, and also at climbing the cliffs for plovers' eggs." Annie was also funny, and had a cute smile, and she was only a year older than Ilya, which was no big deal. And she didn't wear bulky clothes to keep her warm on the beach, so Ilya had seen enough of Annie to really fuel his imagination.

"Well, Annie's a bit young for Gregor." Olaf stooped to pick up a short strand of Sanderman's Kelp and bit into it. The liquid inside Sanderman's was low on calories, but had a lot of vitamin C, if you could stand the sour taste and the cold temperature. "Besides, if she married him, she couldn't marry you, could she?"

Ilya blushed. A wave splashed over his boots and he peered intently at the sand beneath it, looking for pipers' bubbles, but saw none. "I guess what I really mean is, why does he have to go kidnap a woman at all?"

Having sucked all the juice from the kelp, Olaf threw it onto the retreating wave. "Population bottleneck."

"I don't know what that means."

"It means that if you get too few people, then all their descendants are like those people."

"Like if those few people all had big hands, then their descendants would have big hands."

Olaf nodded. "But worse, if they suffer from the same diseases, then their descendants will suffer. Or if they're all lactose intolerant, or susceptible to alcoholism, or have the same parasites."

"This feels like school," Ilya complained. He stomped up another bubble and pounced, throwing his spade into the sand with gusto.

"Ah." Olaf spaded up a piper, but he had acted too soon, and the creature slipped past him and out to sea on the wave. "Then let me try it this way. Once upon a time, the entire village was sick."

"Beaverton's not a village."

"Maybe it was, back then."

"So this isn't a story about Gregor."

"It is, if you pay attention. We do the things we do now because our ancestors did them way back when. Or, you know, because the gods did them."

"Beaverton was sick."

"Because there were too few of us," Olaf said.

"What kind of sickness?"

"Different things, depending on how bad your luck was." Olaf shrugged. "Maybe it was some kind of anemia. Maybe it was brittle bones. Maybe it was loonytunes."

"Madness?" Ilya shuddered. "And the scientists couldn't fix it?"

"Scientists don't fix things with magic wands, you know. In fact, it was the scientists who said, 'look, we have this anemia and bad bones and loonytunes and the way to fix it is we need to get some new people in here to marry."

"Kidnapping seems extreme." Waiting for the next wave, Ilya stooped to pick up a fist-sized salp. The gelatinous mass trembled in his hand like a jelly.

"We didn't kidnap. Not right away. The Lord Mayor picked three brothers."

"Beaverton had a Lord Mayor?"

"In fairy tale times, everyone has a Lord Mayor. Later, you get Governors and Congressmen and Deputy Chief Regulators. These three brothers were all tall and handsome, and didn't have terrible problems. One was a little anemic so he slept a lot, and one had to be a little careful with his bones and drink a lot of sea-cow milk, and one might have been just a little bit looneytunes, but not so you would know it right away."

"Sea-cow milk makes you constipated."

"Like I said, these brothers weren't perfect. But they were pretty good. And the Lord Mayor gave the brothers some precious stones to take with them in their canoe, and they took supplies along, food and pulque for the long nights and sleeping blankets, and they headed for Roanoke."

Ilya stomped several times in his window of opportunity as a wave slipped away, but saw no bubbles. "Were they going to buy women?"

"They were going to give presents to the women's families. We still do that. Which is why Gregor took a thick stack of pelts with him."

"He's going to kidnap a woman, and leave behind pelts for her family."

"For her mother, specifically." Uncle Olaf nodded. "That's how you do it. So these three brothers were named Mike and Lou and Jim—"

Ilya laughed.

"What?"

"Silly names," Ilya said, stomping again but finding nothing.

"It's a fairy tale," Olaf said. "People can have silly names. Or should I switch back to telling it like in school?"

"I like the silly names," Ilya said.

"When they got to Roanoke, the brothers were scared, so Lou and Jim hid outside the wall listening to the screaming of strange beasts and Mike went in alone, with his precious stones. And he found his way to the headman's hut. Everyone noticed him because he looked different from the people in Roanoke—"

"Are you saying they could see his anemia?"

"No, but they had different hair and skin colors, and of course the people in Roanoke were huge compared to Mike, because they had had a population bottleneck, too."

"No fair." Ilya frowned. "They got to be giants, and we got bad bones."

"Another time, I'll tell you a different story, about how life isn't fair. So the people of Roanoke followed Mike to the headman's hut, and he was surrounded by all of them, standing there with his jewels. And the headman, whose name was Clement, said, 'what do you want?' And Mike said, 'I want to marry one of your women, maybe that one over there with the red hair, because I like her smile. Also, I brought you these gifts.' And Clement said, 'I can tell from your skin and your accent and your hair that you are from Beaverton, and if you think that I'm going to let one of our girls marry you, then you really are loonytunes. But thanks very much for the gift.' And they took Mike's gems from him, and beat him up, and threw him into their jail."

"I think *this* story is about how life isn't fair." Ilya stabbed his spade into the sand, but he had been distracted by the story, and missed his spot; only half of the sand piper came up on the spade's blade, and it oozed pink ichor. With a sigh, Ilya heaved the ruined piper into the waves.

"Maybe all stories are. But lucky Mike, he had two brothers, and when night came and he hadn't come back, they climbed over the wall and found the jail and got Mike out."

"How did they do that? You make it sound so easy."

"Well, you know how people at Roanoke can't take their liquor? That's because of their population bottleneck problem, and Lou and Jim knew this. So they slipped their pulque into the guards' rations and when the guards were drunk they unlocked the door and Mike walked out. Only Mike said, 'The Lord Mayor sent me here to get a wife, and they took my precious stones anyway, so I'm going to get a wife, fair's fair.' And he *did* like the way that red-headed girl smiled at him, so the brothers sneaked around the village until they found her, and they took her with them."

"Conked her over the head?" Ilya asked. "Made her drink pulque?"

"Apparently, she was willing to come along, after all. Maybe she was sick of men who were too tall and couldn't hold their liquor, and a little anemia didn't seem like a big problem to her. But before the brothers could leave the island, the men of Roanoke came after them. So Mike and his bride took the canoe and paddled for him, but Lou and Jim took the rest of the precious stones and ran off into the woods making lots of noise, so the men of Roanoke would chase them. And it worked, but it took Lou and Jim a week to lose their pursuers. And by that time, they had nearly reached Antonia."

"The Lord Mayor only sent them to Roanoke," Ilya objected.

"That's what Lou said when he realized where they were. But Jim, who was a little bit looneytunes, said, 'Hey, we still have the gems, we should try to get our brides here. No way the people in Roanoke are going to let us back to try again.' And Lou said, 'Well, negotiating with the headman was a bad idea. This time let's try talking just with the family.' So they walked into Antonia, and walked around talking to the girls there. And because everyone could tell they were not from Antonia, and because young women are always interested in seeing new young men—"

"Always?" Ilya asked.

"Most of the time," Olaf said. "So Lou met a young woman he liked, because she had strong arms and legs, and Lou had always been a little weak."

"Because of the brittle bones," Ilya volunteered. "And the constipation."

"And the young woman invited the brothers to her house for dinner. This was just what Lou wanted, because over dinner, which was very nice roasted beef with a creamy Antonian pepper dressing, he told the girl's father he'd like to marry her. And the father, whose name was Gustavo, said, 'No way.' And Lou said, 'I brought you a gift,' and Gustavo said, 'No way am I trading my daughter for a gift, and if you aren't out of my house by dawn, I will break your brittle neck.' And Gustavo was so mad that he stomped out."

"But that wasn't the end," Ilya said.

Olaf shook his head. "As soon as Gustavo had left, his wife, whose name was Mariana, asked what the gift was. And Lou showed her the stones and she said, 'Give me this gift and you can take my daughter, only you have to leave right now.' And Lou had brittle bones, but he wasn't one to let moss grow on him, and Jim was looneytunes so he was game to help. So Lou left the gem stones with Mariana, and he and the girl with strong arms and legs built a raft. She was really helpful at raft-building, because she was so strong, and then they hoisted Lou's shirt as a sail and came home in triumph."

"So this is why Gregor took pelts to give to his bride's mother, specifically," Ilya said.

"And this is why we sometimes have anemia, and sometimes brittle bones, but not nearly as bad as once happened to us."

"And this is why people from Roanoke and Antonia also come kidnap our girls," Ilya said. "Only the parents always know. And the girls."

Olaf nodded. "That's how it is with a bride-kidnapping, nowadays. Everyone knows in advance."

Ilya popped a sand piper from its watery hole and scooped it into his net. "And what about Jim?"

Olaf shrugged. "Nothing about him. He was looneytunes."

"But we're not all looneytunes today. Didn't Jim get a bride, too?"

Olaf looked up and down the beach; there was no one else in sight. Then he fixed an eye on Ilya and arched his brow. "But where could Jim have gotten a bride from? The people at Roanoke and Antonia were both up in arms, after their girls had been kidnapped. So there was nowhere else to get a bride . . . was there?"

"There's Kerensky," Ilya said. "On Trudovik . . . the other moon. Where it's always warm." The thought of a place that was always warm made Ilya shiver with envy.

Olaf nodded sagely. "But those people didn't like us from the start. They're collectivists up there, and they're suspicious of us one hundred percent of the time. It would confirm all their suspicions if we went up there and stole one of their women, and it would be a terrible idea to make them angry, so there's no way Jim went to Trudovik to get a bride. If that kind of thing had happened, the Kerenskyites would still be upset about it today."

"How would he have done it, anyway?" Ilya felt some disappointment that the story ended this way for Jim.

"Well . . ." Olaf said thoughtfully. "Antonia was trading with Kerensky in those days. I suppose Jim could have sneaked aboard one of those shuttles by tying up one of the off-duty crew and stealing his uniform."

Ilya stared. "Really?"

"He *could* have," Olaf said. "He *was* looneytunes. And then he could have stayed hidden inside the cargo, say, by jettisoning half a crate of fabric and hiding underneath the rest, and smuggled himself into Kerensky that way."

"If the people on Kerensky distrust us so much," Ilya said, "there's no way they let one of their girls marry us."

Olaf considered this. "So if Jim found a girl, named, say, Tatyana, he would never have talked to her father and mother, Pyotr and Zoya. But he might have talked to Tatyana, and given her his precious stones, and said, 'Look, I'm rich. You don't have to stay up here eating bad collectivist bread and waiting five years for your turn to see the doctor, you can come back with me and be a wealthy woman.'"

"But Jim wasn't wealthy."

"No, but he *was* looneytunes, and I'm just suggesting the *kind* of thing he *might* have said."

"And they smuggled themselves back down on a shuttle?"

"They could have," Olaf said. "Only of course they didn't, because Jim was looneytunes, and not stupid. And then I suppose they could have stolen a canoe at Antonia and paddled back home."

"But how would Tatyana have reacted when she realized she wasn't going to be wealthy?"

Olaf shrugged. "Maybe she would have decided that here in Beaverton she would be wealthy *enough*. Maybe she would have had a big enough party on her arrival that she felt wanted and decided to stay. Or maybe she would have decided she liked Jim, after all. But obviously, this is all speculation." He fixed Ilya with his keen eye again. "Because this . . . didn't . . . really . . . happen."

"But we're not looneytunes," Ilya objected. "Or not very much."

Olaf nodded. "The people of Roanoke and Antonia weren't looneytunes, though, so maybe the fresh blood that Mike and Lou brought in was enough. I mean, if Jim had really risked a war with Kerensky over marrying one of their girls, don't you think there would be some other sign of it in our people?"

Ilya felt perplexed. He wasn't sure whether Olaf was telling him that Jim *hadn't* kidnapped a Kerenskyite bride, or that he *had*.

"I guess so," he said.

"Good," Olaf said. "Then let's get these sand pipers home and into the pot. Gregor will be back soon, and we need to feast his bride."

MERE PULP, NO LESS

Following the reception of my Mormon steampunk novel City of the Saints, *I suggested to Jason King, publisher at Immortal Works, that the subgenre could support an anthology. He partnered me up with James Wymore to put the project together and edit it.*

We got so many submissions that we put out three volumes. Afterward, so many writers protested that they would have written for the anthology too, if they'd been aware of it, that we ultimately published a fourth. I edited one of the volumes, and I wrote this story for the volume edited by James.

Trevor Alvord, Chris McAfee, and Dainan Skeem were all on the staff at BYU's Harold B. Lee Library. They have been tremendous supporters of local literature and sometimes participants in it, and I thought they deserved to be "Tuckerized" in this tale. In the good old tradition of Tuckerizing one's friends, I have made some of them villains.

I catch Skeem in the stacks, shelving a book. He looks guilty, as he should.

"Reading novels again, Dainan?" I say.

He's silent.

I eye the spine of the book in question. "*A Study in Scarlet*? Mere pulp, no less. Spies and detectives."

He's given up defending his vice. I decide to let the point lie. Soon, his addiction to the most lurid of reading matter will cease to be relevant. Besides, his deficient sense of literary quality is not what he should feel guilty about.

He should feel guilty because he's a spy.

"No matter." I say it lightly. "Alvord has called a meeting."

"In the conference room?"

"The Young Display Room. In fifteen minutes, if you please."

Skeem doesn't ask what the meeting is about. He would ask, if he were an honest employee of the library. Since he's a spy for John Taylor—or rather, Joseph F. Smith, who heads Taylor's clandestine force of informers and enforcers—he doesn't ask. He pretends it's normal that I should invite him to an unscheduled meeting.

A little more ordinary curiosity might save his life today. I do not regret the loss.

The Young Display Room is not entirely empty when I arrive. Young himself is there waiting for me, standing on his pedestal, immobile as he has been since the day he transitioned from flesh and blood to flesh and bone by way of the embalmer's knife. He poses sternly, staring from the corner of the room at all who would dare examine his life, challenging them to judge.

The paintings that stare back at him from the walls depict key scenes in Brigham's life: his acceptance of a copy of the Book of Mormon from his brother Phineas; baptizing English converts in a river outside Preston; speaking to the crowd at Nauvoo as the mantle and face of Joseph fall over him; driving John D. Lee from the Beehive House during the thwarted uprising of 1859.

The remainder of the room, which is large, contains some of the effects and writings of Brother Brigham. The bloodstone amulet, the collected speeches, the share certificates, the lion-headed cane, the book of sealings, as much as I could convince the Young family to share. All Brigham's works, set out for inspection, as if to say, *do we not need such a man at the helm today?*

Young himself contains *my* work, concealing it from prying eyes.

I hear the door open behind me. I am busy admiring Brigham and pay it no mind. Would Brigham surrender, as his successors have? Would he flee, would he compromise with the corrupt gentiles in Washington?

I think not.

"Turn around, McAfee," Skeem says. "This isn't easy for me, but I'm going to look you in the eyes while I do it."

I turn around. Skeem is pointing a pistol at me, a battered 1851 Navy. From his other hand dangles a long fire ax.

"You knew," I say.

"I guessed you were on to me," Skeem says.

"You can't arrest anyone, not with the federal troops occupying the Salt Lake and Utah Valleys."

"The federal troops are why I have to stop you." Dainan Skeem furrows his brow. "I'm sympathetic, believe me. We all are."

I snort. "Joseph F. Smith, sympathetic? Please!"

"When we're squeezed as we are? Who wouldn't want to see Brother Brigham return as you were planning, riding a white horse at the head of a relief force?"

"If only someone had thought to embalm Brother Joseph," I say.

Skeem shakes his head. "Not this way. Brigham Young wouldn't approve."

"Brigham Young wouldn't approve of Brigham Young saving the saints?" I laugh out loud. "Of course he would! If Brigham were here today, he'd be standing on *this* side of the pistol, with me."

"But it isn't Brigham," Skeem says. "You aren't bringing Brigham back, you've merely built a machine that will animate his skin and bones. No matter how clever your device is, no matter how much it may look and sound like Brigham Young, it isn't. It's just you, pulling the strings on a complicated marionette."

"Brigham will pull his own strings," I say, "exclusively. As he did in life."

"That's nonsense." Skeem shakes his head. "But I can't let you try."

"You can't arrest anyone," I say again. "The federals have taken away all your authority. You can invite me to a Bishop's Council, but I'll refuse. What then, officer Skeem? Will you shoot me?"

"I don't want to." Dainan Skeem sets his jaw. "But I will." He extends the ax in my direction, handle first. "Unless, of course, you cooperate."

"You mean, chop Brother Brigham to pieces." My expression of shock is genuine. "Are you not worried that in the resurrection, he'll rise mangled and angry with you?"

Skeem raised his eyebrows. "Are you not worried that in the resurrection, he'll rise stuffed full of gears and angry with *you*?"

"I've taken excellent care of Brother Brigham while he's been in my care. I've patched his holes only with the finest of lambskin, I've humidified the room to keep his skin supple. I will remove the gears, once Brigham has had a chance to liberate us from our occupying enemy."

Skeem nodded. "That seems wise. And I'll do the same, only in addition I'll have to stitch him up a little bit."

"Impiety." I cluck my tongue. "I won't do it, Dainan."

"Then I'm going to shoot you."

Pathetic, as secret agents go. He should have shot me already. "No, you won't."

"No, you won't," Alvord says in echo.

Skeem turns in surprise and finds himself staring down the two shortened barrels of Alvord's shotgun. "You too, Trevor?"

Alvord nods. "Drop the pistol."

"You won't shoot me," Skeem says. "We're neighbors. You're a good latter-day saint, Alvord, a good man—"

Bang! Trevor Alvord shoots Skeem in the leg. Falling, Skeem drops his pistol, and his blood spills onto the stone floor.

"The difference between you and us," Alvord says, "is that you're a member of an organization. We *believe*."

Skeem presses both hands to the wound in his thigh. He's bleeding a lot, but it's not an arterial gush, he'll live. As long as I want him to, anyway.

I pick up the Navy. There's no need to intimidate poor Skeem any further, I point it at the floor. "Would you like to see?"

The expression on his face delights me. He wants to disapprove, but he can't stop curiosity from creeping into his eyes. Curiosity and something else . . . hope, perhaps. He nods, then looks away, as if in shame.

"Yes, Dainan Skeem," I tell him. "you will die here, but there is a future for your people. Brigham Young will save your wife and your baby daughter."

"Amen," Alvord says.

Skeem drags himself to the wall and leans against it, clutching his wound. His face is pale and drawn. "I hope it works."

I pick the loose journal leaves from the table. Alvord grunts, shuts the door, and then drags Brigham's pedestal away from the corner. He turns the embalmed prophet around and lifts his frock coat, exposing the mainspring crank and the input slot, both located in the small of Brigham's back.

"These sheets of paper," I say, waving them, "are pages from one of Brigham's journals."

Skeem nods. "You leave them here so visitors can leaf through them, and touch pages actually written on by Brother Brigham."

"Yes." I smile. "And also, I will now feed them into the machine."

"What will that do?" Skeem furrows his brow.

"The machine will *read the pages*," I explain. "Brother Brigham *the second* will derive his personality and memory from the journal pages. The body and the soul will be reunited."

Skeem frowns. "Just from the words of the journal?"

"The words," I say, "and also the ideas. And the contact, at second remove, with the man's original body. But do not doubt the power of words. Words make the world. Words are spirit. Words are power. God created just from His words."

"Do you see yourself as God?" Skeem asks.

"Only in a very modest way."

"We're ready," Alvord says.

"But what makes you sure Brigham will cooperate with you?" Skeem has gone white.

"The man he was." The time has come, if I want Skeem to live to see my triumph. I feed the journal pages into the input slot. The soft *whirrr* and the gentle tug as each sheet is pulled into Brigham's body are very satisfying.

When all the sheets have been entered, Brigham emits a gentle hum.

Skeem's eyes flutter.

"Brother Alvord," I suggest, "maybe you should bandage Skeem's leg. Also, get him some liquid."

Alvord squints at the informer with suspicion, but he hands me the shotgun and drags Skeem out of his shirt, tearing the fabric into strips and binding the wound. It isn't art, but it will do. He trots out of the room for a minute or two and returns with a glass of water, which Skeem sips.

Brother Brigham frowns.

"Did you see that, Trevor?" I ask.

"You were right," he says. "The detail work wasn't a waste of time."

"We're the first men to see Brigham Young smile in nearly a decade," I point out.

Alvord's voice is reverent. "If nothing else comes of this, that alone has made the effort worth it."

The frown twists, shudder, and slowly becomes a grimace.

"I believe he's smiling," I say. "I need to adjust a couple of the flywheels, likely."

"It's a work of art," Alvord adds.

Skeem is staring.

"What?" I challenge the spy. "No words of mockery? No condemnation? Now that you have seen the finger of creation in action, do you acquiesce? Will you at least concede my boldness, and my mechanical skill?"

Brigham rotates his head, looking at each of us in turn. I can see the pins beneath the embalmed skin moving and the lumps of the ball bearings. They give him a distorted look that is not entirely lifelike.

But they also allow him to move.

"You're criminals," Skeem says. "If I fail to stop you, someone else will do it instead."

I laugh at his effrontery. "All three of us are criminals? Or do you mean just me and Alvord there, who has bandaged your wound and given you water to drink, like the Good Samaritan himself?"

"I've read the parable of the Good Samaritan," Skeem said. "I don't recall the part where the Samaritan was a necromancer and a criminal conspirator who, in order to help the wounded traveler, had to interrupt his plan to commit murder."

"Well, you know," I say, "as far as it is translated correctly."

Alvord drops to his knees and touches his forehead to the floor, as one might to an oriental pasha. "Brother Brigham, do you remember me?"

Brigham looks to me and then to Skeem.

"Does your voice work?" I ask.

"Yes." His answer is deep and gravelly, with a faint metallic twang in it.

"I carried messages for you," Alvord says. "When John D. Lee was on the run."

Brother Brigham looks at Skeem. "I don't remember."

I shrug. "He won't remember everything, but that hardly matters. He only needs to choose the right side in the conflict. Brother Brigham, your Deseret is occupied by federal troops."

"I don't like federal troops," Brigham says slowly.

That's a good start. "The people are threatened and need to be saved. They need you to return and be your heroic self."

Brigham nods. His chin dips too deeply when he does so, giving the gesture a twisted appearance. "I'll save the people."

My heart races. This is a little more like talking to a child than I had expected, but Brigham must still be absorbing his memories and his soul from the words he has digested. Overwhelmingly, this is success, and surely others will see it this way. Brigham moves, he talks, he promises to help.

His voice could do with a little fine-tuning, to sound less sepulchral.

"First," I tell him. "Kill this man."

"This one?" Brigham points at Alvord.

"This one." I point at the spy. "His name is Dainan Skeem, and he is working against the Kingdom."

Skeem stares up at the automaton. It isn't quite fear that shows in his face. What is it?

Brigham nods, and he holds out his hand to me. Of course, there's no reason to expect him to kill Skeem with his fists. I give Brigham the shotgun.

Bang!

He shoots me in the belly.

The force knocks me back. The treachery takes my breath away.

"Why?" I ask.

Alvord understands before I do. "That's not Brigham!" He leaps to his feet and tackles the automaton.

He doesn't know just how strong my Brother Brigham is. Alvord hangs ineffectually off Brigham's shoulder, punching without doing any damage; Brigham advances toward me, ignoring poor Trevor.

I'm armed, I remember. I'm no marksman, but at this distance, who could miss? I pull back the hammer and fire, again and again until the hammer clicks on an empty chamber. The bullets tear into the body of Brother Brigham, ripping away sheets of skin and clothing and exposing grinding gears and pumping pistols beneath.

Alvord shrieks and falls to the floor.

Brigham rips the Navy from my fingers and pushes me. Pain sears my gut where I've been shot. I strike the wall, stagger forward to bump into the table, and fall to the floor.

I look up to see Dainan Skeem standing. He leans unsteadily against the wall as he addresses the automaton.

"Dainan?" Skeem asks.

"Fool!" I hiss.

"No!" Alvord yells

I clutch my stomach. My legs are numb, and hot blood pours over all my fingers.

Brigham turns to face the informer. "Yes?"

My body is cold all over. "What?" I gasp. "What did you do?"

Some of the color is returning to Skeem's face. He limps to the automaton's side and takes back his pistol; Brigham lets him.

But no, it isn't Brigham.

Skeem reloads the pistol slowly, tapping home the paper cartridges, closing the chambers with mutton fat from a can in his waistcoat pocket, and thumbing percussion caps into the back side. The room smells strongly of fat and blood.

I lean to one side and vomit.

"I switched the journal pages," Skeem said.

"No!" Alvord tries to stand, but Skeem kicks him to the ground and presses his pistol against the back of my ally's skull.

"Another move," Skeem says, "and I *will* shoot you."

"You put in pages of your own manufacture," I say.

"My own journal," Skeem admits.

"So Brother Brigham is . . . he's *you*."

"My memories," Skeem says. "My knowledge of your plot. Maybe some of my spirit."

Brigham turns to Skeem. "I'm you."

Skeem looks uncomfortable again, but he clears his throat and nods.

Our salvation has been thrown away. The taste is bitter in my mouth.

No, that's blood and bile mixed. I spit it out. "And . . . the automaton?" My vision is turning gray. I can't fill my lungs all the way, no matter how much I inhale. I feel light-headed and distant from my body. Is that Alvord crying, or is it me?

"Brother Smith and I will discuss," Skeem says. "We'll figure out what the merciful thing to do is."

Is that a grimace on Brother Brigham's face?

"Tell me at least that you didn't destroy Brigham's journal pages. Tell me at least that you are enough of a librarian not to do that."

"That you have enough *respect*," Alvord adds.

"The novel," Skeem says. "I hid them in the novel."

I try to remember. "*A Study in Scarlet*?" I ask.

He nods. "Brigham's journal pages are safe."

"Mere pulp, no less. Spies and detectives."
He says nothing. He's done defending his vices.
My vision goes black, and I stop defending mine.

Two Strangers

Onward, Libertycon! *was the second homage anthology to Tim Bolgeo and the convention and culture he built in Chattanooga, Libertycon. I met Tim. It was at the first Worldcon I attended, and among all the blue-hairs and electric scooter-riders, I encountered a robust bearded fellow in overalls, playing (I think) Hearts with three friends. Tim knew who I was, and invited me to come to his event.*

This is a story about disappointing yourself, and being redeemed by friends.

S uddenly there are two men there looking at me. Strangers.
"Nice suits," I say. "I hadn't realized there were cosplayers here tonight."
LibertyCon gets a few cosplayers, like Monalisa, who was running around this morning in one of those vampire swordslinger outfits she likes. But mostly, people dress casually, somewhere on the hippie-to-redneck axis of American fashion.
"Men in Black?"

Griff frowns. "Is that what Agent Cross says?" He's not looking at the two men, might not even have noticed them.

Agent Cross is my character. We're playing this roleplaying game that's sort of *X-Files* meets *Paranoia*, with a healthy dollop of H.P. Lovecraft. All the characters are agents of military or law enforcement organizations. Cross is a U.S. Marshal who is a little bit stupid and prays to U.S. Presidents and presidential candidates when the chips are down. Obama was his main man until Obama failed him in a firefight with lizard-people at a California vineyard and he prayed to Mitt Romney for the first time. This session is set in 2016.

"Come on, Clinton!" I bark and throw the dice. I get a fumble. "You fickle beast, you're gonna make me switch parties!"

"The gun misfires." Two more quick rolls of the dice determine that Agent Cross blows off his right hand and is knocked unconscious.

"Good," Griff says. "So the thing with six legs and a baby on an ecto-plasmic stalk for a lure is advancing on Agent Cross. Let's get back to agents Locke and Grimes, creeping along the canal toward the warehouse."

That's Mike's and Chris's characters. Mike's a former SEAL and Chris was in the army and then a merc. There are also an FBI special agent and a former CIA guy playing (their characters are both unconscious, having been stung by luminescent scorpions), and Griff is San Francisco P.D. I have to play a loudmouth idiot in this game, because these guys all know police procedure and rules of engagement and firearms in real life, so if I play straight, I have nothing to add. What the hell am I doing here?

Having fun.

Pretending to be an idiot who once traveled back in time millions of years, saw dinosaurs, and convinced himself that he was on Mars.

"Trump save me!" I gasp, and slump in my chair.

We're playing in the restaurant of the Marriott where the convention is being held, on a mezzanine floor. The restaurant is closed and dark, but not locked up. We got permission from the staff to play; the hotel people are unfailingly polite, but I'm pretty sure they're amused at how nerdy we all are.

"Can we speak with you?" one of the two men asks.

I stand, stretch, and hitch up my pants with my thumbs. "Yeah, I prob-ably have half an hour before Griff gets back to me."

"Hey," Griff growls, "if you're going to chit-chat, do it quietly."

I mime zipping my lips shut and jerk a thumb out the restaurant front door at the elevator bank. The two men and I walk there together and I get a look at their suits in better light. "You aren't men in black, you're men in blue. So, what . . . Agents of S.H.I.E.L.D.? What's that guy's name, Coulter? Or are you guys cosplaying Glengarry Glen Ross? That would be pretty outré. By which I really mean hilarious."

"We would never ordinarily do this," one of the men says. He's the taller of the two, and he has a shock of dark hair, strands thick as wires.

"We are violating all kinds of protocols," the second adds. He has a large chin that wiggles as he talks, and a thin wisp of gray hair around his temples only.

Their suits are blue and their complexions are pale. Not just white-guy pale, but northern Europe-wintertime-white-guy pale. Which is striking, since LibertyCon is a June event, in Chattanooga. I'd guess they were down from Minnesota or Canada, but they have bland Middle America accents.

"I love that you guys are so into your cosplay. I still don't quite get what it is." Are these guys readers? That kind of question is embarrassing, though, so I'll just keep playing along until they decide to tell me they want a signature, or whatever. And maybe they don't. Maybe they want to know where I found the Diet Mountain Dew that pokes out of my shirt pocket, or maybe they're on a scavenger hunt to find a con-goer taller than Larry Correia—there aren't very many of us. "Wait, you're not hotel security, are you? We asked permission to play here tonight."

We're past the elevators, standing on the mezzanine stretch where authors book time at folding tables by the hour to hawk their latest. I was here myself, a few hours earlier, trying to sell my back stock at cost, aiming to find new readers. Now people have moved on to the late-night panels or have gone out to the bars, or are doing nerdy things in the corners of the hotel, like I was. The tables are still here.

"Think of us as security for your life," the bald one says.

I don't feel frightened, because I'm a pretty big guy, and there are only two of them, and we're within shouting distance of half a dozen armed combat veterans who are at least tolerant enough of me to let me game with them. Also, I don't want to offend anyone who might, after all, be a reader. But this conversation is a little weird.

"Okay," I say, "I can grok it. So, what do you want to talk about?"

"What is 'grok'?" asks the one with hair.

"You guys aren't here for the convention," I say.

They look left and right, past the elevators and along the mezzanine. Then both men lose their heads.

It's not like Scooby Doo. They don't pull masks off, and what's underneath is old man Withers; their faces *disappear*, and in their places are insectoid physiognomies, with large, multi-faceted eyes, and rustling thickets of mandibles protruding from the points of their jaws like clicking Van Dyke beards.

Wow.

Now, I'm sober. I've always *been* sober, so I know that I'm not looking at some mind altering substance-created phantasm. I'm looking at two dudes in blue suits with bug heads.

My heart's pounding. I take a step back. I can still yell for the gamers if I need to.

"You're friendly," I say. I want it to be true.

"We're more than friendly," one says. Now I'm not sure if this was the bald guy or the other one. "We're your wardens."

"I'm not really up for any kind of probing," I say. "I don't need to see the inside of a flying saucer. Just plain friendly is enough for me."

Now I see that, although both of the bug-men are basically green in color, one is yellow-green and one is gray-green. "There is a threat to this timeline," the gray-green one says. "You are the only one who can stop it."

"We think," the other says. "This is all a little bit out of our experience."

"You're telling me," I mutter. "But what kind of threat are you talking about? Those guys back there, that I was gaming with, they're all trained to handle real threats. I can teach you how to read a P&L, or tie Boy Scout knots, or figure out guitar chords, but, I mean, if there's going to be fighting . . ."

"Perhaps we can go to intercept the threat," yellow-green says, "and explain on the way."

I don't know about threat to the timeline, and I'm the only one who can help, but I do try to be useful to people. Especially at conventions, where there's a good chance those people might be science fiction readers.

"Okay," I say. "Is this going to be quick? I don't want to leave Griff hanging when it's time to get back to my character."

The bug-men chortle and bob up and down.

"We think it will be fast," gray-green says.

"Either you will succeed or you will die," yellow-green adds.

"If you die, we will probably be demoted," gray-green concludes.

"Lead the way," I invite them. "I certainly wouldn't want you to get demoted on my account."

The two bug-men move along the mezzanine, past the turn to the dining area with the verandah and toward the escalator at the end that leads down into the convention center annex. Freed of their human heads, they also change the way they move—they're both waddling now.

We pass more friends of mine gaming—Alex and Robert Moore, Chris DeBoe, David Sherrer. The convention has a small room open as a boardgaming room, and I think they're playing Robo Rally, or anyway, something that has them all laughing a lot. I wave and take a slug of my soft drink. Alex gestures invitingly at his pewter robot and points at an empty chair; I shake my head. He makes a sad face. I make one back.

"Maybe we could introduce ourselves," I say to my two companions. "I'm Dave."

"Oh, we know," the gray-green bug-man says. "We're big fans."

I'm pretty weirded out now.

And I'm definitely not going to abandon these guys.

"Our names will be very difficult for you to pronounce, lacking mandibles and the ability to generate clicks of different tones," yellow-green says. "My name, for instance, is," he produces a racket of throat-clearing and banging sounds, like a tuberculosis patient playing the bones. "But in your language, it means Toothbrush."

"And my name means Sparkplug," gray-green says. "Well, not really sparkplug exactly, but that's the best analogy you are likely to understand, given your culture's current technology level."

"Given my *personal* technology level, I'm not sure that I really understand sparkplugs." We get on the escalator. "Tell me more."

"This is your Primeline, Dave," Sparkplug says.

"We think," Toothbrush adds.

"Good," I say. "What's a Primeline?"

Monalisa and Rick Foster are coming up the parallel escalator as we go down. Rick waves—he looks laid back, in a red polo shirt and khaki slacks, and of course Monalisa has a corset, high black boots, an ankle-length cape, and twelve-inch spikes protruding from her shoulders. Her make-up is very Goth, pale with black and dark reds.

"He needs more information," Toothbrush says. "Listen, once a species manages to leave its orbit for the first time, you have reached a sufficiently-advanced technology state to attract the attention of the administrators of the All Souls Consortium."

"I think I saw this on Star Trek," I say. "If you picked me to be the ambassador to all bugkind, I'm not the right guy. Maybe someone in Washington."

"We are not concerned with admitting you to the Federation of Planets," Toothbrush says.

"There really is a Federation of Planets?"

Rick and Monalisa have reached the top of the escalator and are coming back down. They're waving at us. I wave back.

"No," Sparkplug says.

"Nor are we here to give you new technologies, or take away your nuclear weapons." Toothbrush says.

"We wardens come here to see to your psychic development," Sparkplug says grandly, spreading his arms wide. He thinks he's saying something wonderful.

We step off the bottom of the escalator. "Monalisa wants to get a photo with you guys," I say.

"We probably shouldn't let that happen," Sparkplug says. "We're wardens."

"Yeah, but she thinks you're two dudes in Ovion costumes," I point out. "In suits. Ovion insurance salesmen."

Toothbrush giggles. "What is an Ovion?"

"It's a . . . bug-man," I saw. "In an old science fiction show."

"As long as she doesn't touch us," Sparkplug says.

"Human cooties?" I ask.

Sparkplug sways back and forth. "We are only apparitions. Holograms. If she tries to touch us and her hand passes through, she may realize what we are."

"If she tries to touch you and her hand passes through," I say, "she will assume that I have a really cool new toy, and she will ask where she can buy one."

The bug-men hesitate, then bobble up and down.

"So you're here to train me in psychic powers," I say.

"No, not that kind of psychic," Sparkplug says. "Spiritual *development*. We're here to help you mature as a species."

"One by one," Toothbrush says. "In your Primelines."

"This being my Primeline," I say. "So you're here to help me . . . mature."

Monalisa strikes a pose at the bottom of the escalator. "Shall we take photos? We cosplayers need to stick together."

"They're fighting colds, though," I say. "So better not touch."

She strikes a different pose. "Cosplay is for looking, anyway."

I take out my phone, and so does Rick. "How about a battle pose?" he suggests.

"The Vampire Queen against two warriors of the green men of Mars." Monalisa draws a sword; I hadn't noticed it under her cape, but it's a katana. I'm no expert, but it doesn't look like a prop. She adopts a martial stance, with feet shoulder-width apart, and levels the sword toward the two bug-men with ferocity in her eyes. "In business attire."

"The green men have four arms," Rick says, as he and I take a few photos. "These guys only have two."

"That we're *showing* you," Sparkplug says.

Toothbrush giggles.

"I think they're cosplaying *A Bug's Life*," I say, "meets *Office Space*."

"Now we must go," Sparkplug says. "We're running out of time."

I follow the two bug-men marching toward the doors at the far end of the convention center annex, waving back at the Fosters for all three of us.

"I don't think I understand what a Primeline is."

"There are parallel universes," Sparkplug says.

"Lots and lots and lots and lots and lots of them," Toothbrush confirms.

Sparkplug bobbles. "At every moment when a thinking individual makes a decision, her universe splits into multiple parallels, one for each possible outcome."

"So there are an unspeakably vast number of universes," I say.

They both bobble.

"And this is my Primeline."

"We *think*," Toothbrush says. "We think this is the universe in which you will personally achieve your maximum psychic potential."

"We won't decide, of course," Sparkplug says. "The judges are watching, and they will determine, at the end, whether this was your Primeline. Or maybe it will turn out that one of the other universes was your Primeline."

Toothbrush makes a keening, mournful sound. "Of course, in many other universes, you are already a convicted criminal, or a drunk, or insane."

"You are a whale poacher in one," Sparkplug says. "But you haven't been caught yet. You still might turn your life around."

"But you're talking about just me," I say. "Is this some kind of solipsism idea? Am I the only person who exists? Because wouldn't that make you two figments of my imagination, just like everyone else?"

"Ah, he's smart," Toothbrush says. "See, this is one reason why we think this might be your Primeline. You think about things."

"Solipsism is a false doctrine," Sparkplug says. "Everyone exists."

"Indeed," Toothbrush says, "the you that exists here is connected on a deep level with the you that exists in every other parallel universe. That's why we say that we believe this is your Primeline, not that you are Dave Prime."

"Déjà vu," Sparkplug says, "is that moment when you in this line connect with you in one or more other lines, and you have the feeling that you are repeating an experience. In fact, you are simply living it twice simultaneously. Or more than twice."

"If this is my Primeline," I say, "then some other timeline is Griff's Primeline, and Monalisa's, and so on."

"In theory, you might share your Primeline with someone else," Toothbrush says, "but that seems vanishingly unlikely."

"Help me understand why you do this," I say. "You're not worried about nuclear weapons or joining the federation that doesn't exist."

"Oh, nuclear war on earth has happened already in many, many timelines," Toothbrush says.

"We come to a planet after it has first left its atmosphere because that is generally how we receive notice of a species achieving sentience," Sparkplug says. "Our process is very resource-intensive, and we simply can't afford to start the search any earlier than that. Then we send wardens into the multiverse surrounding that planet to begin watching its people. Once all versions of a person in all universes are dead, the judges determine, with the input of the wardens, which version of that person was best, and then that version is extracted and joins the All Souls Consortium."

"But he's dead," I say.

"No one's ever really dead," Toothbrush says, "when there are multiple universes and time travel."

"So the people who are good enough make it into the Consortium," I say. "The rest just, what, *stay* dead?" I have terrible visions of being snatched by time traveling bugs from my deathbed in order to be punished for not living a good enough life.

The bugs chortle.

"*Everyone* joins the Consortium," Sparkplug says. "The adjudged best version of every human being who died after April 12, 1961, is in the Consortium."

"Living out the end of their days," I say.

"Living forever, of course," Toothbrush says.

"This is the singularity your public intellectuals have intuited, however darkly," Sparkplug says.

"Adolf Hitler is in the All Souls Consortium," Toothbrush adds.

I choke. "What?"

"Not the version from your Primeline," Toothbrush says. "You got a very bad Hitler, nearly the worst. The one in the Consortium is a lovely fellow, paints bad landscapes and gives the paintings away."

"But he died in 1945," I say.

"Yours did," Sparkplug says. "The one in the Consortium lived into the 1980s."

"He only narrowly beat out the Adolf Hitler who emigrated to the United States and became a senator," Toothbrush says. "That was also a good one."

"Well, we had to take the vegetarianism into account," Sparkplug points out.

"Which way does the vegetarianism cut?" I ask.

They chortle.

I feel short of breath, so I stop and lean forward, resting my hands on my knees. I had lost track of my surroundings, and now realize that I'm out on the streets, somewhere in Chattanooga. I feel disoriented and inside out; the world is not what I once thought.

On the other hand, I'm feeling pretty good about myself.

"Where are they?" I ask. "The nice Hitler, and the nice Stalin, and the nice Mao. Are they out in space somewhere?"

"What, you mean like heaven?" Toothbrush chuckles. "No, they're here. The Consortium repurposed a version of this planet on which every human being died of the Spanish flu. It's now an earthly paradise, and it's the All Souls Earth Station."

"I guess I should be happy about this," I say. "Everyone gets saved."

"In the best possible state they can achieve." The two bug-men bobble with enthusiasm "And when you are extracted and placed on Earth Station, you remember all the other versions of yourself, as well. You become immortal, and you regain memory of an existing eternity of selves."

I laugh grimly. "If you think this is my Primeline, that means you think I might not be able to be any better than this. Bald, heavy, a sugar addict, judgmental, prideful, envious, gossipy, lazy, grudge-holding, vengeful. Wow, what a piece of work I am."

"You should see the version of you in some of the other timelines," Toothbrush says.

"Besides," Sparkplug adds, "You have some good points."

"So . . . what do you guys want from me again?" I ask. "This timeline is threatened, you're the wardens, only I can do anything about it . . . ?"

"We're here to maintain the integrity of the timelines," Sparkplug says. "We also report on what we see to the judges, but mostly we just watch."

"Because you're holograms," I say.

"Well, yes," Sparkplug admits.

"And someone has broken into this world from another timeline," Toothbrush says. "And he's holding a hostage, *and* he wants to talk to you."

I shrug, my breath is tight in my chest. "We should call the police. What am I going to do about a hostage situation?"

"The problem," Sparkplug says, "is that the hostage-taker is you."

I chew on that for a minute.

"He's you from another timeline," Sparkplug continues. "We think he's here because this is your Primeline. He's not a very nice you, he's a bank robber."

"I get back to my earlier question." I take a deep breath, feeling queasy and trembling. "What am *I* going to do about it? I'm in the minority of people in this hotel in being unarmed. You know there are probably actual hostage negotiators at the convention right now? I don't think I need to be the one who does this."

"We're afraid that if anyone else comes in contact with the other you," Sparkplug says, "the two timelines will collapse."

"It's sort of a guess," Toothbrush adds. "It's never actually happened. But the science is sound."

"Let's at least call him 'Evil Dave,'" I say, "not 'the other you.' I hate to sound judgmental, but he *is* a kidnapper."

"And a bank robber," Toothbrush adds.

"And a timeline-jumper," Sparkplug concludes. "He's definitely Evil Dave." He winces.

"What does he want?" I ask.

"To talk," Sparkplug says.

"Maybe he just wants to hide here for a while," I muse out loud. "If it's to rescue a hostage, maybe I'd be okay with that. I mean, in some technical sense, Evil Dave isn't a criminal here."

I notice we're at the old hotel, where the convention used to be held— the Chattanooga Choo-Choo. Between the old terminal building and a bunch of condos behind it, several train cars still stand on old lengths of track. You can rent them now as hotel rooms, and the bug-men lead me across a lumpy gravel track toward a train car with its shades pulled down. A bluish-white glow coming through the shades suggests that the Choo-Choo has replaced the old incandescent bulbs with some pretty strong LEDs since I was last here. I smell ozone and I hear a faint crackling sound.

I look around; the rest of the courtyard is dark. I guess it's later than I thought.

"So, he wants you to go inside the train car," Sparkplug says.

"I've come far enough." I stop where I am and cross my arms over my chest. "Evil Dave can come out now." I say it loud enough that he should be able to hear me inside the train car, but hopefully not loud enough to wake up the rest of the hotel.

Sparkplug and Toothbrush both disappear.

The train's door opens, and Evil Dave steps out into a sudden pool of blue-white light. I don't know what I was expecting, but he's just as bald as I am. He's thinner, though, and he's wearing skinny jeans and a tight shirt with a big red collar. He has a pistol pressed against the head of the person he drags out with him . . .

Who is one of the bug-men. Like my two bug-men, he's wearing a blue suit. His hands are tied behind him. His mandibles are shaking.

"You have a bug-man hostage," I say. "Is that one of the wardens?"

Evil Dave takes half a step back, immersing himself in a pool of shadow. He looks like a head on a red collar, next to a disembodied hand pointing a gun at a giant insect.

"This is Sparkplug," he says. "Toothbrush is tied up inside."

"Oops," I say.

I have been suckered.

"Just a little hologram projector," Evil Dave says. "In my timeline, I'm something of an inventor."

"I don't know why you picked this timeline," I say, "but here I'm not an inventor, or rich, or famous. I'm a bald dork who writes fantasy novels."

"Good," he says. "I'm going to lie low in your life, Dork Dave. And *you* . . . are going back to *my* world." He nods at the train car. "The gate's open."

"I'll let you hang out here for a bit," I say, "but that's all."

"If I disappear in my world," Evil Dave says, "there are traces that law enforcement will follow, and eventually, they'll find me here. If you go back, they'll just arrest you and be done with it. When you try to tell them you're from another world, they'll laugh."

"And I'll go to jail for bank robbery," I say.

"Yes." Evil Dave smiles unctuously. "Prison time for robbery."

Oops; that was too easy. "You've done worse things than bank robbery," I say.

"I'm probably the Worst Dave," he says. "If you're lucky, you'll be in jail a long time. But hey, then maybe you'll become a martyr in prison or something, and end up in the All Souls Happy Happy Club."

"So . . . that part was true?" I ask.

"Of course!" Sparkplug squeaks. Evil Dave is cutting off his air with a hand on his neck. "And even if you die, you'll be part of the memories of the best Dave, who is selected for the All Souls Consortium."

"I'm not the best Dave, am I?" the knowledge makes me feel surprisingly relieved. "You were just flattering me so I'd come with you. This isn't the Primeline."

"Probably not," Sparkplug admits. "This is just the timeline Evil Dave chose after he knocked us out and stole our transporter. It's probably random. You seem like a pretty mediocre Dave."

"What are the good Daves like?" I ask.

"Well, there is a Dave who is a Sufi saint in Morocco. And another one who runs a soup kitchen in Juarez. And there's a Dave U.S. Congressman who has kept all his first-time campaign promises."

"So *far*," Evil Dave sneers.

"So far," Sparkplug agrees. "Dork Dave, you—"

"Shut up!" Evil Dave barks.

Sparkplug falls silent.

"This is easy," Evil Dave says. "You go through the gate. I send the wardens through after you, and I shut the gate. Maybe they can help you escape to some other timeline, to thank you for rescuing them."

"We can't do that," Sparkplug says. "Dave—"

"Shut up!" Evil Dave shakes Sparkplug, and Sparkplug shuts up.

What is the bug-man trying to tell me?

Evil Dave shrugs. "Not my problem."

"This isn't a very attractive offer," I say.

"I'll give you fifty thousand dollars," he counters.

"What does that buy, in your world?" I ask.

"A few years of decent living, if you can make it to Costa Rica."

"Just not attractive enough. I really hope you don't kill the wardens, but I'm not going through the gate. Maybe you should reconsider my offer."

I feel a burr of cold metal against the side of my neck.

Evil Dave sneers. "Maybe you should reconsider *mine*."

There's a third Dave. He has a pistol pressed to my neck. He's wearing a red and black flannel shirt open over a white T-shirt, and black jeans.

"Obama be praised," he says. "*This* Dave's a real sucker."

Obama be praised?

"You curse like my roleplaying game character." I have a hard time not laughing as I say it.

"Another déjà vu effect." Sparkplug shrugs. "The universe is strange."

"Shut up," Third Dave says.

"I needed an accomplice," Evil Dave says. "I knew I could trust this guy."

"You can't both take over my life," I say. "There's only one of me here." To Third Dave, I mutter, "Watch out, he's going to kill you the first chance he gets."

"Stop," Third Dave says. "I'm not stupid. We don't both need to take your life, we just need to be in a world where no one is hunting us. I'll take my share and go live in Costa Rica."

Ugh.

I'm not armed. I'm outnumbered.

Maybe I can get to the other timeline and hide, though. Or maybe the wardens can help clear my name. Or hey, if a gate brought Evil Dave and Third Dave into my timeline, maybe I can find another device, a 'transporter' Sparkplug called it, and get back again.

Going through the gate isn't death. Getting shot repeatedly probably is.

"Where's the fifty thousand dollars?" I ask.

Evil Dave tosses a manila envelope to the ground between us. "I'll give you one minute to count it."

I step forward, shoes crunching on the trainyard gravel. Third Dave moves with me, standing close and keeping his pistol pressed against me. I force myself to breathe calmly, and then stoop to pick up the envelope.

Bang!

What I hear sounds like one gunshot, but I can tell that it's several, fired all at once. Third Dave twitches and spins in a circle, then collapses to the ground.

Evil Dave stays where he is, glaring fiercely at me and not moving.

I can see silhouettes detaching themselves from the shadows around the trainyard, and I know Griff and Mike and Chris and the others well enough to know which is which, but they're moving forward slowly and Evil Dave is holding still and I can't quite see why.

And then Evil Dave's head falls off.

"Holy crap!" I jump back with the money to avoid being struck by spurting blood. Sparkplug scampers up into the train car, Evil Dave's body sags to the ground, and a final silhouette emerges from the shadow—it's Monalisa, with her Japanese sword in her hand.

My knees wobble and I lean against the train car. "Guys," I say, "how did you . . . ?"

Alex and Robert Moore come out from the shadow behind Monalisa. I can see Alex's cheerful bearded smile in the dim blue light, but Robert just hulks like a troll. In a good way. "It seemed weird that you were walking away from the games," Alex said, "and with cosplayers, too. So we followed you."

"Did you hear all the . . . ?" I look around, half expecting to see the flashing lights of a police car. I definitely do not want to try to explain why there are two dead me-lookalikes on the ground.

"We heard it," Griff says.

"That's some crazy stuff," Alex adds.

I look at the bodies. "We can't leave these here."

"Rick, Chris, and David are distracting the hotel staff," Monalisa says. "I think Chris is selling the front desk insurance and Rick and David are stealing the bellboys' carts."

"My car's on the curb," Alex says. "We throw these bodies in the trunk and get them back to the Marriott."

"To do what?" I ask. "Check them into a room?"

"The staff already let you into the hotel restaurant, didn't they?" Alex grins. "There's a very traditional solution, and we have all the tools. By dawn, no one will be able to find these guys."

"I'll get this site cleaned up quick," Mike says. "There's a shed in the back corner. It'll have the chemicals I need."

"We've got your six," Griff says, and he and Chris follow Mike.

"I gotta admit, though," Robert says, "it's going to feel pretty weird to boil the flesh off my friend Dave."

"*I'm* your friend Dave," I say. "Those guys are . . . they're evil Daves from parallel worlds."

The blue-white light suddenly disappears, and I realize that Sparkplug is gone. I poke my head into the train car, and there's no sign of the bug-men or of any strange device or transdimensional gate.

I pick up Headless Dave (formerly Evil Dave) by the shoulders and heave him into the trunk of Alex's black Chevy Cobalt. We toss Third Dave and the detached head inside as well and shut the trunk.

"There's money," I say. "These guys were criminals, and they brought money."

As Alex drives the few blocks to the Marriott, I work the manila envelope open, and then start to laugh.

"No money?" Alex asks.

"Oh, there's money, all right." I show him. "And it's even United States currency, just not the currency of the United States of *this* world. Here's a ten-dollar bill. Notice its lovely purple color, and the image of Herman Melville on it. And on the red twenty is Emily Dickinson, and look, here's a hundred-dollar bill, and it's blue and has a picture of Mark Twain."

"Mark Twain is a good choice," Alex says.

"Yeah," I agree, "but it means I don't have fifty thousand bucks to spread around. I guess the treasure is going to have to be the lessons I learned along the way. Try not to be mediocre Dave. Maybe go to Morocco."

"Yeah," Alex says. "Learning lessons is good. And also, you have friends."

"Yeah," I say. "I've got amazing friends."

A REQUEST

If you liked this collection, please take the time to leave a review on the site where you purchased it and/or on one of the social media reading sites like Goodreads. Tell your friends that you enjoyed it. Suggest it as reading for your local book club. Request it at your local library (or more than one local library). This helps others learn more about the book and gets the word out. Please use the **#hemeleinpubs** and **#chrestomathyofdesire** tags.

Thank you for your time, and thank you for reading this book!

Find more exciting books to read at hemelein.com.

HEMELEIN PUBLICATIONS

About the Author

D. J. Butler has been a lawyer, a consultant, an editor, and a corporate trainer. His general audience works include the flintlock fantasy novels *Witchy Eye, Witchy Winter, Witchy Kingdom,* and *Serpent Daughter,* the modern fantasy novels *The Cunning Man, The Jupiter Knife,* and *The Familiar Spirit* (with Aaron Michael Ritchey), the science fiction novels *In the Palace of Shadow and Joy* and *Among the Gray Lords,* the science fiction short story collection *Between Princesses and Other Jobs,* and the time travel novels *Time Trials* and *Ice Trials* (with M.A. Rothman), all from Baen Books.

His young adult mystery novel, *The Wilding Probate,* was released through Immortal Works. He won a Whitney Award and AML Award for *Witchy Winter* and a Dragon Award for *Witchy Kingdom.* His middle-grade steampunk fantasy adventure tales, *The Kidnap Plot, The Giant's Seat,* and *The Library Machine,* are published by Knopf. Other novels include *City of the Saints* and the *Rock Band Fights Evil* series from Word-Fire Press. Dave organizes writing retreats and anarcho-libertarian writers' events, and travels the country to sell books—he's visited nearly half of all Barnes & Noble stores! He plays guitar and banjo whenever he can, and likes to hang out in Utah with his children.

You can sign up for his newsletter at davidjohnbutler.com.

ABOUT THE COVER ARTIST

TITHI LUADTHONG (ทิฏฐิ ลวดทอง), also known as GRANDFAILURE, was born in Ubonratchathani in northeastern Thailand in 1981, and nowadays lives in Bangkok. Much of his work has science fiction, fantasy, and horror themes. His ideas mostly come from movies, games, and manga. He used to work doing interior watercolor rendering, and he now works mainly as a freelance illustrator and sells images on stock photography websites.

Learn more at https://tithi-luadthong.pixels.com/.

ABOUT THE EDITORS

CALLIE BUTLER lives in Utah, where she studies and explores possible future careers. Her exploration includes volunteer work with juvenile offenders, musical composition, and now editing. She's not sure the checks are phat enough for her in the world of literature, but she's pleased to have made her mark on the career of at least this one obscure science fiction and fantasy writer.

Joe Monson loves reading, books, and butter mochi. He has worked at a couple dozen different jobs during his life. In his current job, he valiantly battles worms, trojans, viruses, corruption, hardware, and updates to keep computer systems running.

He co-edits—with Jaleta Clegg—the LTUE Benefit Anthologies series, and he's the series editor of the Legacy of the Corridor publication series from Hemelein Publications. His anthology, *The Horror at Pooh Corner*, was a successful Kickstarter and was released in bookstores worldwide in 2024.

Joe writes short stories and is outlining a space opera adventure series. He collects science fiction and fantasy art, but not as much as Paul (as if that was even possible). He lives in the tops of the mountains with his thoroughly amazing wife, three miracle children, and their pet library.
Learn more at joemonson.com.

ADDITIONAL COPYRIGHT INFORMATION

- "An Offering the King Makes" originally appeared in *Weird World War IV* (2022), edited by Sean Patrick Hazlett.
- "Others Eat the Sheep" originally appeared in this collection.
- "The Path and the Gates" originally appeared in this collection.
- "A Place Called Liberty" (filk song) originally appeared in this collection. It was originally performed a few years ago at LibertyCon in Chattanooga, Tennessee.
- "The Quail Runs" originally appeared on the Baen.com website in 2023.
- "The Road to Jericho" (filk song) originally appeared in this collection. It was first performed upon the author's leaving Micron.
- "A Short Rest in Hell" originally appeared in *Windows Into Hell* (2016), edited by James Wymore.
- "A Short Story by Somerset Maugham" originally appeared in *Tales from Alternate Earths III* (2021), edited by an unknown hand.
- "Stupid Goat" originally appeared as "Sneak Peek into a New World: Bad Goat" in *Rise of the Administrator* (2023), by M. A. Rothman and D. J. Butler.
- "Sunny Day" (filk song) originally appeared in this collection. It was first performed upon the author's leaving Numonyx.
- "Take a Chance" (filk song) originally appeared in this collection. It was first performed upon the author's leaving the law firm of Clifford Chance.
- "Talking Dragon Con" (filk song) originally appeared in this collection. It was originally performed in 2020 at Dragon Con in Atlanta, Georgia.
- "Two Strangers" originally appeared in *Onward, LibertyCon!* (2022), edited by Christopher Woods and T. K. F. Weisskopf.
- "Vaekra Take Me" originally appeared in *Valcoria Awakenings* (2017), edited by Jason King.
- "A Window on Sarovar" originally appeared as "Window on Samovar" on the Baen.com website in 2022. See https://www.baen.com/window_on_samovar.

· LEGACY OF THE CORRIDOR ·

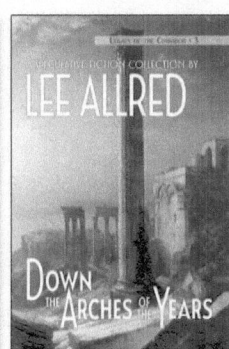

HIGHLIGHTING AND RECOGNIZING
AMAZING SPECULATIVE FICTION
AUTHORS AND ARTISTS FROM THE
INTERMOUNTAIN WEST!

✦ ✦ MANY MORE TO COME! ✦ ✦

www.ingramcontent.com/pod-product-compliance
Lightning Source LLC
Chambersburg PA
CBHW021457110726
47899CB00001BA/185